DETEST-A-PEST: CASE #2

ARACHNID

2.0

DARKNESS CRAWLS

Lee Gabel

FRANKENSCRIPT

Frankenscript Press
Box 717, #105 - 1497 Admirals Road
Victoria, BC, Canada V9A 2P8

ARACHNID 2.0

Cover illustration and design by Lee Gabel
Interior paperback layout by Lee Gabel

Cover images supplied by DepositPhotos
Icons by Font Awesome Free (fontawesome.com/license/free)
Spider icon by IconScout.com

ISBN: 978-0-9918498-9-5 (ebook)
ISBN: 978-1-9991856-0-2 (paperback)

Want to join Lee's Reader Group or find out more about Lee and the books he writes? Please go to:
LeeGabel.com
LeeGabel.com/facebook
LeeGabel.com/twitter
Or follow Lee at BookBub - LeeGabel.com/bookbub

ARACHNID

2.0

DARKNESS CRAWLS

Titles by Lee Gabel

Detest-A-Pest Series
Molerat 2.0 (Coming 2020)
Arachnid 2.0
Vermin 2.0

Standalone
Snipped
David's Summer
Tied

For Ernest, who pointed me
in the right direction.

CRACKED

True silence is rare. There's always something going on somewhere, if you stop to listen. And in the pre-dawn hours of Saturday morning, the sounds of sizzling spiced fillings and lively conversation floated from the back door of Taco Siempre.

Javier kicked the door closed. He preferred quiet and timed his smoke breaks to coincide with dawn breaking across Pacoima and the San Fernando Valley. He pulled a hand-rolled cigarette from a pocket in his denim shirt and perched it between his lips, igniting the end with a flip from his trusty Zippo. He sat on a sun-bleached plastic chair and balanced a tin can ashtray on the arm rest. The smell of fresh corn tortillas, chilis, and cumin rising from an exhaust vent nearby mixed with the sweet tobacco smoke of his first drag. As relaxation washed over his body and mind, his eyes took to the skyline emerging in dark blues and hints of orange.

Local birds had already begun their early morning wakeup songs. Javier was not a birdwatcher, but he knew enough to recognize the American robin with its musical *cheerily cheer-up cheer-up* call.

Halfway through his cigarette, the robins fell silent in unison. He cocked his head to focus on the sudden lack of sound and realized all birds had ceased their morning calls, leaving only the constant thrum of early morning traffic.

Over the span of six seconds, no time to react, a low rumble rose from beneath Javier's feet, culminating in one strong shake. He felt the ground jolt and heard a crack like a whip. The ashtray fell off the armrest, spilling its burnt offerings into the back stairwell to the restaurant's kitchen.

Javier bolted upright, jettisoning the chair away from his legs. One car alarm wailed in the distance, breaking the silence, but birdsong remained absent. He jumped into the stairwell and pulled open the kitchen door.

"Did you feel that?" His shoulders rose and fell with each excited breath.

Edmundo and Reja turned from their cooking stations with confused looks on their faces.

"Feel what?" Edmundo said as he stirred a spiced chicken mixture in a skillet. "And no smoking in here. You know the rules. If Carlos finds out—"

Javier tossed his cigarette out the door and exhaled. "I think there was an earthquake." Javier's eyes darted between the two cooks. "Got to be."

Balls of masa harina sat in ragged rows on Reja's work surface. She placed one into a press and flattened it into a tortilla. "Didn't feel a thing."

Javier crossed the kitchen and pushed through the swinging doors into the customer area of the restaurant. "Hey! Did anyone feel the earthquake?"

Taco Siempre was one of a few 24-hour Mexican food joints in the Pacoima area and had the good fortune of being consistently busy. Folks stopped their conversations and looked up from their meals. Some responded "no", while most shook their heads or simply didn't offer any response.

Carlos, the night manager, stood at the cash register making change for a customer and cast a perplexed look at Javier. The speakers in the corners continued to play their piped-in music.

"No birds," Javier said to himself before returning to the kitchen. "There's no birds."

Reja looked at Edmundo, then at Javier. "What have you been smoking? And can I have some?"

"I'm serious," Javier said. "Come see."

Both Edmundo and Reja knew Javier well enough to know he wouldn't stop. Edmundo shot a look at Reja. He turned the stove off, slid the skillet off the heat and followed Reja and Javier out the back door.

Javier stopped at the top of the stairs, Reja and Edmundo standing just behind. "Listen."

The three stood in silence.

"See?" Javier stepped forward into the back parking lot, gravel crunching under his feet. "There's always birds singing by this time."

"What's that then?" Reja said.

Javier turned to face her. "What?"

Reja held up a finger and shushed him. Faintly at first, birdsong rose from the surrounding trees, followed by the robin's overpowering call.

"I believe those are birds," Edmundo said.

"They weren't there a few seconds ago."

Carlos appeared in the kitchen doorway and knocked the frame. "What is everyone doing back here? People are hungry."

Reja and Edmundo returned to the kitchen.

"You believe me, right?" Javier said.

Edmundo fired up the stove again. "Yeah, sure Javi."

"It's was probably one of those little quakes we always get," Reja said. "They don't do nothing."

Javier washed his hands and returned to his station to prep tomatoes, peppers, lettuce, and grated cheese. He looked out the back door, the framed sky glowing in brighter blues and oranges.

I'm not crazy, he thought. *I know what I heard*

GLASSES CLINKED AND rattled in the kitchen cupboards down the hall from Jack's bedroom. His phone vibrated a random, audible path across his bedside table, but it was the barking of neighborhood dogs that cracked his eyelids and pulled him from sleep. He grabbed the phone, fumbling with groggy coordination.

"4:08 a.m. Magnitude 2.9. San Fernando Valley," the phone read.

Ugh. I got to change the tolerance on that app, Jack thought as he silenced the notification and placed the phone back on the table.

He rubbed his eyes and groaned. Jack had to be up for work in a couple of hours and even though he turned eighteen in four months, fractured sleep had always caused him to feel like a bag of shit the next day. He envied classmates that could pull all-nighters and still function.

Jack laid in his bed and stared at a strip of moonlight slashing the wall, dividing one of his many Mythbusters posters in two. Being an inventive teenager and creative with his hands, working at M5 Industries was his dream job.

The house and surrounding neighborhood fell silent once again, except for his own breathing. Or maybe it was the house he heard breathing. The few dogs who had howled earlier were back to dreaming of open fields and unlimited rabbits.

Jack wondered where his parents were. Luberon? Lyon? Cannes? They had left on a twelve week cycling tour of France and its major cities a week earlier. Their itinerary was stuck on the fridge with a "Cycle the Patagonia" magnet from their last cycling tour. He rarely looked at it. Jack preferred to imagine his parents rolling through the picturesque French countryside he had seen in so many magazines and brochures for the past month. Their research had been relentless. His sleep addled mind calculated that they must be finishing lunch. Somewhere.

Jack had the run of the house and could host a wicked back

to school party if he wanted to, but he wasn't into the party scene. His independence meant too much to him to blow it on a party. And he knew how out of hand those kinds of parties could get.

Jack liked his alone time. He was comfortable in his own skin and knew how to take care of himself. His parents had done a good job in that department. He closed his eyes, his thoughts drifting toward his last year of high school. He'd be a senior, although the title didn't mean much to him. He'd soon be free to follow his own path. Maybe be a star employee at M5 Industries if he was lucky.

Even after eleven years of school, he didn't have many friends. Jack preferred quality over quantity. He spent his summers with his best friend Bradley, but this year Bradley had had the opportunity to meet his dad in New York City for the first time in fifteen years. Jack shortened the nearly three thousand miles of distance between them with sporadic emails and texts.

According to Bradley, he'd been helping his dad manage an apartment building, including acting as exterminator, and had one hell of a story to tell involving rats.

Even though Jack enjoyed his own company, the summer had dragged. He hadn't thought he'd miss Bradley, but texting, email, and the occasional voice call couldn't hold a candle to hang time in person with his best bro.

He immersed himself in work at Food Fresh Market during the day, and with his inventions at night. Jack didn't know it yet, but his ingenuity would soon be tested in unexpected ways.

A TEN MINUTE drive from Jack's House, Hansen Dam Golf Course backed onto the south face of Hansen Dam. The beautifully landscaped grounds offered two unique nine-hole courses, separated by varied elevation and strategically placed trees, predominantly oak and palm.

Each morning during the summer, coinciding with dawn, the automatic irrigation system watered the fairways in preparation for each day's use. Worms, grubs and insects squirmed to the surface and made an all-you-can-eat buffet for birds of all varieties, including finches, sparrows, scrub-jays and robins. When it came to worms and grubs, robins made formidable hunters, ruthless and efficient, seeking out prey using visual and auditory cues.

The watering had just finished its automatic cycle, but instead of flying down to the greens to begin their early morning feast, the birds remained in the trees. They all sensed danger and stopped their singing, like a hive mind thinking and acting as one, sensing sound and vibration beyond human sensitivity. The birds were unable to pinpoint the source of the danger, but knew it was there and chose to remain under cover of their leafy roosts.

Two miles underground within the Sierra Madre Fault Zone, a perpendicular slip caused two walls of rock to shift and open up. The slow rumbling and release of kinetic energy travelled to the surface. A half-minute later, the golf course and surrounding area felt the full force of the rock plates settling into stasis, echoing a loud impact like a dump truck slamming into a concrete wall.

Many birds took to wing at the startling impact, but not the robins. They remained perched in the trees, waiting.

As earthquakes go, this one was considered minor and it didn't take long for wildlife to return to their regular routines. A robin launched itself from an oak branch, landing close to the first hole, where the manicured lawns met the rocky scree of Hansen Dam's south face. Thanks to the recent irrigation, the pickings were good.

The robin ran through the wet grass, stopped, and cocked its head from side to side as it surveyed the ground for movement. Worms and grubs were plentiful, and the bird continued its hunting routine until its keen eyesight spotted something different, a spider, one fully as large as the robin's head. It hustled toward the crunchy delicacy, paused, re-evaluated its path, and scurried forward.

The spider, whose body was covered in dense, whisker-like hairs, sensed the bird's approach, but instead of retreating, it lowered its body and retracted its legs like a shield-carrying warrior preparing for battle.

The robin stopped its attack just short of where the spider sat and tilted its head, looking down on what appeared to be easy prey. Convinced the timing was right, the robin opened its beak and jutted its head forward to snap up the spider.

As if anticipating the bird's move, the spider spun itself around, raised its abdomen and shot a thick, gauzy cloud from its spinnerets to encompass the robin's head and the tops of its wings.

Immobilized and unable to see, the robin struggled to break free of the webbing trapping its body. Several spiders with the same quill-like hairs on their backs appeared from beneath the turf and joined the defending spider, as if they were called by some unknown, unified force. With quick precision, the spiders worked together to encase the robin in a tight silken sac.

The bird writhed within its wrappings until the first spider, the largest one, sank its fangs through the sac, the bird's feathers, and into its neck. As the spider's poison seeped into the bird's bloodstream, swelling and paralysis set in and within seconds the bird's struggles ceased.

The spiders connected threads to their newly captured prey and dragged the robin's paralyzed body below the grass, back into the ground.

MOST OF SAN FERNANDO VALLEY'S 1.8 million people slept through the earthquake that shook that night. The tremor was but a small and consistent blip on the valley's seismographic history, one that residents had come to expect and ignore, taking for granted their lack of danger.

The next morning, the Los Angeles Daily News reported the same information Jack had seen on his phone hours earlier. The quake was minor, almost negligible, and nothing like the magnitude 6.6 tremblor that hit the valley in 1971, a quake that was half a million times stronger and produced half a billion dollars worth of damage at the time.

The Hansen Dam, built in 1940 by the U.S. Army Corps of Engineers, was later determined to be the epicenter of the recent quake and sustained no visible damage to any surrounding structures. But the quake had cracked a channel a foot wide and a thousand feet down into the earth's crust at the border between the dam and Hansen Dam Golf Course to the south. Dank air rose to the surface filtered through ancient cave systems never before explored.

With the golf course at their front door, the spiders feasted on small mammals and birds, but they still preferred cool darkness. Working together using a combination of pheromones and touch, the cluster built a central nest close to water, prey, and constant shade from the sun. Multiple tripwires fanned out from the nest in all directions and made hunting more effective when the spiders behaved as one coordinated organism. Together they hunted and fed on the liquefied flesh of their prey.

The spiders' central nest was a perfect hatching ground and the queen—the most aggressive female in the cluster—wasted no time constructing and filling egg sacs. The male spiders chosen by the queen to fertilize her eggs were later cannibalized by the cluster. With an incubation period half that of a typical spider and a limitless supply of food, the central nest expanded from a cluster to a crowded colony. Emboldened spiderlings cast their silken webs to the wind and the San Fernando Valley became their new fertile hunting ground. But the connection to the central nest—and to the queen—remained.

And their connection, like the gossamer thread of their webs, grew stronger each day.

THE BRONX

*I*F YAH SEE *one rat, there's ten yah can't.*

Captain Hook's words had left an impression on Bradley during his summer stay at Sam's Bronx apartment. And the Captain's words were reinforced during every supply run to Hunts Point Hardware. Bradley thought the store should make it their slogan and put it on their checkout bags. The Captain was content to repeat it to every living soul. His war injury had done nothing to diminish his ability to prattle.

But after all the extermination work Bradley and his father Sam had done, rats continued to show up in the apartment building. No Gambian white-tails at least, and no hordes, but one special rat continued to elude their traps. A female, the queen, the "holy grail" when it came to wiping out an infestation.

What Bradley and Sam had succeeded in doing over their ten weeks together was reduce the food supply available to the rats. They plugged access holes in all the apartments and regularly checked the garbage chute for blockages. Sam attempted to convince the landlord to install a new, more secure dumpster, but the apartment at 616 Casanova—and most properties in the red light district of Hunts Point—were not a high priority. If the improvement had no immediate return on investment, it was dismissed.

The only major repair approved by the landlord was to the massive access hole under Sam's kitchen sink. It had been repaired with new drywall, but as cheaply as possible. Sam had no faith in its structural integrity and had reinforced the wall further with a sheet of 16 gauge steel, paid for out of his own pocket. Any rat could chew through that thickness if they wanted to get at what was behind it, but so far none had tried. The extra layer gave Sam some much needed peace of mind, even though he had grown more comfortable around rats with each passing day.

With food in scarce supply, the remaining rats became bolder. The queen rat ventured away from its nesting area and chewed an undiscovered access hole in the closet of Sam's bedroom, which had doubled as Bradley's room over the summer. Each night under the cover of darkness, the queen ventured out into the bedroom, hallway and kitchen beyond, looking for an easy meal.

As with the rats, the tenants got smarter as well, starting with Sam. He had upgraded his garbage container to a lockable can with a flip-top lid and recommended the rest of the building's tenants do the same. He bid farewell to the days of hanging a garbage bag from the under-the-counter door.

Even with increased garbage security, the queen rat still managed to find enough to eat, but it was forced to expand its diet. Instead of the plentiful garbage delight it was used to, the queen kept the apartment clear of insects and spiders.

Tonight, the queen spotted a juicy house spider the size of a silver dollar under the kitchen table. Following the baseboards, the rat paused at the doors under the kitchen sink, rising on its haunches and trying to catch the scent of something better. It caught the faintest odor of ripe food from the lockable garbage can but had already tried breaking into its polished steel shell during previous outings. Slim pickings tonight, except for the spider.

The rat stood up on its hind legs, surveying the kitchen by habit for any predators from above. It scurried across the open linoleum of the kitchen, close to where Sam had encountered the horde of Gambian white-tails two months earlier. The rodent paused near one of the metal chair legs and sniffed, whiskers quivering, watching. The spider held its ground.

The rat bolted toward the spider and a second later both were scrambling across the floor, the rat in hot pursuit.

The spider made it to the corner of the kitchen and headed up the wall, but not far or quickly enough to escape. The queen rat jumped and knocked the spider to the floor. The spider reared up on its back-most legs and quivered its front legs, nimble chelicerae twitching beneath its eight symmetrically arranged eyes.

The rat paused, surveying the spider's display of defiance before continuing its pursuit. Both creatures ran along the baseboard until the queen cornered its prey. After a split second hesitation, the rat pounced.

In defense, the spider jumped and landed on the rat's back, sinking its fangs into the rat's fur. The spider's venom was not powerful enough to affect the rat in any significant way, but the rat took no chances. It rolled its body, knocking the spider toward the wall again.

The rat brought its paws down, pinned the spider to the floor, and sunk its incisors through the spider's head and eight eyes.

The spider drew its legs close to its body in reflex and was dead a second later.

The queen rat picked up the spider and held it like a blueberry. One bite crushed the spider's head. The rat systematically pulled off each leg and ate it, followed by the thorax and abdomen. A crunchy snack. The rat licked its paws, washed its face, and set out on the hunt once more.

SAM STOOD IN the doorway of the bedroom and watched Bradley collect his belongings, stuffing shirts and dirty underwear haphazardly into his two suitcases. As much as he looked forward to being back in his own bed again, he'd miss his son more. If it meant Bradley could stay longer, Sam would happily continue to sleep on the lumpy TV room sofa he had gotten used to during Bradley's visit. But Bradley would be beginning his senior year of high school back in Los Angeles and Sam knew that was important to him.

Sam focused his attention on Bradley's right bicep, the bottom of his new tattoo just barely visible. "How's the arm feeling today?"

Bradley raised his t-shirt sleeve and craned his neck to get a good view. Slight redness was still visible around the solid black areas of the stylized rat and the red circle-backslash overtop. "Still a little sore."

"Your mom's going to be pissed."

A sly grin broke across Bradley's lips. "I know."

"Ah, to be a fly on the wall when she finds out."

Bradley laughed. "I could live-stream it, if you want."

"Nah," Sam said. "That'd be a waste of… bandwidth?"

"Yup. You're getting it." Bradley bumped fists with Sam. "You'll be an expert in no time."

Sam shook his head subtly. "Doubt it. I have no plans to get a cell phone any time soon."

"But Dad, we could text each other, send each other photos of dead rats. It'd be cool."

Sam imagined connecting with his son any time he wanted. But he could already do that now with the old push-button phone in the kitchen. Still, all the teenagers seemed to live through their phones and part of him wanted to meet Bradley at his level.

"I'll think about it," Sam said.

"Cool. You got my number, right?"

Sam thumbed back down the hallway toward the kitchen. "It's written down on a piece of paper by the phone. And it's in here." He tapped his temple.

"You won't forget?"

Sam shook his head. "Mind's like a steel trap." He smiled at Bradley, seeing parts of himself and of Claire in the teenager, the good parts.

"What?"

"Nothing."

"No, tell me."

Sam paused before dodging the question. "You're a good kid. Don't let anyone tell you different." He looked at Bradley's luggage. "You finished packing?"

"Yup."

"Hungry?"

"I could definitely eat."

Sam looked at his watch, the glass face scuffed from his years at Franklin Correctional Facility. The analog face read just past six o'clock. "When does your flight leave?"

Bradley dug out his plane ticket. "10:25 tonight."

"Could you stand one more pizza from Kingsley's? Maybe some fried chicken?"

Bradley's stomach growled, as if on cue, and he grinned.

"I'll take that as a yes," Sam said. "Let's eat there this time. Get the authentic Kingsley's experience."

Bradley lead the way out of the apartment. Sam followed, locking up. The two of them headed out into the late afternoon autumn sun, up Casanova to hang a right onto Spoffard Ave. Kingsley's Fried Chicken and Pizza was a few blocks away.

Kingsley's focused on take-out but had three booths inside

for dine-in customers. Images of all Kingsley's offerings were plastered to the windows beneath buzzing neon signs spelling out their best sellers.

"They sell breakfast?" Bradley raised his eyebrow.

"Breakfast, coffee, *and* donuts," Sam said. "But I stick to what made them famous."

Sam opened the door and the smell of hot oil, chicken, spices and baking pizza crust filled their noses. It felt just as hot inside the restaurant as outside, maybe a bit hotter.

A stout man with closely cropped hair and a graying goatee stood behind the counter. An equally heavyset woman and a younger man worked in the back preparing the food. All their aprons were stained with grease and tomato sauce.

"Sam!" said the man behind the counter. "Good to see you, brother."

"Hey, Marcus. Busy tonight?"

"Kingsley's always be busy." Marcus laughed. "What can I do you for?"

Sam scanned the menu board, looked at his watch, then turned to Bradley. "What do you think? The works?"

Bradley nodded. "Let's do it."

"Okay. Get one of the booths," Sam said to Bradley before turning to Marcus. "We'll have the large Superbox and pizza combo. Pepperoni and mushroom. And two Cokes."

Marcus pulled two cans of Coca Cola from the cooler and motioned toward Bradley in a booth taking in the restaurant's vibe. "Who's the kid?"

"That's my son, Bradley. He's been visiting from L.A. for the summer."

"Shit, son, you been holdin' out on me."

"Sorry, we've been busy." Sam leaned toward the counter and lowered his voice. "You have any Kingsley's t-shirts left? Extra Large?"

"Sure do."

"I'll take one. A souvenir for Brad."

"Free advertising for me in L.A." Marcus chuckled, his belly rising and falling with the laugh. "I like the sound of that." He punched the order into the cash register. "Anything else?"

Sam shook his head.

Marcus hit a button on the register, causing it to rattle out a final total.

Sam took out his wallet and pulled out two twenty dollar bills. "Keep the change."

"You sure, now?" Marcus eyed Sam's wallet. "You're not going to get yourself into any… trouble?"

"Nope," Sam said. "I got it covered."

"Hey, thanks Sam. Wish all my customers were like you. I'd be retired to the Bahamas by now." Marcus laughed, his whole body shaking in response.

"The Bahamas, huh? Sounds nice."

"Someday, my friend." Marcus reached under the counter and pulled out a white t-shirt, emblazoned with the restaurant's official logo: a chicken giving a thumbs up, wearing a black leather jacket and a golden crown, and standing behind a pizza. Surrounding the logo in a circle were the words "Kingsley's Fried Chicken and Pizza". Sam stuffed the shirt under his own plaid flannel work shirt.

"I'll give you a holler when your order's up." Marcus turned to the cooks in the back and announced the order.

Sam took the Cokes and slid into the opposite seat of the booth Bradley had picked. "Well? What do you think?"

Bradley looked around, taking in the details of the restaurant. "It's like a McDonald's, except way smaller."

"But unlike McDonald's, this place has character." Sam cracked the tab on his Coke and took a swig. "It's not run by a corporation. And the food's better."

Sam sat across the table and watched his son; a young man he'd thought he'd never get a chance to know. He owed the opportunity to Claire, as strange as that idea was, and reminded himself to thank her the next time they spoke. If there was a next time.

Bradley noticed the silence as he broke the seal on his Coke. "Are you okay?"

"Never better," Sam said. "Hey, did you say goodbye to Hope?"

Bradley tried to look nonchalant. "Yeah, I saw her in the hallway this morning. She wished me good luck."

Sam grinned. "You like her, don't you?"

"Well, sure. What's not to like?"

"Not much, I guess."

Sam and Bradley drank their Cokes.

"Can I ask you a question?"

Bradley set his Coke down on the table. "Depends on what."

"You have someone special back in L.A.? Besides Mom?" Sam winked.

Bradley groaned. "Mom? *Please*."

"I mean a girlfriend?"

"Or boyfriend."

Boyfriend? Sam was just about to respond when Marcus approached the table with their order.

"One Superbox and one pepperoni and mushroom pizza," Marcus said. "Fresh and hot, the Kingsley way."

"Smells great, Marcus," Sam said. "Thanks."

Marcus caught Bradley's gaze. "Spread the word about Kingsley's in L.A., okay Brad?"

Bradley furrowed his brow, his eyes flitting between Sam and Marcus. "Um, okay?"

"That's the spirit." Marcus chuckled. "Let me know if there's anything else you need." He tapped Sam's shoulder.

"Will do." Sam opened the Superbox, chose a piece of chicken, and asked through a bite, "You were saying?"

Bradley pulled out an unevenly sliced piece of pizza. "About someone special?"

"Yeah. Girlfriend? Boyfriend?"

Bradley took a bite of his pizza. "I had a girlfriend for most of the last school year, but she dumped me a couple months before school ended."

"Why? Without getting too personal."

"No, it's okay," Bradley said between bites. "She was kind of a control freak. I didn't like how she treated people. I was going to dump her but she kind of beat me to it." Bradley chased his mouthful of pizza with a gulp of Coke. "I guess we both had the same idea."

"What was her name?"

"Alexis." Bradley dug into his pocket and pulled out his phone. After a few finger taps and swipes, he presented a photo of Alexis. "She lives with her foster parents."

"She's certainly an attractive girl."

"Yeah, she's got looks, but that's about it," Bradley said. "I guess that's why I like Hope. She's got so much more going on."

"Maybe Alexis needs control because most of her life has been so out of control." Sam set his chicken down. "Living in the foster system can be hard."

Bradley shrugged. "Yeah, maybe." He took another bite of his pizza and caught a hot spot. As he pulled his mouth away, a big glob of tomato sauce, cheese and pepperoni landed on his shirt, front and center.

"Shit…" Bradley took a quick look around to make sure no one had heard him. "Sorry." He looked down at his chest and picked up the pizza toppings. They left a large greasy, tomatoey stain. He gave his raccoon tail hanging at his belt a cursory inspection. "At least the shirt's black."

Sam pulled the Kingsley's shirt out from under his flannel button-up. "I was going to save this as a surprise, but I'll give it to you now." He held up the white t-shirt for Bradley to see.

"That's awesome." Bradley looked to the counter to see Marcus nodding and grinning and giving him a thumbs up. "Spread the word in L.A. Got it. Love the logo."

"Maybe you can open up my first L.A. franchise," Marcus called out across the restaurant.

Bradley smiled back. "Maybe." He turned to Sam. "Thanks, Dad, but I think I'll wait to put it on."

"Yeah, sure." Sam secured the t-shirt under his flannel and looked at his watch. "We'd better chow down or we'll miss your flight."

Sam and Bradley dug into their meals, switching from chicken to pizza on a whim.

"Anyway, sorry about Alexis," Sam said with his mouth full of food.

Bradley shrugged. "I'm so over her."

Sam held up his can of Coke. "To my son. I hope your senior year is full of adventure."

"And to my dad, the bravest man I know." Bradley tapped his can against Sam's and they both drank.

SAM AND BRADLEY returned to the apartment with a Superbox partially filled with chicken, mashed potatoes and pizza. The quantity of food Marcus had brought them had exceeded their appetites and Sam couldn't help but wonder if Marcus had thrown in a little extra in response to his tip.

"Get your things ready," Sam said. "We should leave soon if you want to catch your flight. I don't want to piss Claire off."

Bradley looked at the time on his phone. "We got lots of time. It's not even eight o'clock."

"We should be at JFK an hour and a half before take-off. Plus, there's travel time… and traffic."

"Seriously?"

Sam walked toward the refrigerator. "Humor me. I'm still relearning this city."

"Okay, but not before I have one more slice of pizza." Bradley slipped his hand into the Superbox and pulled out a jagged piece of pizza, the topping barely staying on.

Within minutes of their returning from their farewell dinner at Kingsley's, the queen rat caught the scent of their leftovers. The smell of fried chicken and pizza was too enticing to ignore. She emerged from the access hole in the bedroom closet and scrambled under the bed and across the floor.

Sam placed the Superbox into the fridge, finding one suitable spot beside a half-full jug of milk. The contents of the fridge bore a striking contrast to its contents at the beginning of summer. No rotting or rancid processed meats permeated the space. There was even a container of salad. Bradley had been a good influence on him, and Sam hoped he could continue the habit of healthier eating.

Bradley crammed pizza into his mouth as he walked to his bedroom, sauce and cheese oozing onto his fingers.

When the sight of human feet appeared at the bedroom door, the queen rat froze, black eyes watching, whiskers quivering at the scent, mouth salivating.

"Hey." Sam stepped into the hallway from the kitchen. "Try on your new shirt." He threw the ball of fabric at him.

"Watch it. I'm eating!" Bradley raised his hands out of the way and let the t-shirt drop to his feet. "I don't want to get it dirty too."

He took another bite and balanced the remaining pizza on top of the open suitcase lid. The queen rat watched Bradley's every move from the protective shadows under the bed. He looked at his greasy, saucy hands and contemplated washing them.

Screw it. It's black for a reason.

Bradley pulled off his already dirty shirt, careful not to snag it on his raccoon tail, and wiped his hands clean. He threw the inside-out shirt into his suitcase.

The rat stretched its body out, trying to get closer to the beckoning scent without leaving the safety of its hiding spot. The dirty shirt smelled a lot better to the rat than the crust balancing on top of the suitcase lid. Chicken, grease, baked goods, all mixed together.

Bradley picked up his new Kingsley's t-shirt and pulled it on. It still smelled like fried chicken. "What do you think?"

"Turn around."

Centered on the back of the t-shirt were the words, "FRY THE BEST - FORGET THE REST" in big, bold red letters.

Sam chuckled and clapped. "Fantastic."

Bradley grabbed the remaining piece of pizza on the suitcase lid and walked to the bathroom to look at himself in the mirror. "This shirt rocks, Dad. Thanks."

Sam appeared at the doorway to the bathroom. "I couldn't resist. I've been eyeing those all summer." He looked at his watch. "We should go. Get your stuff and we'll hit the road."

Sam patted Bradley's shoulder as he left the bathroom to collect his luggage.

Bradley popped one last bite of pizza into his mouth as he zipped the lid of the second suitcase. He slung his leather jacket and day pack over his shoulder, picked up his luggage, one suitcase in each hand, and met Sam by the door to the apartment.

"Let's go."

Sam locked the apartment, leaving it empty and quiet. He took one of Bradley's bags as they both stepped toward the foyer, out the front door and down the steps to the wrought iron gate. He held the gate open for his son and followed him to Sam's old Ford F-250.

One bag at a time, Sam raised Bradley's luggage over the side of the truck bed. Bradley opened the passenger door, tossed his day pack into the footwell and put on his leather jacket. He slid into the passenger seat.

"Your truck have a name?"

Sam pulled himself into the driver's seat and closed the door with a heavy *clrunk*. "Nope."

"You should call it Rusty."

"That's not bad." Sam inserted his key and turned the ignition. The starter whined until the engine turned over, revving into a rolling rumble. Sam patted the dashboard. "Attaboy, Rusty." He looked at Bradley. "Got everything? Ticket? This is your last chance."

Bradley leaned down and partly unzipped a pocket on his day pack. He pulled out his plane ticket as proof. "Got it."

"What about your phone?"

"Surgically attached to my hip." Bradley managed a smile. "But I thought you knew that."

"What about your bags?"

"I checked everything." Bradley locked gazes with Sam for a couple of seconds.

"I could always mail back the things you've forgotten, *if* you've forgotten anything, that is."

"Or I could just come out and visit you again."

Sam felt emotion rise in his throat.

"That'd be okay, right?" Bradley said.

"Sure." Sam swallowed hard. "That'd be perfect." He revved the engine and the faded orange truck, mottled with rust, pulled away from the curb and headed for John F. Kennedy International Airport.

THE SETTING SUN had already dipped below the horizon when Sam drove Bradley to JFK. The view over the East River from the Trogs Neck Bridge was spectacular, with the cloudless western sky spreading out in hues of yellow, orange, red and blue.

"It's going to be a great night to be flying," Sam said.

Bradley glanced out the passenger window to take in the vista. He pulled out his phone and by habit looked for the window switch on the car door.

Sam laughed. "It's a hand crank."

Bradley grinned back. "I know that." He rolled down the window to take an unobstructed photo. The warm wind mixed with the ocean scent of Long Island Sound flowed through the cab of the truck. He closed his eyes and inhaled a deep breath.

Sam cast a glance at him. "Smells pretty nice, huh?"

Bradley nodded, rolled up the window and rested his head against it.

Sam saw a hint of sadness in Bradley's face. He felt it too but chose not to bring it up.

"Are you by the ocean?" Sam said. "Back in L.A.?"

Bradley kept his eyes closed, facing the passenger window. "There's no ocean near the San Fernando Valley. Closest beach is in Santa Monica about an hour south. There's an outdoor aquatic center pretty close to where I live, but it's not the same." He heaved a sigh. "I'm landlocked and it's hot as fuck…"

Sam smiled ever so slightly.

"Sorry. Slipped out. It's so hot during summer. I thought I'd escape most of it by being here, but it wasn't very cool here either."

"I wouldn't know. This was my first summer on the outside in 15 years."

Bradley's eyes settled on the prison tattoos escaping from the cuffs of Sam's work shirt, just barely visible by the dashboard lights and dimming dusk. He turned his head to the window again, his thoughts straying toward how his life might have turned out differently if Sam had been around for all his summers. Bradley felt a wave of sadness wash over him as he pushed the "what ifs" out of his mind, choosing to focus on the future and his final year of school.

Bradley remained quiet for the rest of the ride and Sam didn't try to force conversation. At one point, to try and break the silence, he flipped on Nash 94.7 FM right in the middle of "Five More Minutes" by Scotty McCreery. A good song but the wrong time for it.

"A pause button would be nice," Sam said in a low whisper as he turned the radio off.

Sam navigated onto Belt Parkway and soon after JFK Expressway, the F-250 rumbling and rolling in a predictable fashion. The sprawling JFK International Airport loomed in the distance. It wouldn't be long before Sam would have to face a moment he had grown to dread.

A creature of habit built up from years of routine, Sam found the same parkade he had used when he had picked Bradley up ten weeks ago. So much had changed between them since then, and changed for the better. But the parkade looked the same.

Sam pulled into a parking stall. "This is it." He reached out and gave Bradley's left shoulder a light squeeze. "I'll get your bags." He slid out of the truck and slammed the door with a familiar *clrunk*.

Bradley grabbed his day pack and exited the truck. The parkade was filled with vehicles, but only a few visible travelers making their way to Terminal 8. Bradley's feeling of sadness and isolation amplified.

Sam checked his watch. "It's a few minutes after nine. We made pretty good time." He heaved Bradley's bags out of the truck bed and headed toward the main entrance of Terminal 8. Sam tried not to walk too fast or slow. He didn't want to appear eager, because the truth was Sam would have preferred Bradley to stay.

Bradley followed a step or two behind.

After passing through the sliding doors of the entrance, Sam turned toward the escalators to the departures level. "What airline are you on?"

"American."

Sam spotted the ticket counter for American Airlines. "Let's deal with your bags." There was no one lined up in the winding queue. "Aren't you glad we're early?"

"I guess so." Bradley said in a hushed voice. He stepped up to the counter and presented his ticket and travel documents.

Sam spotted a Visa card in Bradley's wallet. "You have a credit card?" Sam gave Bradley a playful nudge to try and ease the tension. "You've been holding out on me."

Bradley shrugged. "Mom got it for me. It only has a five hundred dollar limit."

"I might have to get myself one." Sam lifted both bags onto the scale. The agent tagged each bag with a flight information ribbon and deposited the luggage onto the trundling conveyor belt behind the counter. The bags soon disappeared into the massive unseen machinery of JFK's luggage processing area.

Sam stepped away from the ticket counter. "So, what do you want to do now?"

Bradley shrugged, stowing his ticket and wallet.

"We could get a snack or a drink."

"I'm kind of full from our dinner at Kingsley's," Bradley said. "Which was dope, by the way."

Sam returned a small nod. He could see the conversation was becoming uncomfortable for Bradley. It wasn't easy for him either.

"Okay. Let's get you through security," Sam said. "I've never been big on long drawn-out goodbyes." As soon as the words left his mouth, he could see the relief on Bradley's face. "You're definitely a chip off the ol' block." Sam smiled and placed his arm over Bradley's shoulder as they walked.

Sam stopped just in front of the entrance to the security checkpoint. "This is it."

"I guess so." Bradley shifted from foot to foot, his hands fiddling with his raccoon tail attached to the side of his jeans, his eyes flitting, not settling on anything or anyone.

"Can your old man give you a—"

Before Sam could finish his request, Bradley stepped forward and wrapped his arms around him, squeezing tight. Sam reciprocated, taking in the hug and filing the memory away for darker times.

Bradley stepped back and wiped a tear away with a stealthy twist of his wrist. "It's been really great, Dad."

Sam smiled. "Yeah. It has."

Bradley took a step toward the security entrance. "You got my phone number?"

Sam tapped his temple. "In here. Steel trap, remember?"

"Speaking of traps, let me know if you spot any Gambians."

Sam raised his eyebrows. "I hope I don't, but I will. For sure."

"Say goodbye to the Dobbies for me," Bradley said. "And I forgot to check their trap this morning."

"I'm on it. I'll let t hem know."

"And get a cell phone."

"I'm working on it."

Bradley sent Sam a "thumbs up" and headed for the security checkpoint.

"Hey, Brad."

Bradley turned immediately, as if he was expecting Sam to say something.

"Call me any time. Day or night."

Bradley nodded.

"I mean it."

"Okay," Bradley said.

"Goodbye, son."

"Bye, Dad."

They both waved at each other. Bradley turned and walked into the security checkpoint and disappeared into a sea of people.

Sam stood outside the entrance for a long time. He closed his eyes and pulled up the memory of their farewell hug. It turned out he wasn't such a bad father after all. He'd just needed a chance to prove himself.

Sam retraced his path out of Terminal 8 back to his truck. Along the way, everyone he saw seemed to have a cell phone. He unlocked the truck's driver-side door and stepped up to his seat.

Can I afford to have a phone? Sam admitted the thought of sending Bradley a text message right now was appealing. *Can I afford not to?*

He started the truck's engine, pulled out of his parking space and began his journey home.

SAN FERNANDO

ONCE THROUGH SECURITY, Bradley found Gate 37, sat, and pulled up the photo app on his phone. Flipping through the images, most were of Sam and him, working alongside each other. Bradley found his favorite photo of Hope, wearing the same Ramones shirt she had worn when he first met her. He pinch-zoomed to her face and studied her.

He flipped to the next image, one of himself giving the camera two thumbs up, with a baited rat trap in front of him. The amber pendant given to him by Washington during his friend's last moments of life hung loosely over his t-shirt.

Bradley's hand went instinctively to the pendant around his neck. He felt the smooth, rounded ball of amber through the fabric of his Kingsley's t-shirt.

Even though he tried not to, his mind revisited Washington's death. It was one of the most horrible experiences of his life so far, one that he would never forget. Bradley didn't want to believe it had been suicide but something else, something deeper. Maybe in time he'd understand why Washington had sacrificed himself. For now, it would remain a mystery. He doubled his efforts to focus on the man Washington had been *before* the Gambian white-tail invasion.

When his flight was called for boarding, Bradley sent a text to Claire. "On my way. See U 2morrow." He found his seat, which happened to be next to a window, fastened his seatbelt and promptly fell asleep. When Bradley next awoke, the plane was landing in Los Angeles. He had slept through the entire flight. That was the good news.

The not so great news? Now he had to face his mom.

WITH HIS DAY pack slung over his shoulder, Bradley recalled how he had played a cat-and-mouse game when he'd first met Sam, making him sweat a little. No such luck with Claire. She was waiting front and center at Arrivals, wearing tight jeans and a plain purple t-shirt, waving excitedly.

"Brad!" she called out. "Over here."

As much as Bradley wasn't looking forward to seeing Claire, it was good to be home, despite the heat of Los Angeles and soon, the valley. He smiled and waved back.

Claire threw her arms around his neck, gave him a kiss on the cheek, and hugged him tight. One thing was for sure: both Sam and Claire knew how to hug.

"Let me look at you." She took a step back and scanned him from head to toe. "I think you've grown." She reached up and ruffled his hair. "Your *hair* has definitely grown. We'll have to get *that* dealt with before school starts."

Bradley swept his mussed hair out of his eyes. "I think I'm going to grow it out long this year."

Claire cast him a sideways look. "We'll see about that."

As the crowd thinned, a man remained standing by Claire's side, a man unfamiliar to Bradley. He wore black brogues, sharply pleated tan pants and a red golf shirt. All that was missing was a set of golf clubs and a sun visor over his curly blond hair.

Claire followed Bradley's stare, prompting her to take a step closer to the man. She placed her hand on the small of his back.

"Brad, I'd like to introduce you to Roy," Claire said.

Roy stuck out his hand. "Nice to meet you, Brad." Roy's bleached smile in his tanned face looked oddly fake to Bradley. "I've been hearing good things."

Bradley took Roy's hand and shook it.

Ugh. Limp. Not a good first impression. Bradley forced a smile. "Thanks. How do you know my mom?"

"Roy and I have been seeing each other, honey." Claire looked up at Roy and touched his chest lightly. "We met a week or so after you left for New York. On the jogging trail near Hansen Dam."

Roy gazed at Claire and grinned. "Your mom is quite a woman."

"Oh, Roy. Stop."

Is this guy for real? Bradley contemplated turning around and catching a flight back to New York. "I need to go pick up my luggage."

"American Airlines, right? This way." Roy grabbed Claire's hand and led her and Bradley to the luggage claim area.

Bradley avoided conversation as he kept an eye out for his two suitcases. He pulled out his phone and texted Jack. "@LAX. Want to hang later?"

Claire approached Bradley and touched his shoulder. "Are you okay, honey? You're awfully quiet."

"I'm just tired," Bradley lied. "I didn't sleep at all." He spotted his luggage and grabbed his bags. Roy didn't offer any help.

"Well let's get you home, then," Claire said.

The sooner the better.

Bradley slipped his day pack over his shoulders, stacked his bags, and rolled them out to the parkade. Claire rested her head on Roy's shoulder a few steps ahead.

Bradley didn't like his mom's "new development" one bit. He

clenched his jaws and looked for their charcoal gray Nissan Pathfinder.

After several minutes weaving around parked vehicles and other travellers, Claire and Roy approached a bright red vehicle.

"Where's Gandalf?" Bradley looked left, right and back in the parkade for the SUV that he had ridden in his whole life. He was looking forward to driving it when he got his license.

"Don't get mad, honey. We traded in the Pathfinder for a hybrid." Claire pointed to a small Nissan Leaf. "Isn't it sweet?"

This can't be happening, Bradley thought. He'd be the laughingstock of the school. No one who cared about their senior year reputation would be caught dead in a little hybrid. But there it was, Claire and Roy beaming next to it like it was their new baby.

"I can't believe you traded in Gandalf the Grey... for this." Bradley looked at Claire, no longer trying to hide his disappointment. "You *loved* Gandalf."

Claire's smile faltered for a moment. "It was time, Brad." She looked up at Roy, finding her smile again. "Plus, Roy got me a great deal. He works for Sylmar Nissan."

"*Roy* sold you the car?" Bradley shot a look at Claire, then daggered Roy. "I bet you got a nice *commission*, huh?"

"Bradley!"

Claire took at step forward, but Roy stopped her, shaking his head. "It's okay. He's just looking out for you." He opened the back hatch and extended a hand. "Let's get you loaded up."

Claire got into the driver's seat and closed the door. It took a little juggling to get both suitcases to fit in the back.

"They fit fine in Gandalf."

"It's all good." Roy closed the back hatch and took a calming breath.

As the back hatch swung past his line of sight, Bradley thought he saw a subtle undulation in one corner of one of the suitcases, but he was too annoyed to pay it much thought. "So, did you sell my mom the car *before* or *after* your first date?"

"Look." He motioned Bradley aside and lowered his voice. "That's none of your business, but just so you know, I *split* the commission with your mom." The two stared each other down for a moment. "Now please, get in the car."

Bradley opened the back passenger door, threw his day pack onto the back seat, and sat down, slamming the door behind him. He buckled his seat belt and looked out the window.

"Hey." Claire gave him a puzzled look through the rear-view mirror. "You okay, hon?"

Bradley looked at Claire's eyes reflected back at him, then returned his stare out the window. He could see Roy watching him through the passenger side mirror. He crossed his arms and recalled his first meeting with Sam over two months ago, which was similar in a lot of ways except one. Sam wasn't intentionally being an asshole.

"Yeah, I'm fine. Just tired I guess."

Claire nodded. "We'll be home soon." She pressed the ignition button, the start-up chiming from the dash. It was a stark contrast to Sam's old Ford F250. She backed out of the parking stall and began the hour long journey back to the valley.

The new car sounded like the Japanese bullet trains Bradley had seen in a documentary at school. It was an electronic whirring that rose in pitch as the little car accelerated. It was a cool sound, almost pleasant. He closed his eyes and imagined himself in a sci-fi movie. Anything to diffuse his annoyance toward Roy.

"Oh, I love this little car." Claire looked to Roy and squeezed his knee. Roy smiled back. "It's so zippy."

Once out of the LAX parkade, Claire navigated onto the 405. Normally by seven thirty in the morning, the freeway would be approaching gridlock. But being a Sunday, there was no delay as the little car zoomed north through the Sepulveda Pass, toward the Santa Monica mountains and the San Fernando Valley beyond.

DESPITE THE PUNGENT new car smell and having no pillow, Bradley slept during the ride home. He awoke as Claire passed through Sherman Oaks.

Twenty minutes and I'll be home. Bradley rubbed sleep from his eyes.

Claire spied him in the rearview mirror. "There he is. You nodded off for a bit."

Bradley yawned. "This car is so quiet. You should hear Dad's truck. Probably drive you crazy." He smiled at the thought before remembering who he was talking to.

Shit. I hope I haven't opened a can of worms.

As if on cue, Claire tensed up, her hands gripping the steering wheel more tightly. She deflected her eyes away from the rearview mirror and tried to keep a scowl from creeping onto her face.

"So... how *is* Sam?" Claire spoke through clenched teeth. Even Roy noticed the change in her tone of voice.

"Mom, we don't have to talk about this. I know how you—"

"No, I'm fine," Claire said. "It was going to come up eventually. Better sooner than later."

Bradley paused, trying to gauge Claire's level of aggression.

"Besides," Claire continued. "If you hadn't connected with Sam this summer, I would never have met Roy." She reached out and squeezed Roy's hand and offered him a smile. Bradley thought it looked forced.

"Well, Dad is doing really well." Bradley stretched his shoulders and leaned his head against the car window, replaying memories of the last ten weeks. "He's the building superintendent of an apartment in the Bronx. And we just finished exterminating a rat infestation that you'd have to see to believe."

Claire's eyes widened. "You killed animals?"

"They're *rats*, Mom. Besides, if you had seen them, you would have wanted to kill them too."

"Every animal is placed on this earth for a reason."

"I hear the rats in New York are pretty bad," Roy said.

Claire turned her head and daggered Roy with narrowed eyes. "Don't you take his side."

"I'm not. But it's true, isn't it?" Roy looked back at Bradley.

"They're bad everywhere," Bradley said.

"Not here, in the valley."

"Don't count on it."

"Stop it," Claire said. "I don't want to talk about this anymore."

"Anyway, Dad's doing fine." Bradley watched Claire's eyes in the rearview mirror. "I'd like to see him again next summer."

Claire cast a quick glance at Bradley.

"Maybe sooner," he said.

Silence hung in the car like fog.

"We'll see." Claire signaled and switched lanes.

"Isn't the Bronx a hotbed for prostitution and drugs?" Roy said. "See any hookers, Brad?"

Bradley remained silent, visions of Carmela in her tight white tank top and red hot pants bubbling up even though he fought hard to suppress them. He still found it hard to believe that Sam *knew* her.

Claire gasped. "Brad! You didn't—"

"No, Mom." Bradley looked away, embarrassed, but caught Roy's smirk in the passenger side mirror. "Give me a little credit."

"I think Sam is a bad influence on you."

"He's a better man than this jackhole," Bradley said in a hushed voice.

Roy turned his body almost completely around in his seat, brows raised in surprise and anger. "What did you say?"

Bradley faced Roy. "I said soon I'll be old enough to do what I want."

"Hmm. I heard something different." Roy settled back into his seat. "You better watch your mouth."

"I'll get right on that," Bradley said. "By the way, remember that rubber rat?"

Claire's gaze locked with Bradley's, a combination of anger and guilt simmering behind her eyes.

"You didn't tell me that Dad was *afraid* of rats, like *really* afraid," Bradley said. "Thanks for that. Went over *so* well."

"Watch the road," Roy said, breaking Claire's focus on Bradley in the back seat.

"What? Oh…" Claire returned her eyes forward.

"He's over that now, though," Bradley said. "His fear of rats."

Claire straightened her posture. "Wonders never cease, do they?"

Silence returned to the car, something Bradley was coming to prefer. If home life was going to be nothing but angst and arguments, he'd take silence in a heartbeat, especially if the arguments were about Sam.

Claire didn't like silence and turned on the radio. It was tuned to 104.3 MYFM, just as it had been in Gandalf before Bradley's trip. "Ironic" by Alanis Morissette floated out of the little car's stereo system.

"So, anything interesting happen while I was away?" Bradley watched Claire shoot a quick look of warning at Roy. Busted. He knew the look because he had used it dozens of times with Claire when he'd gotten into trouble with Jack.

Claire stammered and turned down the volume of the radio.

Bradley recognized it as a stalling tactic. "Um, we had an earthquake a couple of weeks ago. That's about it."

"Did you feel it?" Roy looked at Claire with a lascivious grin. "Because I certainly felt the *earth move* that night."

Gag. The thought of Claire doing anything sexual with this douche-bag turned Bradley's stomach. He didn't get what his mom saw in the guy.

"Nope." Claire sent Roy eyes of admonishment. "*Didn't* feel a thing. It *wasn't* very big. But I remember hearing about it on the radio. Do you remember the magnitude?"

Roy looked out the passenger window, sulking.

Score a point for Mom. The corners of Bradley's mouth turned up into an almost-grin.

"It wasn't more than a three, if I recall," Claire said.

"I'll talk to Jack about it." Bradley closed his eyes and rested his head on the window again. "He tracks that kind of stuff."

Traffic continued to be light as Claire left the 405 and headed east down Ronald Reagan Freeway toward the suburbs of Pacoima, Lake View Terrace, and finally Stonehurst.

1068 Sheldon Street. The house that Bradley had grown up in. It was a small light-yellow rancher with an even smaller backyard where Claire managed to cultivate a select crop of vegetables, fruits, and flowers. She'd have more workable earth if it wasn't for the shed in the corner of the yard, but it held all the necessary tools and materials she needed to keep her green thumb healthy.

A white wrought-iron fence joined brick pillars four feet tall at the corners of the property. Smaller brick pillars framed the gate in front of the house. The Hansen Dam Golf Course lay about half a mile west and the Hansen Dam Recreational Area, with its outdoor public pool and dozens of trails, sat just north of that.

Claire turned down a side alley and stopped the car in front of a detached garage on the back edge of the property. Bradley was used to her parking Gandalf in front of the house, but apparently the new electric car needed to be plugged in to charge every day.

"Roy, do you mind?" Claire looked at him with eyes considerably brighter than they had been moments earlier.

Roy grunted and got out of the car. He twisted a lever on the garage door and opened it. Claire rolled forward silently and killed the engine. The low whine of the electric engine faded away.

Bradley grabbed his day pack, slid out of the car, and maneuvered to the back. The Leaf took up a lot less space than Gandalf had.

"Need some help with those?" Roy said.

"No, I got it." Bradley didn't wait for the back hatch to fully open. He had his luggage in hand before Roy had even taken a step forward to offer help.

"Suit yourself." Roy watched Bradley walk down the alley and around to the front of the house, his arms straining under the weight of his suitcases.

Claire stepped up beside him. "You're a big change for him. He'll come around. Just give him time."

Roy clenched his fists, leaving nail grooves in his palms. "I hope you're right."

IT FELT A little strange to be back in his own room again, walls covered with rock and roll posters, his shelves of books, his clothes dresser, a few plastic models, and a laptop on a desk in the corner. Part of him expected bare walls and a broken-in bed, just like in New York.

It was obvious Claire had been in his room. His bed was made, more precisely than he would ever do himself, and the window was open, allowing a warm August breeze to move through the space.

Bradley stripped off his jacket dropped it to the floor. He heaved his two suitcases up onto the bed and made a beeline to the desk in the corner. He pulled open the drawer and reached into the back right corner.

For a moment, fear took hold of him when he didn't immediately find what he was looking for. Bradley ran his fingertips across pencils, erasers, rulers and other school-related paraphernalia before they fell upon a familiar rectangular object. Then another thought dawned on him.

Did Mom move my condoms? Bradley pulled out a small box and looked inside to take inventory. *They're all there.* He let go a sigh of relief as he placed the box back into the drawer. Maybe things had shifted around since the last time he had used one.

The last time. Bradley laughed. It was months ago, just before he and Alexis broke up. *At least it wasn't drugs.* Having condoms made him a responsible young adult.

At first Bradley thought the noise he heard next was the wood of the drawer scraping as he pushed it back into the desk. The drawer had always stuck in spots. He stood and cocked his ear to one side and heard the sound again.

Scritch-scritch-scritch.

Bradley turned and faced the room, listening.

Scritch-scritch.

This time, in addition to the scratching, he saw the fabric of one of his suitcases move in time with the noises.

"What the hell?" Bradley stepped to his bed to get a closer look at the suitcase. There was something moving inside.

Scritch. Scritch-scritch.

He rotated the suitcase to get better access and slowly began to pull the zipper open.

What the actual fuck am I doing? He took a deep breath, unzipped the suitcase's lid, threw it open, and stepped back.

Nothing. No movement. No noise.

Bradley padded forward on the balls of his feet, closer to the open suitcase. He could see all his clothes, just as he had packed them in New York.

Nothing appeared to be wrong. He reached in, pulled out a shirt, and shook it out in front of him. It passed inspection: he threw it on the bed and grabbed another shirt. He looked at both sides for holes and found none. He tossed it aside. Odors of fried chicken, pizza, dirty clothes, and something else—*urine?*—rose from the case.

He spotted his "Home is where the WI-FI connects automatically" t-shirt. Bradley pulled a corner of the shirt and the suitcase exploded in a frenzy of motion. A rat leaped to the edge of the suitcase. Its tail swished back and forth in angry twirls and he could hear the familiar *chi-chi-chi-chich* of the rat's grinding incisors. Bradley stumbled backward, his feet tangling in his jacket, and fell to the floor.

The rat jumped from the suitcase to the clothes dresser and scurried out the open window. Everything happened so fast that Bradley wasn't sure if it had been real.

"Brad?" Claire called from elsewhere in the house. "Is everything alright?"

It was real. Brad sat on the floor, catching his breath.

Claire popped her head into his bedroom. "What are you doing on the floor?"

"I tripped on my jacket." Bradley rolled onto his knees and grabbed Claire's extended hand for balance. He stood and brushed himself off.

"What is *that?*" Claire's concern was replaced by anger.

"What are you talking about?"

"This." Claire pulled back the right cuff of his t-shirt, revealing his anti-rat tattoo.

Bradley sighed. He had hoped to ease into the topic later, but as usual, things were not going as planned.

"It's a tattoo," he said.

"I *know* what it is. I suppose that's Sam's doing?"

Always trying to blame Dad. "Actually, no. I got it done myself." Bradley stood his ground. "Dad had nothing to do with it."

Claire was livid but had difficulty finding words. "This isn't over, mister. Not by a long shot." She stomped back down the hallway.

"I'm not removing it," Bradley called back. "It's my choice." He expected a response, or even Roy to pop his head in where it didn't belong, but was met with silence.

Bradley replayed the path he remembered the rat taking just moments ago and stepped to his bedroom window. The back yard looked just as it had every August, with assorted vegetables (tomatoes, peas and onions this year) growing in their designated patches of earth. The shed just behind the garden needed a new coat of paint.

And the rat was gone.

Was it a white tail? God, I hope not. Bradley couldn't remember. Everything had happened too fast. The rat hadn't appeared big enough to be a Gambian, but he couldn't remember for sure.

His phone chimed in his pocket. He pulled it out. There were several texts waiting from Jack.

His latest text read, "Breakfast burrito?" Jack had a one track mind when it came to food. Go Mexican or go home. His favorite spot was Taco Siempre, close enough to walk or bike to.

"Sounds good," Bradley texted back. After his dustup with Claire, getting out of the house would help him cool down.

"C U in 5." Jack texted. Translation: He was planning to drive. Jack had had his driver's license since April. Bradley had to wait another couple months before he could apply. As envious as he felt, this also meant that he didn't need to walk or ride much. Jack loved driving almost as much as Mexican food.

Bradley slipped his wallet out of his inner jacket pocket,

pocketed his phone, and headed for the front door of the house. He slipped on his shoes without tying them.

"Going to grab some food with Jack," Bradley called back before stepping out into the morning sunshine. The faster he was out of earshot the better. He stopped and sat at the curb, tying his shoes as he waited.

Bradley didn't have to wait long. He heard the rusted-out muffler of Jack's orange 1982 Honda Civic before he saw it. The Civic zoomed around a corner onto Sheldon Street and barreled toward the house, accelerating instead of slowing. A budding daredevil, Jack applied the brake at the last moment. The little orange car came to rest about three feet from where Bradley sat.

Jack leaned out the driver's side window. "See that? Didn't leave rubber. Hop in."

Bradley pulled open the passenger door with a creak and slid into an aftermarket bucket seat. The two teenagers gave each other dap.

"It's about damn time, bro." Jack pulled away from the curb, accelerating down the street. "Was starting to wonder if you were coming back."

"New York is cool and all," Bradley said as he buckled himself in. "But I'd never want to live there."

"Let me guess. Too many rats?"

Bradley laughed. "You could say that. So, are these seats new?"

"Damn straight. Got them put in a couple weeks ago. But if you checked your texts, you'd know that."

"Sorry. There was no Wi-Fi and data charges were killing me."

"No Wi-Fi? For the whole summer?" Jack ran his fingers through his short afro. "Damn. I think I'd go nuts."

"I got used to it."

Jack wove his way through Stonehurst and west along

Glenoaks Boulevard toward Pacoima, the Civic's belching muffler alerting everyone along the way.

"You got to fix your muffler."

Jack shrugged as they passed the southern edge of Hansen Dam Golf Course. "I'll get to it eventually. Hey, you heard from Alexis?"

"Fuck, no. That was the only plus to having no Wi-Fi all summer."

"You will."

JACK PULLED INTO the small parking lot in front of Taco Siempre. The smell of Mexican seasoning, cumin, chili, and cilantro drifted through the car.

"Smells like heaven," Jack said. "Hope you're hungry 'cause I'm buying."

"We'll see about that."

Jack slid out of the open driver's side window like it was second nature.

"What's up with that?"

"Damn door wouldn't latch, so I welded it shut."

"I bet that goes over well on dates."

"Dates? I don't got time for dates."

Bradley pulled open the door to the small restaurant and the smells intensified. His stomach growled, almost loud enough to be heard above the sounds of sizzling from the back kitchen.

A corkboard hung on the wall beside the entrance where various announcements and business cards from the community were tacked. Bradley noticed a couple missing pet posters before his brain skipped back on track.

"What did you mean I'm going to hear from Alexis?"

Jack's eyes focused on the menu board. "Food first. Know what you want?"

The breakfast selections were limited to two items: breakfast burrito and breakfast plate. Bradley shrugged indifference.

Jack turned to the young woman behind the counter. "Hey, Sofia. Could I get two breakfast burritos, a side of guac, and two coffees."

Sofia punched in the order on the cash register. "That's $18.93."

Jack had pulled out his wallet and was handing Sofia a twenty before Bradley could protest. "Keep the change."

"Gracias," Sofia said with a smile. "I'll call you when your order's ready."

Jack nodded and headed toward one of the few empty tables available. Even at eight-thirty on a Sunday morning, Siempre was hopping busy. He slid onto the red form-fitting melamine bench seat, with Bradley taking the opposite side.

"Thanks, man," Bradley said. "I'll get the next one."

"Deal." Jack clasped his hands behind his head. "I must have some Mexican blood in me because damn, I love this food."

"I hadn't noticed."

Both teenagers laughed and bumped fists.

"So, what were you saying about Alexis?"

"I'm surprised she wasn't waiting on your doorstep," Jack said. "You haven't gotten texts? Because I've been getting them all damn summer. It's like I've been your secretary. Fucking annoying."

Bradley pulled out his phone. There were no new texts from Alexis. He placed the phone on the table. "What was she saying?"

"She wanted to know where you were, to tell you that she's sorry, crap like that."

"You didn't—"

"Hell no. We both know she's crazy." Jack studied Bradley's

expression and saw the gears turning in his head. "Don't even think about getting back with her."

"No, I won't," Bradley said. "Just curious."

"You know what they say about curiosity."

"Jack?" Sofia called out from the front counter. "Order's up."

Jack stood up to go get the food.

"You know what they say about satisfaction." Bradley grinned.

"No." Jack pointed at Bradley. "Just no." He lifted the tray off the counter and inhaled the aroma deeply. "Smells great. Thanks, Sofia."

Sofia nodded.

Jack transported the tray back to the table and both teenagers dug in. He lifted the additional cup of guacamole.

"You want some guac?"

"Nah." Bradley took his plate and coffee off the tray. "Good call on the coffee."

"I figured you needed something to wake you up after your flight."

Jack peeled back the paper on his burrito and took a large bite, savoring the flavors. "I got to learn how to make this. Maybe Sofia is single."

"I thought you didn't have time for dating."

"If it was Sofia, I'd make time."

Bradley laughed and cut into his burrito. "I wonder if they have rats in a place like this?"

"I doubt it," Jack said between bites. "The food doesn't last long enough to attract rats."

"You'd be surprised."

"Right now, I don't give a damn." Jack chomped another bite.

"Hey, take a look at this." Bradley raised the right cuff of his t-shirt and exposed his anti-rat tattoo.

Jack's eyes went wide. "Bro, that's sick."

"Souvenir from New York."

"Bet your mom freaked."

"Yup."

"So, what's the big deal about New York City rats?" Jack crammed in a mouthful of burrito.

"Actually, these ones were hybrids. Part Gambian, from Africa, and part Bronx," Bradley said. "Strong and smart as fuck."

Jack pumped his fist. "Africa, for the win."

"One of the exterminators, Washington, he invented all his own tools," Bradley said. "There was this big, electrified cage he called the Kill-O-Matic. We lured thousands of rats into that thing and fried them."

Jack's attention took priority over food for a moment. "Thousands?"

Bradley nodded. "I wish I had video of it. Then again…" He trailed off, his hand instinctively touching the pendant under his shirt. Bradley removed it from around his neck and set it into his palm. "He gave this to me."

Jack took the pendant with careful fingers and examined the rat skull encased in amber closely. "That's seriously cool." He handed the pendant back and Bradley placed it around his neck.

"Washington was a cool guy." Bradley sipped his coffee. His shudder from its strong flavor also disguised his reaction to the memory of Washington's death. "You would've liked him."

"Wait." Jack raised his eyebrows. "Would have liked?"

"He was electrocuted. Right in front of me."

Jack stared and his jaw slackened. "You're shitting me."

Bradley shook his head. "He died inside his own invention. But he took a lot of rats down with him."

"Damn."

A somber tone fell over the table. "Sorry. I shouldn't have said anything."

"Don't worry about it, bro." Jack drank from his coffee. "I

would've done the same thing. Lucky we don't got rats in the valley."

"We do now," Bradley said. "One of those bastards hitched a ride back in my suitcase."

"A…" Jack searched his memory, then snapped his fingers. "A Gambian hybrid?"

"I don't know. It was too fast."

"Tell me more about the cage."

Bradley could tell Jack was switching into "idea mode".

"The Kill-O-Matic?"

"Yeah." Jack continued eating his meal, mouth full but ears open.

Bradley had barely opened his mouth when his phone lit up and began vibrating on the table.

"What the?" The phone was showing weeks of unanswered texts from Alexis popping up in rapid succession.

Jack halted his chewing. "What?"

Bradley held up his phone's display as more texts appeared, getting more and more recent.

"Oh, shit," Jack said.

Oh, shit is right, Bradley thought.

Predator

CLAIRE NEVER LOCKED the shed in the back yard. She needed tools and supplies from it far too often to bother. Without a lock, the rain and heat-warped doors offered a gap at the bottom about an inch wide. Just the right size for a hungry and recently escaped rat.

After scrambling out Bradley's bedroom window and scaling an electrical conduit to the ground, the rat followed the foundation of the house until it could find cover in the garden foliage. The rat's nose quivered madly as sorted through the scents to determine the best source of food.

The rat bypassed the onions and tomatoes completely, focusing on low-hanging pea pods. It gnawed a stem, picked up the fallen pod and began to eat.

Under normal circumstances peas would have sufficed, but the rat could smell something else, something more tantalizing. It dropped the pea pod to the dirt after eating half and searched under cover of shadow for the source of this intoxicating smell.

The rat followed its nose until it found itself at the foundation of the shed. It stood on its haunches, looking across the back yard and to the open window through which it had recently escaped.

The odor was strong here. The rat was close. It surveyed the yard, the front of the shed, and the surrounding trees for danger. Raptors were always a threat.

Satisfied it was safe, the rat scurried along the front of the shed and wriggled through the uneven crack between the double swinging doors.

What little light there was in the shed entered through vented openings near the roof joists, one on each wall. The dim environment proved little challenge to the rat's eyesight. So close to such a heavenly smell, the rat's snout kicked into overdrive.

The rat shot across the shed to the right wall and followed the exposed floor studs until it found what it was looking for: a bag of premium bird seed, chock full of shelled raw sunflower seeds. It gnawed the corner of the bag until a small torrent of seeds cascaded onto the wooden floor.

The rat picked up a seed from what seemed to be an endless supply and consumed it without pause. It was about to pick up another seed when something in the shed moved. The rat froze in its tracks, listening and watching.

After half a minute, the rat returned to its feast, searching with its paws for another seed. After its third helping, the rat saw something that it had missed on its way in. The rat had been so intent on finding the sunflower seeds that it had bypassed a plum lying on the slats of the floor.

Rats love plums and this new delectable find would be the perfect dessert. It kept its body low and stretched its neck forward, sniffing and testing the nearby air.

In the blink of an eye, the plum was no longer a plum, but the abdomen of a large spider. Its eight spindly legs mobilized from underneath its body and long whisker-like hairs sprang up from around its thorax and abdomen, acting like feelers.

The rat was quick, but the spider was quicker. It shot a jet of sticky silk from its two spinnerets, covering the rat's eyes, snout, and whiskers. Unable to see, the rat reversed itself into the open floor of the shed and emitted a raspy wail. The spider jumped on top of the rat and punctured its neck with its venom-filled fangs. The rat's wail morphed into a short-lived shriek.

The effect was instantaneous. The rat lost control of the left side of its body and rolled onto its useless limbs. Its right legs spasmed as the rodent tried to regain control of its body.

The spider crossed the rat's body from side to side, front to back, until all remaining air in the rat's lungs was squeezed out by a thin but tight net of silken webbing.

Several more spiders emerged from the shadows, each attaching their own threads to the paralyzed rat, and together they dragged the cocoon into a corner of the shed and deep within a woven funnel-like structure.

FOR ALMOST TWO years, Jack had begun his days at five-thirty in the morning. Working at the local Food Fresh Market had helped him finance his customized Honda Civic and buy the supplies and equipment he needed for his inventions. He was the only teenager he knew at Washbrook High that worked before school started.

Jack got up, took a quick shower, and threw on his Food Fresh shirt and comfortable jeans. He ran his fingers through his tight afro curls, noting a need for a haircut soon.

He finished the carton of milk with his cereal and saw that the fridge looked bare. He'd need to make a grocery run at the Food Fresh sometime today.

He slipped out his phone, called up his banking app, and checked his expense account. Being the beginning of a new week, funds for running the household should have been automatically deposited overnight by his parents. For a moment, the Internet hiccupped as he waited for the app to load. But the screen updated as it usually did, showing his weekly allowance. His parents had made it clear that the money be used for household bills and supplies first. Any remaining balance by the time Sunday rolled around was his to keep, and Taco Siempre got a fair share of it.

Jack grabbed his wallet, keys, and a banana for the road. He locked the house, jumped into his Civic through the passenger side, and sped off toward Food Fresh Market. He woke up every dog along the way.

His shift started at six and he made sure he was always a few minutes early. The neon "OPEN" sign for the market was still off, as were most of the lights inside. He backed the Civic into the stall furthest from the store, cracked open the skin of his banana, and ate it in three bites.

Will I be stocking shelves or delivering groceries today? If he had his pick, Jack would much rather deliver groceries. Anything that let him zoom around town got his vote.

"This Is America" by Childish Gambino played from his phone played wirelessly through the speakers in the dash. Jack had modified a set of Bluetooth headphones and connected it to an old cassette adapter. He could have bought a dedicated Bluetooth cassette adapter to achieve the same result, but he had wanted to build something himself from parts he had on hand. It worked well, other than some dropout when traveling over bumps, and saving fifty dollars made the solution even sweeter.

The lights within the store's sign flickered and buzzed on, the neon "OPEN" glowing red in the dawn light. An animated neon arrow pointed toward the main doors. Less than a minute later, the fluorescent lights within the store cascaded on, one aisle at a time. Jack turned off the music, grabbed his keys, and locked the car. As he crossed the parking lot, he took in the blue sky and fresh morning air.

The double doors slid open automatically as Jack strolled inside. It was always a strange feeling walking into the market before the rest of the employees and customers had arrived. *Almost apocalyptic,* he thought.

He headed to the manager's office situated at the back of the market. The staff schedule and daily employee tasks were posted on the wall next to the door. Jack poked his head into the office.

"Hey, Mr. Toscano."

"Mr. Johnson." Giovanni Toscano, a bald, portly man with a thin black mustache and a heavy gold chain around his neck, spoke without looking up from his work.

"What's up for today?" Jack said to himself as he scanned the task list for his name. As it turned out, he was responsible for a few deliveries and a pickup from a local boutique egg producer. *Not bad*, he thought. He'd have just enough time to get everything done before the first day of school.

Jack grabbed a cart from the front of the market and collected the items for the three deliveries he was scheduled to make, separating the items into plastic boxes as he went.

By the time he was finished, several cashiers had arrived, including Tasha. She was a year older than him and worked full time. It was her rich, dark eyes that got him every time. He'd gladly stand in line to have her ring in his groceries, even if other lines were shorter. But he always lost his voice when he stepped up to the till. He never knew what to say.

This morning Jack was first in line. He lifted each box to the conveyor and Tasha began to ring through the delivery items to their associated delivery accounts.

"Three deliveries today, huh?" Tasha smiled. "Beautiful morning for it."

Jack felt as if his knees would buckle. He couldn't hold her gaze, so he traced the length of her tightly braided cornrows with his eyes until they touched the nape of her neck.

"Your hair looks nice." Jack cast his eyes to the floor and groaned to himself. *Your hair looks nice?* Tasha had had her hair in cornrows for over a month and he couldn't be sure that he hadn't made the same compliment already.

Tasha tilted her head slightly and grinned as she bagged his orders and placed them back in the plastic boxes. "Thanks." She pulled the receipts from the cash register and tucked them into an envelope reserved for deliveries. "Drive safe, Jack."

He nodded, loaded the boxes back into the shopping cart, and exited the store. He couldn't wait to get back to his car, but at the same time, he didn't want to leave. He paused and shot a quick smile at Tasha. The first few customers had already begun filtering in from the parking lot.

Jack loaded the boxes into the back of the car, then slid behind the wheel. He watched the entrance to the market just long enough to see Tasha serving another early-bird customer.

Using a mapping app on his phone, Jack planned his route for maximize efficiency. He started the Civic and the engine settled into a low rumble. "Act A Fool" by Ludacris, an oldie but a goodie, pumped from the car's speakers as Jack peeled out of the parking lot. Thirty-five minutes later he was parked at Unbeaten Farms, loading eggs separated by the dozen into the back of his car.

Back at the market, Jack parked in back and moved a wheeled pallet next to his car. He loaded the eggs onto it, wheeled it through the cooled storage room and into the market's public area.

Jack rolled the eggs through the fruit and produce section, passing Tasha on her way back from the staff room. In his distraction he clipped a display of bananas with the pallet and one carton of eggs fell to the floor. He heard at least one distinct crunch.

"Shit." Jack stopped and secured the pallet.

"Sorry," Tasha said. "Need some help?"

"No." Jack could feel the burn of embarrassment creep up his neck. "I got it, thanks."

"Okay." Tasha continued up the aisle toward the front of the store.

Jack lifted the lid to inspect the contents of the fallen carton.

Dented in one side, only three eggs had broken. He'd pay for the dozen and take the rest home. Luckily, he needed eggs anyway.

Jack visited the staff room, tore off a strip of paper towel and returned to the scene of the accident to pick the broken shells out of the carton.

He pulled the first eggshell out of the carton and jerked back when a swarm of glistening black spiders scurried away in all directions. Jack scrambled backward in shock and disgust.

The spiders disappeared into the shadows of the surrounding fruit displays quicker than the words "what the fuck" had escaped from Jack's mouth. But there was something about the spiders, something about their backs that seemed odd. He filed the observation in the back of his mind for later.

He approached the second broken egg and flicked it with his finger. The cracked shell rattled in the carton. Jack picked it out, leaving a yolky mess behind. He tested the third egg in the same way and was relieved to find no eight-legged surprises underneath. He soaked up the rest of the spilled whites and yolks and set the carton aside.

Jack deposited the shell remnants into a nearby garbage can in the rear warehouse. He stuck his head into the office on the way back. "Mr. Toscano, I broke some eggs. But I'll buy the carton, I need groceries anyway. Can I store them in back?"

"Sounds good." Giovanni gave Jack a "thumbs up" without averting his eyes from his computer monitor.

Just as Jack stepped away, Giovanni called him back.

"I have one more delivery, if you have time," he said. "Mr. Moody. It's all packed, ready to go at the front."

There weren't many rules that went with working at Food Fresh. Honesty, punctuality, and "the customer is always right" were standard. But one unwritten rule topped the list: you *always* had time for Giovanni. If you didn't have time, you *made* time. Second on the list of unwritten rules: you *never said "no"* to Giovanni. To preserve their own sanity, Jack and his coworkers had an unwritten rule of their own: avoid Giovanni as much as possible.

No such luck today. "Sure, Mr. Toscano."

It wasn't that Mr. Moody's orders were complicated. Quite the opposite. The old man ate the simplest of foods. It was everything else about him that gave Jack the creeps. He couldn't imagine a worse way to start his first day back to school.

Jack picked up Mr. Moody's delivery from the front of the store, managing only a wave to Tasha as he walked by. He carried the delivery box back to his Civic and placed it on the back seat.

He dug out his phone and texted Bradley. "Want a ride?"

BRADLEY WOKE BEFORE his six-thirty alarm feeling exhausted. His sleep the night before had been fractured, not by worries about school, but by jet lag mixed with anxiety about running into Alexis. He ran scenario after scenario through his head, trying to come up with the best response. One idea his fuzzy brain kept returning to was to continue ghosting her, but that would become a ticking time bomb. Bradley decided not to seek out trouble, but if trouble found him—and Alexis's kind of trouble *always* found him—he'd face it head on.

He got up, showered and dressed, and wandered into the kitchen. His residual anxiety had spoiled his appetite for breakfast, so he chose coffee instead. The same modern Mr. Coffee drip brewer sat on the counter as before his New York trip.

At least some things haven't changed around here.

Bradley scooped enough coffee grounds into the filter cone for a full pot, filled the water reservoir and set the machine to brew. He was looking forward to better coffee than the swill that came out of the Mr. Coffee from the 1970s that Sam used.

While the coffee brewed, Bradley made himself a ham and cheese sandwich and threw it into a paper bag, along with an apple and most of the few Oreos that remained in the bag. He noticed that Claire had stocked the fridge and pantry with food he liked, and he felt a little guilty about their argument the night before. But not guilty enough to put the Oreos back.

A pot of hot coffee would be a nice peace offering.

Bradley added two ample teaspoons of sugar to a mug and waited for the brewing to complete. He stood at the kitchen window and watched the back yard wake up.

His hand went instinctively to the raccoon tail hanging off his belt loop. He pulled it through his hands and fingers. The soft feeling of fur calmed his anxiety about Alexis.

Mr. Coffee beeped and Bradley poured himself a mugful. The coffee's rich aroma filled the kitchen and it wouldn't be long before the smell would pull Claire and Roy out of sleep. He raised the mug to his lips and took a tentative sip.

The raccoon tail worked wonders, but coffee amplified his relaxation as well as his awareness. It was a better combination.

Through the kitchen window, Bradley spotted a raccoon wandering through the garden. Claire would have a hissy-fit if she knew some creature was eating her vegetables, but this raccoon had other ideas.

Is that the same raccoon I saw after being jumped last spring? Probably not, but the thought reassured him, and Bradley treated it as a sign of good things to come.

He stood at the window drinking his coffee and watched the raccoon wind its way to the front of the shed. The animal pawed at the doors until it had created an opening large enough to squeeze itself through.

Bradley thought of telling Claire but decided against it. There wasn't any food inside the shed worth eating anyway.

Bradley's phone chirped in his pocket and his body stiffened.

What if it's a text from Alexis? He took a gulp of coffee to prepare his nerves before pulling out his phone to look.

"Want a ride?" Jack's text read.

Bradley heaved a sigh of relief and texted back a "thumbs up" emoji.

"ETA 8 mins," Jack's reply read.

Bradley downed what was left of his coffee, grabbed his bag lunch, day pack, and shoes, and headed out to the curb.

THE RACCOON HAD been drawn to the shed by the scent of the premium sunflower seeds. Once inside, it rummaged around looking for the source of the smell. Other equipment stored in front—a lawn mower, earthenware pots and assorted tools—blocked the path of the larger animal. The bag of sunflower seeds remained unattainable for now.

Instead, the raccoon found an open bag of allium bulbs and began eating.

Deep within the darkness of the shed, behind the bag of sunflower seeds, the tunnel of silken webbing had increased in size. Hundreds of gossamer trip wires lead out and around the opening.

Glints of oily black attached to eight gunmetal legs moved forward in small bursts. The cluster of spiders held their distance, choosing to observe instead of attack. The raccoon was much larger than any prey they had captured so far.

The raccoon, unaware of the lethal threat behind it, finished its snack and pushed its way back through the double doors of the shed. Getting out of the shed was easier than getting in.

The spiders retreated into the dark and lay in waiting. Spiders survived on patience, but hunger would force them to hunt. Escaping the shed would be more difficult next time.

First Day

The shady refuge of the trampoline provided a favorite summer haunt for Winston the cat, when Elizabeth and Jacob Hyland weren't using it to reach for the sky. He spent most of his sunny days snoozing in the cool grass with warm summer breeze buffeting his fur. It was cat paradise.

When Winston didn't show up for breakfast, Liz and Jake's alarm bell went off.

"He always eats with us in the morning," they had said to their mom.

By lunchtime the two set out to find him.

"Win-boy! Winner!" their concerned voices called out. Liz and Jake circled the house, then expanded to side streets around the neighborhood. They even took his Pyrex food dish out and rapped the edge with a spoon. The invitation of food attracted other neighborhood cats but not Winston. Not today.

Liz and Jake went to bed that night without their favorite pet and their sleep did not come easily.

No one had thought of checking under the trampoline. If they had, they would have found gauzy webbing and wisps that led to the corner of the yard, between the neighbor's garage and an old refrigerator with its door stuck open. They would have found Winston's body inside, tightly wrapped in a silken cocoon and covered with black spiders, cultivating him for food.

But no one found Winston. The spiders consumed him over several days, leaving nothing but a sack of bones.

JACK PULLED UP to the curb in front of Bradley's house, facing the Civic in the opposite direction as all the other cars parked on the street. Jack liked to stand out.

Bradley threw his pack into the footwell and hopped inside. "Thanks," he said as he gave dap to Jack.

"Got to make a short delivery first." Jack scanned the street around him for approaching vehicles, then pulled out, accelerating fast.

"Where?"

"Moody's place."

"Damn. Lucky you."

"Don't I know it." Jack hooked his thumb at the back seat. "The guy eats nothing but oats, bananas, and milk. Oh, and vodka, but I don't get to deliver that."

Bradley twisted in his seat to see the box. There was an aerosol paint can next to it. "The guy must be totally bunged. Maybe a rat will come through his toilet and bite him in the ass."

"They can do that?"

"Saw it with my own eyes."

"Shit, I don't even want to imagine Moody's toilet."

Bradley loosened his seat belt, reached back, and picked up the paint can. "What's this?"

"That's one of my latest inventions. See the lever?" Jack pointed to a metal rod at the base of the can. "Squeeze it."

Before Bradley could work his hand around to the lever, a small black spider crawled onto his hand from the opposite side of the can.

"Holy shit!" He dropped the paint can and recoiled his hand, squirming in his seat as the spider fell on his lap. Bradley brushed it into the footwell and stamped it into a dark, greasy stain.

Jack laughed. "Don't like spiders?"

"Not when they sneak up on you."

"You going to clean that mess up?" Jack nodded at the remains of the spider now embedded in the passenger side floormat.

"Are you serious?"

"Damn, bro," Jack said between chuckles. "I've missed having you around. Now back to what matters. Squeeze the lever."

Bradley raised the paint can in front of him. It didn't take much pressure to move the lever. It triggered a spring-loaded arm that flipped out, unfolding a stencil of a Wi-Fi symbol in front of the spray nozzle.

"Tag and run with one hand, bro." Pride showed through in Jack's voice. "Fold it back away for quick and easy storage."

"You sound like a commercial."

"I can't sell it without talking about it."

Bradley folded the arm back down until the lever clicked, then triggered it again. "Love the Wi-Fi symbol."

"It's small and recognizable. You can swap it out for whatever shape you want, as long as it's not too complicated."

"Cool." Bradley placed the spray can on the back seat. He scanned the joins and shadows of the seat for any other unwelcome eight-legged creatures just as Jack pulled into Moody's rutted driveway. The house, a dilapidated rancher from the 1950s, was in serious need of paint and a new roof. All the windows had curtains covering them and the surrounding lawn was overgrown with weeds.

"Love what he's done to the place."

Jack killed the engine and pulled himself through the driver-side window. "The guy never leaves the house." He flipped his seat forward and lifted the delivery box out the window. "If I'm not back in ten minutes, call the cops."

It must have been Bradley's expression, because Jack laughed as he walked away from the Civic. "Bro, you crack me up."

Jack carried the box down the driveway and up a short rickety staircase to the left of the ramshackle garage. He knocked on the back door before taking a couple of deep breaths of fresh, clean air, a scarce commodity inside Mr. Moody's house.

Jack waited a moment and listened before knocking again.

"Yeah, yeah, I'm coming," a hoarse voice said from behind the door. "Wait a goddamn minute, will yah?"

Sounds of deadbolts sliding and unlatching echoed through the door. The doorknob turned, the door opened a crack, and stopped.

Silence, then a voice. "What're yah waiting for?"

Jack pushed open the door and received a blast of warm ripe air, pungent with a mixture of body odor, shit, and rotting fruit. He gagged and struggled to control his nausea.

The morning sunlight slashed through the dark mudroom that led into the kitchen. The air was thick with haze and everything looked dirty and diseased.

"Well, don't just stand there, boy." Mr. Moody sat in a motorized wheelchair that looked as if it had become one with his body. The old man was grossly obese, his soiled pajamas stretched tight across his body, stained yellowish brown at the crotch. His breathing rattled in his chest and Jack imagined his lungs half-filled with diluted oatmeal. The glasses he wore tethered around his neck with rotting cords doubled as a trough for fallen food.

Jack carried the delivery box into the mudroom. "Where do you want this?"

Mr. Moody grunted. "Kitchen counter. Same as always."

Jack set the box down and unloaded the bananas, oatmeal

and milk onto the counter. "You want me to put the milk away for you?"

"I don't want yah touching my food any more than yah have already, boy."

Fine by me, you fat fuck. "That'll be $11.23."

Mr. Moody grumbled something unintelligible and drove his wheelchair down the hallway into an adjoining room. Sounds of crashing dishes pierced the dank darkness. "Boy!"

Jack gritted his teeth at the man's overt racism and tip-toed down the hallway. This was the furthest he had ever ventured into Mr. Moody's house since beginning his deliveries and the walls felt like they were closing in on him.

Mr. Moody's foot had caught on a woolen afghan, toppling a stack of dirty dishes. But it was the hundreds of porcelain doll heads that caused a scream to build in the back of Jack's throat. Every free space, table, and shelf was occupied by pale miniature heads that seemed to glow in the dark, some cracked, some with pieces missing, all with wide-open dead-black eyes that seemed to track his every move.

"I'm stuck, boy." Mr. Moody's voice distracted the terror rising in the back of Jack's mind. "Want yer money? Pull yer thumb out of yah ass and unstuck me."

Jack knelt next to the wheelchair. The yellow, fungus-encrusted toenails of Mr. Moody's right foot were tangled up in the afghan's weave. One by one, Jack extracted Mr. Moody's toes, trying not to touch his feet any more than necessary.

Once freed, Mr. Moody navigated around a couch and retrieved his wallet. "Don't got no twenty-three cents."

"Eleven is fine." Jack didn't care that he'd have to make up the difference. All he wanted was to get the hell out of the house.

Mr. Moody handed Jack a wad of bills.

"Thanks, Mr. Moody." Jack jammed the bills into his pocket without counting them and headed for the door, sunlight, and salvation just beyond. He grabbed the delivery box as he passed through the kitchen.

"Them bananas better be fresh," Mr. Moody said, following Jack with his wheelchair.

"Shipment came in yesterday." Jack closed the back door behind him and stopped on the bottom step, taking in the sweet September air like a drowning man pulled to safety.

JACK JOGGED DOWN the driveway to the Civic, threw in the delivery box, and jumped into the driver's seat.

"Holy shit. I think I need a shower."

"I was this close to calling the police." Bradley held his thumb and index finger an inch apart. "Seriously, man."

"You got any hand sanitizer?"

"That bad?"

"You don't want to know." Jack started the engine and backed out of the driveway. "Fucking gross. But he does have a lot of cool shit in his garage. Like turn-of-the-century kind of shit. Remind me to show you some time."

"When were you in his garage?"

"You know, odd jobs. I have no problem taking his money," Jack said. "Even if he is an asshole. But going into his damn house? Fuck that shit."

Jack worked the gear shift of the Civic's standard transmission like a pro. He envisioned himself a Formula-1 racer, the aftermarket accessories reinforcing the image. What the Civic really needed was a new coat of paint.

"We had earthquakes while you were gone."

"Yeah, my mom mentioned that," Bradley said. "Nothing too big, she said."

"There was one quake. Woke me up." Jack geared down and

turned onto a side street like the car was on rails. "Compared to the others, it was big. A 2.9. I crunched the numbers and it was over two standard deviations above the mean for the summer."

"In English, please. You know math ain't my thing."

"It wasn't typical," Jack said. "If I graphed it, you'd see it right away."

Bradley gave Jack a sideways look.

"I got it on my phone. I'll show you later." Jack slowed the Civic at a four-way stop and looked for approaching vehicles. "Speaking of phones, did you get any more *ex texts* since yesterday?"

Bradley shook his head. "No." He grabbed his raccoon tail and let the fur slip through his fingers.

Jack tapped on the steering wheel and smirked. "You're so fucked."

"I'm so fucked," Bradley said in unison.

The two teenagers laughed and tapped fists. Jack accelerated away from the four-way. Washbrook High School could be seen in the distance.

"You shouldn't have ghosted her, bro."

Bradley protested. "I didn't do it on purpose. How was I supposed to know she'd go ape-shit on me?"

"I don't know, but there are few things worse than a Latina on the warpath."

"Says the guy who has no time for girls."

"Hey, I don't need to date to know the facts." Jack turned into the school's student parking lot and found a spot on the far edge. "Girls hold all the cards."

"Whatever."

Both teens rolled themselves out of the Civic's passenger door. Bradley swung his day pack over his shoulder and watched Jack grab a pad of paper and a pencil from the back seat.

"You sure come prepared."

Jack gave him a shove as the two walked toward other

students hanging in front of the school. "You know what the first day is like. We don't do shit. Besides, what can *they* teach *me?*"

"Wow. Look at Jack's *massive* ego."

"Shut up." They both laughed.

Bradley passed a lamp standard with a paper notice taped to it.

"HAVE YOU SEEN BARKLEY?" the top of the notice read in bold black letters. A black and white photo of a cat was framed underneath with contact details below that.

Bradley hooked a thumb at the notice as they passed by. "What's up with that?"

Jack shrugged. "Pets started disappearing about a month ago."

Bradley snapped his fingers. "There were posters in Taco Siempre yesterday."

"They're popping up everywhere," Jack said. "I been seeing them a lot on my deliveries."

"Weird." For once, Bradley was glad Claire hadn't let him have a pet.

The school bell rang the day into session and students funneled in through the main doors.

"Later, bro." Jack grinned and raised his middle finger at Bradley. They had been giving each other middle finger goodbyes since Grade 8, confusing anyone witnessing the exchange. To Jack and Bradley, the gesture was as harmless as a wave, but they liked to screw with people's heads.

Bradley returned the gesture. "Later."

The friends disappeared into the school in opposite directions. Washbrook High could accommodate over one thousand students from grades nine through twelve. The size of the school and the number of students made it easy to fly under the radar and blend in. That was Bradley's first order of business.

His phone chimed in his pocket. He slid it out and on the display was a text from Alexis.

"WHERE U BEEN???" it read.

Shit.

Bradley tapped "NYC" and hit "send." He set the phone to vibrate and dropped it back into his pocket.

BRADLEY FOUND HIS old homeroom from last year easily enough. They tended not to change from year to year since students were divided by alphabetical order based on last name. This also meant that he wouldn't run into Alexis. Delarosa was worlds apart from Shaw, alphabetically speaking.

After confirming his homeroom assignment with the one he had received by email, Bradley followed a mass of students up the south stairwell to the second floor, where most of the grade eleven and twelve classes were located. Lockers in varying states of disrepair and decoration lined both sides of the hallway. The lockers should have been cleaned up over the summer break, but in Bradley's view, they all looked the same.

Mr. Silver's classroom was two doors down from the stairwell on the right. The windows faced east and were blessed by the morning sun. Mr. Silver, a man who never said "no" to a doughnut, sat reading with his feet up on his desk.

The only aspects of Mr. Silver that seemed to change from year to year were the book he was reading and the length of his beard. He had played Santa in previous years, but this year he could pass for a younger, slightly rounder Jeff Bridges. His typical attire consisted of pressed khaki pants with a buttoned shirt, a tie, and a brown leather vest, all one size too small. He looked like he was going to pop at any minute. Instead of a book, he held an e-reader.

Bradley pointed to the device in Mr. Silver's hand. "Moving up in the world."

"Birthday gift from the missus." He flipped the device around in his hand. "Jury's still out. I miss the smell of paper."

"You'll get used to it pretty fast." Bradley found a seat at the front. "What're you reading?"

Being an English teacher, Mr. Silver usually chose a classic novel like *Murder on the Orient Express* or *The Picture of Dorian Gray*, which was why his answer surprised Bradley.

"Jaws. Peter Benchley."

"The movie's awesome."

"The book is better." Mr. Silver placed the e-reader on his desk. "I've been immersing myself in genre fiction this summer. I'm hooked."

"Great."

"Do you have English with me this year?"

As the classroom filled with students, Bradley's conversation with "a teacher" threatened his "coolness factor." He pulled out his phone and dialed back his conversation. "Think so."

"Good," Mr. Silver said. "We're going to have some fun this year."

Bradley nodded and went back to his phone.

"You're going to want to put that away." Mr. Silver motioned at the phone.

Bradley took a hint and stuffed it back into his pocket. Students talked amongst themselves in small groups, some standing, some sitting in or on top of desks, excitement evident in their voices.

Mr. Silver looked at his watch, cracked his knuckles, and stood. "Take a seat, everyone."

Most of the students still standing found open spots to sit. "I see we'll need a few more desks. Duly noted. Can I have someone close the doors?"

Two students at the back rose from their desks and closed the doors at the back of the classroom.

Mr. Silver placed a cardboard box on his desk and picked up

a clipboard and a pencil. "To those just joining us, welcome to Washbrook High. To everyone else, welcome back. Did everyone have a good summer?"

The class mumbled various forms of "yes."

"Great. I hope your time here will be both fun and productive. We don't have much time, so when I call your name, raise your hand and say 'here.' "

Since Bradley first started at Washbrook three years ago, there had always been a high number of last names beginning with "S." Jack had once calculated and graphed the distribution curve of last names to try and predict homeroom assignments. Most of the time, he was accurate. Math certainly had its uses.

One by one Mr. Silver called out the names on his list. When a student responded, he noted their name on his clipboard and handed them a combination lock from the box. A paper tag with a locker number hung from the lock loop.

This year Mr. Silver's homeroom was entirely comprised of students with last names beginning with 'S.' When Bradley heard his name called, he raised his hand and took his lock.

"Trillian Stark?" Mr. Silver was answered with silence. "Is there a Trillian Stark here?"

Bradley looked around the classroom, as other students did the same, shrugging their shoulders.

Mr. Silver made a note on his clipboard and finished taking attendance. He exchanged the clipboard for a stack of paper and pencils from his desk and handed a portion to the first student in each row. "Take a sheet and pencil and pass the rest back." After a flurry of paper, everyone had a sheet. "Those with phones, place them face down on your desk, or leave them in your pockets. We won't need them for a while. And don't think about taking the pencils. They all have tracking chips in them. I will find you." Mr. Silver used that same joke every year and it received the same response: not a peep.

He looked out at the students in front of him, many staring

back with apathy, and smiled. "Don't worry. I'm not going to ask you to write down what you did over the summer." A sigh of relief drifted through the classroom. "However, I would like you to write your name at the top of the sheet and list what you read over the summer."

A grade nine girl sitting in the front raised her hand.

Mr. Silver consulted his clipboard. "Ella?"

"Can it be anything?" Ella asked.

"Yes. Books, magazines, anything." Mr. Silver took his seat behind his desk as the room fell into a hush of pencil scribbles.

One of the doors at the back of the classroom creaked open and an unfamiliar girl entered. Everyone in the class turned around to look. Her dark brown eyes didn't seem to mind the weight of everyone's stares.

The girl was dressed in graffiti-covered Doc Martens, black jeans, and a white t-shirt with the words "lit happens" scrawled across it. Her hair was shaved close to the scalp on one side with the hair on the other side divided into long rainbow-colored sections. Each ear supported half a dozen earrings and a black knapsack with string straps hung off her shoulders.

An image of Hope back in New York flashed through Bradley's mind and his heart skipped a beat. The new girl's fashion sense wasn't as hardcore as Hope's, but he couldn't help but wonder if she had any tattoos.

"You must be Trillian," Mr. Silver said.

The girl nodded.

"Come on up." Mr. Silver took a pencil and piece of paper, as well as a lock from the box, and handed the items to the girl. "Write your name down and what you read during the summer. I expect great things."

Trillian gave Mr. Silver a confused look.

"Your shirt gave me a clue," he said. "Take a seat."

Bradley seized the opportunity and rose from his desk. "Take mine." He offered a shy smile to Trillian and handed his paper and pencil back to Mr. Silver. "I'm done." Without a smile, Trillian gave Bradley a once-over, settling a moment longer on the raccoon tail hanging from his belt loop.

Trillian lowered her head, her colorful locks falling and hiding her face like a curtain, and joined the other students completing their assignment. Bradley grabbed his lock and day pack and headed to the back of the classroom to wait for first bell.

Mr. Silver picked up Bradley's paper. In one line of non-cursive rushed lettering were the words: "I read the instructions on rat trap packages." He found Bradley at the back of the room with his eyes and gave him a sideways look with a dash of raised eyebrow.

Bradley shrugged and offered a grin back. It was the truth.

The first bell rang.

"Leave the sheets *and the pencils* on the desks, please," Mr. Silver said. "I'll see some of you later today, but most of you later in the week. Have a great first day."

Everyone collected their locks and belongings and exited into the hallway to find their lockers.

Bradley looked at the tag attached to his lock loop. Locker number 323 was located about a dozen spots past the first entrance to his homeroom. He pulled open the mildly dented and scratched locker door and was pleasantly surprised to find the interior reasonably clean. There was the usual wear and tear, but without any potentially embarrassing leftover graffiti. Bradley had seen some lockers that looked like they had been hit by a battering ram.

On the back of the lock was a sticker with the lock's combination. He peeled it off and stuck it in his day pack. Bradley spun the numbers and popped open the lock loop on the second try. He hung up his coat and pack took out a binder full of blank paper and a pen.

Bradley was about to slip his phone out of his pocket to

check his class schedule when Trillian walked out of homeroom in search of her locker.

Stay cool, Bradley thought as he busied himself, rummaging needlessly inside his day pack. He offered a shy wave as she passed by.

Trillian noticed Bradley's greeting and stepped up to locker 327 without reciprocating. She looked at the combination on the back of her lock and tried to unlock it. Her first two attempts were unsuccessful.

"Stare much?" she said.

Bradley realized he had been gawking and straightened himself up. "Sorry." He closed his locker door and locked it. "For the second number, remember to turn past the first—"

Trillian glared at Bradley. "Mansplain much? I'm not a troglodyte. I *know* how these work." Her rich brown eyes connected with his for only a second before they settled back on the combination lock. Her third try was unsuccessful, and she kicked the base of her locker door.

"No worries," Bradley said. "Just trying to help." He headed toward the south stairwell.

Trillian sighed. "Hey."

Bradley spun around, hoping he wasn't too quick.

"Sorry," she continued, fumbling with the lock. "Everything's new. I don't like new."

"Just go slow." Bradley saw confusion in her face, then grinned. "The lock, I mean."

Trillian worked the lock for the fourth time, slowly and deliberately, and its loop sprang open. "Good advice." She had nothing to deposit into the locker, so she locked the door closed.

"Take the sticker off the back. The school's full of assholes."

"Right." Trillian peeled the combination sticker off, rolled it into a tiny ball and flicked it down the hallway where it rolled into the stairwell and disappeared.

Mr. Silver poked his head out of the classroom. "You two better get moving. You'll be late."

They both walked toward the stairwell.

"What's your next class?"

Trillian plucked her phone out of her knapsack and found her course schedule. "Biology with Miss… Fiscara?"

"Me too. Come on." Bradley led the way, with Trillian matching his stride as they both descended the stairs. "We call her Miz Viscera, by the way."

"Viscera?"

"As in guts. Internal organs. You know, biology."

Trillian raised an eyebrow. "Oh-kay."

"She's cool. You'll like her."

As Bradley and Trillian disappeared down the stairs, their voices echoing back, a Latina girl stepped to the top of the stairwell. She wore an all black ensemble comprised of a sleeveless t-shirt and shorts, black and gold Air Jordans, and a black Coach purse slung around one shoulder. Her dark brown hair framed her caramel face, bangs in the front, a long braid in the back that ended just past her shoulder blades. Her eyes were deep brown, but if asked, Bradley would say they were black as night.

She held a notebook and pen in one hand, her face flushed with anger. She balled up her free hand hard enough to turn her knuckles white.

She extracted her phone from her purse and keyed in a text. "Found him."

By the time Bradley and Trillian arrived for Biology class, there were a few vacant desks available. Bradley found a seat in the middle row, third from the front. Trillian ended up a few desks farther back in an adjacent row.

Miss Fiscara perched herself on the edge of a long table in the back corner of the classroom, directly in front of two large terrariums. She held a file folder in one hand and tapped the eraser end of a pencil against her leg with the other.

Of all the teachers at Washbrook High, Wendy Fiscara had casual dress on lock with jeans, a t-shirt, and red Converse high tops. Always red. Her straight black hair fell loosely around her shoulders and her Kate Spade frames, also red, boldly framed her face. Today, her white t-shirt was emblazoned with "Has anyone seen my tarantula?" in red panic-stricken lettering.

"Nice of you to join us, Mr. Shaw and Miss…?" She tilted her head and looked a question at Trillian through her rectangular-framed glasses.

"Stark."

"Right." Fiscara made a checkmark in her file folder. "Trillian Stark. The new girl."

Trillian sighed and sank into her desk, her emotional armor beginning to weaken from inquisitive eyes.

As Miss Fiscara stepped to the front of the class, Bradley saw Alexis stroll in, fresh lipstick applied and not a hair out of place. Her eyes narrowed and flitted between Bradley and Trillian.

Bradley looked down at his hands clasped on his desk and felt the heat of impending doom rise on his neck.

"Brilliant." Fiscara made one last mark in her file folder and dropped it on her desk. "All sentient organisms accounted for. Find a desk, Miss Delarosa."

Alexis went out of her way to walk down the center aisle. She paused at Bradley's desk, looking down on him. After a moment, he stared back, unwilling to back down. She moved farther down the aisle. She kicked the metal leg of Trillian's desk as she passed and found a seat at the back of the class. Alexis slung her Coach purse on the seat back and slapped her notebook and pen on the desk.

"Before we get started, some may have noticed a few new additions to the class since last year." Fiscara pointed to the terrariums at the back of the class. "I'll get to that in a moment. We have a new student."

Trillian groaned and set her head down on her desk. This was one aspect of new schools that she hated: the dreaded introduction. But over the years, she had developed a reliable method of cutting it short.

"Trillian?" Fiscara stepped to her right to get an unobstructed view of Trillian's desk. "Please stand and introduce yourself."

Trillian let go an exasperated sigh as she pushed herself out of her desk. "Hi. I'm Trillian. My parents, who abandoned me when I was five, named me after a character in *The Hitchhiker's Guide to the Galaxy*. My favorite color is all of them. I like long walks on the beach but there's no beach in the valley. Last year I lived in Lakewood, but my foster family didn't want me anymore. I move around a lot. It sucks because—"

"Trillian, if I may interrupt, have you read *The Hitchhiker's Guide to the Galaxy*?"

"No. I think that'd be weird."

"I think you might like it," Fiscara said.

"What's with the rainbow?" a voice from across the classroom said.

"*Lez-be* friends," Alexis said, shielding her mouth with the back of her hand. Laughter chittered through the class. Bradley turned and glared at Alexis. She returned his gaze with a raised middle finger.

Trillian noted the exchange and ignored the laughter. "Mediocre minds," she said to herself, but loud enough for Bradley and Alexis to hear.

"What was that?" Alexis leaned across her desk toward Trillian. "Speak up, *Rainbow Brite*."

"Miss Delarosa," Fiscara said. "Let's start the year on the right foot, shall we?"

Trillian turned her head, slow and determined, and looked down at Alexis. "I said *mediocre minds.*"

Alexis sat back and looked around the classroom. "What's that supposed to mean?"

Trillian nodded and grinned. "Exactly."

Fiscara felt the animosity building between the two girls. "Thank you, Trillian. We appreciate the detail. Please take your seat."

Alexis watched with disgust as Bradley gave Trillian a "thumbs up" sign. She had missed something and was determined to find out what.

"This year, we'll be focusing on invertebrates," Fiscara said. "Can anyone tell me what an invertebrate is?"

A girl in the front raised her hand.

"Abigail?"

"Any animal without a spine?"

"That's right." Fiscara looked around the room. "Can anyone name an invertebrate?"

"You spineless, Rainbow Brite?" Alexis whispered at Trillian.

"Alexis?" Fiscara walked down the aisle to where Alexis sat. "Have something to share?"

"No."

"Anyone else?" Fiscara walked to the terrariums in the back of the class, opened the lid, and reached in. The class was more interested in what Fiscara was doing than in answering her question. "Whoever said *spider* would be correct."

She picked up a tarantula from a secluded corner of the right-hand terrarium and carefully placed it into a smaller plastic container. The tarantula's legs and body alternated between black and orangey-red and its entire body was covered in a fine but husky fur.

"Ladies and gentlemen, this is Killer." Fiscara beckoned her students to come closer. They hustled from their desks and surrounded Fiscara and the spider. "She's a Mexican Redknee tarantula and she'll be sitting in all year long, so don't get out of line."

She held the container up for everyone to see.

Abigail stared at the large, hairy arachnid in the container. "What does it eat?"

"Good question," Fiscara said.

"Kiss-ass." Alexis shoved Abigail aside.

"All Killer needs is a couple of crickets every week or so. We'll make up a feeding schedule." Fiscara lifted Killer out of the plastic container and placed her in her palm. Students who were closest backed up. "Occasionally, she'll eat a pinky mouse as a treat."

"They eat meat?" someone said from within the crowd of students.

Trillian shot a surprised look at Bradley and they both shared an uneasy smile.

"Oh yeah," Alexis said. "That's what I'm talkin' about. Let's see that thing eat a mouse."

"That's animal cruelty," someone else said.

"That's nature." Fiscara shrugged. "Tarantulas eat mice in the wild."

Alexis turned to look back at Trillian, a scowl crossing her lips. "Do they eat anything *larger*?"

"No. She won't overeat and she won't bite unless provoked."

"Too bad," Alexis said.

"Is it true that the average person eats five spiders in their lifetime while they're sleeping?" Abigail said.

"That's a myth someone made up to vilify the spider," Fiscara said. "However, due to their sheer numbers, spiders could consume every man, woman, and child on the face of the earth in one year."

"What? I'll never sleep again," someone said.

"Relax. Spiders don't eat people." Fiscara placed Killer back into the terrarium and closed the lid. "Everyone back to your seats."

"They almost look cute," Trillian said.

A shiver moved through Bradley's back. "I wouldn't want to wake up next to one." He ran his fingers across his raccoon tail.

"Maybe you *will* wake up next to one," Alexis said to herself.

"Most spiders are harmless." Fiscara moved to the front of the class. "However, there are some species out there that can kill a person in seconds." Most students stared back blankly at her. "Lucky for us, those spiders are not indigenous to this region."

Fiscara wrote "Invertebrate" on the chalkboard and drew a basic sketch of a spider underneath. She spent the rest of the class going through the parts of a spider, the mechanics of how they move, their diet and habitat.

Alexis missed most of what was said, instead choosing to focus on Bradley and Trillian and trying to interpret their body language. What little she saw she didn't like.

The bell rang and everyone collected their notebooks and various supplies before heading to the doors.

"For next class, research the origins of a deadly spider," Fiscara said. "Most lethal spider wins a pinky mouse."

Bradley shivered again as he left to go to his next class. Trillian followed and observed his hand instinctively going to his raccoon tail once more.

Alexis followed them both out and watched them disappear into the busy hallway crowd. "Mediocre minds, huh," she said to herself. "We'll see about that."

It was last class before lunch and Alexis had become bored with Math. She faked a bathroom emergency and had spent the past half hour playing games on her phone.

Now Alexis stood outside Mr. Silver's English class, filing her manicured nails with an emery board and waiting for her best buds Deirdre and Caitlin.

Ever since ninth grade, the three girls had been inseparable. Alexis liked to surround herself with people whom she saw as inferior to herself, in looks, height, weight, and fashion. She made an exception for intelligence because Alexis could use that to her advantage.

Deirdre and Caitlin fit her criteria perfectly. Deirdre stood half a foot shorter and several pounds heavier than Alexis and Caitlin had a bad case of acne. Alexis once told Caitlin that her acne was God's way of trying to burn her face off.

Despite the insults, Alexis offered bad-ass status at school and free makeup supplies from her foster mom's salon. It took little time before they became Alexis's soldiers, enacting most of Alexis's dirty work.

The bell sounded and the doors to the classrooms on the south wing of the school burst open almost in unison. Deirdre and Caitlin were among the first students to exit and Alexis grabbed their arms and pulled them across the hallway.

"Hey!" Deirdre tried to pull away. "Don't squeeze so hard."

"Don't be such a pussy." Alexis backed the two girls against the lockers. "We got to teach Brad a lesson."

"Why? You dumped him," Caitlin said. "Why are we wasting our time with that dick?"

"Because I said so." Alexis was about to lay out her plan when Trillian walked out of Mr. Silver's class. The two locked eyes, trying to stare each other down. "And that *bitch* is the reason why."

"That's the new girl." Caitlin cast her mind back. "Trillion? Is that right?"

"She's mostly zeroes." Deirdre laughed at her own joke as she watched Trillian open her locker to exchange something inside.

"I think Mr. Silver likes her." Caitlin loved to start illicit gossip.

Alexis pushed Caitlin back into the lockers with two fingers. "Who gives a shit?"

Caitlin fell quiet and shrugged.

"Listening?" Alexis scrutinized each girl as they nodded in affirmation. "Okay, here's the plan." She scanned the hallway for any sign of Bradley, then huddled close with the other two girls.

BRADLEY RAN UP the south stairs two steps at a time. His class right before lunch happened to be Home Economics, which made him hungry at the best of times. Having the class scheduled right before lunch just made it worse and he was ravenous. He unlocked his locker, threw his books inside and grabbed his bag lunch.

The hallway was deserted. Everyone was outside enjoying what was left of the September weather. Bradley strolled down the hallway and took a detour into the boy's bathroom. He placed his bag lunch next to the sink and stepped up to the urinal.

The door to the bathroom squeaked open. The sound of shuffling shoes—too many shoes—echoed in the small space. A second later, someone kicked Bradley's feet apart and forced him forward into the urinal wall. He had just enough time to raise his hands to the wall to protect his face. He turned his head to the right, cool tile against his cheek, and felt a body press itself against his back. If the attack hadn't been so unexpected, he might have been turned on by it a little. But the smell of jasmine, specifically Dolce & Gabbana, turned his stomach. The perfume was a dead giveaway and brought with it a flood of bad memories.

Alexis.

"You been ghosting me, asshole?" Alexis's hot breath floated past his right ear.

"I told you." Bradley spoke through clenched teeth. "I've been in New York."

"What, you can't text in New York?"

The door to the boy's washroom swung open and struck the back of Deirdre's shoes. She turned to the teenage boy wanting to get in. "Occupied, *bitch*," she said before pushing the door closed.

"I couldn't afford it and the Wi-Fi sucked." Bradley tried to push back but Alexis had him at a disadvantage. "Besides *you* dumped *me.*"

There was a time earlier in the year when Bradley had wanted Alexis back. He hadn't understood why she'd dumped him. Now he realized things had played out just as they should have.

Alexis jammed her elbow into Bradley's ribs, causing pain to radiate across his back. "Just because we're not together doesn't mean you get to *ignore* me."

"You're crazy," Bradley winced. "I don't even like you anymore."

A subtle *click* echoed through the bathroom. Alexis raised a switchblade up to Bradley's face. His wide eyes and sweating brow reflected off the blade's stainless steel surface.

"What are you going to do with that?" Bradley increased his struggle. Alexis signaled Caitlin for back up. She positioned herself next to Alexis, securing Bradley's body against the urinal and wall.

"You're in a tough spot."

Bradley could hear the grin on Alexis's face.

"You've let it all hang out. Be a shame if your *fun* was cut short."

"Do it," Deirdre said. "Cut his dick off."

Alexis dragged the blade tip across Bradley's cheek, leaving a white scratch line behind. "Who's the girl?"

Thoughts of losing his manhood cluttered Bradley's brain. "What girl?"

"Don't jerk me around," Alexis said. "Rainbow Brite."

"Oh. She's new." Bradley's saliva and sweat made the tiled bathroom wall slick against his face. "Never met her before today. I swear."

"You look like best friends."

"I offered to show her to her first class."

Alexis brought her mouth to Bradley's ear. "You better not be lying." She bit his earlobe hard enough to draw blood. Bradley grit his teeth and stifled a scream. Caitlin watched with surprise and awe as blood began to trickle down Bradley's neck.

Alexis lowered the switchblade down to the belt-line of Bradley's jeans. He twisted his body but couldn't clear the sides of the urinal. He was trapped.

"Stop squirming," Alexis hissed, "or I might take more than I came for."

Bradley tried to look down, but the knife was out of view. "Don't do it."

"Oh, I'm going to do it alright." Alexis hooked the blade through one of Bradley's belt loops and cut through it with a flick of her wrist. His raccoon tail fell to the dirty tiled floor. "I never understood that fucking tail of yours… Dee."

Deirdre stepped away from the bathroom door.

Alexis motioned at the tail. "Flush it."

Bradley thought of protesting more but chose to remain silent. Anything he could have said at that point would have made things worse.

Deirdre plucked the tail up off the floor with two fingers and walked to the first empty toilet stall. She disappeared and a moment later the sound of the toilet flushing and choking down its contents rose from the stall. Deirdre emerged empty-handed.

"You fucking bitch." Bradley's voice was low and full of anger.

Alexis gave him one final push and backed away. Bradley almost spun around to confront his attackers head on, but remembered he was still exposed down below. He adjusted himself, zipped his fly and turned around.

"What are you going to do now?" Alexis said. "Hit a girl?"

Bradley remained silent, holding his rage at bay.

Alexis spotted his bag lunch on the counter next to the sink and grabbed it. She gored the side of the bag with the knife and cut a hole in the bottom, causing the contents to fall to the floor. The apple bounced and rolled under one of the toilets. "I hope you're hungry."

The three girls sauntered to the door. Diedre stepped on Bradley's sandwich, mashing it into the grout between the tiles.

Alexis stood in the bathroom's entrance. "You better think twice who you hang with."

Bradley propped himself up on the countertop and stared into the sink.

"Later, lover boy." Alexis, Deirdre and Caitlin disappeared down the hall, laughing and talking excitedly.

Bradley pushed open the door to the first toilet stall. The bowl was filled with clear water. Not a trace of his raccoon tail. He was filled with feelings of fierce independence instead of revenge, which surprised him.

He stepped back to the row of sinks, looked in the mirror, and said to himself in a low whisper, "You're not the boss of me, Alexis Delarosa." He washed his hands and face, dried himself off, and left.

BRADLEY FOUND A place to sit on the grass, close to the outdoor equipment storage and edge of the basketball courts. The sun spread warmth on his back and helped him relax. He watched other students sit and talk in groups and often wondered what it would be like to be part of a "tribe."

His phone chirped in his pocket. A text from Jack.

"10-20?" the text read. Jack liked to seem like an enigma to most people. He tried to respond in 10-codes whenever he could.

"Near ball courts," Bradley texted back.

A shadow drew out on the grass in front of him. Bradley turned back to look and was blinded by sunlight filtered through rainbow-colored hair. It was the graffiti-covered shoes that gave Trillian away.

"Hey."

"Hey," Trillian said. "Mind if I sit?"

Bradley shrugged.

She placed her knapsack on the grass and sat beside Bradley, her arms around her knees. Silence held between them, but it wasn't uncomfortable.

Jack pushed open the double doors that led to the basketball courts. He spotted Bradley right away, then saw Trillian, *a girl*, sitting next to him.

Jack and Bradley had an agreement that they would never interrupt the other if one was "making a move." The fact that Jack hadn't had a girlfriend yet didn't matter.

The two appeared to be in a deep conversation so Jack detoured around the corner of the school toward his car in the parking lot. Sun, music, and racing seats. Couldn't go wrong with that.

"Thanks for being nice to me this morning." Trillian guided her colorful hair behind her ear. "When people see me, they assume I'm unapproachable."

"People are assholes."

Trillian looked along Bradley's belt-line. "Where's your raccoon tail?"

Bradley's hand went to the belt loop that Alexis had cut and rolled the frayed denim between his fingertips. "Like I said, people are assholes."

Trillian could read between the lines. "Well, I thought it was cool."

"Thanks." Bradley tore out a clump of grass by the roots. "And sorry about your parents."

Trillian hung her head down. "Thanks."

"My dad's been absent all my life, until this summer."

"At least you get a second chance."

Bradley looked at her. "What happened?"

Trillian focused on the far side of the field. "No offense, but I don't want people to know the real me unless they pass my inspection."

"I haven't passed yet, huh?"

Trillian shook her head.

A moment of silence passed between the two teenagers as a daddy longlegs spider crawled up onto one of Trillian's shoes. She reached out and intercepted the arachnid, letting its thin, spindly legs carry its round body over her hand.

"It's hard to imagine that this little guy has been around for over four hundred million years," said Trillian. "Not too bright, though."

"Smart enough to outlast the dinosaurs." Bradley watched Trillian transfer the spider from hand to hand. He was reminded again of Hope back in New York and smiled.

Trillian felt his gaze. "What?"

Bradley shrugged. "You just remind me of someone I used to know."

She could have probed for more information, but instead offered the spider to Bradley. "Want to hold it?"

"Nah."

"They don't bite, and they aren't venomous." Trillian looked at the spider closely. "That's a myth."

"I don't have anything against spiders. They're just not my thing."

Trillian set the spider down and watched it crawl away.

The end of lunch break bell rang and everyone headed for the doors. Alexis stood on the landing between the first and second floor of the south stairwell. Through the window she spotted Bradley and Trillian.

"You don't listen too well, do you Brad?" Alexis said to herself.

DEIRDRE AND CAITLIN were on their way to class when Deirdre's phone buzzed in her back pocket. She slid the phone out.

"Message from our fearless leader." Deirdre held up her phone so Caitlin could read the display.

"Get the bitch's locker combo," the text read.

"How come she never sends me texts like that?"

Deirdre and Caitlin reversed direction, heading back to Mr. Silver's classroom on the second floor. "Because between you and me, I'm the brains and you're the muscle."

Caitlin gave Deirdre's shoulder a shove. "I got brains."

"Oh yeah? How are we going to get the bitch's combo without getting caught?"

Caitlin worked on the question longer than Deirdre had patience for. "See?"

"So, what's *your* plan?"

They rounded the second floor landing and up the second flight of stairs. "I can pick any lock if I have the right tools and enough time."

"But class starts in, like, three minutes." Caitlin looked at her phone's clock. "I can't be late for math."

Deirdre was busily tapping and swiping on her phone. "I'm going to let technology do the work for me."

"You better hope that she hasn't gone already."

The two girls arrived on the second floor and walked past the bank of lockers outside of Mr. Silver's classroom.

"You stand here with your back to the lockers." Deirdre framed up the shot on the phone's display. "Pretend like I'm shooting a video."

"How do you know…" Caitlin looked over her shoulder, scanned the hallway, then back at Deirdre. "How do you know what locker is hers?"

"I pay attention." Deirdre held the camera up as the hallway began to fill. "Now, do as I say."

Caitlin gave a goofy salute and spoke through her front teeth. "Yes, Cap-ee-tain."

"Such a dork." Deirdre spotted Trillian emerge from the stairwell to the second floor. "Shit, there she is. Act natural."

"What do you want me to do?"

"I don't know. Talk about your classes."

Deirdre positioned herself and Caitlin several feet away from Trillian's locker and tapped "record." She framed Caitlin in the shot but included Trillian's combination lock in the lower right corner of the frame.

Trillian spun the dial on the lock and popped open the lock loop. It was over in less than five seconds.

"I think I got it." Deirdre moved her finger across the phone's display, a smile breaking across her face. "I'm so brilliant," she said to herself. The ultra high definition video showed Trillian spinning her locker combination in super slow motion. The numbers were easy to read.

"Got what?"

"I'll show you later." Deirdre ran down the hallway. "Don't be late for math," she called back.

Caitlin headed in the opposite direction toward the stairwell. She passed Trillian and offered her a smile. Caitlin had meant it to be mischievous, but it ended up looking friendly.

Deirdre arrived at her history class just as the bell rang. Unable to wait, she stood outside the classroom door to watch the video she had just recorded.

Her history teacher, Mrs. Medina, despised cell phones and took offense that these intrusive devices were becoming a part of history, shaping it even. She stepped to the entrance to the classroom and saw Deirdre buzzing with excitement over her phone.

"Deirdre?" Mrs. Medina glanced at the phone with disgust. "Are you planning on joining us?"

"Just one second, Mrs. Medina." Deirdre kept her eyes on the phone's display, her smile growing wider.

Mrs. Medina crossed her arms and glowered at her. "If you aren't in this classroom in three seconds, both you *and* your phone are getting detention for a week."

Deirdre wanted to play the video again but knew Mrs. Medina meant business. She dropped her phone into her bag and found an empty desk near the back of the classroom.

"Nothing, except history, should be that important." Mrs. Medina closed the door hard and walked to the front of the class.

"Oh, I'd say this is pretty *fucking* important," Deirdre said to herself. She pulled a notebook out of her bag and slid it onto her desk.

"Something to share, Deirdre?" Mrs. Medina looked across the classroom at her.

"Nope." Deirdre grinned back, doing her best to push down her excitement. Alexis would be pleased.

SEARCH

CLAIRE HAD ENJOYED her summer more than expected. She loved Bradley and would do anything for him, but having two months to be an adult again, without any teenaged angst, was a refreshing change. She could be spontaneous and do what she wanted, when she wanted. And she would never have met Roy otherwise. The decision to send Bradley to visit Sam in New York had been a good one.

She had arranged to take the first week of school off from the hospital to make sure Bradley settled into the routine of his final year. However, his first day had begun without a hitch. Bradley was handling himself just fine.

After school began, the rest of the day was hers to play with. Waking up to fresh coffee this morning had been an unexpected treat that Claire hoped would continue, but she tempered her expectations knowing that one day didn't make a trend. Bradley was still a teenager.

After Bradley had left for school, Roy joined her in the shower, and they ended up having perfunctory sex. Awkward and inconvenient was how Claire described shower sex most of the time. But at least Roy was interested in her as a sexual being and she was getting the physical contact she needed.

To make the most of her week off, she headed out to her first love, her garden. The tomatoes would need weeding, and a few would be ripe enough for picking. Claire threw on a pair of loose denim overalls and her button-up gardening shirt and headed to the back yard. She opened the shed and grabbed her wide-brimmed gardening hat and a hand-held claw.

She knelt between the tomato plants and began excavating rogue weeds by the root. She didn't bother with gloves. The fresh earth felt like heaven in her hands. Half an hour later, Claire had amassed a pile of weeds and the soil around the tomato plants was once again a rich, oily black.

One plant was weighed down with ripened tomatoes and risked collapse. Claire stowed the claw in a breast pocket of her overalls and walked back to the shed.

She stood in the entryway of the shed and scanned the right-hand wall reserved for hand tools. The pruning scissors should have been hanging next to the claw, but an empty space was there instead. Roy must have misplaced them somewhere else in the shed.

Her left foot brushed against the cocooned rat next to her feet, vibrating the webbed tripwires leading away from it. Black spine-backed spiders advanced out of the darkened funnel next to the cocoon.

Had Claire worn her rubber boots, she would have been in no danger. But today she had chosen open-toed flip-flops. Good for the spiders. Bad for her.

The first spider out of the funnel leaped and landed on her left foot, past her purple-painted toenails and above the foot strap. It sank its fangs into her skin and scrambled back into the darkness to wait.

Claire felt a tickle, then searing pain as if a red-hot needle had been jammed into the top of her foot. She stumbled back out of the shed, landing hard on her backside.

She drew her foot close and looked at the skin. Two small punctures could be seen. Her eyes darted around the shed, looking for bees or wasps. Perhaps she had disturbed an unseen nest.

Then she saw her assailant, a mean-looking black spider with what looked like quills emerging from its back. The spider advanced to the front of the shed, soon joined by others. Claire grabbed her gardening claw from her front overall pocket and swung it at the leader of the cluster. The spiders evaded her attacks with easy agility.

Her foot began to feel hot and the skin around the punctures morphed into a spreading swollen red before her eyes. The clock was ticking, and she only had a few minutes, perhaps seconds.

Claire hobbled to the house and into the bathroom. From the medicine cabinet she uncapped an epi-pen and jammed it into her left thigh, holding it there for a few seconds to administer the drug to her system. She moved to the bedroom and pulled a belt from the closet, cinching it around her left leg, just below the knee, as tight as she could stand.

Claire grabbed her purse, hopped across the back yard to the garage and opened the door. She unplugged the Leaf, dumped herself into the driver's seat and backed out.

She drove herself to the hospital, sweat drenching her face and stinging her eyes, her left leg numb from the knee down. But the tourniquet wasn't working. She could feel hot pain seep up her leg, past the tightened belt and into her thigh like sharp claws in her flesh.

Claire could barely walk when she arrived at Sun Valley Medical Center. She parked askew at the Emergency entrance, called Roy but got his voice mail.

"At hospit… Aller-gee. Stung or…" Claire's thoughts were becoming clouded. Words that made sense refused to vocalize. She sent a text to Bradley before run-hop-stumbling in through the automatic doors.

Shari, a nurse at the Admitting desk, recognized Claire immediately. "You're not scheduled—"

"I'm… p-patient." Claire's panicked voice was raspy and her

breathing wheezy and labored. "Allerg… stung by s-sp-sp spome…"

Shari grabbed the intercom. "Code blue, emergency!" She ran around the desk, grabbed a stretcher and helped Claire onto it. Her left leg was almost unrecognizable, swollen red, the skin tight and shiny. She was unable to bend her knee.

"Epi-pip-pipp…" Claire's speech slurred as a doctor and other emergency support staff pulled her stretcher into a curtained section of the emergency ward.

Shari looked Claire directly in the eyes while holding her forearm to measure her pulse. "epi-pen administered?"

Claire nodded, her ability to speak gone. Tears streamed from her eyes and soaked the pillow behind her head.

"How long ago?" Shari maintained eye contact.

Claire began to shake.

Shari held up her hand, all five fingers spread. "Five minutes ago?"

Claire stared back at her, terror in her eyes.

Shari held both hands up. "Ten minutes?"

Claire managed a nod.

Dr. Nikki Holbrook pulled back the privacy curtain. "What have we got?"

"Not sure, Nikki," Shari said. "Claire's been stung by something. Epinephrine auto-injected about ten minutes ago."

Dr. Holbrook and three nurses transferred Claire from the stretcher to a bed. She removed the belt from Claire's leg. "I want albuterol, five milligrams nebulized and point-five milligrams of adrenaline every ten minutes if no improvement."

She took Claire's pulse and examined her leg closely from her knee down to her toes. "There appear to be two puncture wounds just above the arch of the foot." Dr. Holbrook looked at Shari, concern in her face. "Claire wasn't stung. She was bitten."

BRADLEY HAD ARRANGED to meet Jack in the parking lot after school. Jack was already out in his Civic, reclining in the front seat and listening to music.

He wove around parked cars to the Civic's stall, threw his day pack into the back seat and plopped himself in the passenger seat.

Jack took one look at him and knew something was up. "Bad first day?"

"Good and bad." Bradley closed his eyes. "Highlight of the day was meeting a cool new girl. She's smart. You'd like her."

"Did you eat lunch with her?"

"We hung out, yeah."

"Girlfriend material?" Jack grinned and flashed his eyebrows.

"Don't know yet," Bradley said. "Definitely friend material though. We exchanged numbers."

"And the bad?"

Bradley shook his head, almost imperceptibly. "Alexis is going to be a problem."

"I told you."

"Yeah, you told me." Bradley opened his eyes to the Civic's textured roof. "What you didn't tell me is she's a fucking psycho. She pulled a knife on me in the guy's bathroom."

Jack's eyes widened. "Holy shit."

"Cut my tail off and flushed it." Bradley looked at Jack. "She thinks she can control me."

"Fuck that."

The two teenagers bumped fists in agreement.

"How about you? Your day go well?"

"Good. Flew under the radar. Got all the courses I wanted." Jack laughed. "Shit, bro. We sound like an old married couple."

He turned the ignition and revved the Civic's engine a couple of times. A blue cloud belched out from the tailpipe.

Bradley watched the smoke drift away. "You're burning oil."

"Tell me something I don't know." Jack reversed out of the parking stall and navigated his way to the street, where he accelerated to just above the speed limit in what seemed like seconds.

"While I was waiting, I graphed the summer's earthquakes," he said. "I'll show you when I get to your place."

"Why does that not surprise me?"

"You see different things when you make pictures out of the data."

Bradley stared out the window and saw several "missing pet" notices stapled or taped to trees and telephone poles. He reached down for his raccoon tail. When his hand came up empty, his thoughts led him to the raccoon he'd seen in his back yard. Could it have been a sign of something to come?

"Earth to Brad." Jack poked his shoulder. "Come in, Brad."

"What?"

"I said did you ever read about the Sylmar quake?"

Bradley shook his head.

"1971. A 6.6. One of the worst earthquakes in California's history. The epicenter wasn't that far from where we live." The Civic rounded a corner onto Sheldon Street.

Bradley chuckled. "You are *such* a nerd."

"And you're listening to a nerd, so that makes you a nerd by association. Anyway, people *died* in that quake. Can you imagine something like that happening today?"

"Honestly, no."

"Well, bro, we're due for one." Jack pulled the Civic over to the curb. "See? Look." He held out his phone and showed the graph of the summer's earthquakes. The 2.9 magnitude quake stood out like a sore thumb. "You got emergency supplies?"

"I don't know," Bradley said. "I'll mention it to my mom and check the shed later."

Jack's stomach growled. "I think there's a taco in my future."

Bradley grabbed his day pack out of the back seat and stepped out of the car. "You think?"

"One-hundred percent probability."

Bradley stepped onto the sidewalk. "Nerd."

Jack laughed and peeled out down the street.

Bradley raised both hands, middle fingers extended. He heard Jack tap his horn and saw him flash a middle finger out his driver-side window before turning out of sight.

The house was quiet. Bradley dropped his day pack in his room and went to the kitchen to find something to eat.

"Mom?"

No answer.

He grabbed some Oreos from a new package and stepped out the back door, across the back yard to the garage. The Leaf was gone.

The shed's doors were open, illuminating the interior with afternoon light. Bradley stepped inside. Smells of gasoline and musty fertilizer assaulted his nose. And the smell of something else, low and unpleasant underneath it all. It sent a shiver down his back.

He closed the shed doors and returned to the house, making a mental note to ask Claire about earthquake supplies. Bradley preferred to be prepared for anything.

On his way back to the kitchen to get more Oreos, Bradley's foot kicked a small, blue plastic object down the hallway. He picked it up, his blood running cold.

The cap to Mom's epi-pen.

Bradley ran back to the bathroom and saw Claire's used epi-pen on the floor next to the toilet. As he picked it up, his phone chimed an incoming text as if both were connected by his touch.

On his phone's display were three emojis that confirmed his worst fear:

A spider, a syringe and a hospital symbol. But the spider should have been a bee. That sequence of emojis was what Bradley and Claire had agreed upon to indicate a bee sting when he got his first cell phone six years ago. But spiders don't sting, do they? They bite.

Oh shit.

Bradley dialed Jack. "I got a big favor to ask. It's a matter of life and death."

IN LESS THAN ten minutes, Jack reappeared in front of Bradley's house. He reached over the passenger seat and pushed open the door.

"This is becoming a habit." Jack grinned.

"Sorry. I didn't know who else to call," Bradley said. "A taxi would have taken too long."

"Don't worry about it. You'd do the same for me."

"Absolutely. Things will change in November."

"Pay for gas every once in a while, and we're cool." Jack sped down Sheldon Street toward the hospital. "So, what's up?"

"It's my Mom." Bradley kept his eyes on the hospital ahead. With its five floors, Sun Valley Medical Center was the tallest building in his immediate vicinity. It had been convenient to live so close to the hospital growing up when Bradley had had his fair share of cuts and broken bones. "I think she was bitten by a spider."

"But the hospital? For a spider bite?"

"She's allergic to bees and wasps," Bradley said. "I guess

spiders too." He spotted a raccoon scampering down the sidewalk like a stray dog. His hand went to find his raccoon tail at his belt, but the emptiness he found did nothing to calm his mood. "It's called anaphylaxis. If spiders are like bees, she could die from it. Thankfully she got to her epi-pen in time."

"Shit, bro." Jack floored the gas and the Civic tore down the street.

"Easy, man. I don't want to die getting there." Bradley gripped the passenger door handle. Now out of the residential area of Stonehurst, industrial buildings flew past his window. "And don't get a ticket."

"I've never gotten a ticket in my life." Jack gripped the steering wheel and grinned.

"You're kidding, right? You've been driving for six months."

"My driving record is spotless."

Bradley shot a dubious look at him. "In words you'd understand: Not enough data."

Jack laughed as he turned right onto San Fernando Road. "I got you here, didn't I? And in one piece."

"Yeah, you did."

"Damn straight." Jack signaled and turned left into the parking lot of Sun Valley Medical Center.

"Thanks, again."

Jack nodded as he trolled for a parking space.

"Let me out and I'll get a permit." Bradley waited for the Civic to roll to a stop before getting out. He found a permit machine, inserted his credit card, and punched in some time. A second later a paper permit popped out.

Bradley scanned the parking lot and spotted Jack waving about a hundred feet away. As he ran toward him, Bradley was reminded how lucky he was to have a friend like Jack. A friend who would drop everything for him.

Bradley handed the permit to Jack and he placed it on the

dash of the Civic. "You know I'm just fucking with you, right? About the speeding?"

"You do it because you care," Jack said, closing the passenger side door and locking it. "So do I." They both trotted toward the main entrance. "Let's find your Mom."

As Bradley approached the main entrance of the hospital, he spotted movement out of the corner of his eye. He turned his head to see Roy running toward him from the parking lot. He was dressed in a red color-coordinated jogging outfit with a white sweat band around his head. Bradley waved at him but either Roy didn't see his wave or chose not to respond.

Roy made it to the double sliding doors at the same time as Bradley and Jack. He pushed in front and speed-walked toward the Emergency waiting area.

"What the hell!" Jack stepped back and eyed Roy's awkward run down the hallway.

"That's Roy." Bradley shared Jack's disapproval.

"What? You *know* that asshat?"

"Unfortunately, yeah," Bradley said. "He's dating my mom. They met while I was in New York."

"Damn, bro. Sorry. Seems like a douche."

"That's accurate, according to *my* data." Bradley picked up his pace. Jack matched it. "He probably wants to show me up."

Bradley didn't recognize Shari, the nurse behind the Emergency Admitting desk.

"Where can I find Claire Shaw?" Bradley tapped his hands on the countertop.

Jack looked around the emergency area. Behind the curtained bays he could hear cries, pulse meters, and other intense sounds of doctors and nurses saving lives. The smell of antiseptic accosted his nose. "I don't like hospitals," he said in a hushed voice to no one in particular.

"You must be Bradley," Shari said. "Last bay on the right."

"Thanks. How is she?"

"You better talk to the doctor."

Bradley and Jack hustled down the hall. The curtains to the last emergency bay were open and Roy was leaning over the bed, holding Claire.

"Mom?" Bradley stepped toward the bed, Jack close behind. Claire's legs were raised and covered by the bed sheet. Although he couldn't see it directly, the profile of Claire's left leg under the sheet looked different than the right.

Roy stiffened and stepped back, his eyes narrowing on Bradley's approach. Claire raised her arms for a hug.

"I got your text." Bradley stepped up to the bed and embraced her. "Are you okay?"

"I've been better."

Bradley sat on the edge of the bed. "What happened?"

"Isn't it obvious?" Roy crossed his arms over his chest. "She was stung."

"Bitten," Claire said.

Roy looked confused. "What? But your voice mail said you were stung."

"Maybe. I was having trouble talking."

"Bitten by a spider?" Bradley asked.

Claire nodded.

"How do you know that?" Roy stepped forward, closing the distance between himself and Bradley.

"Mom texted me."

"And you thought it would be best if you kept that information to yourself?" Roy took another step forward.

Jack could see the makings of a brawl and stepped in to diffuse it. "Easy, man."

Roy looked down on Jack. "Who the hell are you?"

"I'm Jack, Brad's best friend." Jack extended his hand despite his dislike for the man. Roy ignored the gesture.

"Don't be a jerk," Bradley said. "I didn't text you because I don't know your phone number."

"Guys. Please." Claire looked at the three of them. "I don't want World War Three breaking out in Emergency."

An air of guilt floated through the bay.

"It was a spider," Claire said. "A lot of them. I tried to kill them, but they were too fast."

Dr. Holbrook emerged from the hallway and presented herself at the foot of the hospital bed. "I'd like to have a word with Claire alone, please."

"It's okay, Nikki," Claire said. "No secrets here."

"Alright." Dr. Holbrook cleared her throat. "How's your pain level?"

"Maybe a seven out of ten."

"I'll see what I can do," Dr. Holbrook said. "Your spider bite has caused necrosis in isolated areas. Your allergy to bees didn't help. And it's serious. There is a chance that you could lose your foot, or worse, your leg."

"All that from a spider bite?" Roy shrugged.

"Don't underestimate a spider's bite." Dr. Holbrook focused on Roy before settling on Claire again. "Their venom is largely misunderstood, so treatment may change over time. Presently, we've administered an antivenin and antibiotics, and we'll keep your leg iced, but we'll need to keep you under observation to make sure the current treatment is working. Surgery may be required if the wound doesn't heal on its own."

"Damn," Jack whispered as he tracked his eyes over Claire's shrouded legs.

"What kind of spider causes this?" Bradley asked.

"Probably a black widow," Roy said, self-assured.

"No. Black widow bites are not necrotic." Dr. Holbrook said. "Usually bites like this come from Brown Recluse spiders."

"I'm a gardener. I know what those spiders look like." Claire said. "The spider that bit me… I've never seen anything like it before."

Roy, Bradley, Jack, and Dr. Holbrook exchanged looks.

"I'll arrange for some pain control. And as much as I hate to say it, we're going to have to wait and see how this develops." Dr. Holbrook made notes on Claire's chart. "By the way, your epi-pen probably saved your life."

"What's next?" Bradley asked.

"Go home and let your mom rest."

With Claire out of immediate danger and in good hands, Bradley relaxed and realized he had a real-life candidate for his biology assignment on "most lethal spider." But he needed more research.

Roy jangled the Leaf's key fob at Bradley. "Let's head out. You mom needs her beauty sleep."

My mom could lose her leg, you fuckwit, Bradley thought. What Claire saw in the guy was anyone's guess.

"I was going to go with Jack." Bradley hooked a thumb at Jack, who was standing just outside the main entrance.

Roy shook his head. "No can do. Your mom wanted me to take you."

Bradley grit his teeth. "Just a second." He walked over to Jack. "Thanks for the lift. I owe you one."

"No bigs, bro." Jack bumped fists with Bradley.

"I got to go home with *the douche.*" Bradley looked over his shoulder at Roy. His red jogging suit made him look like a bundle of sweaty twizzlers.

"He's quite a catch."

"My mom should have thrown him back."

Laughter caught Roy's ears. "What's so funny?" Bradley and Jack stifled their chuckles and looked at him as Roy's eyes flitted between them.

"Nothing," Bradley said. "Inside joke."

"Didn't your mom ever teach you any manners?"

Bradley let the question slide.

Jack extended his hand again and grinned. "Nice to meet you, Roy."

Roy eyed Jack with distrust. He grabbed his hand and gave it a limp shake. "Let's go, Brad."

"See you at school."

Bradley followed Roy out toward the parking lot. "Yeah, later." He raised his middle finger at Jack.

Jack raised his arm and flipped the bird back at Bradley. Roy caught the gestures and poked Bradley in his shoulder.

"Ow. What the hell?"

"What was that?" Roy glared at him.

"Nothing." Bradley rubbed his shoulder. "What do you care?"

"I don't." Roy swept his arm around him like he was in a dealership showroom. "It's everyone else. That kind of shit sends the wrong message."

"Boo hoo."

"You better watch yourself, Brad."

Bradley stopped to face Roy, making sure to look him in the eye. "Don't touch me again."

They both shared a tense moment before continuing out into the parking lot. Roy clicked the rear hatch button on the key fob and waited. The Leaf soon identified itself with its hatch raised to the sky. He closed the hatch again and corrected his course.

Once inside the Leaf, Roy turned to Bradley. "Give me your phone."

"What? Why?"

"So I can text or call you if I need to."

"No. Just give me your phone number."

Roy's jaw tightened and he grudgingly dictated his number as Bradley dialed. The phone in Roy's pocket began to ring.

Bradley ended the call. "Happy?"

Roy started the Leaf and drove back to Claire's house in silence.

Halfway home, Jack zoomed past in his Civic, his middle finger jutted out the driver-side window and a wide grin on his face.

Bradley smiled back.

Thank God for Jack.

ROY PULLED INTO the garage and shut off the Leaf. Bradley unbuckled his seat belt and moved to open the door, but Roy grabbed his shoulder and held him in place.

Bradley looked at Roy's hand, then at Roy, noting that he had a firm grip when it suited him.

Roy let go and raised his hands in surrender. "Sorry. Didn't mean to touch you." He sighed. "I'm on your side, Brad."

"I think you're on my mom's side. Not mine."

Roy shook his head. "No. You and your mom are a package deal. I knew that going in."

"Sure doesn't feel like it." Bradley looked out the windshield at the work bench, covered in old paint cans, brushes, and assorted tools. He had used that paint to cover his bedroom walls with navy blue. Roy had no idea.

"This is new to me," Roy said. "Your dad's got pretty big shoes to fill."

"You'll never fill my dad's shoes." Bradley opened the car door and crossed the back yard to the house. He was surprised to see the sun dipping toward the horizon. He had spent more time at the hospital than he had realized. Bradley opened the back door, kicked off his shoes, and headed to his room.

He heard the back door open, close, and lock. Bradley found Roy hanging his jacket up in the mud room off the kitchen.

"What are you doing?"

Roy untied his runners. "I'm going to be staying with you until Claire is well enough to come home."

"Why? I'm almost seventeen. I can take care of myself."

"I'm done talking." Roy pulled off his head band and unzipped his jogging suit, revealing a mass of chest hair greased with sweat. "It was your mom's idea. Take it up with her." He walked past Bradley and down the hallway to the master bedroom. "I'm going for a quick shower."

"Good. You *stink*," Bradley said under his breath. He opened the pantry and grabbed the bag of Oreos. One left. He jammed it into his mouth, placed the empty bag in the garbage and rummaged through the pantry shelves looking for more snacks. The food would kill his appetite for dinner, but Bradley didn't care. Anything that Roy could come up with was bound to suck.

Bradley found a box of peanut butter Ritz Bits and shook it. *About half full,* he thought. He stood at the kitchen sink and popped a couple of the crackers into his mouth. Stale but palatable.

From the kitchen window, Bradley noticed that the door to the shed was still open, just as it had been earlier that afternoon. He sensed movement, but the sun had dipped below the horizon and cast the back yard into growing shadows. He took the box of crackers, slipped on his shoes, not bothering to tie them, and crossed the back yard to the shed.

Something fell inside the shed, clattering onto the planked floor. Bradley slowed his stride over the grass and tried to discern any movement in the shadows.

Failing to see anything, he heard the patter of feet and low chittering emanating from deeper within the shed. Bradley's first thought was of...

Rats.

He pulled out his phone and turned on flashlight mode. He directed the light beam across the walls, floors, supplies, and tools within the shed. Bradley caught two red eyes peering back at him.

But the eyes were too big to belong to a rat. Bradley tucked the box of Ritz Bits under the arm holding his phone, so he could grab crackers with a free hand while still holding the light.

He tossed a cracker into the shed. The two halves of the cracker separated and rolled in opposite directions, one further into the shed and one closer to the doors.

The two red reflective eyes stared back at Bradley, blinking occasionally. He moved the light off the opening of the shed and onto the grass in front, but there was enough ambient illumination to see detail where the unidentified eyes sat.

A black nose with quivering whiskers poked through the space between a stack of adobe pots and a collection of work-worn shovels. Two paws reached out and grasped the nearest half of the cracker and pulled it back into the dark. Sounds of chittering and crunching floated back.

It wasn't a rat, but Bradley would know those paws anywhere. It was a raccoon. *His* raccoon.

He squatted and tossed another cracker into the shed. With every second, the raccoon's confidence grew. The animal crawled forward and grabbed the second cracker. This time, the raccoon ate the crunchy treat in full view. Once done, it sniffed for the remaining half of the first cracker, finding it and gobbling it quickly.

The raccoon sat up on its haunches, sniffed the air, and chittered. Bradley had a flash of the white-tailed rats he had encountered back in New York. He grabbed a couple more crackers and tossed them toward the raccoon. One landed at the creature's feet and it foraged under its tail for the morsel. Bradley focused his phone's light on the raccoon and its current treat.

The other cracker rolled right, into the shadows of the shed by the raw sunflower seeds, and out of Bradley's line of sight. It bounced against the woven funnel and bumped against several of the silk trip wires. A large black spider emerged in a defensive stance, advancing with small bursts of speed. It caged the cracker with its oil-black legs and the whisker-like quills on its thorax and abdomen folded down smooth.

Bradley watched the raccoon sniff around for the last cracker. Its nose and whiskers quivering, the animal poked his head near the bag of sunflower seeds.

What happened next both surprised Bradley and horrified him. The raccoon's contented chittering changed to a shrieking worse than anything he had ever heard in his life.

The raccoon reared back into the shovels, knocking one over. Its head, eyes, and nose were covered in a thick and gauzy white substance.

Bradley lost his balance and fell backward. The crackers spilled on the lawn and he dropped his phone in the grass. Retrieving and retraining the phone's light revealed a large, black, quilled spider joined by at least a dozen other spiders. The arachnids swarmed the raccoon and burrowed into its fur, creating an inky and lethal necklace. With one coordinated strike, over a dozen pairs of fangs injected poison into the raccoon's bloodstream.

Bradley stared in horror at the raccoon as it began to convulse. The spiders wasted no time encasing the animal in inescapable webbing.

He dug his heels into the grass and pushed himself backward away from the shed, the intensity of his phone's light weakening with every step until it was of no use anymore.

He could still hear the final moments of struggle from within the shed as he ran toward the back door of the house, tripping once on his shoelaces along the way. He burst into the house and yelled the first thing that came to mind.

"DAD!"

"ROY!"

Bradley heard the door to the master bedroom open and heavy footsteps travel down the hall.

Roy entered the kitchen shirtless, wearing jeans and a t-shirt hanging from his back pocket. He held a towel and was drying off his head.

Gross. Chest pubes. The sight of his hairy chest made Bradley want to gag.

"What do you want?" Roy looked Bradley over from head to toe and back. "You hurt or something?" He looked at the phone in Bradley's hand. "Why is your light on?"

"I just saw a bunch of spiders kill a raccoon."

"What? What are you talking about?"

"Out in the shed." Bradley walked to the back door. "Come on. I'll show you."

"Spiders don't kill raccoons," Roy said. "They eat other insects."

"These ones did."

"Bullshit."

"See for yourself." Bradley stepped out into the back yard shadows. He expected Roy to stay in the house, but he followed a moment later.

"You better not be fucking with me."

The two approached the shed. Bradley held his free hand back as a warning. "Don't get too close."

"Or what?" Roy tilted his head and gave Bradley a dubious look. "I'm going to get eaten by spiders?"

"Yeah. It's possible."

"Give that to me," Roy scoffed and grabbed Bradley's phone out of his hand. He trudged toward the shed aiming the phone's light toward the entrance. "Spiders, my ass."

"Wait! Don't go—"

Roy ducked and stepped into shed, his feet falling firmly on the planked floor. He scanned the floor and walls with the light. He stepped and crouched left, then right, pushing tools and pots around looking for anything out of the ordinary.

"I don't see any raccoon anywhere."

Bradley stepped forward to get a closer look. Roy was right. There was no carcass.

"It was just there." Bradley pointed to the location he last saw the raccoon. "They must have dragged it into their lair."

"Lair? This is ridiculous. I'm missing the game for this?" Roy slapped the phone into Bradley's hand and stomped back to the house, slamming the door behind him.

Bradley approached the shed but didn't go inside. He listened for any strange noises, but all he could hear were crickets in the night.

I know what I saw.

Bradley cast his mind back to his time lapse video experiment with the white-tailed rats in New York over the summer. There was no way he would enter the shed now, but maybe there was another way.

He left the shed doors open, ran back to the house and down the hall to his bedroom. Roy had planted himself in front of the television and was watching football.

"You took your shoes off, right?" Roy called back from the living room. "Don't want dirt tracked all over the damn house."

"Fuck you, you douchebag," Bradley said to himself. He dug through his closet until he found what he was looking for: a selfie stick.

Bradley stood in front of the shed, his phone attached to the selfie stick. The light on the back of the phone cast a blue-white light into the interior of the shed. With every movement and step, shadows grew and shifted. Even with the light, there were dozens of darkened places for nimble spiders to hide.

The sun had completely disappeared below the horizon, leaving an orange-blue cloudless sky that on any other day would have been worth admiring.

Bradley launched his photo app and engaged video mode. He pressed record and stepped onto the leading edge of the shed's floorboards. He positioned the phone between the earthenware pots and the shovels.

He was flying blind and couldn't see if the phone was recording anything useful. He wished he had one of the remote cameras they had used to battle the rats in New York, but this would have to do.

Bradley raised the camera out and moved toward the right side of the shed. He crouched and brought the phone's camera around the pots, over scattered tools on the floor and behind where the sunflower seeds were stored. His movements combined with light from the phone threw shards of illumination on additional tools, bags of seed, and the back walls of the shed.

The light on the phone dimmed.

"Shit." The phone had had plenty of power the last time he checked. The light didn't draw that much power, did it?

Bradley guided the phone out from behind the front row of pots. As he retracted the phone, he saw the real reason for the lack of light. A half dozen large black spiders, maybe more, clung to the phone, covering the light and the phone's display.

He dropped the selfie stick, stood, and backed into the shovels behind him. The phone hit the floor, startling many of the spiders across the floorboards into hiding. The phone no longer obscured, a beam of cool white light illuminated the roof of the shed and blinded Bradley momentarily.

The shovels behind him bounced off the back of his head. But they seemed soft and had a heaviness to them, not like shovel handles at all.

Bradley spun around to find teardrop-shaped cocoons looped and lined up in a neat row, raised to the rafters, just high enough to be hidden by the top front-facing wall of the shed. The first gauzy cocoon terminated with a coal-black snout and whiskers protruding from the bottom. It was his raccoon. Attached to that was another cocoon of similar shape but with a rounder head, perhaps a house cat. Bradley couldn't be sure. Next in line was his stowaway rat, its tail glued to a cross beam with layer upon layer of webbing. A fourth cocoon enveloped something smaller than a rat, perhaps a bird.

"How the hell…?"

The light on the floor flickered. Bradley looked down and saw large black spiders advancing over the phone across the floor toward his feet, their quills pulsing over their abdomen.

He ducked out of the shed's entrance and onto the lawn, his heart jackhammering in his throat. He picked up a brick from a nearby flower bed and threw it into the shed, smashing several earthenware pots.

The spiders scattered back into the depths of the shed. Bradley grabbed the selfie stick and adjusted the holder on the end for a better angle. He raised the phone up behind the front wall of the shed so that he could remain outside and recorded video of the hanging cocoons.

A spider three inches across dropped onto his phone and began to crawl down the stick. He shook it off and onto the concrete paving stone pathway at the front of the shed.

Bradley raised his shoe and stomped the spider. It crunched under his foot like he was stepping on a crab, leaving a dark smear on the concrete.

He kicked the doors to the shed closed and locked the latch.

Bradley stood on the lawn, slicked with sweat and breathing heavily.

These were the spiders that had bitten Claire. He was sure of it. He had the evidence.

But these spiders looked like they came straight from a science fiction novel. Quills on their backs? Like a porcupine? He had never seen anything like it.

Tomorrow he would find some answers.

School Assignments

Doug Schroeder and Bob Thurmond worked together at Pacoima Paper Products. They had been golf buddies for years and decided to play the back tees that day at Hansen Dam Golf Club. Hole sixteen bordered the southern edge of Hansen Dam and was the shortest hole on the back nine at one-hundred eighty-five yards. The fairway was lined with oak and palm trees.

Bob selected a three-iron from the golf bag secured in the back of the cart. He knelt to place his tee and ball and centered his tremendous bulk over it.

He surveyed the fairway, tested the wind, and settled his stance. His golf ball was obscured by his overflowing belly.

"You got to lay off the pasta. And the beer." Doug was the very opposite of Bob, thin as a rail and a man of many words.

"Silence." Bob stepped back to see where his ball and tee sat, then stepped forward again.

"It's affecting your game."

Bob looked at Doug over the frames of his aviators. "I've got a system that works. Now shut up." He rocked the three-iron in his hands twice before sweeping the club back then forward in a powerful arc.

The golf ball shot down the fairway and almost immediately both men knew the trajectory was botched. The ball hooked left and overshot the green by a dozen yards, rolling into shrubs and rough along the dam's southern slope.

Bob replaced his club into his bag and joined Doug in the golf cart.

"What'd I tell you?" Doug navigated the gently winding path to the sixteenth green. "You keep this up, you're going to owe me beer for life."

"I'd buy you beer for life even if we didn't play golf." Bob smiled. "Because I'm a magnanimous human being." He looked at Doug. "You, on the other hand, are one annoying motherfucker."

Both men chuckled as they pulled up beside the putting green.

"I believe furthest away from the hole goes first."

"Funny guy." Bob slid off his seat, pulled his pitching wedge out and trudged to the treed and bush-lined rough where he last had seen his ball.

"You're going to have to get on your hands and knees," Doug said. "I'd better not take a photo and post it online."

Bob cocked his head and glared at him. "Why do I subject myself to this abuse?"

"Because you know I love you like a brother."

"Oh, is *that* why?"

Doug didn't need to see Bob's eyes to know he had reached the end of his rope.

"Get over here and help me look for my ball," Bob said. "And hold the jokes if you value your life."

Bob and Doug scanned the rough. It took about a minute of searching before Doug spotted the golf ball, low and about three feet in.

Bob knelt and leaned into the shrubs, but the ball lay a few inches out of reach. He pushed his body farther into the bushes and his fingers brushed over the dimpled surface of the ball.

An excruciating pain shot through Bob's arm, beginning at the fingertips of his right hand and settling in his shoulder. He screamed, fell backward, and rolled away from the bush, clutching his right hand.

Doug's eyes widened with horror as he witnessed Bob's right hand swell up, almost in real-time. "What the hell did you touch?"

"I don't know but it hurts like a son-of-a-bitch." Bob's right hand looked like a poorly constructed balloon animal, scarlet red with the skin stretched so thin it looked as if it might split and pop at any minute.

Doug fell to his knees beside his fallen friend and watched helplessly as the redness and swelling moved up Bob's arm.

Bob clutched his forearm like he was trying to stop the pain from moving further. "For Christ's sake do something!"

Doug pulled out his phone and dialed "9-1-1."

Hector Delarosa stood in the main equipment shed taking inventory. He had just finished applying a second round of new environmentally-friendly pesticide along the borders of the front nine.

He closed and locked the doors to the shed. The slow rise and fall of sirens sounded out in the distance.

Hector stood five-nine, overweight for his height (technically obese his doctor had said), with a black goatee that matched his crop of short hair. Usually a jovial sort, Hector got along with most everyone.

His walkie-talkie chirped then crackled, "We got a situation on sixteen." It was only then that Hector realized the sirens' intensity was increasing. He quickened his pace and hopped into his maintenance cart.

When Hector arrived at the sixteenth hole, the course's general manager Maria Gonzales was already on the scene.

"Stay with them!" She ran to Bob and Doug's golf cart and peeled out toward the main clubhouse and parking lot.

Hector approached the two golfers. Bob lay on his back, shivering uncontrollably, even with a blanket laid over him. "What happened?"

"Something bit him."

Bob's swollen right arm flopped out from beneath the blanket. Purple veins spidered out from his fingers and knuckles, across the red, swollen skin of his hand and forearm. The whole limb looked like a caricature.

Hector's eyes bugged out at the sight. "Bitten by what?"

Doug tucked Bob's arm back under the blanket without answering.

"Clear a path!" Gonzales led two paramedics with a wheeled stretcher up the path to hole sixteen and across the green to where Bob lay. One paramedic began measuring Bob's vital signs while the other prepared the stretcher.

Gonzales pulled Hector aside. "Do you know what's going on here?"

Hector pointed at Doug. "That guy over there said he was bitten."

"Bitten by…?"

"That's the question everyone's asking."

Gonzales paced back and forth, wearing a path into the finely manicured grass. "This better not come back to bite us in the ass."

"I don't see how it can."

"You know. Bad press." Gonzales stopped in the middle of the rut she had worn into the grass. "You've been using that new environmentally-friendly pesticide?"

"InsectaHex? Yeah. All summer." Hector pointed along the leading edge of the dam. "Both the front and back nine perimeter."

"Well, something got through."

"Want me to dig up the industrial strength stuff?" Hector lowered his voice. "You know, Emtix? The stuff that's illegal now?"

Gonzales crossed her arms. "I thought that shit was dealt with, as in *gone*."

"I was keeping it for a special occasion."

"Like when I fire your ass for violating city ordinances?"

"I'll dig it out and get rid of it," Hector said. "But I'll need a hazmat suit."

"I don't care how you do it, just do it."

"Alright. In the meantime, I'll rope off the area and find out what we're dealing with." Hector nodded toward the sixteenth green.

"Good." Gonzales approached the paramedics as they fastened Bob to the stretcher. "Is he going to be okay?"

"He should be," said a paramedic. They rolled Bob across the green and onto the path back to the parking lot. "Looks like a bite of some kind. Worst case he could lose his hand, but we'll know more when we get him looked at by a doctor."

"Great. A golfer loses his hand on my course. Fucking great." Gonzales turned toward Hector and pointed her index finger at him. "Keep me informed," she said before following Doug, Bob and the paramedics to the parking lot.

Hector gave her a thumbs-up before walking back to the bushes where Bob had lain minutes earlier. He pushed back the leaves on the bushes and searched the green shadows.

There was nothing there.

ALEXIS FOUND HERSELF sitting at the dining room table working on her biology project. There was something about researching the most lethal spiders in the world that appealed to her.

When Lucia arrived home from the salon with groceries for dinner, she looked twice to make sure she wasn't hallucinating.

"Is that my kid?" Lucia displayed a mock look of surprise. "Doing homework on the first day of school?"

"Don't get used to it," Alexis said, an undercurrent of disdain in her voice.

"I can dream." Lucia looked over Alexis's shoulder as she put away groceries. An image of a spider on the laptop's screen stared back at her. She shivered. "I don't like spiders."

"Lots of people don't. But they're misunderstood," Alexis said. "The more I learn about them, the more I like them."

"What's to like? They're ugly, big, and hairy."

"You could say the same thing about Hector."

"Hector doesn't have eight legs." Lucia placed boxes of cereal into the pantry.

The door to the garage opened. Sounds of random whistling, almost a melody but not quite, floated out from the hallway. Hector stepped into the kitchen and pecked Lucia on the cheek.

Lucia wafted air from her nose. "Someone needs a shower."

Hector tried to kiss Alexis, but she ducked his attempt. "I'll get you one of these days, Lex."

"I don't want your old, slobbery, stanky-ass kisses."

"Don't know what you've got 'til it's gone." Hector peered into the grocery bags looking for a snack but got his knuckles playfully rapped by Lucia. "And watch your tongue. I ain't *stanky-ass*."

Hector tried again, snagged a celery stick, and crunched it as a taunt. Lucia waved her knife, raised her eyebrows, and shot him a look. "Shower, *stanky-ass*."

"Did you know that at any given time, a person is always about ten feet away from a spider?" Alexis said.

Lucia shivered again. "Thanks for that."

Hector stood in the kitchen and watched Lucia and Alexis interact. It was one of the great pleasures of his life. Applying to the foster-parent system in San Fernando was Lucia's idea and one that neither of them regretted. He only wished that they had become Alexis's "forever parents" sooner. No child should have to grow up in the system.

"And they puke out digestive juices to help—"

"Okay. Enough spider facts for now." Lucia kissed the top of Alexis's head. "It's good to see you interested in school."

Alexis pushed her away. "Too bad everything else is totes basic."

"Got to start somewhere."

"Speaking of spiders, I got a story to tell." Hector disappeared down the hallway again, crunching his celery stick as he went. "Going to change."

"And shower!" Lucia called back. She placed lettuce, tomatoes, green onion and a cucumber on the counter. "Can you put the homework on pause for a second? Help me make a salad?"

Alexis groaned and closed her laptop.

"Got some new samples from the salon," Lucia said, grabbing Alexis's attention.

"Oh, what did you get? Can I see?"

"Help me first."

Lucia handed Alexis a peeler and the cucumber. "Peeled and sliced, please."

Alexis held the cucumber's cool, firm length in her hand and began to strip off the skin in long strips.

Lucia grabbed the head of lettuce and cut it in half. "Did you see Brad today?"

Alexis's brain went from the cucumber to Bradley and from there it was a short skip to Trillian. She cut a thick strip off the cucumber.

"Easy, Lex," Lucia said. "Not so deep." She looked at Alexis and tried to gauge her feelings. "Bad day?"

Alexis finished peeling the cucumber and switched the peeler for a chef's knife. The wide blade gleamed in the kitchen light. She chopped the cucumber harshly, dividing wide uneven chunks of the vegetable on the cutting board.

"You could say that." Alexis continued to chunk the cucumber.

"Are you two going to get back together?"

Alexis slammed the knife down on the cutting board. "Brad's an *asshole*. I'm glad I dumped his sorry ass."

Lucia switched her gaze from Alexis to the cucumber chunks and back.

Alexis returned her stare. "What? Butt out of my life! I can't deal right now." She stormed off down the hallway. "Spider!"

"What?"

"SPIDER!" Alexis called back. "In your LETTUCE!"

Lucia glanced down at her cutting board. A spider had crawled out from the heart of the lettuce. She let out a yelp and threw her knife, missing the spider by inches. It scrambled off the counter, dropped to the floor, and disappeared.

"I certainly know how to clear a room," Lucia said as she took several calming breaths.

Alexis slammed her bedroom door closed and flung herself onto her bed. Thoughts of Bradley and Trillian together swirled in her head. "That *bitch* stole him from me."

A text alert chimed from her back pocket. She slipped the phone out and rolled onto her back.

"Got the bitch's combo," Deirdre's text read.

I was just thinking of you, Dee, Alexis thought. She sent back a "thumbs up" emoji and tossed her phone beside her on the bed. She closed her eyes and was asleep in minutes.

A KNOCK ON the bedroom door roused Alexis from sleep. Hector poked his head into the room.

"Dinner, Lex."

Alexis rubbed her eyes and picked up her phone. No alerts since she dozed off. She stretched, slid off the bed and walked to the dining room, fighting grogginess the entire way.

Lucia plated up spaghetti with meatballs and marinara sauce. Alexis took her plate and sat down at the table across from Lucia.

"Looks great, Babe," Hector dished himself some salad, giant chunks of cucumber plummeting into his bowl like sodden stones.

"The cucumber… compliments of Lex."

Alexis glared at Lucia, who in turn smiled sweetly back at her.

"How'd you know I liked lettuce with my cucumber?" Hector winked at Alexis, his good nature dulling the chip on her shoulder.

"A warning," Lucia said as she served herself. "There may be spiders in the salad."

Hector froze.

"Thanks to Lex, I scared the first one away, but there might have been more that I didn't see."

"I'm going to pretend that I didn't hear that," Hector said. "I've had enough of spiders for one day… Ah shit."

Lucia glared at Hector. "Watch your mouth!"

"Sorry," Hector said. "Just forgot to get rid of some insecticide today. Old stuff. It's been banned and against the law now."

"Why was it banned?" Alexis asked.

"It was great at killing insects, but extremely toxic to mammals." Hector shivered. "It's like liquefied cancer. Very potent stuff."

"Well there's no pesticide in our salad," Lucia said. "Bought it from the Food Fresh today, locally sourced."

Lucia handed the salad to Alexis. She dropped a serving of

greens with large chunks of cucumber into her bowl, causing it to flip and twirl on the table. She looked at Lucia and smirked.

Lucia chased a cube of cucumber, made slippery by the salad dressing, around her bowl until she finally speared it with her fork. "Lex is studying spiders for Biology class."

"Maybe not for the whole year, but Viscera is starting with them." Alexis twirled spaghetti on her fork. "She's even got a big-ass tarantula in the class."

"Language," Hector said as he crunched a cucumber chunk.

"Shouldn't talk with your mouth full," Alexis said.

Hector waved his index finger at her.

"Viscera?" Lucia rolled the name through her memory. "You mean Fiscara?"

"Oh. Yeah. Viscera's her nick. A biology joke."

"No, I get it," Lucia said. "I hear she's good."

Alexis shrugged. "Maybe. I don't know."

"Any friends in your classes? Deirdre? Caitlin?" Hector sliced a meatball and missed Lucia's 'cease and desist' signals. "Brad?"

A hush fell over the table. Lucia looked at Alexis and Hector alternated his attention between the two.

"Did I say something wrong?"

Alexis forced a smile. "It's okay Dad. I broke up with Brad months ago. I'm so over him."

"Really?" Lucia stared at Alexis, a look of astonishment on her face. "Didn't seem that way an hour ago."

"So? I was tired."

"Want to hear my spider story?" Hector shoveled spaghetti and half a meatball into his mouth and began to chew.

Lucia turned to Hector. "Sure, why not."

Hector pointed at his mouth and made a point of chewing and swallowing. "Didn't want to talk with my mouth full." He grinned at Alexis, but she stared at him stone-faced. Lucia had impatience written all over her face.

"Whoa. Tough crowd tonight." Hector sipped his water. "So,

I had just finished spraying the border of the front nine, when I get a call on the walkie. Situation on hole sixteen. I high-tail it over there and a golfer was laid out on the grass, his hand swelled up like a pumpkin."

Lucia was just about to take a bite of pasta, paused and set her fork down. "Is it going to be one of *those* stories?"

"Nah, that's the worst of it." Hector settled into his chair and propped his elbows on the table. "The medics said the guy was *bitten* by something. So, Gonzales was all up in my grill about finding whatever it was that bit him. Y'know, bad PR and all that."

"Let me guess." Alexis gave Hector a look of apathy. "You found a spider."

Hector grinned, his eyes widening. "No. That's the thing. I didn't find any spiders or nothing."

"But...?" Lucia said. "There always a 'but.' " She placed the forkful of noodles into her mouth.

"But..." Hector paused for dramatic effect and ended up annoying Lucia and Alexis even more. "What I did see, and pardon my language Lex, would turn your shit white."

Alexis crossed her arms against her chest, a poster child of doubt and boredom. "So, what did you *see*, Dad."

"A string of cocoons, maybe four or five, kind of like sausage links, leading up the face of the dam and disappearing into the rocks."

Lucia shivered. "What, like cocoons for flies?"

"No. For other stuff. I didn't get too close, but I saw what looked like birds, mice or maybe a rat. And they were the size of sausages."

"Yeah, you already said that," Alexis said.

Hector gulped some of his water. "I poked one with a stick and this slimy stuff dripped out."

Alexis exchanged a look with Lucia, their combined "bullshit meters" going off the scale. "How do you know it was a spider?"

"What else wraps their prey in cocoons? Besides, I wasn't going to get close to it." Hector's body shuddered. "You didn't see that guy's hand."

All three sat at the table in silence, all with fading appetites.

The phone rang. Hector walked to the counter and picked it up. "Hello? Oh, hey." He walked back to the table and sat. "No, not at all. Just finishing dinner."

Alexis and Lucia heard low, distorted conversation filter out of the phone's speaker against Hector's ear. His jaw slackened, like he was going to say something but changed his mind. The color drained out of his face just before he hung up the phone and placed it on the table.

"What is it, Hec?" Lucia said. "You're scaring me."

"That was Gonzales." Hector looked at Lucia, then Alexis. "That golfer I was talking about... he died."

Whatever doubt remained for Alexis about Hector's story had disappeared along with the color in his face. But instead of fear or sorrow, an idea popped into Alexis's head and she had to force herself not to smile.

BRADLEY SAT IN English class and watched the analog clock on the wall, comparing it to the time on his phone. Back and forth. Check and recheck.

The classroom clock is slowing down. He was sure of it. And if he'd been asked what had been covered during class, he wouldn't have had a clue.

The bell rang. Students collected their belongings and shuffled to the exits. Mr. Silver strolled to the back of the class, straightening desks as he went.

"Looking forward to hearing about your book choices," he said as students filed past him. Bradley avoided eye contact as he moved toward the exit. "Brad, a word?" Mr. Silver pointed to a desk. "Take a load off."

After the last student left the classroom, Mr. Silver sat on the desk in front, his left foot propped up on the seat.

"Any ideas what you're going to pick?"

Bradley shook his head.

Mr. Silver crossed his arms. "You don't have any idea what I'm talking about, do you?"

"No." Bradley picked at a fingernail. "Sorry, Mr. Silver. I've got things on my mind."

"I know you're a good student," Mr. Silver said. "And it's the first week of school. So, I'm going to cut you some slack and give you a warning."

"Thanks."

"Here's the assignment. Pick a theme and four fiction books that fall under that theme. We'll get to the details next class."

Bradley raised his eyebrows. "A theme like…?"

"Like love conquers all, coming of age, good versus evil, that kind of stuff."

"Okay." Bradley sat and rattled his fingers on the desk.

"Go on." Mr. Silver sensed his impatience waved him off. "Get out of here. But next time I want your full attention."

Bradley collected his books and headed out of the classroom. He visited his locker to grab his day pack, threw his books into it, and hoofed it down the hallway. He thought it was weird that an English teacher's classroom was on the opposite side of the school as the library.

Trillian topped the south stairwell and spotted Bradley's hurried walk. Instead of calling out, she followed him.

On his way, Bradley passed students placing posters on the walls for the first dance of the year. *REMEMBER SEPTEMBER*, *EQUINOX ROCKS*, and *ROCK 'N' FALL* graced the tops of paper broadsheets in capitalized, autumn-colored letters.

Apparently, no one could agree on a name. Friday, September 21 was just over two weeks away.

Bradley had purposely not mentioned the spider video to Jack or Trillian. It was difficult keeping it to himself all day, especially after watching the video the previous night. Every bone in his body wanted to share, but he wanted more credible information than what he could find on the Internet. Fiscara preferred books over the Internet as well, so his trip to the library would serve double duty.

Being the second day of the new school year, the library was a dead zone. The librarian, Mr. Lovecraft, who was quick to point out to anyone within earshot that he was not related to the horror writer, was surprised to see a student so soon.

"Good afternoon. Can I help you find something?" Mr. Lovecraft never remembered students' names, but his knowledge of books, specifically the books in the Washbrook High School library, was close to encyclopedic.

"Uh, yeah. I'm looking for anything about spiders."

"Fiction or non?"

"Non."

"Follow me." Mr. Lovecraft stepped out from behind his desk. His tall, thin frame blazed a trail through the stacks of books until he faced a section filled with reference books on invertebrates. "I've seen a few students checking out books on spiders yesterday and today."

"Probably from Miss Fiscara's class," Bradley said. "We're studying spiders."

"Ah yes. Wendy." Mr. Lovecraft flashed his eyebrows. "She does love her creepy crawlies. I'll leave you to it." He began to walk back to his desk, stopped and turned. "I roll up the carpet at four."

Bradley nodded. "Thanks." He scanned the spines of the limited selection of books in front of him. Most were superficial, suitable for Grade 9 students. Bradley wanted details. He pulled a few books out: *Spiders: Consummate Killers*, *The Audubon Society Field Guide to North American Spiders*, and *The World of the Spider*. Not the best selection, but a start.

He carried the books to a study desk and sat down. His phone chimed.

"Bro, where R U?" Jack's text read.

Bradley tapped out a reply. "At library doing bio research."

Jack's response popped up a second later. "Defo lame. LOL Catch U L8R."

Bradley pocketed his phone and picked up the thickest book first, the Audubon Society Field Guide. The book was tall and narrow and fit nicely into his hands.

He flipped through the book, noting the section focusing on spiders. Pages and pages of full color photographs flew by his fingers.

This is going to take forever.

Bradley's phone chimed in his pocket again. Maybe Jack had changed his mind. The display showed a text from Trillian instead.

"What are you doing right now?" Her text read.

"Homework." Bradley texted back.

"Want some help?" Trillian's semi-hushed voice said behind him.

Bradley swung around in his seat and knocked one of his books to the floor. Trillian was standing a few feet behind him,

"You shouldn't sneak up on people," he said. "How long have you been standing there?"

"Not long." Trillian looked at the fallen book. "Working on your bio assignment?"

Bradley shrugged, picked up the book from the floor, and turned back to the Audubon Guide. "Sort of."

"Sort of?" Trillian pulled up a chair and picked up a book. "What do you mean, *sort of?*"

Bradley hesitated and directed his eyes across the library.

Trillian read the conflict on his face. "Hey, if you want me to go, just say the word."

"No, it's okay. It's just…" Bradley reached for his phone. "It's just that I wanted to know what I was dealing with before talking about it with you."

Trillian raised a brow and cast him a glance of curiosity mixed with trepidation. "Talking about… *what* exactly?"

Bradley loaded the shed video from the previous night. He slid the phone to Trillian and pressed play. "This. I know you're more of a spider expert, so I wanted to be more knowledgeable."

The video began to play. "You're giving me too much credit. I'm no spider expert." The phone's video showed Bradley scanning the contents of the shed, shadows dancing and stretching with every movement. "What is this?"

"I recorded this last night in the shed behind my house. Keep watching."

Trillian's eyes became like saucers when the first spider lead a cluster of others behind. Their dark, oily sheen caught reflected highlights from the phone's light.

"What the hell is *that*?"

"That's what I'm trying to find out." Bradley flipped through the Audubon Guide. "They're definitely spiders."

"What's on their backs?" Trillian squinted at the phone's display. "They look like quills, like from a porcupine."

"Yeah, they do a bit. I can't find anything that looks similar in this book."

Trillian handed back the phone. "They're spiders, and also porcupines. You should call them sporkies."

Bradley slid the video scrub bar forward and placed the phone back down in front of Trillian.

"What the hell, dude!" Trillian looked around the library and lowered her voice. "Is that a…" She cocked her head to one side. "Is that a *raccoon*?"

"Yeah. I think that's a cat next to it. Then a rat and a bird… or something else."

"Your sporkies did this?"

Bradley smiled at the nickname. "I guess so?"

Trillian paused the video and took a closer look at the cocoons. "That's way fucked up." She looked at him and placed her hand on her mouth. "Sorry."

"No bigs. I don't care if you swear."

Trillian scrubbed the video to the beginning. "They're coming from that tunnel in behind. You can kind of see it." She paused the video and pointed out the detail. "Look up the funnel web spider."

Bradley flipped to the page in the guide describing funnel web spiders. "It looks kind of the same, except for the quills, but this can't be a funnel web spider. They only exist in Australia." He flipped a page. "There's a funnel weaver native to North America, but it doesn't look the same at all."

"You should talk to Fiscara."

"I'm going to, but you don't know what she's like," Bradley said. "She's going to want more info. She's insane about details. I wanted to do some digging myself first."

The video ended, pausing the screen on the final image of the cocoons hanging from Bradley's shed.

"Consummate killers." Trillian looked at the phone's display, then to the book on the table. "Yeah, I'd say that's accurate." She glanced at Bradley, a subtle grin crossing her lips. "You going to be much longer?"

"Uh, I don't know—"

"Walk me home?"

"Okay." Bradley collected his things. He piled the books on the table and was about to reshelf them when he heard Mr. Lovecraft call across the library.

"I'll take care of them," he said. "You kids go on home."

"Thanks, Mr. Lovecraft."

Trillian pulled Bradley aside. "Lovecraft?" she whispered. "As in the horror writer?"

"No relation, apparently."

Bradley and Trillian left the school to begin their walk home. Along the way, they passed another "Missing Pet" poster. "Have you seen Winston?" the poster read, this one penned by a young hand. Underneath the title was a black and white photo of a handsome tabby cat. Deep down, Bradley already knew what had happened to Winston.

On any other day, he'd be filled with nervous excitement to be alone with a girl, but today his thoughts were consumed with spider venom and identifying this new type of spider. His mom's life may depend on it.

THE PHONE TRILLED in Bradley's ear.

A click. "Hey, bro. What's up?" Jack said.

"Want to help me on a fact finding mission?" The pause in Bradley's ear grew longer by the second. "Jack?"

"Uh, weren't you just at the library doing exactly that?" Jack's lack of interest came through loud and clear. "Sounds like work, bro. Why don't you call up that new girl you've been hanging with?"

"She's nice but I don't know her well enough yet."

"Your *fact finding mission* would be the perfect opportunity to get to know her," Jack said. "You do want to *know* her, right?"

"Yeah, I guess." Bradley looked out his bedroom window at the locked shed. "Look. I need to find the source of the spider that bit my mom. And I need to do it fast."

"That's easy. It came from your back yard."

"There's more to it than that. You've seen all the missing pet posters around the area," Bradley said. "Don't you think that's weird?"

"I get it. You need wheels."

Bradley could hear Jack's grin through the phone. "Yes. I would not turn down an offer of your superior driving skills."

"All you had to do was ask."

"I'll sweeten the deal." Now it was Bradley's turn to grin. "We begin and end this mission at Taco Siempre."

"Exploiting my weakness for Mexican food. Well played, bro."

"Consider it payment. And a thank you," Bradley said. "What are you doing right now?"

"I've got work stuff to do. First thing after school tomorrow?"

"Thanks, man." Bradley hung up the phone and loaded his shed video. He paused it on a good shot of a sporky, its black armored exoskeleton and spines highlighted against the shadows of the shed, and captured a screen shot. He sent the image to Jack.

A few seconds later, a text from Jack appeared. "WTF is that?"

"A sporky."

Jack texted back, "???"

"I'll fill you in tomorrow," Bradley tapped with his thumbs. He stared at the image, the arachnid's eight soulless eyes staring back at him, through him. He shivered and turned off his phone.

THE THURSDAY END-OF-DAY bell rang. Bradley crested the south stairwell and found Jack waiting by his locker, practically vibrating.

"Bro what took you so long," Jack said. "I'm in agony. Let me see that video."

Bradley looked up and down the hallway, now filled with students rushing to their lockers and collecting their things before heading home. There was no sign of Trillian or Alexis either, which would have complicated things. "Not here. I'll show you in the car."

"Screw the cloak-and-dagger shit, Brad." Jack said. "You want a ride or not?"

Bradley pulled Jack close and lowered his voice. "If this got out it could cause mass panic. You want that?"

Jack shrugged him off. "This better be good is all I can say."

Jack lead the way down the stairwell and out of the school to the student parking lot. Bradley stopped at the lamp standard with the missing pet sign on it. He pulled out his phone and took a photo.

Jack unlocked the passenger door of his Civic, shuffled across into the driver's seat, and started the engine.

"What about the video?"

"I'm hungry. The video can wait." Jack grinned. "First stop, Taco Siempre, right?"

"That was the deal," Bradley said. "Don't speed like a bat-out-of-hell. If I see any posters, I'll need to stop and take a photo."

Jack navigated out of the school parking lot, onto the street and floored the gas. The Civic's tires squealed, leaving tread marks on the pavement and a plume of blue, acrid smoke as Jack and Bradley flew down the street.

"I thought you said you weren't going to speed," Bradley said, gripping the door handle.

"You know me. Slow's not in my vocab," Jack said. "But don't worry. I'll stop for your missing posters."

Five minutes later, Jack and Bradley were inside the

restaurant. Jack craned his neck, scanning the front counter and into the kitchen.

"Damn. Sofia's not working today." He stepped to the counter and ordered a burrito. "You're not getting anything?"

Bradley shook his head and paid the cashier. They took a nearby booth and Jack waited for his name to be called.

"You know, this video might not be the best thing to watch while you're eating." Bradley cued up the shed video on his phone.

"Show it to me now, then." Jack beckoned with his hand. "We've got about two minutes." Bradley slid his phone across the table and Jack tapped play.

"Do you have issues with spiders?" Bradley asked.

"They've never bothered me any."

As the video played, Jack's face moved from boredom to curiosity to confusion and horror.

Bradley glanced at the screen. "That's a *sporky*. A spider porcupine. Trillian came up with that one."

"Good nickname. She's the new girl?"

"Yeah," Bradley said. "Did I tell you that she's in my homeroom?"

Jack was unable to tear eyes away from the video. "That's convenient. Lucky you… How did you get this video?"

"Slightly modded selfie stick," Bradley said. "We used video to figure out what was going on with the rats in New York too."

"Jack?" the cashier called out from the front counter. "Order for Jack?"

"Damn. I like how Sofia says it." Jack paused the video and went to grab his order. He returned, his burrito unwrapped before he sat down.

"What are your feelings toward spiders now?" Bradley looked at him with a twinkle in his eye.

"I'm fine with spiders."

"Liar."

Jack shrugged and tapped the play icon, continuing the video where he left off. He took a bite of burrito, chewed, and swallowed. He took another bite.

Bradley watched as Jack's chewing slowed, then stopped completely.

"What?" Jack managed to speak through a mouthful of partially chewed burrito. "No way. Is that a…"

"A raccoon? Yep."

Jack locked eyes with Bradley. He took a sip from his drink and swallowed his mouthful. "Are you shitting me? 'Cause if you are—"

"I'm not."

Jack watched the rest of the video without eating or saying a word. When the video was over, he handed the phone back to Bradley.

"So, you're saying these things, these *sporkies*, bit your mom?"

"Yeah. And they can kill a raccoon."

Jack picked up his burrito. "Well, I better eat fast so we can go and find more of those posters."

Bradley watched Jack wolf down the rest of his food. The shed video had lit a fire under his ass. Maybe it was because he lived alone most of the time and if he was bitten, there would be no one around to help

"What's gotten into you?"

Jack looked at him, cheeks filled with burrito. "What?"

"I practically had to drag you out here to help me," Bradley said. "Now you're totally into it."

Jack swallowed and wiped his mouth. "Something clicked." He stood and headed for the door.

"What?" Bradley wanted an answer, but Jack was already out in the parking lot, sliding into the driver's seat from the passenger side. He followed him outside and into the Civic. "Spill it."

"Okay. When I was at work the other day, I knocked over

some eggs and a whole bunch of spiders ran out of the carton," Jack said. "It happened so fast, but I think they looked like the spiders in your video."

"Sporkies."

"Whatever." Jack started the Civic's engine and revved it. "They were smaller though." He backed out of the parking lot and turned onto the street. "We only found one other poster on the way here. Maybe we'll find more going the opposite direction."

Jack's intuition was spot on. Using an alternating east-west search pattern, they found half a dozen more posters, all featuring small dogs or cats. Adding to the one from the school and Jack's Food Fresh encounter brought the total up to eight.

"You doing anything right now?"

Bradley shook his head.

"Let's visualize the data."

Jack drove to his house. After setting up drinks and snacks, Jack opened his laptop on the kitchen table.

"We'll reverse search the phone numbers for addresses and create a map out of it." Jack called up an online phonebook in his Internet browser. "What's the first phone number?"

Bradley read off the phone numbers from the poster photos one by one. All but two were mobile numbers and didn't have addresses associated with them.

Jack dropped pins for the addresses they did have onto an online map, as well as the locations where each photo was taken. With each pin, a visual pattern developed.

"Holy shit." Jack stared at the laptop screen. "What's the next location?"

Bradley read out the longitude and latitude numbers. "34.256° N, -118.377° W."

A dotted, ragged line of location pins moved from close to the Hansen Dam Golf Club, past Washbrook High, and a few blocks past that.

The hair on the back of Bradley's neck stood on end as he lightly traced the path on the laptop screen with his finger. "It goes right through the school grounds and my house. I don't want those things in my back yard, do you?"

Jack tapped his finger on the screen. "They're not in my back yard."

"How do you know?"

"What we're seeing is inconclusive. With a data sample this small, it could mean anything."

"You want more data, don't you?"

Jack smirked. "I *always* want more data."

"Do spiders migrate?"

"Bro, you're asking the wrong person."

Bradley motioned at the laptop. "Do a search, brainiac."

Jack typed in Bradley's question and a list of results flashed across the page. "Looks like they do. It's called 'ballooning' and they do it in search of better hunting grounds." Jack exchanged looks with Bradley. "Distances travelled range from a several feet to hundreds of miles."

Bradley swallowed hard. "I don't know about you, but that doesn't help me feel any better."

Jack flipped back to the map page in his browser and typed in Bradley's email address. "I just shared the map with you."

Bradley's phone chimed and buzzed in his pocket. "Got it." He looked at the time on the clock hanging on the kitchen wall and confirmed it with the time on the laptop. "Hey man, I got to get going."

"Sure. Want a ride?"

"Nah, thanks," Bradley said. "It's not far."

"Even with ballooning killer sporkies everywhere?" Jack grinned.

"You sure got a way with words. I think I'll be okay." But the image stuck in the back of Bradley's mind like a waiting predator.

Jack gave Bradley dap and raised his middle fingers at him.

Bradley hoisted his day pack onto his shoulder and returned the gesture.

"Later, bro."

"Yup." Bradley closed the front door and began the short walk home. The sun had started its slow track to the horizon.

He pulled out his phone and dialed Claire. The number trilled twice before switching to voice mail. He left a message, then tried Sun Valley Medical Center. A nurse from reception told him that they couldn't reveal any patient information over the phone. Bradley thanked the nurse and hung up.

Everything felt different now that he suspected a community-wide infestation of spiders. Shadowed areas, under cars and bushes, in mailboxes, his shed back home, they all seemed more dangerous now. He quickened his pace.

He had to become hyper vigilant, and in hindsight, recording the shed video had been irresponsible. If he had been bitten there was a good chance that he would have died. But after all the combined research, he still didn't know definitively what kind of spider had bitten Claire.

Luckily Bradley knew someone who could answer all his questions.

BRADLEY'S STOMACH GROWLED loud enough for Mark Everett, the student sitting next to him, to notice.

"Aren't you hungry?" Bradley whispered.

Mark shrugged and switched his attention back to Fiscara, who was standing at the chalkboard finishing up the breakdown of a tarantula's inner anatomy. When Fiscara got started on a subject, she didn't stop until she had exhausted every detail.

Bradley's biology class was right before lunch on Fridays. The class had gone long and was five minutes into the lunch break.

Everyone was on edge, shifting in their seats, waiting for Fiscara to finish up. Sounds of lunchtime antics filtered through the closed door from the hallway beyond.

Bradley doodled in his notebook, drawing sporkies in as much detail as his memory would allow. His brain was full and sketching relaxed and distracted him from his ravenous stomach.

Trillian on the other hand was a machine. She wrote notes at a furious pace as Fiscara spoke, stealing a glance at Bradley every so often. A mixture of curiosity, concern and admiration showed on her face.

Alexis occupied her familiar seat in the back of the class. Her notebook was closed. Instead of taking notes, she watched Bradley, and more importantly, watched Trillian watching Bradley.

"You're going to get yours, *bitch*," Alexis hissed to herself.

"Thanks for your patience. I know it's lunchtime and we went long. I'll make it up to you," Fiscara said. "For next Friday's class, I'd like to see a short paragraph describing each major internal organ of the tarantula. You can hand in your 'most lethal spider' assignments on your way out."

There was a flurry of paper and books as the students packed up their belongings. One by one the students placed their assignments on Fiscara's desk as they rushed out of the classroom.

Bradley hung back, waiting for the class to clear out a bit more before he approached Fiscara. Soon it was just the four of them in the classroom, Fiscara, Bradley, Trillian and Alexis.

Trillian sidled up to Bradley. "You going to show her?"

He shot a wary glance back at Alexis, who was collecting her things. "She's stalling." Bradley dug through his day pack, feigning a search for his assignment.

"I thought you'd be the first out of here, Mr. Shaw." Fiscara sat at her desk. "I've been listening to your stomach roll and rumble for the past half hour."

"Yeah. Sorry. I wanted to talk to you about the lethal assignment." Bradley approached Fiscara's desk, Trillian close behind.

Alexis stood and sauntered toward the front of the class, her ears in eavesdropping mode. She held a makeup mirror and lipstick in her hand, concealed against her purse.

Bradley grabbed his phone from his pocket and unlocked it. The shed video was loaded and ready to go, having preloaded it before the class. "My mom was bitten by a spider a few days ago. She's still in the hospital."

"I'm sorry to hear that, Mr. Shaw."

"Just Brad."

"Okay, Brad."

Alexis pushed Bradley aside and dropped her assignment on the stack. She turned and bumped the corner of a desk on her way out and dropped the mirror and lipstick onto the floor. She crouched to pick the items up, her ears perked. But there was no talking to be heard.

She turned to see Fiscara, Bradley and Trillian staring at her.

Fiscara raised her eyebrows. "Everything okay, Miss Delarosa?"

Alexis popped open the mirror and refreshed her lipstick, taking her time. "Don't mind me. Just want to look my best." She pressed her lips together and wiped a smudge from the corner of her mouth.

Bradley crossed his arms, waiting, clearly annoyed. A subtle yet satisfied grin crossed Trillian's lips as she stood behind Bradley. No one caught it except Alexis, just as Trillian had hoped.

"Bye, lover boy." Alexis kissed the air and offered a small wave before strolling out of the classroom.

Fiscara shook her head. "Could that girl be any more self-absorbed?"

"Probably," Bradley said.

Trillian stifled a giggle.

"I'm sorry about your mom, Brad. Spider bites can be serious." She looked at Bradley, then Trillian and back. "Was there anything else?"

"Actually, there is." Bradley placed his phone on Fiscara's desk. "Can you ID this spider?" He tapped play.

As Fiscara watched, her brows furrowed in confusion.

"We thought it might be a funnel web spider," Trillian said, excitement evident in her voice. "But they're only found in Australia."

"I need to know what it is." Bradley spoke in earnest. "Knowing could help my mom."

"Where did you get this video?" Fiscara scrubbed the play control to find a good view of the spider.

"The shed in my back yard."

"We call them sporkies," Trillian said. "A cross between spiders and porcupines."

Fiscara studied the still image on the phone. "I can see why."

"Did you see the end?"

"No. Is there more?"

Bradley glanced at Trillian, then faced Fiscara again. "Just skip to the end."

Fiscara moved the play control to the end of the video and let it play. When the video reached the end, she took off her glasses, rubbed her temples, and placed her hands in front of her mouth, as if she was praying.

"I need to see this in person," she said after a moment.

"Sure." Bradley nodded.

"How about tomorrow morning?"

Bradley thought about how Roy would react to an unannounced visit from his biology teacher on a Saturday morning. He could text or call him right now or tell him at dinner.

Fuck Roy.

Bradley nodded. "Sounds good." He jotted his address on a scrap of paper.

"See you tomorrow."

Bradley and Trillian walked toward the classroom door.

"Aren't you two forgetting something?"

The two teenagers looked at each other, confused for a moment until Bradley clued in.

"Our assignments!"

Fiscara smiled and pointed her index fingers at them. "Bingo."

They pulled out their assignments, placed them on the top of the stack of papers, and left the classroom.

Fiscara put her glasses back on and leaned back in her chair. She pulled a red apple from a lunch bag by her desk and took a large bite. The crunch echoed across the classroom.

She looked at Bradley's assignment on the top of the stack, then past it to focus on the terrarium at the back of the class.

"You don't eat raccoons, do you Killer?"

BRADLEY WOKE ON Saturday just before eight thirty in the morning. He hopped out of bed and dressed quickly. He chose a clean pair of jeans and a stylish button-up shirt. He wanted to look good for Fiscara, but not too good. He didn't want her to think that he was trying to impress her.

The smell of coffee, bacon, eggs, and toast lured him to the kitchen. For a moment he thought Claire was home.

"Mom?" The image evaporated as soon as Bradley entered the kitchen. "Oh. It's you."

Roy stood at the stove, wearing a coordinated orange track suit with Claire's "Kiss the Cook" apron tied in front. A white baseball cap with the words "World's Greatest Jogger" embroidered on it completed his morning ensemble.

"How about 'good morning, Roy,' or a 'smells great, Roy.' "

"Morning." Bradley crossed the kitchen, grabbed a coffee mug from the dish strainer and poured himself a cup. He stirred in two tablespoons of sugar and took a sip.

Ugh. Rotgut. No amount of sugar could salvage this abomination.

Bradley set the cup on the table, lifted a bowl from the cupboard and filled it with Cheerios. He splashed some milk on top and sat down to eat.

"Don't you want some bacon and eggs?" Roy scraped scrambled eggs into a serving dish.

From his vantage point, Bradley could see charred bits mingled with the rest of the eggs. "No thanks."

"Your loss."

Not likely, Bradley thought as he munched on his cereal.

Roy laid overcooked bacon beside the eggs and placed the entire unappetizing heap on the table. Even the toast was well done. He grabbed a cup of coffee and some condiments from the fridge and sat down.

"Breakfast of champions." Roy served himself a large portion of eggs, bacon, and toast. "I ran 15 miles this morning. What did you do?"

"Slept," Bradley said through a mouthful of Cheerios.

"You should come jogging with me in the mornings," Roy said. "Increased circulation is great for the brain."

Bradley dug through the toast to find the least burnt piece and spread a thick layer of peanut butter on it.

Roy gave Bradley a once-over. "You're all dressed up. Expecting anyone?"

"My bio teacher's dropping by," Bradley said between bites. The peanut butter barely covered up the acrid taste of the burnt toast. "I told her about the spiders in the shed and she wanted to take a look for herself."

"She's coming here?"

"Yeah. I can't take the shed to school."

"Smart ass." Roy shoveled in a mouthful of eggs followed by a swig of coffee. "By the way, your mom has to stay in the hospital for at least another week. But you'd know that if you had actually checked up on her."

"I called but her phone was off and visiting hours were over."

"Uh huh." Roy's lips were peppered with bits of burnt bacon. "Likely story."

"It's true." Bradley gritted his teeth. "Want to see my call history?"

Roy shrugged and continued stuffing his face with burned breakfast.

The doorbell rang.

"She's here now?" Roy said, mouth full.

"That's what I said."

Bradley brushed off his hands and went to the front door. On the front step stood Fiscara *and* Trillian, who was smiling at Bradley's expression of surprise.

"Look who I found on the way here." Fiscara nodded her head at Trillian.

"I wanted to see the freaky-ass cocoons for real," Trillian said.

Roy appeared by Bradley at the door. "I see why you dressed up," he said loud enough for only Bradley to hear and nudged him in the ribs.

"This is Roy, a friend of—"

Roy stuck out his right hand. "I'm Roy, the man of the house."

Fiscara met his hand with hers and shook it briskly. She wiped a sheen of transferred bacon grease off her hand and onto her jeans.

Roy cast an eye of uncertainty at Trillian as he retracted his hand.

"I'm Trillian. A friend from school."

Bradley opened the front door as wide as it would go. "Come in. I'll take you to the back yard." He led Fiscara and Trillian through the house via the kitchen. "Don't mind the mess. We were just finishing breakfast."

"So, you're a biology teacher, huh?" Roy walked in tandem with Fiscara. "I'm the top salesman at Sylmar Nissan. I could get you a deal."

Bradley rolled his eyes in disgust. "My mom's in the hospital and he's hitting on Viscera," he whispered to Trillian. "He's such a douche."

"How is your mom, by the way?" Trillian glanced at Bradley though her rainbow hair.

"She's okay, but she needs to stay in the hospital longer," Bradley said. "That's why I need to know what kind of spider this is. The doctors need that kind of info." He led Trillian and the others across the back lawn toward the shed.

"…and when I showed Bradley what was in the shed," Roy said, "I told him to bring in the pros. And here you are."

"Ugh. Liar," Bradley whispered. "Roy didn't even believe me."

The group gathered at the locked doors to the shed.

"Roy? You were the last one in the shed, right?" Bradley stood expectantly. "Can you please unlock it?"

Roy tapped his track suit with his hands. "I left the keys inside. Let me go—"

"That's okay." Bradley pulled out his set of keys. "I'll just use mine since I have them on me at all times." He unlocked the doors, feeling the heat of Roy's glare on the back of his neck. "Stand back. Sporkies could be anywhere."

Roy furrowed his brow. "Sporkies?"

"That's what we call them," Trillian said. "A spider with quills."

"Like a porcupine. Very descriptive," Fiscara said.

Bradley pulled the doors open as he stepped back. A blast of foul-smelling air floated out of the shed. "God damn. What the hell?" He placed his hand over his nose and mouth.

Fiscara nodded. "That's the smell of decay, putrefaction, probably from the larger animals you showed me. But it normally takes longer than this. If I had to guess, it's the digestive enzymes from the spiders that is accelerating decomposition."

"Wouldn't that take a lot of enzymes?" Bradley asked. "I can understand a bird or rat, but a raccoon?"

"It could be that the enzymes are extremely potent." Fiscara pointed at a puddle of crimson fluid collecting on the floorboards. "Something's been leaking. Not surprising since it would take a lot of spiders to completely consume a raccoon."

"Or several *really big* spiders," Trillian said.

Roy crossed his arms, impatient. "We don't get really big spiders here."

"How do you know that?" Bradley asked.

"I've read things online."

"You read?" Bradley laughed. Roy shot him a glare.

"Actually, he's right." Fiscara pulled out a penlight and scanned the interior of the shed. "Of the almost fifty thousand species of spiders on the planet, most really large spiders live in the southern hemisphere."

Roy's anger at Bradley dissipated and an air of smugness crossed his face instead.

"But the big spiders aren't usually the lethal ones." Fiscara stepped closer to the doorway to the shed, crouched, and looked up. The four cocoons still hung in place. "Got any trash bags?"

Bradley disappeared into the garage and returned with a couple of black garbage bags.

"Spiders go where the food is plentiful," Fiscara said. "Let's take away their supply." Fiscara grabbed a rake from the left side of the shed.

Trillian watched Fiscara work. "What's with the rake?"

"We don't want any surprises." Fiscara smiled as she rapped the wall and ceiling of the shed, her flashlight trained on the rake's handle.

"See? What did I tell you?" Roy said. "There's no spiders in there."

"What made the cocoons, then?" Bradley shook out a garbage bag and pointed at the shed's entrance. "Have you even looked at them?"

"You two clearly have issues," Fiscara said. "But it would be great if you both shut the hell up."

Bradley's and Roy's jaws dropped almost in unison. They glanced at each other as a red flush spread across Bradley's cheeks.

"Thank you. Now let's get back to business—"

Trillian's eyes widened as she pointed. "Look out!"

A black spider about four inches across dropped down within half a foot of Fiscara's right shoulder. The weight of the spider on its silken thread caused it to bounce a few times before it continued its descent onto her middle back.

"Wait!" Fiscara froze. "No sudden moves. Can anyone see it?"

Trillian stepped slowly around Fiscara and saw the spider perched near the base of her ribs. "Oh fuck." The quills on its back were flipping in and out as its eight legs stepped up Fiscara's back.

"You got to knock it off me before it gets to my neck." Fiscara maintained her cool and looked at Roy and Bradley. "Any ideas?"

Roy shrugged.

Bradley's gaze darted around the shed before settling on the garden hose. "I have an idea."

"Move fast, but slowly... got it?" Fiscara sent Bradley an intense gaze. It was clear to him that she was barely holding on to her fear.

"I think so." Bradley turned to Trillian. "Pick up the sprayer. I'll go turn on the water. When I give you the signal, blast it."

Trillian nodded.

Bradley walked quickly until he was far enough away that running wouldn't pose a threat to Fiscara. He reached the side of the house and cranked the tap's valve open.

Trillian saw Bradley give the thumbs up and squeezed the sprayer's trigger. Nothing happened. She tried the trigger again with the same results.

The spider moved up Fiscara's back. "Hurry up or I'm toast."

Bradley followed the hose with his eyes and spotted a kink blocking the flow of water. He ran to it and straightened the hose.

Trillian squeezed the sprayer and the nozzle spurted loudly then ejected a wide, fine mist. "Shit!"

"Come on guys," Fiscara spoke through her teeth.

Trillian fell to her knees and aimed at the ground. She twisted the nozzle until the spray was focused into a single, powerful stream.

"Hurry. I can feel it on my shoulder blade."

The spider, its quills expanding and contracting like a fleshless rib cage, approached the top of Fiscara's shoulder.

Trillian aimed the stream of water at the spider, carrying it off like a sailboat in the wind and drenching Fiscara in the process. She dropped to the pavement as the spider landed in the grass near Roy's feet.

"Kill it!" Bradley yelled.

"No!" Fiscara began to protest but Roy had already brought his shoe down on top of the spider, an audible crunch resonating from under his foot.

"Damn." Fiscara rolled onto her back, then sat up. "We could have had a live specimen to study."

"Maybe there's more," Trillian said. "It's possible."

"More than possible." Bradley twisted the water tap closed.

"I've seen enough missing pets posters to know that there's a problem."

Roy held out his hand to Fiscara. She took it and he helped pull her up. His gesture could have been considered chivalrous had it not been for him staring at the shirt plastered to her breasts. "Thanks."

She turned to Bradley, pulling her wet shirt off her chest. "What missing pets?"

"I noticed one a few days ago," Bradley said. "Then I started seeing more and more of these posters. Jack and I, we plotted a bunch on a map."

Bradley dug out his phone. He pulled up his mapping app and the saved map that he and Jack had worked on the day before. The number of locations had more than doubled since Thursday. "Holy crap."

"What?" Trillian studied Bradley's face.

"Jack's been busy. There's way more data here than what we collected on Thursday," Bradley said. "Jack loves data."

All four looked at the phone's display. There were enough location pins on the map to show a scattered line, from the golf course, through his yard, and around the high school. It reconfirmed what Bradley had suspected before.

"There's a lot around the school." Bradley pinch-zoomed the map to show more of the school.

"If the missing pets are due to spider attacks, it may be because of ballooning in search—"

"In search for food!" Bradley grinned with enthusiasm. "I was reading about this yesterday."

"Bonus points for you," Fiscara said.

"There's so many of them, and probably more we don't know about." Trillian pursed her lips in thought. "Do spiders usually work together?"

"Most spiders are solitary creatures, but there are a few species that live communally, working together to capture larger prey and defend themselves." Fiscara tapped her lips with her index finger. "The type of spider you showed me on that video doesn't jive with those species."

"Maybe this is a *new* species," Trillian said.

Bradley and Fiscara shared a glance. Roy yawned.

"It's a possibility. But before we can act on this, you're going to need to confirm that there are actually spiders at these locations." Fiscara looked at Bradley and Trillian. "You two up for the task?"

They looked at each other, then back at Fiscara and both nodded. "Yup," Bradley added.

"I'll keep my eyes open, too," Roy said in an attempt to stay relevant in the conversation.

"I'll give you a little slack on your assignments. If you need it that is."

"Thanks," Trillian said.

"Okay, let's get those cocoons down." Fiscara returned the rake to the shed and took out a long shovel instead. "Roy, you hold my light." She handed him her penlight, then faced Bradley and Trillian. "You two hold the garbage bag up so these corpses don't fall too far."

Bradley grabbed one side of the bag and Trillian took the other. "Ready?"

"Yeah, but I better not get slimed." Trillian wiped a bead of sweat off her forehead with her outstretched bicep. "I'll be going home smelling bad enough as it is."

"You could shower here if you wanted to," Bradley said. "That's okay, right? Roy?"

"Huh?" Roy was staring at the translucent wet fabric of Fiscara's t-shirt as it hung loosely off her shoulders. "Oh, yeah. Right."

Bradley rolled his eyes and smirked at Trillian. They raised the garbage bag up under the raccoon's corpse.

"Roy?" Fiscara caught Roy's sightline before he could look away. "Stop staring at my tits and shine the light up *here*."

Caught in the act, Roy straightened up and redirected the penlight's beam at the ceiling of the shed. "I wasn't staring."

"Here goes nothing." Fiscara positioned the shovel's blade above the first cocoon and scraped the top. It dropped into the bag like a cluster of rotted fruit. Bradley and Trillian were unprepared for the sudden weight and the bag slipped out of their grasp and hit the ground, half in and half out of the shed's entrance. A greasy pop sounded from within the bag, followed by an intense odor of sickly sweet rot.

When the smell hit Roy's nose, he buckled over and vomited onto the grass.

Bradley's mind flashed back to the dumpster in the Bronx when Sam was fishing out Piper's carcass. He'd never forget the smell of decomposing flesh.

Trillian and Fiscara shared a look as they watched the men fight against waves of nausea.

"Mind over matter, I say." Fiscara winked at Trillian. "Let's get the rest of these cocoons down before the men pass out."

Trillian giggled.

Bradley grabbed the garbage bag and together with Trillian they raised the bag up once again.

"Light?" Fiscara looked at Roy, sitting on the grass wiping his mouth. He held up the penlight with a shaky hand.

In rapid succession, Fiscara scraped the dead cocooned animals into the garbage bag. Bradley knotted the bag and placed it in a second bag, knotting that as well. The smell of death and rot still hung thickly inside the shed.

"Where did you say the nest was?"

Bradley pointed to the right side of the shed. "There, behind the pots."

Fiscara shifted the lawn mower and the larger pots to one

side. The woven funnel opening to the nest was now clearly visible.

"There you are, my pretty." Fiscara crouched to get a good look. "Sure looks like a funnel web's nest... if I could *see* it. Roy, sorry buddy but you're fired. Trillian? Could you?" She motioned toward the penlight.

"Oh, sure." Trillian took the light that Roy had already held out to her.

"I'm out of here." Roy trudged back to the house. "I'll be inside if anyone needs me."

The others watched Roy until he had disappeared inside.

"I don't know what my mom sees in him," Bradley said.

"He's a real catch, that's for sure." Fiscara looked back into the shed. "Trillian? Light. Or I'll have to fire you too."

Trillian targeted the beam on the nest opening. Fiscara poked the shovel blade into the opening of the nest and a solitary black spider burst forth. Sensing it was outnumbered, the arachnid scrambled backward, over the shovel and into the deep shadows of the shed.

"Unless we clear out the entire shed, we'll never find it."

Bradley shook his head. "Ain't going to happen. This is ground zero for my mom's garden oasis. She'd never go for it."

"Well then... plan B." Fiscara used the shovel to extract the funnel web, doing her best to keep the nest as intact as possible. "This will make for a nice addition to the class, don't you think?"

Bradley leaned forward to get a closer look. "Are there eggs in that nest?"

"If we're lucky, an egg sac." Fiscara smiled, wide and confident. "If they *are* a new species, the discovery could put Washbrook into the spotlight. And we'd all get credit."

Trillian shrugged. "I think I'd rather just not get bitten." Bradley presented his fist and she bumped it.

"You got to think beyond Washbrook and what a discovery like this could mean to your future career."

"What career?" Bradley said. "I don't even know what I want to be when I graduate."

"Me neither," Trillian added.

"You got to start thinking about it sometime and it may as well be now." Fiscara looked around the back yard. "Got a box I can put this nest in?"

Bradley disappeared into the garage and returned a few moments later with a tattered cardboard U-Pick berry box. He dropped it on the ground.

"Perfect." Fiscara placed the nest in the box.

"Don't you have a lid?" Trillian asked.

"I didn't see any evidence of spiderlings, so I think I'll be fine." Fiscara alternated her gaze between Bradley and Trillian. "Well don't just stand there. We all have work to do." She walked toward the side gate. "I expect a full report next class."

Bradley and Trillian watched Fiscara walk around to the front of the house.

Trillian raised her eyebrow. "Is she always that bossy?"

"Yep." Bradley pulled out his phone. "Where do you want to start?"

An Expanding Web

AFTER A SECOND breakfast of Cheerios, peanut butter on *unburned* toast, and coffee, Bradley and Trillian walked to the outlying pins on the map. They had to be careful not to trespass. Two unknown teenagers digging around on private property would have raised red flags quickly. But sometimes there was no other option.

The first three addresses were a bust. Either the pets disappeared from another location, the spiders' nests were too cleverly hidden, or the spiders had moved on.

At the fourth address, the homeowner caught Bradley and Trillian in their back yard.

Bradley was quick with a response. "Sorry Ma'am. My baseball landed in your yard and I'm just looking for it." It was a blatant lie that worked well enough to become the standby excuse.

"Make it snappy." The homeowner watched them like a hawk from her porch as Trillian and Bradley looked around the yard's open areas for their "missing" baseball.

A Yorkshire Terrier stood next to her and barked the whole time. Memories of Bradley's summer in the Bronx continued bubble up unexpectedly and an image of Carny, the little Bichon Frise, popped into his head as they left the yard, zero for four.

Trillian caught his smile. "What?"

"That dog reminded me of this yappy little dog that lived in my Dad's building in the Bronx. Barked at everything."

Trillian cocked an eyebrow. "Lived?"

"Yeah. After the paramedics took away his owner's remains, the little dog—"

"Wait. *Remains?*"

Bradley nodded. "Rats killed him and ate most of his body. That dog chased the ambulance down the street and never returned. Funny and sad at the same time."

Trillian stared at him.

"Remind me later to tell you about how I spent my summer vacation," Bradley said with a smile.

"How about you tell me now?"

"Because I think our odds just got better." Bradley looked from his phone to the house they stood in front of and recognized it immediately.

It was Mr. Moody's house.

"Come on," Bradley said as he walked down the long driveway. "But keep it down. The guy who lives here is an asshole who would call the cops on us in a second."

Trillian's eyes scanned the front lawn overgrown with weeds and the windows shrouded with stained curtains. The house looked like it would collapse at the slightest touch.

The small back yard was in even worse condition than the front. In the corner sat a rusted out 1955 Chevy truck without doors or wheels. An overgrown apple tree stood close by, with a heap of rotting and fermenting fruit in the grass beneath.

Trillian reached up and pulled an apple off a low hanging branch.

"You're not going to eat that, are you?"

Trillian shrugged. "Why not? It's just an apple." She bit into it, crunching a mouthful of fruit as apple juice ran down her chin. "They're really good. Try one."

She reached up to grab another apple and froze when she saw

cobwebs. "Shit." Trillian spat out her mouthful and examined the apple in her hand for spiders. Instead of taking a chance, she tossed the apple aside. "We got nests in this tree."

As the two of them stepped back, the intricate web of funnels interwoven between the branches became more obvious.

"I'm surprised we missed that coming in," Bradley said.

"But are they the right spiders?"

"Let's find out." Bradley grabbed a nearby stick and poked at a nest entry hole. A black spider scrambled out and ran down the stick toward Bradley's hand.

He jettisoned the stick away from his body and stepped back. The black spider flashed its quills in the grass and began spiraling back up the trunk of the tree.

"I'd say that's a yes."

"Let's get out of here," Trillian said. "This place gives me the creeps."

Bradley took out his phone and snapped a photo of the tree and the spider. "Best idea ever," he said as the two of them headed back to the street.

BRADLEY AND TRILLIAN continued their search, working their way east to west through Stonehurst toward Hansen Dam Golf Club.

The more houses and yards they searched, the easier identification became. One house had a layer of webbing and nests underneath a trampoline in the back yard. An image of kids being overtaken by those awful black spiders with their half-inch fangs made both Bradley and Trillian shiver with revulsion. They agreed to inform the residents.

Bradley knocked on the front door. There was no answer. He tried again with the same response.

"We got to tell them somehow."

Trillian reached into her knapsack and pulled out a notebook and a pen. "Write them a note. Use your baseball excuse."

Bradley scrawled a warning notice about the spiders, folded it in half three times and tucked it in between the door and frame.

"I hope they take it seriously." Bradley handed back the notebook and pen.

"What else can you do?" Trillian skipped down the front walk to the street. "Let's get moving. I don't want to be doing this on Sunday too."

"You mean you're not having the time of your life?"

"Ha ha. Come on."

A telephone pole next to another pinned address had webbing surrounding the transformers.

"I hope those ones get fried," Trillian said, looking up at the grey cylinders humming with electricity.

"Electricity is good for that." Again, Bradley was reminded of his visit to New York and the electrified cage known as the Kill-O-Matic.

By the time the two of them had reached Washbrook High, a spider infestation was becoming more and more evident. Bradley wasn't a data geek like Jack, but he knew at least half of the pinned addresses so far had nests clearly visible. He thought that was worth considering and he hoped that Fiscara would see it that way too.

The high school had turned out to be a bonanza of nests despite the map. On Bradley's phone, pins were clustered *around* the school, but the nests they found were on *school grounds*. Trillian was the first to spot one, woven into the top corner of the far soccer net. An oak tree near the basketball courts had several branches covered in webbing. The best find of the day was located on the school building itself.

"Holy shitballs, look at that," Trillian said.

Bradley laughed. "Shitballs?"

"Just look." Trillian pointed at the alcove underneath the home economics classrooms. Maintenance equipment and spare desks and chairs were stacked within, all surrounded with a locked chain-link fence. As the two of them made a closer approach, Bradley saw what Trillian was talking about.

"Holy shitballs," he said grinning.

Trillian gave Bradley a playful shove to one side.

A gauzy funnel built from interconnecting strands of silk stretched from a recessed ceiling light to the walls and equipment surrounding it. It looked a like a stack of do-it-yourself bug tents. Near the back of the funnel hung a small, spiky teardrop-shaped object.

Trillian pointed at it. "See that thing inside?"

Bradley squinted and nodded.

"I bet you that's an egg sac."

Bradley looked at her. "How many eggs are there in an egg sac?"

"A thousand, maybe?" Trillian clicked her tongue. "I remember reading that the other day."

"Can you imagine a thousand of those sporky things crawling around in the school?"

Trillian swallowed hard. "Unfortunately I can."

Bradley cast her an uneasy glance. "Me too." He took a photo with his phone.

A bird landed on the chain-link fencing ten feet away from them, then launched itself inside the enclosed storage area.

"Hey look!" Trillian said. "An American Goldfinch."

"How do you know that?"

"The yellow body and black wings and head are the dead giveaway." Trillian shrugged, a little self-conscious. "What can I say? My dad… taught me." Her voice hitched.

Bradley followed the bird as it hopped and flew around the area, collecting bits of paper and twigs. "What's it doing?"

"Probably building a nest."

The goldfinch hopped onto a chair leg and began to peck at one of the funnel web's supporting strands. From the center of the funnel, near the recessed light, a spider appeared. It moved down the funnel in repeated quick-then-slow movements.

"Look." Bradley pointed through the chain-link at the top of the funnel web. "Mama spider's come out to play."

The bird continued to peck at the webbing, pulling small pieces off with its beak. It looked like the bird was growing a little white beard. The spider, now out of the funnel opening far enough to reveal the quills on its back, crawled to the roof of the funnel and continued its approach.

"No. Not the goldfinch." Trillian watched the spider advance until it was within striking distance. She turned and rested her back against the chain-link fencing. "I'm not watching."

Bradley zoomed in on the bird with his phone and tapped "Record." The spider spun its body around, aimed its spinneret, and a jet of silk flew out. The sticky stream missed the bird's head but stuck to its wings.

The goldfinch tried to fly away, but with one wing impaired, it flapped around in a frenzied circle and stuck to the side of the funnel. The spider repositioned itself with quick linear movements and shot a gooey strand of silk, this time encasing the bird's head. It was all over. Fifteen seconds later, the spider had the bird wrapped in a tight bundle and was drawing it up into its central nest. It reminded Bradley of a tamale from Taco Siempre.

"Is it over?"

Bradley nodded. "But I got it all on video if you want to watch."

"No, thanks." Trillian crossed her arms. "We need to get rid of those things."

"And before that egg sac hatches."

"Do you think we have enough data for Viscera?"

"Probably," Bradley said. "But I'm going to do a bit more looking."

"Brad, I like hanging with you, but I'm really tired." Trillian stifled a yawn. "I think I'm going to go home."

"Where do you live?"

Trillian thought for a moment. "On Bromont, I think?"

"That's on the way. I'll walk you home."

"Thanks." Trillian smiled.

The two of them exited the school grounds and headed down Stonehurst Avenue.

Once they were out of sight, Alexis stepped out from behind a large oak tree next to the school. She had been following the two for over an hour.

"So oblivious," Alexis said to herself. She walked over to the enclosed area, hooking her fingers through the chain-link and squeezing until her knuckles turned white.

She followed the strands of webbing, from the upturned chairs and desks, all the way up to where they converged on the recessed light. The egg sac dangled just within the opening.

Alexis's eyes settled on the chain-link door's padlock, and she began to formulate a plan.

It didn't take long to get to Trillian's house on Bromont, a few blocks from Washbrook. It was a modest white rancher-style home with a contrasting orange adobe-tiled roof. A portico covered the main entrance on the right side, next to the driveway. A three-sided bay window in the front faced the street and a neglected garden.

Bradley looked at his phone. "You're lucky. There don't seem to be a lot of spiders around your area."

"Good." Trillian sighed. "This is me."

Bradley looked at the house and smiled. "Cool."

A moment of awkward silence settled between them.

"So...?"

"So, eight o'clock, Monday morning, okay?" Bradley said. "We'll talk to Viscera?"

"Yeah, okay." Trillian said as she headed up the driveway to her door. "Bye."

"Trillian?"

She turned around. "You can call me Trill for short. If you want."

"Okay. Trill. Thanks for helping."

"Sure." Trillian opened her front door and disappeared inside.

Even though the map on his phone showed most of the concentration of missing pets east of where Trillian lived, Bradley continued his trek along one of the many trails that snaked through the Hansen Dam Golf Club and recreation area.

He passed through the front nine and scaled the rocky scree that lined the east side of the dam. The two-mile long concrete walking path was eerily silent. Not a soul walking, running or cycling across the dam tonight.

It's Saturday, almost dinner. Why am I here?

Fiscara wanted data. That's why. And boy she was going to get it. Of course, there was another reason. Roy. Going home meant having to see—and possibly talk with—Roy. It was the last item on his priority list.

Bradley stood at the top of the dam and took in the view. The San Fernando Valley sprawled out before him and the vantage point offered just enough altitude to see the entire city up to the Santa Monica Mountains. He was able to spot Trillian's house and his own, just barely. Jack's house was too far.

With the sun low in the sky, Bradley began his walk home. He selected a couple extra addresses to investigate that weren't out of his way.

The first address had a "BEWARE OF DOG" sign next to the yard. Bradley and dogs didn't get along. Frenzied barking from behind the fence erupted as he passed the house on the sidewalk. The dog was alive so there was a good chance that the spiders' nests were in a secluded spot.

The next address had a neighborhood barbecue in full swing. The smells of burgers and ribs made Bradley's stomach growl in protest, reminding him that he had skipped lunch.

He consulted his phone. More than three quarters of the addresses had been covered.

Good enough for school.

In Bradley's eyes, the evidence was overwhelming. The missing pets posters could be tied to the presence of spiders by a margin of three to one. And some of the addresses had been inaccessible.

But what would Fiscara think?

IT WAS AFTER 10 p.m. Saturday evening. Deirdre and Caitlin, both dressed in dark clothing, waited outside the school just off the student parking lot. The moon cast the school grounds in a blue light, but Deirdre preferred to skulk out of the moonlight's reach, in even darker shadows.

"Where the hell is she?" Deirdre paced back and forth, checking her phone constantly. "She's the one who set this stupid meeting up in the first place."

"She'll be here. Cool your jets." Caitlin sat with her back against the concrete steps to the north stairwell. Even though it was still officially summer, the air developed a chill at night that was absent a month ago.

"I could have been watching Saturday Night Live."

"Sit." Caitlin pointed to the ground next to her. Deirdre

paused, then sat reluctantly. "And put your phone away. She'll be here."

The two girls faced the night sky, peppered with starlight. Deirdre was consumed with aggravation and closed her eyes.

"Satellite." Caitlin pointed out a small, fast moving object moving across the black expanse of sky.

"Huh?"

"Never mind."

Deirdre pulled out her phone again to check the time. "If she's not here in two minutes, I'm going to bail. I've got more important shit to do."

"More important than what?" a voice said from the corner of the school. Alexis stepped out into the moonlight, a backpack slung over her shoulders. Her face looked pale as a ghost and gave Caitlin a fright.

"Finally." Deirdre stood. "We don't have all fucking night."

Alexis stared down on Deirdre, using her height to her advantage. "You better watch your mouth or I'll kick your ass."

Deirdre backed down, but she was still annoyed. Her fuse tonight was even shorter than usual.

Alexis glared at Caitlin. "You going to sit on your ass all night?"

Caitlin rolled her eyes and stood. "Happy?"

Alexis walked toward the home economic classrooms, Caitlin and Deirdre quick to follow.

"What's so damn important?" Deirdre said.

"I saw the love birds today." Alexis pointed at the maintenance alcove. "Right over there."

Caitlin furrowed her brow. "Love birds?"

Alexis elbowed Caitlin in the ribs. "Brad and that bitch, Rainbow Brite."

Caitlin recoiled more in surprise than pain. "Were they making out?"

"No, stupid. But they were watching something in there."

"What, old desks?" Deirdre pulled out her phone to check her social media feeds.

"Something better."

"Better than old desks?"

"Of course, dumbass." Alexis stopped in front of the chain link fence. "Dee, turn on your light."

Deirdre engaged flashlight mode on her phone and directed the beam into the storage alcove. A vast funnel-shaped web expanded from the desks and chairs right up to the recessed light socket. Both Caitlin's and Deirdre's jaws dropped at the sight.

"Holy shit," Caitlin said.

"The web is thicker than when I was here four hours ago."

"It's a damn spider web." Deirdre shrugged. "So what?"

Alexis pointed toward the convergence of the funnel, her finger poking through the chain-link. "I want the egg sac."

"But the place is locked," Caitlin said.

Alexis dropped her backpack on the ground and pulled out a pair of bolt cutters, a new padlock, and a plastic bag from Lucia's salon. She walked up to the door's padlock, slipped the blades of the bolt cutter around the lock loop and squeezed. The metal loop separated like it was made of plasticine. She pulled the lock from the latch it was hanging from and threw it on the ground.

"You were saying?" Alexis pushed the chain-link door open, its squeaky hinges echoed in the enclosed space.

"So, what now?" Diedre adjusted her phone's flashlight to get a better view of the funnel web.

"We take the egg sac," Alexis said. "Any volunteers?"

"What?" Caitlin stared at Alexis and Deirdre. "Your plan is to just reach up and take a spider egg? You don't even know what kind of spider made that." She waved her hand in the general direction of the web and shivered.

"Sounds like Cait is volunteering," Deirdre said.

"Uh huh." Alexis grinned in agreement.

Caitlin took a step back "The fuck I am." She looked at the

top of the web attached to the ceiling. "I'm not sticking my hand up there."

Alexis grabbed Caitlin's arm and pushed her into the storage alcove. "Yes. You *are*." Always the enforcer, Deirdre stepped into the doorway to block Caitlin's only escape.

"What the *fuck*, Alexis. Come on."

"You're afraid of an itsy bitsy spider? What could they do?"

Caitlin sent panicked looks at the two girls. "Ever heard of a brown recluse? Or a black widow?" She paused for a response but was met with blank stares. "Give me your phone and I'll show you some nasty-ass bite videos."

"She's stalling." Deirdre switched her phone light to her opposite hand.

"No shit, Einstein," Caitlin said. "You would too if you've seen what I've seen."

"We're not leaving until you reach up there and get me that egg sac."

Caitlin glared at Alexis. Her choices were do as she was told or face a crew punishment. In other words, no choice. She looked around the cramped alcove. The chairs and desks were efficiently stacked next to the wall. She grabbed one and began to drag it.

"Not that one!" Alexis placed her hand on the chair, stopping its movement. Caitlin was too preoccupied with unease to understand what Alexis meant.

"Look." Alexis pointed at a web strand attached to the chair that helped secure the large funnel web. "You'll destroy it." She indicated a chair farther along in the stack. "That one."

"Fuckers," Caitlin said to herself. She moved into the alcove, paying more attention to where her body was in relation to the web, careful not to touch it.

"Take this." Alexis handed her a plastic bag branded with Lucia's salon, Forever Stylez. "Put the egg sac in it."

Caitlin reached the chair, lifted it off the stack, and placed it as close as she could get to the web. She stepped up onto the chair, with only an inch of clearance between the ceiling and her head.

From her position on the chair, Caitlin could reach around the opening of the funnel web on its shortest side. But she had a problem. "Someone's going to have to hold the bag open."

"You're up, Dee."

"But I'm holding the light."

Alexis beckoned with hand. "Now, you're holding the bag. I'll hold the light." She took the bag from Caitlin and handed it to Deirdre in exchange for her phone.

Alexis aimed the phone's light at the center of the funnel. Shadows stretched and danced on the ceiling and walls with her movements. Caitlin raised her hand toward the dangling egg sac.

"Bag ready?"

Deirdre nodded even though Caitlin couldn't see her. "Yeah."

"Come on. What's the hold up."

"Fuck you, bitch," Caitlin said. "I'm going as fast as I can."

"Well, go faster." A sly grin spread across Alexis's lips as she panned the light away from the nest's central opening.

Caitlin pulled her hand back, unable to see in the darkness. "What the hell are you doing?"

Alexis brought the light back. "Just testing you."

"I don't need no damn testing." Caitlin scowled over her shoulder down at Alexis. "Don't move the light."

Caitlin moved her hand toward the egg sac, slowly, closer. Even in the cool night air, sweat beaded across her brow and dripped into her eyes, stinging them.

A black spider, the size of a baby's fist and shiny like painted metal, burst to the forefront of the web's opening. Caitlin screamed, pulled her hand away and nearly fell off the chair.

The spider's sudden appearance startled both Deirdre and Alexis, both taking a step back.

"That's it," Caitlin said. "I'm not fucking doing this."

"Yeah, you are." Alexis and Caitlin, both angry now, locked gaze. "Don't even think of getting off that chair,"

The two teens stared at each other. Then Caitlin's face cleared.

"The bolt cutters. Give them here."

Alexis grabbed the tool and handed it to Caitlin. "That's the first good idea you've had all night."

Caitlin ignored the insult and pulled open the handles of the bolt cutters. "Hold the light steady." She raised the tool with one hand around the leading edge of the funnel web and positioned the free handle against the side of the webbing.

"Don't jiggle it." Deirdre raised the bag up to catch the egg sac. "Hurry up. My arms are getting tired."

"Try holding bolt cutters. You're all a bunch of punk-ass bitches," Caitlin whispered to herself. She gently poked the free handle through the gauzy sheet and wrapped her free hand around the grip. With both hands in control of the bolt cutters, she raised the blades up to the egg sac.

"Ready?"

"I'm dying here," Deirdre said.

Raising the bolt cutters caused the handle piercing the web to stretch, forming a larger hole until the web's strands reached their breaking point.

What happened next took place over the span of a few seconds.

A large hole tore through the side of the funnel like a rubber band snapping back into shape. The vibrations along the webbing alerted the spider and it reappeared beside the egg sac, its chelicerae and glistening black fangs pumping up and down.

Caitlin tried to close the bolt cutters, but the spider was faster. It bolted across the blades and down the handle to her left hand. She screamed, her eyes bright with terror, and let go of the cutter's grips. The weight of the tool pulled both the egg sac and the funnel web down with it. Caitlin stepped back into thin air, careening backward into darkness until she landed on the floor with a thud.

The bolt cutters punched a hole in Deirdre's bag, and both the egg sac and the tool fell to the concrete floor. She and Alexis stepped backward, nearly falling over each other as the funnel web's gossamer sheets floated to the floor.

The spider clung to Caitlin's hand during the fall. "Get it off! Get it—" The spider plunged its fangs into the fleshy part of her hand between her thumb and index finger. She screamed again, this time a high-pitched blood-curdling scream.

Alexis and Deirdre exchanged a fearful look in the dimming light from the phone. Caitlin flicked her wrist violently and sent the spider sailing into the darkness. She scrambled on all fours out of the alcove, Deirdre not far behind.

"Where's the egg sac?" Alexis aimed the phone's light every which way with no luck.

"I don't give a fuck." Caitlin sat outside the storage alcove, trembling and holding her left hand. Two black puncture wounds on her skin welled with blood. Under the moonlight, it looked like she was bleeding black ink.

"Where is it?" Alexis waved the phone's light side to side, scanning the cracked concrete floor, the Forever Stylez bag with the bolt cutter underneath, and the toppled chair. She dragged the bag across the concrete to the chain-link fence with her foot. Alexis crouched and lifted one corner. Inside sat the egg sac, one side smashed, the other torn open with hundreds of tiny black spheres spilling out from the sac.

But the black spheres were propelling themselves across the floor and upon closer inspection, each sphere had eight wisp-thin legs attached. Baby spiders not much bigger than black grains of coarse sand scrambled in all directions away from the damaged egg sac.

"FUCK!" Alexis tossed the phone aside, stomped on the egg sac, killing any baby spider in proximity. She ran out of the storage alcove in a rage, dragged Caitlin off balance, straddled her chest, and began smashing her back against the asphalt. "You bitch! You ruined everything!"

Deirdre pulled Alexis off Caitlin and threw her sideways. "Stop it!"

"She fucked everything up."

"Fucked *what* up? You didn't even tell us the plan," Deirdre said. "We're not mind readers, you stupid bitch."

Alexis heaved herself up and stood face-to-face with Deirdre, both girls holding their ground and unwilling to back down.

Deirdre's nostrils flared in anger. "Cait needs to go to the hospital."

"Because of a little spider bite?" Alexis laughed. "Get real."

"Look at her hand."

Alexis turned her head slow, keeping her eyes on Deirdre until the last second. Despite being half a foot shorter, it was common knowledge that Deirdre could beat the shit out of anyone at the school.

Caitlin lay groaning on the pavement. The skin on her fingers was red and drum-tight, and looked like a well-done package of franks. The swelling had moved past her wrist and halfway up her arm. She started to shake and her breathing became raspier with each breath.

Deirdre picked up her phone and dialed "9-1-1."

"Yeah, hi. There's a girl at Washbrook High School that needs help. She's been bitten by a—"

Alexis grabbed the phone and ended the call. "What are you, fucking stupid?"

"I don't want Cait to die."

"She's not going to die."

"How do you know?"

"I just do." Alexis paced back and forth. "Now the police are going to get involved. She'll blab, and rat us out."

"No way," Deirdre said. "Cait has never ratted on us."

"There's a first for everything."

Deirdre grabbed her phone back and pocketed it. "You're a real stone-cold bitch."

"I'll take that as a compliment." Alexis cocked her ear to the sounds of sirens approaching. "Come on. Let's go." Alexis turned and ran onto the sidewalk and down the street.

Deirdre looked at Caitlin, then back at the storage alcove with the door wide open. She ran to the alcove, engaged her phone light and repositioned the fallen chair. She kicked the plastic bag and the cut padlock under the desks and picked up the bolt cutters. She closed the chain-link door and repositioned the new padlock through the latch and locked it. To the casual observer, the alcove looked undisturbed.

The sirens sounded even closer now. Deirdre knelt beside Caitlin's ear. "Ambulance is on its way." Caitlin groaned in response.

With her phone pocketed and the bolt cutters in one hand, Deirdre ran down the street, away from the approaching sirens. Alexis was nowhere to be seen.

She dumped the bolt cutters under a bush three blocks away from the school and continued running. With every step, her thoughts kept drifting back to Caitlin lying alone beside the school until she couldn't stand it any longer. She turned back.

By the time she was close enough to see the school, an ambulance had already arrived, and paramedics were strapping Caitlin to a stretcher. A police car with lights strobing was angled across the street.

Deirdre waited until she saw Caitlin loaded into the ambulance before turning around and walking back down the street. Hearing the receding siren didn't do anything to ease her guilt.

BRADLEY PACED OUTSIDE the front entrance to the school. He looked at his phone. The time on the lock screen read 7:55 a.m. He had arrived ten minutes ago just in case Trillian was early. She wasn't.

When Trillian did arrive, it was 8:02 a.m. "Hey, Brad."

Bradley didn't waste any time. "You said you'd be here at eight."

"It *is* eight."

"It's two minutes *after* eight."

"Whoa. Back off dude." Trillian recoiled and gave him a once-over. "Who pissed on your cornflakes?"

"This is important." Bradley pulled open the door to the school, letting Trillian enter first. A warm and stale smell of dust and floor wax washed over them.

"I know it's important," Trillian said. "But two minutes isn't going to kill us." She gave Bradley a gentle poke on the shoulder. "Chill out."

The two of them navigated the hallways to Fiscara's classroom. There were some early-bird students at their lockers, but the school was largely empty. This was good. Bradley had no desire to draw attention.

They found Fiscara at the back of the classroom feeding Killer. She had set up a second terrarium and placed the remainder of the nest from Bradley's shed inside.

She looked up with surprise as Bradley and Trillian entered the classroom. "You two sure are prompt. Class doesn't start for…" She looked at her watch for emphasis. "…for another day."

"You wanted a full report." Bradley fished his phone out of his pocket. "This couldn't wait until our next class."

Fiscara alternated her gaze between the two students. "Alright. Lay it on me."

Bradley loaded his photo app and handed the phone to

Fiscara. "We found nests in most of the addresses on that map I showed you before. Including here."

"At the school?" Fiscara looked at Bradley with raised eyebrows, before returning to the photos, swiping and pinch-zooming.

"Yeah."

"He got video, too," Trillian added. "Show her—"

"I think I found it." Fiscara sat transfixed by what she saw on the phone's display. "Damn, not an American Goldfinch."

"I know. I couldn't watch." Trillian looked at Bradley, who seemed to be vibrating with nervous energy. "You okay?"

Trillian's question broke Fiscara's focus on the phone. She handed it back to Bradley.

Bradley looked at Trillian with concern. "We have to show—"

"Show me?" Fiscara broke in. "Lead the way."

The three of them left the classroom, Fiscara closing the door behind her.

"Aren't you going to lock it?" Bradley asked.

"There's nothing in there that's worth stealing."

Trillian lead the way until she realized that she didn't know the school as well as she thought. "I think it's under the Home Ec. classrooms but…"

"This way." Bradley took over.

"You were right." Fiscara nudged Trillian. "I know where we're going too."

Bradley led the group out a pair of side doors near the north end of the school and around the corner. Something was different and Bradley noticed it right away.

He grabbed the chain-link fence as he looked through it. "Someone's been here. Look." He rattled the fence then shoved himself away.

"Yeah," Trillian said. "The web was attached to that light up there and connected to all the chairs."

Fiscara looked through the alcove. "It must have fallen down. The wind maybe?"

Bradley crouched down, scanning under the chair legs and spotted a familiar plastic bag. "Someone's been in there."

"But the door is locked," Trillian said.

"Easily cut off with the right tools." Fiscara looked at the padlock. "It's not a standard school-issued lock."

"We could pick it." Trillian looked for approval of her idea.

"We could." Sounds of a souped-up Honda Civic roared into the parking lot and Bradley smiled. "Or we could ask Jack for his help. He's got an ultimate set of tools."

Jack saw Bradley, Trillian and Fiscara standing next to the school and parked the Civic in the closest stall possible. He pulled himself out of the driver's side window.

"What a showoff," Bradley said to himself.

"Brad. Trillian. Miss Fiscara." He nodded to all three. "What's going on?"

"Do you still have your grabber in your car?"

"Yeah, always." Jack looked at the three of them, perplexed. "Why?"

"Can I borrow it for a second?"

"Uh, sure." Jack ran back to his car and dug out the grabber. It was a long aluminum rod with a trigger on one end, pincers on the other, and compact enough to slip through the openings in the chain-link. He handed the tool to Bradley. "So, what's up?"

"There was a huge spider nest here on Saturday and now it's on the ground." Trillian switched her gaze from Jack to Bradley. "I don't know what he's digging at now."

Bradley had crouched down on all fours and was directing the grabber as far as he could. He nudged the bag aside and revealed the cut padlock underneath. Hooking one of the claws into the cut lock loop, he dragged the padlock across the floor and out of the alcove.

Bradley turned the cut lock around in his hand a few times. "Miss Fiscara. Take a look." He tossed the brass and silver lock up to her.

"This is the lock that should have been on the gate," Fiscara said. "Sliced right off."

Bradley fished around under the desks and chairs, determined to retrieve the plastic bag.

Jack squatted next to Bradley. "What's in there?"

Bradley didn't offer an explanation as he latched onto the corner of the bag. "Got it." He pulled the bag out slow so it wouldn't snag on any of the desk and chair legs. Now at the chain-link barrier, he handed the grabbers back to Jack, and pinched a corner of the bag between his thumb and forefingers, pulling the bag as gently as he could.

The logo on the side clearly read "Forever Stylez."

Bradley shot a glance at Jack. "Alexis," he said in a low whisper.

Jack's eyes narrowed. "Shit. That's bad isn't it?"

"Probably." Bradley looked back at Fiscara and Trillian, who were talking about the web inside the alcove. The cut padlock dangled from Fiscara's finger. "Keep this to yourself for now."

Bradley tore open the side of the plastic bag and folded back the edge. The remnants of the egg sac plus a few crushed black baby spiders were smeared along one side of the bag. "Miss Fiscara? I think you're going to want to see this."

Bradley and Jack stepped back to allow Fiscara and Trillian room to observe. Fiscara pulled out a compact magnifier, unfolded it, and leaned down to get a close look.

Trillian backed away. "I wouldn't get too close if I were you."

"Yeah," Bradley said. "I've seen what these things can do."

"They're all dead… and they've all got tiny hairs sticking out of their backs."

"The quills." Trillian shivered at her words. "Sporkies."

Fiscara folded the bag up to protect the remains of the egg sac and picked it up.

"Is that enough evidence?" Bradley asked.

"Short answer? Yes. This is big." Fiscara headed back toward the school entrance. "I'll take it up with Maddox," she called back.

"Maddox?" Trillian sent a look of confusion at Bradley.

"Mad Dog Maddox," Bradley said. "He's the principal."

"He's also an asshole." Jack held the pincers of the grabber in front of his face, triggering them opened and closed. "Remember when he sent me to detention for a week for idling my car next to his?"

Bradley nodded.

"Viscera isn't going to get anywhere with that dick."

The bell rang and the three friends joined other students entering the school.

Maddox better do something, Bradley thought. *Because if the school is the epicenter, then…*

The images in his head went nowhere good.

Fiscara liked to think she was tough but fair, especially where her students were concerned. When designing her class curriculums, she made a point of going a little further than most teachers would. She incorporated assignments that challenged her students, forcing them to think outside the box more, instead of just adding more homework. The evidence that Bradley, Jack, and Trillian had uncovered had both impressed and concerned her. But getting Maddox to understand the danger and act on it would be an uphill battle.

Fiscara wove her way around sleepy students, a common hallway obstacle on a Monday morning. She was happy to see more posters had been taped to the walls since last Friday for the upcoming dance. She always volunteered to chaperone dances because, even though she'd be there in an official capacity, teachers should get to have some fun too.

She spotted Alexis and Deirdre walking the opposite direction. They were missing one member of their trio today.

"Miss Delarosa." Fiscara nodded at her. "How's Friday's assignment coming?"

Alexis passed Fiscara before answering. "Great. Have you marked my *lethal* project yet?"

"You'll know when I'm done."

A grin spread across Alexis's face. "I want that pinky mouse."

"You do, huh?" Fiscara turned and casually pointed at Alexis. "Good luck." She continued forward, but not before noticing Deirdre staring at the plastic bag in her other hand. She was about to say something, but the two girls turned abruptly and disappeared into a crowd of other students.

What's with the bag? Fiscara began to second guess herself. She dismissed it as teenage girl weirdness.

Fiscara turned into the office and offered a little wave at the receptionist, Wendy Bischoffe. They weren't friends but had remained connected over the years upon learning that they shared the same first name.

"Hey, Bish." Fiscara motioned at Maddox's office door. "Is he in?"

"Yes, but knock first," Wendy said. "He's in one of those moods."

"That's a switch." Both women laughed.

Brent Maddox had been principal of Washbrook High School for the past eighteen years. He had been given the nickname of "Mad Dog" early on in his administrative career because of his tenacity, like a dog with a bone. Or as some students had experienced, like a rabid dog when his anger overflowed. Many student caricatures over the years had depicted Maddox foaming at the mouth.

Maddox had served in the military before switching to his school administrative career, a fact he was fiercely secretive about. He held rules, procedure, and discipline in high regard, which made him an efficient—yet ineffective—principal. People skills were less of a priority.

Fiscara knocked on the door.

"It's open," Maddox's deep voice bellowed from beyond the door.

Fiscara flashed her eyebrows at Bischoffe, who mouthed "good luck" and gave Fiscara a thumbs up.

Maddox's office was small and crammed with books, accolades, and memorabilia from his years as an administrator. He didn't believe in "sitting down on the job" and was the only faculty member who used a standing desk. A computer and monitor sat on one side of the desk and a photo of his wife and two children sat on the other.

"Miss Fiscara." Maddox squared his body to face her.

"Maddox." Fiscara placed the Forever Stylez bag on his otherwise tidy desk.

Maddox recoiled at the sight. "What is this… garbage?"

"I have reason to believe that the school has a spider infestation." Fiscara pulled open the sides of the bag to reveal the crushed spider egg sac. "Some students of mine alerted me to the possibility on Friday. I sent them to find more evidence over the weekend and they came back with this." She slid the tennis ball-sized egg sac forward a few inches.

Maddox gave the egg sac a cursory glance. "I don't see any spiders."

"Maddox, this is an egg sac. All the spider eggs within have either been crushed or have hatched and escaped."

"So? We have spiders." Maddox crossed his arms. "What's the big deal?"

"What's the biggest spider you've ever seen?"

"I don't know." Maddox touched his thumb to his index fingertip. "About yay big, maybe an inch and a half?"

"A spider egg sac is usually about the same size as the spider that made them." Fiscara watched Maddox's eye flit to the egg sac on his desk and back to her. "So that means we could have thousands of spiders in the school that will grow to the size of a tennis ball. Sound good to you?"

Maddox shrugged. "Most spiders are harmless."

"These spiders I can't identify. They may be a new species. The school may be sitting on a major discovery, but it could get bad very fast if they start killing kids."

"Wait a minute. Killing kids?" Maddox placed his elbows on his desk and leaned in. "How?"

"Spider bite. If this egg sac is for the same spider I witnessed over the weekend, then killing a kid is within the realm of possibility." Fiscara held Maddox's gaze. "It can kill a raccoon for fuck's sake." She cleared her throat. "Sorry about the language."

Maddox huffed. "See it from my position. The school year is just getting started. Students are settling in. The fall dance is coming up. Closing the school and calling for exterminators and fumigation on account of spiders that you have no evidence of seems a little premature."

"No evidence?" Fiscara pointed at the egg sac. "What do you call that?"

"An empty shell." Maddox scooped up the plastic bag, crumpled it, and threw it into the waste basket next to his desk. "This discussion is over until I see an actual spider. Dead, of course."

Fiscara shook her head. "You couldn't be more wrong about this."

"Was there anything else, Miss Fiscara?"

"No. Thank you for your time," Fiscara said through pursed

lips. She turned and marched out of Maddox's office. He watched her go, a subtle grin on his lips.

STUDENTS AND FACULTY had left for the day and the janitorial staff had just begun their sweep of the school. In two hours, most lights would be turned off, plunging the school into darkness. Principal Maddox's office was one of the last rooms to be cleaned.

Maddox's waste basket was filled to the rim with garbage. Like a time capsule, the layers revealed the days events. Old faculty memos covered a spent pen and the wrappers of two Oh Henry! bars. Maddox had a secret sweet tooth.

At the bottom, covered by the remnants of Maddox's bag lunch, sat the Forever Stylez bag.

Had someone been in Maddox's office at the time, they wouldn't have heard the low, almost imperceptible rustling.

Three black spiders no bigger than a pinky nail emerged from the crinkled Forever Stylez bag. They moved up and through the layers of garbage, one after another.

Once on the lip of the waste basket, the spiders lined up side by side. As if cued by some unknown force, the spiders began to expand and contract, arching their legs and bodies like they were experiencing seizures. From underneath their bodies new spiders emerged. They cast off their newly molted skin and arched their legs. Quills sprang forth from their backs, rising and falling like ribs protecting a lung.

The empty husks of their former bodies fell back into the waste basket and the renewed spiders scaled up the shadowed nooks and crannies of Maddox's desk. They positioned themselves at the edge of the desk and released strands of silk that floated and billowed in the eddies of air circulating in the office.

The silk threads adhered to the adjacent wall, spanning the distance from Maddox's desk. One by one, the spiders leaped from the edge, collecting their silken lifelines close to their bodies until they had positioned themselves on the wall.

In quick succession, the spiders scurried up the wall, onto the ceiling and disappeared into a circular air vent directly above Maddox's desk.

BRADLEY COULDN'T WAIT until his biology class the next morning for an update. After the lunch bell rang, he left his Math class and ran from one side of the school to the other. It was just his luck that Fiscara's classroom was polar opposite to his Math class. At least it was on the same floor.

As he approached the classroom, Bradley noticed that the door was closed.

Please don't be locked.

He reached for the doorknob and gave it a turn. The door's latch slid back easily and allowed Bradley to pull the door open. He knocked on the door too, just to be polite, but Fiscara had heard the door open already.

"Usually people knock first before opening a door." Fiscara remained deadpan.

"Yeah, sorry." Bradley's chest heaved as he caught his breath. "Meant to. Ran all the way here."

Fiscara smiled. "Sit, although I don't have much to tell you."

Bradley leaned against the edge of a desk. "I'm okay. What did Mad Dog… I mean Maddox. What did he have to say?"

"Nothing of consequence." Fiscara propped herself up

against the blackboard and crossed her arms. "He wants physical proof. In other words, a dead spider in hand."

"He's such a f—" Bradley caught himself before the swear left his mouth.

"Yeah. He could have at least called an exterminator to take a look."

Exterminator. It had been a while since Bradley had heard anyone talk about exterminators. His thoughts drifted to his dad and O'Connor back in New York. He knew how they'd deal with things.

"I guess it's going to take someone getting bitten, or dying, before Maddox will listen."

"I hope it doesn't come to that," Fiscara said. "Now get out of here. You got better things to do than hang with your biology teacher."

Bradley walked to the open door. "Thanks, Miss Fiscara."

"Keep your eyes open."

Yeah, you too."

After grabbing his lunch from his locker, Jack met him on the chip trail that circumnavigated the school's back field. Students were already playing soccer at the end farthest from the school.

Jack took one look at Bradley and knew the news wasn't good. "What'd I tell you. Mad Dog's a dick."

"He wants physical proof."

"Like an actual spider?"

"Yeah."

"Well, let's give it to him."

Bradley look at him. "How?"

"Food first." Jack looked at Bradley's bag lunch and flashed his eyebrows. "What's for lunch?"

Bradley had opened his bag to pull out his sandwich when he was pushed from behind. He flew forward, dropping his lunch, but luckily caught his fall with his arms. He looked up to see Alexis and Deirdre charging ahead on the chip trail.

"Chip trail's for runners, asshole," Alexis yelled back.

"Fuck you, Delarosa!" Bradley brushed himself off. "What are you, six?"

Jack handed Bradley his lunch bag. "Let's walk on the grass."

"Good idea." Bradley rubbed his neck as he looked around. "Where's the other one? Caitlin?"

Jack shrugged.

"I better not have whiplash." Bradley reached into his bag and pulled out a sandwich in a baggie.

"Got any burritos?"

"Funny guy." Bradley opened the baggie. "Turkey with mustard, lettuce, and cheddar." He held out half of the sandwich to Jack.

"Basic, but I'll make an exception this time." Jack took a large, hungry bite. With his mouth full, he said, "I do recommend adding burritos to your diet. They're a good source of complex carbs and fiber."

Both teenagers laughed, eating as they walked. Being friends for so long gave them permission to act sillier than normal with each other.

"End of the road, man." Jack and Bradley stood at the end of the field where the chip trail turned and crossed behind the soccer goal posts.

"Do we cross, or go back the way we came?"

Jack watched other students on the field play soccer. One player had secured a break-away and advanced on the goalie. The approaching player foot-handled the soccer ball until the point of no return. He wound his foot back and kicked the ball, sending it high and right toward the goal posts.

The goalie, a stout student sporting a buzzcut and wearing mirrored sunglasses and sports gloves, held his cool. He jumped, reaching for the top of the goal posts and deflected the ball off his gloved fingertips. He fell to the ground and tumbled to his feet. The soccer ball bounced twice and rolled into some shrubs at the far end of the field.

"Now's our chance. Let's go." Jack jogged along the chip trail behind the goal posts, Bradley picking up his pace to follow.

The goalie brushed himself off and trotted toward the bushes. He got on all fours, reached into the bushes, then fell backward and reversed, his face covered in white webbing.

"Holy shit. Look!" Bradley's eyes bugged out. He ran toward the goalie, who writhed on the grass panicking, screaming, and tugging at his face.

Jack was first to see the black spiders on the goalie's cleats and nearly froze in his tracks. "His feet!"

The goalie pulled his sunglasses off, tearing a hole in the webbing big enough to see several black spiders the size of his fist crawling on his shoes. By reflex, he flicked his feet back toward the bushes like he was deflecting a shot on goal. All but one spider flew back into the bushes. The goalie kicked again and propelled the remaining spider forward instead of back, landing on the goalie's head.

"Don't move!" Bradley skidded to the grass in front of the goalie. The eyes, the hair. Recognition. "Wait. Mark, right? Mark Everett? Bio class?"

Mark didn't respond, his eyes glistening with fear.

"Don't move, Mark," Bradley repeated. Other students approached, both curious and horrified. He held up his hands. "Stop! Don't come any closer."

Bradley scanned his immediate surroundings, and at Jack a few steps behind him. "Get something long, a stick or a branch or something."

Jack broke through his fear and scrambled back, away from the goal posts and toward a side street bordering the field. Nothing looked strong enough except for a tree next to the chain-link fence.

"Fuck it," he said and snapped off a lower branch. He ran

back to Bradley and Mark, snapping smaller twigs off the main branch.

The spider moved forward, taking several steps toward Mark's forehead. Its quills pumped up and down, like it was intentionally fanning Mark's fear.

Bradley locked eyes with Mark. "Listen. You *can't* move. Understand?"

Tears from Mark's eyes mixed with sweat from his brow. The webbing covering his mouth inflated and deflated with each panicked breath. Bradley thought he saw acknowledgment and that was good enough for him.

Jack placed the branch in Bradley's hands. The branch was about two inches thick and its bark felt smooth and strong in his hands, apart from the knots where smaller branches had broken off.

"I'm going to play tee-ball with this motherfucker, got it?" Bradley choked up on the thinner end of the branch like he was holding a baseball bat. "I'm probably going to hit your head by mistake, so I'll say sorry now."

Bradley lined up on the spider. A hush fell over the field as all eyes focused on Bradley with the stick. Even the birds seemed to know something wasn't right.

For Bradley, only Mark and the ugly-ass spider on his head existed. He blocked out the rest. "Ready? On three… one."

Bradley moved the branch back in a slow arc.

"Two."

His bicep muscles tensed in anticipation of the swing.

Don't miss don't miss don't miss…

"Three!" Bradley swung the branch toward the top of Mark's head, but his aim was off. The end of the branch clocked the back of Mark's head and bounced up, glancing the spider and knocking it onto Mark's abdomen. The spider landed on its back, its oily black legs pumping and coiling, looking for purchase.

The strike to his head caused Mark to lose consciousness and he collapsed onto his back on the grass.

All eyes remained on Bradley. The spider hooked a leg into the fabric of Mark's shorts and flipped itself over, now inches away from Mark's crotch.

There was no time to waste. Bradley reacted without thinking and swung the branch again, this time connecting with the spider. Its abdomen exploded in a *pop* of bluish-green guts, coating Mark's inner thighs. The rest of the spider sailed up and disappeared into the shrubs.

Bradley peeled the sticky webbing off Mark's face and checked his head for bite marks. His initial search didn't reveal anything, but he couldn't be sure. He turned to Jack. "Call 9-1-1. I'm getting my epi-pen."

Jack dialed. "I need an ambulance… Washbrook High… Uh, possible spider bite." He paced back and forth, listening. "Yeah. An epi-pen… Okay."

Curious students began to crowd Mark, some taking photos and videos with their phones.

"Back up." Jack stepped in and held his arms up. "Give him some air." He looked at one of the students taking photos. "Did you get video?"

"Uh, nope," the student said.

Jack looked at the remaining bystanders. "Anyone else?" Those who were still holding their phones pocketed them and backed away. "No one got video? Now that's some bullshit right there."

Mark stirred and moved his head side to side slowly. He raised his hand to touch the back of his head. "What happened?"

"Whoa, man. Stay still." Jack directed Mark's hands to his side. "You were attacked by a spider." Jack looked over his shoulder toward the school. "Come on, Brad. Where are you?" he said under his breath.

"Attacked by *what?*" Mark appeared confused and couldn't keep his eyes open.

"Easy," Jack said. A flood of relief washed over him as he saw Bradley burst out of the school, hurtle himself down the steps, and cross the field. Sounds of an ambulance siren rose up in the distance.

Bradley slid across the grass next to Jack. "Is he okay?"

"I think so. Ambulance's on its way."

Bradley cracked the cap off the epi-pen. "Sorry again, Mark, but you'll thank me later." He rammed the epi-pen's needle into Mark's upper thigh and triggered the injection of medication with his thumb.

"Holy shit." Bradley removed the pen and tossed it aside. He looked at Jack, a grin sliding across his mouth and breathing heavily. "Tell me you got video of that."

"Um…" Jack shrugged sheepishly.

"What? Damn, dude."

"Sorry. I was freaking out," Jack said. "Everything happened so fast."

Bradley looked to the thinning crowd of students. "Did anyone—"

"Don't bother. Already asked."

"No one got *any* video?" Bradley looked incredulous.

"Apparently not."

"Fuck. Whatever."

The ambulance rolled into the parking lot beside the school. "I'll go get them." Jack ran over to greet the paramedics.

Mark groaned and touched the back of his head gingerly.

"Do you remember anything?"

Mark squinted at Bradley and crunched his brow. "I know you…"

"I'm Brad."

Mark gave Bradley a sideways look. "You saved my life?"

"Maybe." Bradley looked at the red, angry welt on top of Mark's head. "I gave you one hell of a bump, that's for sure."

Jack and two paramedics arrived with a stretcher and lowered it to ground level.

"Your friend here says this teenager was attacked by giant spiders, you hit his head in the process of removing them, and administered an epi-pen," said one paramedic.

"Basically, yeah," Bradley said.

The paramedics exchanged dubious glances.

"I didn't know if he'd been bitten."

One paramedic knelt and recorded Mark's vital signs. She flashed a light in his pupils, took his pulse, and measured his blood pressure. "What's your name?"

Mark looked at the paramedic, confused. "Brad?"

"His name's Mark," Bradley said.

The paramedic glanced at her partner, who was placing both sides of a scoop stretcher along Mark's body. "Likely a concussion."

The paramedics pressed the scoop stretcher together, lifted Mark onto the wheeled stretcher, and strapped him in.

"What's with this school?" one paramedic asked as they rolled Mark back toward the waiting ambulance.

"What do you mean?" Bradley walked with the paramedics, Jack and small group of onlookers not far behind.

"This is the second time in two days that an ambulance has been called to this school."

"When was the first?"

"Saturday night?" The paramedic looked for confirmation from her partner.

"Yeah, about 10:30 p.m.," the other paramedic said.

Bradley shared a knowing look with Jack as his brain clicked into overdrive.

Principal Maddox burst through the main doors of the school and made an intercept course toward the ambulance.

"What's going on here?"

The female paramedic pointed at Mark, who was being secured in the back of the ambulance. "Slight concussion and apparently a spider bite, according to…"

"Brad."

"Is this true?" Maddox glared at Bradley, his hands and arms akimbo like a drill sergeant.

"Yeah, but you know about it already."

"Huh." The female paramedic looked from Bradley to Maddox. "Looks like you got a spider problem, chief." She climbed into the driver's seat and pulled away.

Maddox and Bradley stared at each other.

Bradley pointed at the ambulance turning out of the school parking lot. "Would that be considered evidence? Sir?"

Maddox scanned the group of students, scowled at Bradley, and trudged back toward the school entrance.

Bradley, his confidence boosted by the crowd, called back at Maddox. "I'm going to deal with these spiders with or without your help."

Maddox stopped, turned, and walked back to Bradley, standing nose to nose with him. The crowd of students watched, some with their phones out.

Maddox spoke through clenched teeth in a firm and controlled voice. "You will do nothing of the sort. If there is evidence of a spider problem, I will deal with it. Not you. Understand?"

Bradley stepped backward and shrugged.

Maddox looked at him, then the crowd, and singled out one student recording video on his phone. "Put your damn devices away. There's nothing to see." He turned once again and headed back toward the school.

"That ambulance was the best evidence we've had so far, and you *ignored* it." Bradley watched Maddox walk away.

Trillian moved forward through the crowd and stood next to Jack. "What'd I miss?"

"Mad Dog got *burned*," Jack said grinning. "Brad for the win." The two of them bumped fists.

"But it's not enough. It's not 'proof.' " Bradley air-quoted the word as he watched Maddox pull open the door to the school and disappear inside.

If Maddox wasn't going to do anything, Bradley knew someone who would be happy to help.

BRADLEY SAT ON his bed, the rest of the house silent. He had just spent two fruitless hours calling exterminators all over the San Fernando Valley who either didn't think spiders were a problem, didn't believe his story, or were booked for weeks.

Bradley's phone trilled in his ear. Two rings, then three. He was just about to hang up when the line connected.

"Hi honey." Claire's voice sounded clearer and more upbeat than the last time he had spoken to her, even through the cheap speaker on his phone. And it was a relief to hear her voice again because it had been too long. The spider problem had taken far more of his time than he had anticipated.

"Hi Mom. How are you feeling? How's your leg?"

"I'm doing okay but my leg's seen better days. It's still pretty swollen." Claire sighed. "I miss you guys, you and Roy. But Roy's visited me every day, sometimes smuggling in edible contraband. The food here isn't great."

Roy. He was a constant thorn in Bradley's side. Luckily with school and the influx of spiders, he hadn't seen much of him since Saturday. He could have shared how Roy fell all over himself to impress Fiscara, but kept that little detail to himself.

It sounded like Roy was treating his mom okay, so Bradley decided to cut Roy a little slack.

"Brad?"

"What?"

"I said have you and Roy been getting along?"

"Yeah, Mom. Actually, we have." Bradley smiled because technically that was true.

As long as I don't see him and he doesn't see me, we get along fine.

"What have you both been up to?"

Bradley stammered for an answer. "Uh, we found the spider that bit you."

"You mean spiders. Plural."

"Yeah."

"Did you kill those…" Claire paused, then lowered her voice. "Did you kill those *little fuckers?*"

Bradley pictured Claire surveying her hospital room for potential eavesdroppers and grinned. She rarely swore. "As many as we could. But they're everywhere. All through the neighborhood."

"Well, be careful. I don't want you or Roy getting bit."

"I will." Bradley heard her yawn. "Are you sure you're okay?"

"I'm a little tired. The pain meds make me sleepy," Claire said through a second yawn. "How was the first week of school? Make any new friends?"

"A few. School's okay but Alexis is being a b… a problem."

"You've matured a lot in two months. She's realizing what she's lost." Bradley could hear the smile in her voice. "Maybe you'll get back together."

"No chance."

Claire laughed.

"Mom, are you going to lose your leg?" It was an awkward segue, but a question that had been buzzing around in the back of Bradley's mind since seeing Claire in the hospital a week ago.

"I don't know, hon. I hope not." Claire took a moment of

silence. "The nurse just gave me the hairy eyeball so I'm going to have to cut this short."

"Okay."

"Next time come in person," Claire said. "I'm running low on hugs from my number one son."

"You got it."

"And be nice to Roy."

Bradley balked.

"Brad?"

"I'll try."

"Good. Love you."

"Ditto." Bradley ended the call and laid back on his pillow. The quiet surrounded him.

This must be what it's like for Jack, with his parents away all the time. Bradley didn't like it.

His eyes scanned the room, from his shelves, past his desk, and to his one window that overlooked the back yard. From his vantage point on his bed, he couldn't see the shed, but he knew what lurked there.

Sporkies.

What if Mom loses her leg?

What if they get into the house?

Bradley picked up his phone again and dialed. The connection took longer this time, finally clicking in his ear.

"Hello?"

Bradley smiled. The voice was warm and familiar. "Dad?"

New York 10474

Sam had just sat down in front of the television. A rerun of *Welcome Back, Kotter* was on and it was an episode he hadn't seen yet. That, in itself, was amazing to Sam. *Welcome Back, Kotter* hadn't aired in almost forty years, and there were still episodes that were new to him. He held a bowl of salad with chopped hot dog pieces and Italian dressing on top.

It was healthy, Sam told himself. *The salad made it healthy.*

The phone in the kitchen rang out. Sam had been meaning to install an extension in the TV room, but with receiving so few calls, the job held a low priority for him.

I can just ignore it. But part of being the building superintendent meant being available at all hours of the day and night. If he didn't deal with a problem immediately, the problem tended to get bigger. Who would it be tonight? The Dobbies? Hope?

He set the bowl down on the couch and walked back to the kitchen. He lifted the receiver to his ear.

"Hello?" Sam listened for a familiar voice, but it wasn't the voice he had expected.

"Dad?" Bradley's voice buzzed through the earpiece and Sam made a mental note to buy a better phone.

"Brad?" Sam's eyes flashed wide as an immense smile spread across his face. *But why is he calling me?* His smile faltered. "Are you okay?"

"Yeah." Bradley's voice sounded distant and small.

"Let me guess. It's been a week and you want to return to the Bronx."

"I need your help."

It was clear that Bradley was not in the mood for jokes. Sam cleared his throat. "Sure. Absolutely."

"Two things," Bradley said. "Mom's in the hospital… and are you afraid of spiders?"

"Wait. Back up." Sam paced back and forth, tethered by his inconveniently short phone cord. "Claire's in the hospital? What happened?"

"Spider bite."

"Shit," Sam said, genuinely concerned. Claire may have been his ex-wife, but he still cared about her well-being. "She going to be okay?"

"I hope so, but she might lose her leg."

Sam couldn't wrap his head around how a spider bite could lead to limb loss. "What kind of spider?"

"No one knows, not even my Bio teacher. But they're everywhere, Dad. I've been tracking them."

"Of course you have." A small smile broke through his concern. "How can I help?"

Bradley heaved a sigh of relief. "I was hoping you… and O'Connor… could come out, because no one here is interested in doing anything about it. And these spiders are attacking people now."

Sam wanted to drop the phone and hop on to the next flight to California, but his ex-convict status reared its ugly head. "I'll have to talk to my parole officer… so I may not be going anywhere. And O'Connor might be booked."

"Dad, all I know is we need some kick-ass exterminators with balls. And that's you and O'Connor."

Dad. Sam still felt a shiver when Brad addressed him that way and hoped it never changed. He owed his son so much. He couldn't disappoint him now.

"Since you put it that way." Sam laughed. "I'll do my best."

"Thanks," Bradley said. "But you never answered my question."

"What question?"

"Are you afraid of spiders? Like you were with rats?"

Sam pictured the biggest spider he could remember seeing in his apartment, an inch across and easily squished with the heel of his boot. "No, I don't think so. Should I be?"

"Yes."

THE FOLLOWING MORNING, Sam hopped into his rusted Ford F-250, inserted his key and turned the ignition. The starter cranked a couple of tired cycles and ground to a halt.

"Not today, damn it." He tried the key once more and the starter clicked like a bag of bones. "Nope. You're not going to do this to me, you piece of shit!"

Fate must have been smiling on him when he parked the truck last because it was facing downhill on Casanova Street. Sam popped the gear shift into neutral. He released the parking brake, opened the driver's side door, and gave the truck a push with his foot. The truck began to roll forward, picking up speed.

Without the engine running, the steering and brakes lost their responsiveness. Sam alternated his attention between the speedometer as it climbed toward ten miles per hour and the impending intersection where Casanova crossed Randall Avenue.

He stepped on the clutch and shifted into second gear. "Come on, come on… you rusty bitch."

The speedometer hit five miles per hour, then seven. The

intersection had a stop sign but stopping would kill his momentum and any chance of starting the truck.

Eight miles per hour. Nine.

Sam had neither time nor road left and let the clutch up. It was now or never. The whole truck lurched forward as the engine was forced to turn over and fire. He stomped the clutch again to avoid a stall and for a shuddering moment he thought it wasn't going to work. Then the truck's engine roared to life just in time to brake before the right turn onto Randall.

Sam headed north on Bruckner Boulevard and right on Colgate. It wasn't difficult to find Detest-A-Pest. The familiar rusted-out white van with the hand-painted logo on the side was parked in front of the building.

Towering above the graffiti-style depictions of pests on the front of the building was a caricature of a large black man. He wore Detest-A-Pest coveralls over his muscular body and held a taser rod in one hand and a propane torch in the other. Sam recognized the likeness immediately.

"Washington," he said to himself before releasing a sigh. Washington had been a good man and Sam believed his grisly death could have been prevented.

A familiar voice echoed out of one of the two open loading bay doors. "Well, I'll be dipped in shit. If it ain't Sam Shaw, rat buster extraordinaire."

Sam turned toward O'Connor and smiled. Except for her more pronounced limp, she hadn't changed a bit. Ever stout, wearing snug coveralls and heavy work boots, and chewing on a stub of a cigar. A snap trap was lodged in her breast pocket. She wore a weathered backward baseball cap and her face was smudged with black grease.

O'Connor walked out to greet him. She extended her hand, then grabbed Sam and pulled him into a tight bear hug. "You couldn't keep away from this well-oiled sex machine body of mine, huh?"

Sam laughed. "Same old Bertha."

"Hey!" O'Connor punched him in the shoulder. "Who you calling old?"

Sam pointed at the mural of Washington. "Was just admiring your new addition."

"Yeah." O'Connor looked at the mural, wistful for only a moment. "Jimmy Washington was one giant pain in my ass. I had to do something to immortalize him."

Sam focused on the caricature. Washington's eyes sparkled and he sported a toothy grin a mile wide. "Really captures his character. Found a replacement yet?"

"For Washington?" O'Connor shook her head. "Nah. That lovable asshole is a hard act to follow." She squinted at him. "Why? You looking?"

"No, no. Just curious."

"Well, something caused you drive that rusted bucket of bolts over here... besides this cornucopia of carnal delight." O'Connor ran her hands over her body with a flourish.

"You need to get yourself a man."

"I've got more than enough men. I practically invented the reverse harem." O'Connor winked.

"Then you need a filter."

O'Connor grabbed her cigar with one hand and laughed, clutching her belly with the other. "You're funny. Now spill it."

"I'm getting to it. You always got to drive the bus, don't you?"

O'Connor scrutinized him.

"Brad called me yesterday."

It had started to rain. O'Connor wrapped her lips around the cigar stub and spoke out of the side of her mouth. "Come with me."

She led Sam inside the shop, flipped open the front counter entrance, and trudged into the back office. She dug through her desk, piled high with papers, magazines, and other garbage, and pulled out two used paper cups.

"Coffee?" O'Connor pulled a half-full carafe from the old, stained Mr. Coffee machine in the corner and poured herself a cup. "It's still warm."

"No, thanks."

"So, you said Brad called." O'Connor gulped some coffee. "I miss that kid. How's he doing?"

"Good," Sam said. "But he's got a problem, one that takes a certain type of… *expertise.*"

A wide smile spread across O'Connor's face from behind her coffee cup. "I'm listening."

"Ever dealt with spiders before?"

"Can't say I have, but there's a first for everything." O'Connor set her cup down on the corner of the desk. "There's got to be an exterminator there that he can call?"

"He's being stonewalled. No one believes there's a problem. And we're talking *big* spiders."

"How big?"

"Three, maybe four inches across."

O'Connor nodded. "Yeah, that's big."

"Can you help? I have some money set aside for emergencies and—"

"Save your money." O'Connor placed her finger to her chin like she was deep in thought. "I think I need a vacation. I hear California is nice this time of year."

"Now you're talking."

O'Connor grinned at him. "When do we leave?"

"As soon as possible."

"I smell a road trip." O'Connor pumped her fist. "And I'm driving." She hooked a thumb through her office window at the white 1956 Buick Century parked in one of the two loading bays. "I haven't stretched Bruce's legs for a while. This would be perfect."

Sam shook his head. "We're not driving."

"The hell we ain't."

"I talked to my parole officer and the most time I can get is two weeks out of state," Sam said. "If we drove, we'd be on the road for most of that time."

"You just don't want to be alone with me for that long." O'Connor attempted to pout but Sam saw through it immediately.

"You're such a bullshitter. I want to make the most of my time with Brad, so we're flying."

"I'm still doing all the driving." O'Connor crossed her arms. "We'll take your shit heap to the airport and rent something nice in L.A."

"What happened to *stretching Bruce's legs?*"

"Are you nuts? I'd never leave Bruce at JFK all alone." O'Connor swapped her cigar for a sip of coffee. "And I get to drive in L.A.... *and* pick the rental. You get to pick the motel. That okay with you?"

"As long as we have separate beds."

O'Connor placed the cigar back between her teeth. "Prude." They both laughed.

Sam could see O'Connor's brain working. "You know," she said, "this could be a real opportunity to go worldwide."

"Can you survive without your tools? Nothing in that truck of yours would make it through security."

"I've been in this situation before." O'Connor winked at him and blew a smoke ring. "I've got a contingency plan."

BACK AT THE apartment building, Sam collected some clothes and toiletries and soon realized that he didn't have a suitcase.

He found himself on the third floor, standing in front of

apartment 301, Hope's place. He knocked and tried to conceal his embarrassment.

The pad of light steps approached the door and after the deadbolt retracted, Hope threw open the door.

"Hey, Sam. What's up?"

Sam scanned her ensemble, making sure not to let his eyes linger too long in one spot. Black Vans, black jeans and a red t-shirt loudly proclaiming "Bitch, please! I'm from L.A." Her jet-black hair still fell in a pixie cut but it was an inch or two longer than when she'd moved in two months ago.

"I need a favor." Sam could feel his neck and cheeks heating up.

"Sure," Hope said with a smile. "Anything."

"Can I borrow a suitcase?" Sam flashed his eyebrows and gave her a toothy, slightly goofy grin.

"Going on a trip?"

"Yeah, to visit Brad in L.A." Sam's eyes fell to the inscription on Hope's shirt. "It's kind of a working trip." His eyes flipped back up to her face. "Want to come?"

"Another rat infestation?"

Sam shook his head. "Not this time. You like spiders?"

"Nope." Hope held up her hands emphatically. "Hate them. Kill 'em all with fire."

"All right, then." Sam rocked on his feet. "About that suitcase?"

"Right! Come in for a sec." Hope stepped aside, letting Sam in, then closed the door. She disappeared down the hallway and into a side room. "I'll dig it out."

On the kitchen counter sat a cage with Harriette inside. Sam approached the cage with caution instead of fear, which was a huge difference compared to two months ago. Harriette scurried to greet Sam at the bars, gave her furry white face a wash, then busied herself in her exercise wheel.

"How's Harriette doing?"

"She's great," Hope's voice floated back. "I was just about to clean her cage."

Sam heard Hope walking back to the living area, towing a wheeled suitcase.

"Sorry, this is all I have," Hope said. "It's pretty old, but it's good."

She presented Sam with a suitcase that was hot pink with black and silver trim and adorned with assorted stickers, mostly of Disney, My Little Pony, and Bratz characters.

Sam closed his eyes and laughed. "Jesus. O'Connor is going to have a field day with this."

"O'Connor's going too?"

"Yeah."

Hope smirked. "Lucky you."

Sam retracted the towing handle and lifted the suitcase by its handle. "Thanks. If it gets damaged, I'll replace it."

"Don't worry about it. The thing's practically indestructible." Hope glanced at the stickers. "By the way, I'm not into that stuff anymore. The exterior is more of a time capsule now."

"I get it, not that there's anything wrong with My Little Pony."

"Actually, it's a good look for you."

Sam gave Hope a sideways look. "Bitch, please."

They both laughed and Sam took it as a cue to get moving. He carried the suitcase to the door.

"I see what you did there, Sam," Hope said, following. "Paying attention. That's a good trait."

"I try."

She stepped in front to open the door for him. "Repeat after me. Kill them with fire."

"Got it."

"Be careful. And good luck with O'Connor," Hope said, her eyes matching the warmth of her smile.

"Thanks. I'm going to need it."

"Say hi for me."

Sam strolled down the hallway toward the elevator. He looked back and waved. "Will do."

Back in his own apartment, Sam opened the suitcase and threw his clothes and toiletries inside. Locking the case closed, he noted just how rugged the case felt, despite the color, scratches and ubiquitous stickers.

He locked his front door, tacked a short notice about his travel on the building's bulletin board, and took a moment to prepare for O'Connor's onslaught of jokes. Sam took solace in knowing that in less than twenty-four hours, he'd see his son again.

O'CONNOR PARKED THE F-250 in a stall in the extended lot at JFK International Airport. She killed the engine and wiped tears from her eyes. She looked at Sam and burst out laughing again.

"I never pegged you for a Brony." Her whole body hitched as she wiped her face with her sleeve.

O'Connor had insisted on driving to JFK and Sam had spent the entire trip worrying that they might die in a fiery crash as a result of her uncontrollable laughter. There was something about a pink tween-stickered suitcase in his hand that had set her off.

"Was funny once, *Bertha*." Sam had reached the end of his rope. "Let it go." He slid out of the truck and began collecting their luggage from the back.

"Hey, you're flying on *my* points," O'Connor said. "Least you can do is allow me to laugh at your expense."

"Fair enough." Sam pulled his pink suitcase toward the tailgate, stifling a chuckle of his own. Laughing out loud now would be admitting defeat. He pulled O'Connor's four loaded duffel bags out of the truck bed. "What the hell do you have in these bags?"

"The usual." O'Connor grabbed a bag and placed it on the pavement. The contents rattled like it was filled with oversized cutlery. "My vast wardrobe. This 'n' that. The usual."

"Mind if I take a look?"

"Be my guest."

Sam unzipped the bag already on the ground. It was filled with pellet guns and taser rods. The next bag held four flame throwers. "What the hell are these?"

"Elon Musk was having a flash sale, so I picked some up." O'Connor fished one of the flame throwers out of the bag and cradled it in her arms. "Beautiful piece of engineering. Beats the shit out of my propane torches." She opened the gas valve, flipped off the safety, and pulled the trigger. A hissing blast of orange flame shot forth from the flame thrower's nozzle, a little too close to neighboring vehicles for Sam's liking.

"What the *fuck* are you doing?" Sam looked over both shoulders for onlookers. He pushed the nozzle down. "This is a goddamn airport."

"I couldn't resist." O'Connor grinned around her sodden cigar. "Can you imagine what your infestation would have been like if we'd had our hands on these suckers?"

"Don't care. Turn it off and put it away." Sam surveyed the area again. "I'm still on parole for Christ's sake. I don't want to take any chances."

"Okay, *Dad*." O'Connor placed the flame thrower carefully into its duffel beside the other three.

"No. You don't get to call me that." Sam glared at her as he yanked another duffel bag out of the truck bed. "Got it?"

O'Connor held up her hands, yielding. "It was just a joke."

Sam ignored her response. "I may not have flown in an airplane for over fifteen years, but I know enough to know that most of this stuff won't be allowed in checked luggage."

He unzipped the last duffel bag, which was filled with clothes. Sam zipped it up again.

O'Connor smiled at him. "Like I said before, I have a contingency plan." She patted her breast pocket.

"Please say you got a new phone."

O'Connor nodded and pulled a corner of the phone into view.

"Good. We've got a six hour flight to figure it out." Sam picked up one of the duffel bags filled with weapons. "We'll stow this stuff in the cab behind the seats."

"Whatever you say, Tinkerbell." O'Connor laughed, short-lived due to exhaustion, then rubbed her abdomen. "I got to tell you, that was the best laugh I've had all month. Abs are going to ache for a week."

"You've got abs? More like flabs."

"Hey." O'Connor's mood flipped like a switch. "My Little Pony is funny. Body shaming not so much, even if I'm usually in the mood for it."

Sam stepped to the back of the F-250. He held O'Connor's remaining duffel bag out to her. "Sorry. Truce?"

She took the duffel bag. "Hell... why not."

Sam motioned toward O'Connor's stogie. "Might want to put that away."

She clamped down on the cigar stub with her teeth. "Thought we had a truce."

Sam shrugged as they both wound their way through the parking lot toward the terminal.

"MOTHERFUCKERS. EVERY LAST one of them." O'Connor glared at the flight attendants busy helping other passengers to their seats.

"What did I tell you?" There was a hint of a smile on Sam's lips.

"You're enjoying this, aren't you?"

"Never," Sam said.

O'Connor's first opposition had been the ticket agent, who had requested that she extinguish her cigar. O'Connor argued that since it wasn't lit, it wouldn't bother anyone. The agent let it go.

Coming off that perceived win, O'Connor had faced security and almost came to blows with one officer. Sam had stepped in and smoothed things over, but O'Connor had to throw away her cherished cigar stub.

They were flying an American Airlines Airbus A321, with four distinct seating sections: first class, business class, economy class with extra legroom, and economy class.

Sam and O'Connor had found their seats at the back of the plane, 22E and 22F, just in front of the bathroom bulkhead. O'Connor insisted on the window and Sam made no protest. He wanted to sit, relax, and maybe catch some winks. Even though it was a red eye flight, he hoped to arrive without red eyes.

"Right next to the shitter," O'Connor said. "Good plan. I hear airplane food goes right through you."

Sam tilted his seat back, but it stopped short against the bulkhead. "Not good enough. We can't recline."

"You planning on sleeping?"

"I'm going to try." Sam closed his eyes and pressed the button on his arm rest, returning his seat back the two inches it had moved.

An hour later, Sam opened his eyes to mayhem. It appeared from the steady stream of people standing in line that almost all seventy-two economy passengers needed to use the two rear bathrooms at the same time. A toddler clutching his teddy and smelling of baby powder, sour milk and ripe diaper was slumped to Sam's left. On his right, O'Connor worked at her new phone, a fresh unlit cigar clamped in her teeth.

"Rip Van Winkle awakens," O'Connor said. "Whatever you do, don't wake the shit-demon beside you."

Sam noted the cigar. "You're never going to learn, are you?"

"The flight attendants and me, we got an agreement."

"What's that?"

"They let me have my cigar, unlit of course, and I don't beat the crap out of them with my leg." O'Connor's left prosthetic leg was leaning against the side of the plane, just under the window.

"I was meaning to ask, how is your leg lately? I thought I noticed more of a limp."

"I need to replace the old son-of-a-bitch." O'Connor swapped her cigar with a handful of almonds. "But those new-fangled bionic ones are damn expensive."

"Maybe if you stopped taking jobs for free." Sam grinned, but was quick to deflect. "Just kidding."

"Who says I'm doing it for *free?*" O'Connor grinned back. "Someone, or *something*, is going to pay." She handed some snacks and a can of cola to Sam. "The refreshment cart went by when you were in la-la land. I grabbed you a few things."

"Thanks." Sam cracked his cola and the toddler stirred beside him. He looked across the aisle to what he assumed were the parents, dead to the world, catching flies with their snores. Sam nudged the child gently on the shoulder until the tot readjusted his position, using his teddy as a pillow.

"You're lucky he didn't wake up," O'Connor said. "I don't know how you slept through that thing's shrieking bullshit."

Sam opened a pack of almonds, tossed a couple in his mouth, and looked at O'Connor's phone. "Find anything interesting?"

"I'm amazed at what you can buy on the Internet."

"Contingency plan?"

"Smart ass." O'Connor smirked as she scrolled the display with her finger. "Guns, tasers, torches, porn... pretty much everything we were going to bring with us. But nothing as cool as that flame thrower."

"Wait." Sam did a double take. "Did you say *porn?*"

"Hell yeah. I need my in-between thrills."

Sam held up his hands. "Too much information. Did you find anything on spiders?" He sipped his cola.

"I didn't have much to go on," O'Connor said. "Except you saying they're big-ass spiders."

"Brad didn't know what kind they were."

O'Connor worked her phone with her right hand, her left going to her stump, unconsciously giving it a massage. "Did you know you can buy tarantula burgers in Durham, North Carolina?"

"What the f... How does that work?"

"Looks like just a chargrilled tarantula on top of a beef patty."

Sam chuckled. "Kill it with fire."

"Damn straight. Wanna see?"

Against better judgment, Sam glanced at O'Connor's phone. The photo showed a delicious-looking burger with a hairy grey tarantula perched on top, its legs pulled into its body like a cage.

"What do you think it tastes like?" O'Connor's stomach growled.

"Ugh... was that you?"

"Can't help it." O'Connor licked her lips. "A burger's a burger. Going to add that to my bucket list."

Sam took a swig of his cola. "Whatever floats your boat."

"Is there a meal on this flight?"

"I doubt it. Have the rest of my almonds." Sam handed O'Connor the package. "I'm going to sleep this flight away." He crossed his arms and closed his eyes.

Deep dreamless sleep came fast. The next time Sam opened his eyes, he'd be in Los Angeles for the first time in his life.

A New Crew

Bradley spotted Alexis and Deirdre leaning against their lockers several classrooms down the hallway from his. It was early and the first warning bell hadn't rung yet. He deposited his jacket and day pack in his locker and made a determined beeline toward the two girls.

And they saw him coming too, whispers and smiles shooting back and forth until Bradley was within earshot.

"Well, if it isn't lover boy." Alexis eyed Bradley with a lascivious grin. "Finally find your balls?"

Deirdre stood with a hand on her hip, looking down on Bradley and smacking her lips around a large wad of gum.

There it was again. The smell of jasmine that Bradley had grown to loathe. He swallowed his disgust and took a step forward.

"I need to talk to you."

Alexis shrugged. "So talk."

Bradley looked at Deirdre and she smirked, snapping her gum at him. He scanned left and right, noticing more students in the hallways. He didn't have much time if he wanted this to stay reasonably private.

"What were you doing in the equipment storage area?" he said.

Alexis maintained a cool demeanor. "What storage area?"

"Don't play dumb. You know the place." Bradley could feel

the heat of anger building in his head. "Under the Home Ec. classrooms."

Alexis shook her head. "Don't know what you're talking about."

"Yeah, so skurt, asshat," Deirdre said, punctuating her words with a crack of her gum.

"Sorry but the Forever Stylez bag gave you away." Bradley watched a flicker of insecurity cross Alexis's face. "I'm one of the few who knows… but I can easily change that." Bradley crossed his arms. It was his turn to make Alexis squirm. "A cut lock, trespassing on school property after hours… you'd probably get suspended."

"She dropped some jewelry in there," Deirdre said. "Had to get it out."

Alexis glared at Deirdre, then turned to Bradley. "It was a ring from my grandmother. I couldn't just leave it there."

Bradley raised his eyebrow, already bored with this charade. "And the bag?"

"Used it to carry my tools."

Bradley found it hard to believe anything that came out of Alexis's mouth, but he was drawing blanks for more questions. He alternated his gaze between the two girls, then smiled.

"What if I told you that Caitlin's story doesn't match yours?" Bradley said.

Alexis's eyes narrowed and darkened. "I'd say you're full of shit."

"Where is she today? You three are always together."

"Bathroom? Fuck if I know," Alexis said.

"Maybe I should drop by Caitlin's house… ask her some questions."

"Maybe you should hide and go fuck yourself."

Deirdre guffawed.

Bradley took a step back and pointed at Alexis. "I know what you're doing. And I'm going to find out why." He turned and walked down the hallway.

Deirdre gave Bradley a sarcastic wave. "Bye, *Felicia*."

When out of earshot, Alexis thumped Deirdre in the chest.

"Ow. That hurt."

"You're such a tool. I do the talking." Alexis walked in the opposite direction from Bradley and Deirdre followed like an obedient puppy. "Text Cait and make sure she doesn't talk to lover boy."

Deirdre pulled her phone from her back pocket and began tapping a text with a flurry of thumbs.

"Lover boy's gonna go gaga on *my* biology project," Alexis looked over her shoulder at Bradley, now at the opposite end of the hallway. "It's going to be killer."

BRADLEY AND TRILLIAN descended the stairs to Biology class, weaving their way around students going up to classrooms on the second floor.

He paused just before the open front door to Fiscara's classroom. "Hold up."

Trillian stopped and stepped back. "What's wrong."

Bradley lowered his voice and leaned close to Trillian's ear, catching a light scent of soap and sweet skin. "The storage area… it was Alexis."

Trillian squinted a question at him. "Are you sure?"

"Remember the bag?"

"The one Fiscara took away?"

Bradley nodded. "It's from Alexis's stepmom's salon. Forever Stylez."

"Shit," Trillian said. "What does she need spiders for?"

"That's what I want to know." Bradley looked at the open classroom door. "Act natural."

"What does *that* mean?"

"Whatever you do, don't look at Alexis."

The pair strolled into the classroom and found their seats. Alexis was already seated at her usual spot in the back. Fiscara let in a couple of latecomers, then closed the classroom door.

"I have some disappointing news." Fiscara's eyes flitted over the students.

Bradley managed a casual but confused glance back at Trillian, who offered the same look in response.

"We have a thief in our school." Fiscara crossed her arms and sat on the corner of her desk. "Maybe right in this classroom."

Students looked at each other, surprised. Bradley looked back at Alexis for a moment and found her emotionless, staring straight at the front of the class.

Fiscara continued. "Over the weekend, I brought a spider egg sac to the class to study over the coming weeks. I put it in that terrarium right there." She pointed to the empty terrarium to the left of the one Killer called home.

"At some point yesterday, the egg sac disappeared." Fiscara studied the faces staring back at her. Alexis crossed her arms and slouched in her desk, rolling her eyes and looking bored.

"It is very important that I get the egg sac returned. As most of you have discovered by now with your project research, the gestation period for spider eggs can range from two to three weeks." Fiscara stood and walked to the back of the classroom. "Each sac can hold up to a thousand eggs. Those kinds of numbers hatching in the wrong environment would pose considerable problems. So, if anyone has any information, please let me know. Spread the word, okay?"

Students nodded and murmured various forms of "yes."

Fiscara launched into the day's lesson, focusing on the arachnid digestive tract. Bradley tried to take in the new information, but his brain fought between countless images of large prey, slowly dissolving within tightly wrapped silken webbing, dried spider shit, and Alexis's actions.

The bell signaled the end of class and the students rushed the doors, happy to leave spider innards behind for the rest of the day. Alexis collected her things and bolted as well.

As numbers thinned, Fiscara motioned to Trillian and Bradley. "Have you seen anyone or anything suspicious?"

Bradley cast a quick glance at Trillian, and she nodded, as if to encourage him to speak. "I think Alexis has something to do with… what's going on, but I don't know what," he said. "I am sure she was in the storage area on the weekend."

Fiscara raised her eyebrows. "How sure?"

Bradley shrugged. "Pretty sure?"

"What's your evidence?"

"That bag you took to Principal Maddox, it was from her foster mom's salon."

"Anyone could have put that there," Fiscara said. "That's circumstantial at best."

"I just have this gut feeling."

"Well, keep your eyes peeled." Fiscara tidied her desk. "We don't want to compound the school's spider problem."

Bradley and Trillian nodded and left the classroom.

"We should follow her," Trillian said. "Spy on her house."

"Good idea. Meet in the parking lot after school?"

Trillian nodded. With their hasty plan set in motion, they both headed to their respective classes.

But Alexis had outsmarted everyone and left the school during the lunch break, a good three hours before the end of the school day. She hadn't even told Deirdre or Caitlin her plans that day.

When everyone was sitting in their afternoon classes, Alexis was sitting in a cool, dark corner of her garage, in front of a mason jar with nail holes driven into the lid. Within the jar sat not one but three white silken orb sacs about the size of golf balls. Fiscara's egg sacs, the same ones she had removed from Bradley's shed the previous Saturday.

Alexis didn't know if Fiscara had miscounted the number of egg sacs or was intentionally withholding the correct number. She didn't care either. The sacs were hers now.

Alexis tipped the jar on its side and coaxed the sacs to slide to the lid. With slow and careful turns, she opened the jar and removed one egg sac, placing it gently on a folded terrycloth towel. After closing the lid, righting the jar, and sliding it back into the cold shadows, Alexis paused to examine the egg sac up close. For a moment, she thought she saw the gossamer surface undulate from within.

"A thousand hungry babies," Alexis said to herself as a grin formed across her lips.

O'CONNOR SCROLLED THROUGH listings on her phone. "ZipZoom Car Rental. I like the sound of that."

"Never heard of it," Sam said as he scanned the baggage carousel for his hot pink abomination.

"You've been in prison for fifteen years. What do you know?"

"Touché." Sam spotted his suitcase and O'Connor's right next to it and grabbed both. They caught an airport shuttle to ZipZoom's lot, five minutes east on West Century Boulevard.

"I saw on your website that you rent Mustangs. I want one," O'Connor said to the ZipZoom clerk. "Red. Convertible."

"All of our Mustangs are all spoken for—"

"Then you'll be finding a Mustang from somewhere else."

Sam tapped O'Connor's shoulder. "Borrow your phone?"

She dug it out of her pocket and handed it to Sam. "No porn."

"I'm texting Brad for his address."

O'Connor pointed two fingers to her eyes, then at Sam. "I'm watching you."

As O'Connor continued her "negotiations" with the ZipZoom clerk, Sam stepped out into the Los Angeles sunshine and sat on the curb. He took a deep breath. Scattered clouds drifted through blue skies overhead and palm trees lined the boulevard. He liked what he saw.

As he tapped out a message to Bradley, Sam heard O'Connor's familiar voice boom through the glass.

O'Connor isn't getting what O'Connor wants.

He blocked her bellows from his mind and enjoyed the moment, the sun on his face, even if it was in front of a car rental lot next to one of the largest and busiest airports in the world.

O'Connor stepped out from the rental office, cigar in hand, and sat next to Sam. Her face was flushed, but she appeared calm.

"I got my Mustang."

"Did you murder the clerk, too?"

"Damn straight." O'Connor bit down on her cigar and spoke through clamped teeth. "Tore her a new asshole."

Sam looked around the lot. "So where is it?"

"It's at another lot. I, uh, had to compromise."

Sam looked at O'Connor and began to laugh. "What?" he said between snorts. "The great Bertha O'Connor had to *compromise?*"

"Shut up or I'll tear you a new one, too."

Sam took a moment to calm his laughter. "What did you end up getting?"

O'Connor fell silent and stared toward the boulevard.

Sam nudged her shoulder.

"I don't want to talk about it," she said.

Sam smiled. "Oh, this is going to be good."

The Mustang took over an hour to arrive. In that time,

O'Connor replenished her supplies, buying propane torches and canes with lights in the handles that doubled as tasers. All with her phone.

"Hey, I forgot to show you this." O'Connor unzipped her duffel bag, dug around through the clothes, and pulled out a small silver device. "I didn't leave *everything* back in New York."

She plugged the device into the bottom of her phone and worked the display with her finger, finally presenting the screen to Sam. "Thermal imaging in the palm of your hand, baby."

Sam pointed the phone-device combo at O'Connor, the sky, and around the rental lot. The image on the display showed colors ranging from blues to reds, oranges and yellows. The hotter the surface, the more yellow it appeared in the image, with cooler surfaces appearing deep blue.

Sam shook his head in wonderment. "Today's tech just blows my mind."

"It's great with anything that gives off a heat signature," O'Connor said as she moved her unlit cigar to the other side of her mouth. "Even farts."

"You're shitting me."

"Point it at my ass. You'll know pretty quick." O'Connor handed her phone to Sam, but he waved it off. She disconnected the thermal camera and returned it to her duffel bag.

The ZipZoom clerk poked her head out the door of the office. "Ms. O'Connor, your car has arrived. We're just giving it a quick wash and vacuum."

Less than ten minutes later, a baby pastel blue Mustang convertible rolled up in front of Sam, O'Connor, and the ZipZoom office. The driver left the car running and hopped out with a clipboard in his hand.

"You O'Connor?"

"That's me." O'Connor reached out with her hand. "Hey Tinkerbell, give me a hand."

Sam stood and pulled her up, his mouth agape in surprise as he took it all in. "Karma's a bitch, huh?"

"Shut up." O'Connor signed the form on the clipboard and the ZipZoom driver handed her the keys.

Sam started to laugh. "Hot pink and cotton candy. What a pair." He doubled over in hysterics.

O'Connor grabbed her duffel bag. "Get your shit in the trunk or I'm leaving you behind." She pressed the lock release on the key fob and the rear trunk popped open. "Come on!"

Sam carried his suitcase to the back of the Mustang, chortling all the way, and dropped it in the trunk. O'Connor tossed her duffel bag on top and slammed the trunk closed.

"Get in."

Sam slid into the passenger seat and fastened his seatbelt, pleasantly surprised by the comfort of the leather seats. He looked at O'Connor in the driver's seat—surrounded by baby blue everything—and tried to silence his laughter.

"I never knew you were into pastels," Sam said.

O'Connor kept her eyes forward, her attempt to look cool failing miserably. Even the cigar didn't help. "I wanted red."

"Sure, you did."

It was no use. Sam buckled over his knees, laughing longer and louder than he had in years.

"You're on notice." O'Connor glared at him, her cheeks flushed, as she floored the gas and peeled out of the ZipZoom lot.

BRADLEY WAS FIRST to the parking lot. He leaned against a nearby tree and monitored all the exit doors he could see from his vantage point. Trillian burst out of the south stairwell exit and he waved at her as she hustled to meet him.

"Have you seen her yet?" Trillian said between breaths.

"No." Bradley watched the exodus of students continue. His mind flipped to an image of a ruptured egg sac with hundreds of spiderlings expanding outward in all directions. A shiver ran down his back.

Jack sauntered out of the school, going with the flow like he didn't have a care in the world. He saw Trillian and Bradley and changed his direction to meet up.

"Hey bro… Trillian. What's going on?"

"We're going to tail Alexis," Bradley said without diverting his eyes.

"We think she stole a spider egg sac from Fiscara," Trillian added.

"It was originally from my shed." Bradley glanced at Jack. "From the same spider that bit my mom."

"Shit… How is your mom anyway?"

"Kind of the same."

Jack sat on a concrete parking divider, pulled out a pack of cigarettes, and extracted one with his lips. He held the pack up to Bradley and Trillian, who both declined. Jack removed a lighter from inside the pack and lit the cigarette. He drew in a breath, then released it in a smoky, wispy drift.

Bradley stared at him. "Since when do you smoke?"

"Since my best friend was gone all summer."

"So you take up smoking?"

Jack shrugged. "It relaxes me. Frees my mind."

"You're too smart to smoke," Bradley said. "Analyze the data."

Jack looked up at him and grinned, eddies of smoke leaking from the corner of his mouth. "I'll look into it."

All three watched the school until the numbers of students exiting slowed to a trickle. Bradley nodded toward the main entrance of the school as Deirdre stepped out into the sunshine.

"She's not with her enforcer."

Trillian shook her head. "I think we missed her."

Jack rubbed his cigarette out on the pavement. "Can I give you guys a ride home?" He stood and walked to his car.

Bradley flashed his brows at Trillian, then turned to Jack. "I think we're down for that. Trill?"

Trillian put her hands in her pockets and scrunched her shoulders together. "No, it's okay. I'm going to walk."

"You sure? Jack's got a lead foot." Bradley smiled at her.

"Yeah." Trillian looked to the sky. "It's a nice day."

"Okay." Bradley caught up with Jack and followed him into the Civic through the passenger door. Jack started the engine, rolled down his window, and backed out of his parking spot.

Bradley waved as they passed Trillian walking on the sidewalk.

"Damn bro." Jack glanced into the rearview mirror, Trillian's reflection shrinking with distance. "You should've walked."

"Huh?"

Jack shook his head and chuckled. "Can't you see she's into you?"

"Trill?"

"Yeah. Trill. Who else?"

Bradley twisted in his seat to look through the back window. "Should I go back?"

"Nah, but you got to be more aware."

Bradley faced forward. "Huh. I guess my mind's been occupied with other things."

"Maybe just a bit."

Jack took the corner onto Sheldon a little fast and the Civic's tires squealed against the asphalt. He pulled up to Bradley's house. "What the hell is *that?*"

A baby blue Mustang was parked in front of Bradley's house. Roy sat on the front stoop talking to a man and a short, stout woman.

Bradley's eyes widened. "Dad?" He leaped out of the Civic, walking fast.

"Wait… Dad?" Jack killed the engine and pulled himself out of the driver's side window.

Bradley threw his arms around Sam and gave him a strong hug. Roy eyed the embrace with disdain.

"Hey, son," Sam said, smiling.

"O'Connor!" Bradley hugged her too.

"Brad! How's it hanging?" O'Connor's cigar was now smoldering. "A little to the left?"

"Uh…"

"Just bustin' your balls," O'Connor said.

The three of them laughed.

Jack stepped up the walkway, unsure until Bradley waved him on.

"Dad, O'Connor, this is my best friend Jack."

Jack shook both Sam and O'Connor's hand.

Bradley continued. "He's an inventor."

Sam nodded approvingly. "Good to know."

O'Connor shifted her weight off her left leg and eyed Jack up and down. "The more inventors, the better, I always say."

Sam chuffed. "Since when do you say that?"

"When you're not around, obviously," O'Connor said.

Bradley looked around the stoop. "So where are your bags?"

"Still in the trunk," Sam said, "but we don't need to unpack just yet." He motioned subtly at Roy and winked. Bradley got the message loud and clear.

Roy caught the exchange. "We don't have much extra room."

Jack raised his eyebrows. "That's your car?"

"It's a rental but baby blue is O'Connor's favorite color." Sam laughed.

O'Connor pursed her lips and daggered a look at Sam.

Jack alternated his gaze between Sam and O'Connor. "Are you two… married or something?"

"Married?" O'Connor flew into hysterical laughter as she walked back toward the street. "That's rich. He couldn't keep up with me… sexually speaking." She roared, clutching her gut.

Sam hooked a thumb at O'Connor. "If you haven't realized it yet, she's full of shit."

O'Connor wiped the tears from the corners of her eyes. "So where are these goddamn spiders I'm supposed to kill?"

"Back shed?" Jack looked to Bradley for confirmation.

Bradley nodded. "Yeah. Follow me." Sam and O'Connor followed Jack and Bradley around the front of the house, through the side gate, and into the back yard.

Sam caught up with Bradley. "How's Claire doing?"

"Fine, except for her leg. She still might lose it."

Sam sighed. "Do you think she would mind if I visited her?"

"I don't know." Bradley noticed Roy standing in the kitchen window, watching the group. "But if you go, don't let Roy know."

"Her boyfriend?"

"Boyfriend. Leech. Douchebag. Take your pick. He can be a real dick."

"I hadn't noticed," Sam said.

Bradley appreciated Sam's sarcasm.

The shed stood just as it had been left on the weekend, the doors wide open, but with one important difference: more cocoons hung from the rafters.

"What in the hell is that?" O'Connor squinted at a lumpy teardrop-shaped cocoon.

"The big one?" Bradley said. "That's probably a cat, or maybe a small dog. The other one I think is a squirrel."

"Can we see one of those things?" Sam took stock of the shed's contents.

"Wait!" O'Connor ran back toward the side gate. "I've got just the thing."

Two minutes later, she returned huffing and puffing and

cackling to herself. She had attached the thermal imaging camera onto her phone.

"Whoa." Jack's eyes went wide. "Is that a FLIR?"

"Give the man a cigar," O'Connor said. "But not this one." She pointed at her smoldering stogie with her thumb.

O'Connor stepped up to the open shed. "This is state-of-the-art shit right here." She scanned the area with her phone, the image on the screen producing details in dark blues and purple. "Where's the nest?"

"We took it out on Saturday but—"

"You took it out?" O'Connor shook her head. "For fuck's sake."

Bradley stared at her. "You going to let me finish? You may be the exterminator, but you're not the expert here anymore."

O'Connor removed her cigar and crossed her arms. "Oh, and you are?"

"I know more than what you looked up on the flight over here," Bradley said. "And I have my Bio teacher on board."

"Oh, *burn*," Sam said. Jack smiled too.

"I forgot you grew some balls over the summer." O'Connor held out her arm, signaling Bradley to continue.

"We took a nest out on Saturday, but the cocoons are back. That means a nest is back. Help me move some stuff around and get that camera ready."

Jack and Sam stepped up to the entrance of the shed and joined Bradley, who was sliding items away from the right exterior wall. O'Connor stood to one side scanning the shed for hotspots.

"Move slowly," Bradley said. "Sporkies are fast and scare easily."

"Wait." O'Connor cocked her head to one side. "Did you say *sporky?*"

"It's the name we gave these spiders. Because of the quills on their backs."

"Quills?"

"Yeah, like a porcupine."

O'Connor looked at Sam. "Just what in the fuck did you get me into?"

"Me?" Sam laughed. "As you've made it painfully obvious before, nobody's the boss of you."

She looked at Bradley. "Are these quills poisonous?"

He shrugged. "No one's been stung yet, but the bites are pretty bad." Bradley glanced at the others. "My Bio teacher has never seen anything like them before." He moved a pot away from the right-hand wall, trying to focus on the dark corners of the shed. The bag of sunflower seeds, where the previous nest had been located, was clear of webbing.

Sam grabbed the handle of the lawn mower and rolled it back. "You getting anything on that fancy-shmancy camera of yours?"

"Holy shit. Now I am." O'Connor took an involuntary and stumbling step backward. "Back wall. Center."

Sam shifted his gaze and saw half a dozen black spots spread out and up across the wall. "God DAMN it." He backed out of the shed, knocking Jack aside as he went.

Jack pulled Bradley back out of the shed.

"What did you do?" O'Connor hit record and tracked the flurry of orange and yellow hot spots on her screen as they disappeared into other cracks and crevices in the back wall.

"The lawn mower."

O'Connor stepped up onto the leading edge of the shed's floor. Hand forward and slightly above her head, she angled the camera down at the lawn mower.

"Someone pull the mower back," she said. "Slow."

Bradley grabbed the handle and rolled the mower back toward the entrance. The nest showed up as a hazy grey mass of webbing, stretching as the mower moved back until it tore like old fabric.

The webbing glowed red and orange on O'Connor's phone. The brighter orange and yellow spots had all disappeared.

"Makes you wish they were rats, doesn't it?" Bradley grinned at O'Connor. "At least we'd know how to deal with them."

"I wish I had my flame thrower," O'Connor said. "The little assholes would be toast."

"And if you burned the shed down, my mom would murder you."

"She sounds delightful." O'Connor stopped her video recording. "I'm looking forward to meeting her."

Sam laughed. "I can't wait."

O'Connor raised her eyebrows at him. "I'm serious."

"I don't doubt it," Sam said.

O'Connor ran around to the back of the shed, alternating between what she could see in front of her and the thermal camera's screen. The display showed up a dark blue with tinges of greens where the afternoon sun glanced the siding. She turned the corner and aimed the camera where the shed's back wall met the ground a foot away from the fence. The shadows crawled.

"Bogeys… everywhere," she yelled back and turned her camera to record again.

The spiders blended into their surroundings well, but the hot spots on O'Connor's phone display betrayed their locations as they scattered out from the shed's base, under the fence and into the next yard.

O'Connor stepped on an unseen board lying in the grass and catapulted several spiders into the air, two landing on her chest.

"Shit!" Instinct took over and O'Connor brought her hand up, scooping the first spider away with her phone. She was about to repeat the move when the second spider sprayed her hand with webbing, fastening both the spider and her phone to her hand.

She swung her arm and flung the attached spider against the

back wall like a whip, but the webbing and the spider's clutch was too strong.

"Moth-ther-fuck-ker," O'Connor said between swings, but despite her attempts the spider began to advance up the strand toward her hand.

"Stop," a voice said behind her. Bradley stood with a pair of garden shears. "Back up toward the fence." Jack and Sam poked their head out from around the shed.

O'Connor did as she was told. She steadied her arm and without the added centripetal force of the swings, the strand settled into a gentle swaying motion. The spider scaled the strand to her hand even faster.

"Hurry the fuck up, Brad."

Bradley said nothing as he reached forward with the shears. He centered the blades on the thick web strand and brought the handles together with a forceful chop.

Instead of cutting through the strand, it bent and slipped through the gap between the blades. The black and shimmering arachnid was now less than six inches away from O'Connor's hand.

"Any time, now…" O'Connor's forehead had broken out in a sweat.

Bradley opened and closed the shears twice before remembering the trick Claire had shown him earlier in the year. He twisted the handles in his hands and the blades ground against each other, slicing through the strand just as the spider reached the underside of the shears.

O'Connor stepped back and Bradley dropped the shears on the grass. He tried to stamp it with his shoe, but Jack pulled him back. The black mass propelled by hairy, articulated twig-legs scrambled off the blades and escaped into foliage of the adjoining yard.

Bradley skewered a look at O'Connor. "These things aren't rats. Don't be a hero."

O'Connor gnawed on her cigar, mulling over how to respond, shrugged and said nothing.

All four of them exchanged glances as O'Connor caught her breath.

"What's next?" Jack said to Bradley.

"Face time?"

"Taco Siempre."

"You're on," Bradley said. "I'll call Viscera and Trillian."

"Did someone say tacos?" O'Connor grinned, the recent spider incident fading to a distant memory.

Both Jack and O'Connor's stomach rolled a hungry growl. "Yep. Best in the valley," Jack said.

Bradley tapped out a group text to Trillian and Fiscara as he led the way out of the back yard to the cars in the front.

Roy stood with arms crossed in the kitchen window watching them go—forgotten.

JACK AND BRADLEY burned through the neighborhood streets, with O'Connor and Sam following close behind.

Bradley looked back through the rear window of the Civic. "You better slow down. You're going to get a ticket, they're going to get lost, or both."

Once on Glenoaks Boulevard, Jack floored the gas pedal. "You worry too much. Ol' Stogie back there is keeping up just fine."

Jack pulled into the small parking area in front of Taco Siempre. He was about to pull himself out of the driver's side window when O'Connor flew into the lot, turned and reversed the Mustang into the next stall.

O'Connor hung her elbow out the window. "Nice moves, Speed Racer. Want to race for pink slips later?"

Jack furrowed his brow, then looked to Bradley for clues. He shrugged in response.

Sam and O'Connor laughed, already out of the Mustang.

"Fast and Furious," O'Connor said. "Do a search."

Jack waited for O'Connor to close her door before pulling himself out of the side window. She raised an eyebrow and gave him a curious glance.

"Couldn't afford to fix the latch. So, I welded it," Jack said.

O'Connor turned to Sam. "A showoff *and* he welds."

Bradley held the door open as the others filed in. He stopped O'Connor. "No smoking here. You should put the cigar away."

"It's not lit, for Christ's sake."

"I know, but it won't go over well." Bradley held O'Connor's gaze. "Besides, you can't eat with a cigar in your mouth."

O'Connor tapped Bradley in the center of his chest. "Got a point there." She placed the cigar stub in her front breast pocket. "So, what's good?"

"Everything."

Fiscara and Trillian had beaten them to the restaurant and were already sitting at a table, Fiscara with a coffee and Trillian a soda.

Bradley stepped forward. "This is Miss Fiscara, my biology teacher, and Trillian, another friend of mine."

Fiscara and Trillian stood.

"It's Wendy to my friends," Fiscara said.

Bradley continued the introductions. "This is my dad, Sam, and his colleague, Bertha O'Connor. She's an exterminator."

O'Connor gave Bradley a friendly tap on the shoulder. "It's just O'Connor, numbnuts." She presented her hand. "Detest-A-Pest. New York's finest exterminator."

"Good to meet you all." Sam smiled and shook Trillian's hand, then Fiscara's.

O'Connor rubbed her hands together. "So now that we're all besties, let's eat."

As the six of them stepped to the front counter, Bradley caught Fiscara checking Sam out. She shrugged and flashed her eyebrows, knowing she was busted, and pulled Bradley aside.

"Sorry," she said. "I know that would make parent-teacher interviews weird."

"As far as I know, he's single." Bradley smiled as he observed Sam going through the menu on the wall.

"You mean your dad and mom are…"

Bradley nodded. "And he's got history, so…"

"Enough said."

Everyone ordered their food, paid and returned to the table with their drinks, adults on one side, teenagers on the other.

O'Connor wasted no time breaking the awkward silence. "So?" She turned to Bradley. "You called this shindig and I flew all the way from New York for it. Talk."

Bradley looked around the table, all eyes on him. His mouth went dry even though he was among friends. He sipped from his coffee.

"So yeah. We got a spider problem," Bradley said. "Jack put together a map and Trill and I tracked them down. And they're all like the ones in my shed."

Jack placed his phone on the table, called up the spider map, and slid it over to the adult side of the table.

"We think there's a colony somewhere in the school," Trillian said. "There's a large concentration of nests all around it and we found a nest in the storage area."

"Maddox, the school's principal, isn't going to do anything," Fiscara said. "His head is so far up the school board's ass it's a wonder anything gets done at all."

Sam and O'Connor studied the map on the phone. O'Connor was pinch-zooming and panning the image in and out, left and right.

Sam looked up. "All these are spider nests?"

Bradley and Trillian nodded. "We confirmed almost every location. We've even got photos," she said.

A shiver ran down Sam's spine and his body visibly shuddered. Everyone else noticed.

"You okay, Sam?" Fiscara asked.

"Yeah," he said. "I thought I wasn't afraid of spiders, but hundreds of them all at once kind of gives me the willies."

"Come on." O'Connor slapped Sam on the back. "What's a few spiders?"

"I seem to remember you shitting your pants about half an hour ago," Sam said.

The group was losing cohesion and focus. The teacher in Fiscara took charge. "So, this past summer was drier than most," she said. It was an awkward segue, but it got everyone's attention. All eyes were on her now.

"Like all living things, spiders need water to survive," Fiscara continued. "Migrating to well-maintained greenspaces, like residential properties and the school grounds makes sense. Water and food would be more abundant, allowing the spiders to flourish."

"The school," O'Connor said. "I want to start in the basement."

"What's with you and basements?" Sam asked. "We're not chasing rats here."

"Vermin is vermin in my book. And there's no better place to start than in a dark basement." She slapped her hands on the table. "Where's my goddamn enchilada?" Her voice carried through the little dining area and into the kitchen.

"Cool it, O'Connor." Jack looked back at the counter. "I see our order on the passthrough. They'll call our names when it's ready."

"It better happen soon or I'm going back there and raise some shit."

Fiscara studied O'Connor. "You have many friends back in New York?"

O'Connor looked at her, momentarily confused. "What? No... why?"

"With your sparkling personality, I would've thought you'd be the toast of the town."

"What would your students think of you without teeth?"

Both women regarded each other for a moment. Everyone else at the table exchanged uneasy glances until O'Connor and Fiscara began to laugh. Everyone else joined in.

"Don't cross me, bitch." O'Connor's eyes narrowed.

Fiscara responded in kind. "Or what?" It was clear that she took no shit from anyone, including O'Connor.

A hush fell over the table until both Fiscara and O'Connor broke into laughter once again. O'Connor placed her arm around Fiscara's shoulder and addressed the rest of the table.

"I like her," O'Connor said between laughs. "She's good people."

"Exterminator?" Sofia called out from the front counter. "Order's up, exterminator."

Bradley smiled. "That's us." He slid off the form-fitting melamine seat and beckoned Jack to help. They grabbed their food trays and brought them back to the table.

"Prepare for heaven on Earth," Jack said, doling out the individual orders.

O'Connor ripped open the paper around her enchilada and took a bite. "Not bad, not bad," she said with her mouth full. "Now tell me about your school."

The self-proclaimed group of exterminators discussed their plan of attack, fueled by the best Mexican food in the valley.

Killing with Kindness

The next morning Bradley awoke to a text from Mark waiting on his phone. It took him a second to remember who Mark was.

"We need 2 talk," the text read. It had been sent just after four o'clock in the morning.

What the hell? 4 a.m.? Bradley tapped back a response. "Sure. What's up?"

Mark texted back, "Still in hospital. Drop by after school?"

Bradley felt a little apprehensive about committing. He didn't know Mark and their social circles hadn't crossed during his entire academic life. But what was the harm in talking to the guy?

He texted back, "Sure. R U OK?"

After a brief pause, Mark's response arrived. "L8R." Then nothing.

Bradley swung his legs out of bed and began his morning before-school routine: shower, get dressed, make his lunch and eat breakfast.

As he padded toward the bathroom, he could hear Roy rummaging around at the front door. Bradley looked out over the living room toward the front of the house and saw Roy putting on his shoes.

"Oh hey," Roy said, looking up. "Going for a run. Want to join me?"

Bradley shook his head. "I got to get ready for school."

"Maybe next time," Roy said as he tightened the knot on his remaining shoe.

"You know, there's lots of room here for my dad and O'Connor. They could have crashed here."

Roy looked over his shoulder. "Your dad's a criminal and a drunk, and O'Connor is… I don't know what she is except repulsive. Besides, Claire would never have allowed it."

"You talked to her?"

"I didn't have to," Roy said. "I know what she likes." He stood and let himself out the front door.

"You're full of shit, *Roy.*" Bradley walked to the front door to lock it. As he returned to the bathroom and stepped into the shower, his thoughts drifted back to Mark's texts. What did he want to talk to him about? And why was he still in the hospital?

AT ABOUT THE time Bradley was waking up, Jack sat in his parked Civic at Food Fresh Market, waiting for the store to open. And like clockwork, the lights and neon buzzed to life a few minutes after six. He headed inside to the back of the store.

Jack passed the open door of Mr. Toscano's office, stopping in front of the task boards on the wall: one delivery, then stocking shelves for the rest of his morning shift. Relaxed and easy.

Jack found his delivery book and opened it to today's date.

Mr. Moody. Jack groaned. Maybe the morning wasn't going to be as easy as he thought, but at least he got to drive.

He couldn't dawdle either. Thanks to an online map app on his phone, Mr. Toscano knew exactly how long a delivery should take. Those who made deliveries that took too long were promptly fired.

Jack grabbed a shopping cart and collected the items on Mr.

Moody's list: twenty-four cans of tomato soup and two loaves of bread. The cans of soup were separated into cases of twelve, making collection easier. He checked the items off on the order list and signed the bottom.

Jack rolled the soup and bread to his car, loaded them into the back seat, and returned the cart.

He started the Civic's engine, giving it gas and letting it settle into a low purr. Jack sped out of the parking lot, just slow enough so his tires wouldn't squeal on the asphalt and feeling thankful that he had a job that let him drive, at least part of the time.

Mr. Moody's house looked the same as it had on the first day he'd delivered groceries there six months ago, shortly after receiving his driver's license.

Vegetation grew and died with the seasons and swallowed up more of the property year by year. The grimy windows were no longer approachable. Lucky for Jack, the driveway resisted most of the invasive weeds.

He stacked the two boxes of soup and placed the loaves of bread on top. It was heavy, but the promise of one trip made it bearable.

He ascended the back steps, balanced the boxes and bread on a rickety porch railing and knocked on the door. Mr. Moody was known for taking his sweet time, so Jack had no choice but to wait.

After five minutes, Jack knocked again. He didn't want to be fired for taking too long. Today, Jack should have waited longer before knocking twice.

"For fuck's sake hold on!" Mr. Moody yelled from behind the door. "God-damned entitled motherfuckers, the lot of yah."

Deadbolts disengaged and latches clicked. The door opened an inch and Jack heard Mr. Moody's motorized wheelchair navigate away from it. With the soup and bread in his arms, he inhaled deeply, pushed the door open, and began the ritual of seeing how long he could go without taking a breath.

Not long apparently, especially when carrying almost twenty pounds of canned goods. Jack moved through the warm, moist air, and even though he held his breath, the pervasive odor of the house invaded his nose and caused him to gag. He opened his mouth and took a shallow breath of relief, only to smell the house more. It was reward and punishment all rolled up into one.

Jack made a direct line through the mud room to the kitchen. On his way, he passed several creepy porcelain doll heads adorning the countertops that he didn't remember seeing the last time he was there. Jack ignored them to the best of his ability and focused on finding free counter space. On the back wall of the kitchen sat dozens of black spiders, not immediately obvious in the shadows. Had he not been distracted by the doll heads, Jack would have easily spotted the cluster.

He set the boxes and bread on the counter with a *thud,* next to what looked like the same bananas he had delivered on his last trip. The sudden noise and vibration caused the spiders to scuttle into hidden corners.

The bananas were a rich yellow, evenly dotted with brown spots. A porcelain doll with dead eyes, one half-closed, slumped to one side next to the ripe fruit. It was the only doll head with a complete body, dressed in a torn and soiled frock.

"Watch it, jackass," Mr. Moody said. "Don't be touching Henrietta."

Jack played along. "She's fine, Mr. Moody."

"She better be."

Just for the hell of it, Jack poked the skin of one of the bananas. It tore open easily, the skin appearing to move on its own, and a viscous jaundiced fluid oozed out, almost as dark as the spots on the banana's skin.

"Jesus." Jack stifled a gag.

"What's that, boy?" Mr. Moody squirmed in his wheelchair and ripped a fart. "You say somthin'?"

Jack referred to his order sheet. "That'll be thirty-one dollars even." He turned to face Mr. Moody and noticed that he had a porcelain doll head perched over his crotch. Beside that, affixed to the wheelchair's frame, was a large ring of keys. He averted his eyes to the floor.

Mr. Moody pulled out his wallet from between his right thigh and the side of the wheelchair. He opened it up and dug through the pockets.

"You have a lot of keys."

"Huh?" Mr. Moody paused and looked up. "You tryin' to confuse me, boy?"

"Uh, no. I—"

"How much?"

"Thirty-one," Jack said.

"That's highway robbery, goddammit." Mr. Moody pulled a few bills out and handed them to Jack.

The bills felt warm and moist in his hands and Jack fought the urge to vomit.

"Thank you for shopping at Food Fresh, Mr. Moody."

Mr. Moody grumbled.

Jack headed for the back door but stopped before passing the threshold. "I got to ask… What's the deal with the doll heads?"

Anger flashed across Mr. Moody's face. "None of yer fuckin' business, you little shit! If I wasn't in this chair, I'd—"

"Okay, thanks." Jack closed the door on Mr. Moody's onslaught of vulgarity. He savored the fresh air as he walked to the Civic, but inside the car was a different story.

Jack sniffed the air, then his shirt. His clothes reeked of Mr. Moody's house and school started in less than two hours.

He brought the wad of bills to his nose and its pungent odor was worse than his clothes. He threw the bills into the glove compartment and spotted a small travel-sized bottle of hand sanitizer.

"There is a God!" Jack gave his hand an ample squirt and rubbed the sanitizer all over his hands and part way up his arms. He rolled the window down and started the engine.

If he was fast, he could change his clothes before returning to the market. And if there was one thing Jack was, it was fast.

THE SCHOOL SIGNALLED the end of the day. Alexis collected her psychology books and joined the other students lining up to leave the classroom. She had no time to waste.

The students in front and behind her talked excitedly about the upcoming dance, who was going and with whom.

Inconsequential chitty-chatty bullshit. Alexis would be going stag. There was no point in bringing a boy to mess up her plans. And so far, her preparations had worked out.

She headed out into the second floor hallway, scanning left and right. No sign of Deirdre or Caitlin yet but she had to act fast to avoid them.

Alexis dumped her books into her locker and speed-walked toward the south stairwell. She spotted Trillian leaving her English class and uncharacteristically averted her eyes, hoping that Trillian hadn't noticed her pass by.

She flew down the first flight of stairs, looking back only when she reached the landing between floors. Trillian stood at her locker, her eyes trained on Alexis. She *had* been watching her the whole time.

Nosy bitch doesn't know when to mind her own business.

As Alexis reached the first floor, she heard her name in the hallway.

"Lexi!"

Only Caitlin and Deirdre were allowed to use that nickname. Anyone else would get their tongues ripped out.

Alexis turned to see Caitlin a few classrooms down the hallway. She smiled brightly and waved, her left hand and arm wrapped with a bandage that matched her t-shirt. Deirdre walked next to her, rolling her eyes.

She could include them, but more people just made things more complicated. She stepped through the exterior doors without returning Caitlin's greeting.

Alexis pictured Caitlin's smile dissolving into hurt and confusion as she ran to the street in front of the school and down two blocks to the bus stop. She pushed past other students to get to the front of the line. Those who complained of her intrusion stopped once they saw who it was. Alexis was not one to mess with.

She had timed things exactly right. The #14 bus rolled toward the stop. Just as she stepped on the bus, a text alert chimed on her phone. She found a seat next to the exit and grabbed her phone from her purse.

"Where R U?" Deirdre's text said.

"Doc appt. L8R," Alexis tapped back before silencing her phone and dropping it back in her purse. She didn't want any more interruptions.

She stepped off the bus at the Stonehurst Hills strip mall and surveyed the businesses until she found what she was looking for: Daisy Days Flower Shop.

Inside the small shop, shelves containing different grab-and-go floral arrangements lined both walls. The florists, the walk-in refrigerator, and work surfaces lined with tools and accessories anchored the back of the shop.

Alexis browsed the arrangements. She wanted to find a nice bouquet but didn't have a lot of time. She settled on an arrangement of daisies, tulips, carnations and dahlias in a faux crystal vase. But one flower was missing.

Alexis brought the bouquet to the florist at the back counter. "Can I add three white roses to this?"

"Absolutely." The florist stepped into the refrigerator and returned with three pristine white roses, their petals tightly wound atop sturdy stems. "Would you like the thorns removed?"

"No, that's fine."

The florist inserted the roses into the arrangement, giving them prominence among the other flowers. "You've made a beautiful choice."

Alexis glanced at her phone, noting the time, and smiled.

"Will that be all for you?"

"Yes."

The florist rung up the bouquet on the cash register. "Your total with tax is $34.31."

Alexis removed a collection of bills from her purse and handed thirty-five dollars to the florist. "Thanks. Keep the change."

She stepped out of the flower shop and checked the time again. The hospital was a few blocks away, a short enough distance to walk the rest of the way. Less than ten minutes later, Alexis strolled through the automatic sliding doors of Sun Valley Medical Center.

She inquired at the reception desk for Claire's room, then made her way to the elevator, exiting on the fifth floor. Using the map affixed to the wall beside the elevator, Alexis found Claire's room without difficulty. She calmed herself with a few cleansing breaths before knocking on the door frame and entering the room.

"Alexis!" Claire's expression was a mixture of confusion and surprise. "How nice of you to drop by."

"I know Brad and I have broken up, but I wanted to drop by and wish you well." She set the vase down on the back counter and stood with her back to Claire.

"How's school going so far?"

"Pretty good. Busy." Alexis removed a small glass jar with a perforated screw-top lid from her purse. Within the jar sat an intact spider egg sac. She removed the lid, spread the flower stems apart, inserted the sac within the bouquet, and returned the jar and lid to her purse. The entire move took less than thirty seconds.

"Have you and Bradley talked at all?"

"Not much." Alexis took a paper cup from a dispenser on the back wall and pretended to top up the vase with water. "Most of our classes are different." She raised the vase off the counter and placed it on the rolling tray that fit over Claire's bed.

"It's a lovely arrangement, Alexis. And my first one! Thank you." Claire's eyes misted over.

They'll be perfect for your funeral.

Claire sat up and raised her arms from the bed. "Can I have a hug? For old time's sake?"

Alexis smiled and bent over to reciprocate.

"I've missed you, Alexis," Claire said. "You're one of the good ones."

"Thanks." She stood, looking at Claire's left leg, still overly red and swollen within its white gauze wrap. "How is your leg feeling?"

"A bit better every day," Claire said. "I may get out of here in a week or so if I'm lucky."

Alexis walked back to the bouquet and began adjusting the arrangement. Looking down from the top, she could see the egg sac perched between a multitude of stems, including the thorny roses. She adjusted the roses, watching the thorns rip holes into the wispy exterior of the egg sac. Small spiders the size of inky marbles spilled out into the center of the bouquet.

"I think luck's on your side." Alexis held Claire's gaze for a moment and gave her hand a gentle squeeze. She looked at the clock over Claire's bed. "I've got to get going. Homework, you know."

"Did you want me to let Bradley know you dropped by?"

Alexis stepped toward the door. "No, that's okay. I'll talk to him later."

Claire nodded. "Sure."

"Bye." Alexis waved and stepped out of the room. As she approached the elevator, the doors slid open as if she planned it. She dug into her purse and pulled out the jar and lid.

The elevator opened to the first floor and Alexis dropped the jar and lid into the nearest recycling bin in the waiting area. A subtle grin spread across her face as she strolled toward the main entrance of the hospital.

The main doors slid open and Bradley walked in. The sight of him was unexpected and Alexis had to force herself not to react. They passed each in the vestibule as if in slow motion. He stared at her as he passed, while she kept her eyes front and center.

Despite this small hiccup, Alexis's plan had worked out perfectly. The remaining step, letting nature take its course, was the easy part.

BRADLEY'S LAST CLASS of the day was Entrepreneurship. The class's spirited discussion about the importance of a devoted website went several minutes past the bell. Many argued that keeping things simple was the best route to take, citing examples of social media campaigns that went viral. Bradley had already made up his mind. A website was essential. More visibility drove more sales.

He loaded his day pack with books he needed for homework that night and ran down the stairs two steps at a time. He emerged from the school just in time to see the #14 bus roll away from the bus stop.

"Shit." He looked at the time on his phone. 3:11 p.m. He could still make it. The next bus would be by in fifteen minutes.

Bradley cut across the student parking lot and toward the street, but stopped when he heard a car honk.

"Brad!" He looked to his right and saw Jack behind the wheel of his Civic.

He rolled the car up beside Bradley as he walked. "Hey bro, where you headed?"

For some reason, Bradley didn't want to say where he was going or why. "To the hospital… to see my mom."

"Need a lift?"

"I'm good. The bus will be here any minute."

"Okay. So, I've been thinking about spiders lately."

Bradley chuckled. "No shit?"

"Yeah. I got an idea." Jack hit the brakes and reached into the back seat of the Civic. He presented Bradley with a sketch on a piece of paper. "Take a look at this. It's my most recent invention."

The sketch depicted a modified vacuum that had a funnel attached to the end and a mesh of razor blades embedded into it.

"Looks like a Flowbee on steroids."

"A what?"

"You've never heard of the Flowbee?" Bradley handed the sketch back to Jack. "It's a hair cutting system that you connect to a vacuum."

Jack narrowed his eyes. "You shitting me?"

"Just do a search."

"Anyway, the idea is spiders go in, chopped up spiders come out. You think it would work?"

Bradley shrugged. "It should. Might get messy after a while, though."

"Yeah." The gears in Jack's brain were already working on refinements. "It's a work in progress."

A car rolled up behind Jack and the driver gave a quick honk of his horn.

"Sure I can't give you a ride?"

"Yep."

"Peace, bro." Jack drove away, his left hand out the window, middle finger raised. Bradley reciprocated the gesture with both hands, laughing to himself.

He quickened his pace and arrived at the bus stop with a minute to spare. Even with the number of students waiting, there were plenty of free seats available on the bus.

The ride to the hospital was uneventful. To pass the time, Bradley searched for the Flowbee on his phone and sent a link to Jack with a rolling-on-the-floor-laughing emoji beside it.

He loaded his mapping app and the overlay showing the locations of all the spider nests he, Jack and Trillian had found. Bradley pinch-zoomed and rotated the map, looking for patterns, but all he could see was a concentration of spiders around the school. There didn't seem to be a pattern to it at all.

He pocketed his phone and stepped off the bus in front of Sun Valley Medical Center. It was just over a week ago since he and Jack had stepped through the same automatic sliding doors on his way to see Claire.

I'll surprise her after I talk with Mark.

The doors slid open as Bradley approached and his heart skipped a beat. Alexis passed by on her way out of the hospital, snubbing him completely.

He stopped within the vestibule, watching her leave, his surprise turning to confusion mixed with questions.

Why are you here, Alexis?

After asking for Mark's room, Bradley took the stairs to the fifth floor. He viewed elevators with distrust ever since spending the summer in New York with Sam.

Bradley found the room quickly after exiting the stairwell. He poked his head in. "Mark?"

Mark was sitting upright in his bed staring blankly out the window. He turned toward Bradley and heaved a sigh of relief. "Thank God. I've been dying of boredom here. I didn't think you were going to show."

"Yeah, sorry. I missed my bus," Bradley said. "I tried to text you, but it didn't go through."

"The hospital has this stupid fucking rule about patients and cell phones. The nurse actually took mine away just after I texted you this morning."

"Uncool, man." Bradley walked to the foot of the bed. "How are you doing? And sorry about your head, by the way."

Mark waved him off. "I've seen the videos. You saved my life. That epi-pen shit was epic. Straight out of *Pulp Fiction*."

"There's *videos?*"

"Yeah."

"Any good shots of the spiders?"

"Probably," Mark said. "Someone even made a remix. Imagine shots of you hitting my head edited to 'Baby One More Time' by Britney Spears."

"Shit. Sorry man."

"It's actually pretty funny." Mark chuckled. "They're not even worried about my head anymore. It's my legs they're more concerned with now."

"What? You weren't bitten, though." Bradley searched his memory of the attack. "Were you?"

"No. The spider guts that landed on my legs caused some strange burning. Doctors wanted to do some tests. But it's nothing that's going to keep me in this hellhole much longer."

"So, what did you want to talk to me about?"

"I've heard things going around." Mark held Bradley's gaze. "You think the school's infested, right?"

"Yeah," Bradley said. "I've got some friends helping me, Viscera too. And my dad and his exterminator friend are visiting from New York."

"I want in, too. Only one thing's going to burn my inner thighs, and spiders aren't it, know what I mean?"

"Sure." Bradley laughed, even though he wasn't one-hundred percent sure *what* Mark meant.

"That reminds me. You know who I saw today?"

Bradley shook his head.

"Caitlin. She had her hand all bandaged up," Mark said. "Never realized how hot she is. We talked for a bit. Thought I'd mention it since you're going out with that Alexis chick."

"*Used* to go out." Bradley could have sworn that he caught a whiff of jasmine in the air and shuddered. "She's history."

Mark threw his hands up in surprise. "Dude! What are you doing? She's a smokin' babe."

"With the personality of Hannibal Lecter."

"Who?"

"Never mind."

"So… is Alexis on the market?"

Bradley shrugged indifference. "You'll have to ask her."

"Maybe I will." Mark smiled as his thoughts wandered. "Anyway, like I said before, I want in."

"Good. The more people we have on board, maybe Maddox will finally listen."

The two teens looked at each other and broke out into simultaneous laughter.

"Nah," they said in unison.

The sound of flat-soled shoes running echoed down the corridor, distracting Bradley. A nurse flew by the open door to Mark's room, followed by another.

"Room 513," a nurse said into a small walkie-talkie. "We need the hazmat team immediately."

"What are we dealing with?" a voice on the walkie-talkie squawked back.

Bradley stepped to the door, but was unable to decipher any

other words, except "arachnidism," a word the doctor had used to describe Claire's spider bite a week earlier.

"I got to check this out," Bradley said to Mark as he stepped out into the corridor. Two people in yellow hazmat suits stepped from the elevator and jogged past Bradley toward room 513.

"No worries. I get out tomorrow," Mark said. "I'll text you." But Bradley was too far down the corridor to hear him.

The hazmat team stepped into the room, ignoring the commotion unfolding in the corridor. Bradley inched along the wall across from the room's doorway, managing to widen his vantage point, one step at a time.

First he saw a vase with a flower bouquet, which at first glance seemed perfectly normal. Bradley fished out his phone from his pocket and loaded the photo app. Then a step further the patient's legs came into view. The left leg was larger than the right and elevated. There were small black dots covering the bed sheet, moving away from the bouquet. He took a picture.

One hazmat officer was on the side of the bed furthest from the door, talking to the patient in calm tones. The other was backing up to the door, keeping their eye on the bed sheets and surrounding floor.

Bradley's eyes fell on the toes of the patient's right foot, painted purple and peeking out from under the top bed sheet. He went to his phone and pulled up the last photo, zooming into the foot. Recognition, concern, and terror flooded him at once and his blood ran cold. He launched himself toward the door of the hospital room.

"Mom!" Bradley knew it was Claire before he saw her. "Mom!" He was able to see into the room and lock gazes with Claire for a moment before a nurse held him back. The fear on her face remained etched in his mind like the afterglow of a camera flash.

The second hazmat officer blocked Bradley's path. "It's not safe," she said.

"But that's my mom." Bradley tried to look over the officer's shoulder, but his view was blocked by the officer's bulky yellow suit. "She's been bitten once already."

"Then stay put and let us do our job." The second hazmat officer's voice echoed through the hood and mask she was wearing over her head. "Stay safe for your mom's sake, okay?"

Bradley nodded.

The second hazmat officer ran down the corridor and around a corner.

"Hey, where's she going?" Bradley looked to the nurse, then to the first hazmat officer. "What's going on?"

"Lower your voice, son," the first hazmat officer said. "Loud noises ain't going to help anyone." He motioned at the nurse.

"Let's let the hazmat team do their work," the nurse said. He directed Bradley away from Claire's room just as the second hazmat officer returned, carrying an industrial wet/dry vacuum with coils of flexible tubing resting on top in a spiral. Several seconds later the vacuum's motor spun up to a roar.

Bradley glanced at the nurse. "Can I at least see what they're doing?"

The nurse contemplated the question, but Bradley could see the curiosity in his face too. "Okay, but you stay next to me. Got it?"

Bradley nodded.

The two of them moved back toward Claire's room, maneuvering around the crowd of people collecting at the door.

The wet/dry vacuum had been modified to accept two hoses instead of one and both hazmat officers were wasting no time chasing scuttling black spiders with the nozzles of their hoses. The setup reminded Bradley of Jack's recent invention idea. Great minds think alike.

Bradley locked his eyes with Claire's and tried to convey calm across the divide between them but all he saw was terror in his mother's eyes. The second hazmat officer kicked the door closed to control the scrambling spiders, which at last view appeared to be spreading across the floor in all directions.

Bradley tried to run for the door, but the nurse held him back. He was stronger than he looked.

"Let them do their jobs," the nurse said. "Nothing's going to happen to her."

"Did you see how many there were?"

The nurse cast his eyes toward Claire's door. "I did."

Cut off from all visual clues, Bradley had no choice but to wait. It was the longest twenty minutes of his life.

BRADLEY SAT ON a nearby bench and focused his attention on the door to Claire's hospital room. The crowd in the corridor had dispersed, making surveillance easier.

When the door cracked open, Bradley was first to stand. He made a beeline to the door and pushed it, but the door only opened a few inches more before stopping. He heard laughter emanate from within the room, which eased his worries somewhat.

Bradley pushed the door again, and again it didn't budge. He resorted to knocking. A black woman in a hazmat suit with the hood off poked her head around the door and smiled.

"You must be Bradley," she said.

"Yes, ma'am. Can I come in?"

The black woman turned her head back toward the inside of the room. "Can he come in?" Laughter rose up again. She stepped aside and pulled the door wider. "Your clearance has been approved."

Bradley stepped into the room and met Claire's eyes. The terror was gone and she looked like her old self again, except for her left leg. He was across the room in a flash, bending over to give her a hug and not caring about the two onlookers in hazmat suits.

"We'll be off now, Ms. Shaw," said the Caucasian man, who stood a head shorter than the woman. "No more bouquets, okay? Just to be safe."

Claire nodded. "Brad, this is Harry and Monique. You should have seen them. A symphony of suction."

Monique laughed as she coiled the hose around the top of the wet/dry vacuum. "Just doing our job, although I have to say we haven't had to deal with spiders for a very long time."

"Years," Harry added. "These ones kept us on our toes, super aggressive, but I think we got them all. If you see any stragglers, don't hesitate."

"I won't." Claire held up her phone, then turned to Bradley. "They gave me their direct hospital line."

Harry and Monique left the room with the vacuum and a garbage bag in tow, their boisterous voices still audible even when they disappeared from sight down the corridor.

"Are you okay?" Bradley asked. "You didn't get bit again?"

"No."

Bradley cast a glance at Claire's left leg.

"And no real improvement there either." Claire sighed. "Or if there is, it's damn slow. If the antibiotics don't work, I may lose my leg."

"You won't lose your leg." Bradley looked around the room. "Where's the bouquet?"

"Harry trashed it."

"It was from Alexis, wasn't it?"

Claire blinked in surprise. "Yes, it was. How did you know?"

"I saw her leaving as I got here." The muscles in Bradley's jaws tensed as he gritted his teeth. "She had no reason to be here other than to bring you a bouquet. Doesn't that seem strange to you?"

"No." Claire scrunched her brows together in confusion. "Alexis is a nice girl."

Nice girl. Bradley shivered. "And that bouquet just happened to be full of lethal spiders?"

Claire narrowed her eyes in thought. "What are you saying? That Alexis put the spiders in the bouquet on purpose? Why?"

Bradley said nothing and instead matched Claire's gaze. He knew all the reasons why.

Her jaw dropped just a bit. "No. She wouldn't do that. I could've—"

"Died?"

It was Claire's turn to remain silent.

"I think you dying was part of the plan." Bradley stared out the window. "Some kind of ultimate payback for me actually moving on with my life."

"I can't believe that."

"You need to, Mom, because it's true."

Claire crossed her arms against her chest. "Have you got proof?"

"Jesus, you sound like Maddox," Bradley said to himself. He flipped through the list of circumstantial evidence in his head. "Not exactly, but—"

"Not exactly? That's not very convincing."

Bradley grabbed Claire's hand and squeezed it. "Mom. Do you trust me?"

Claire blinked. "Yes. Of course."

"Trust me when I say that Alexis is dangerous. She's a psychopath, Mom. I'm sure of it. If she shows up again, call security."

"Okay," Claire said.

"Promise me."

Claire swallowed hard. "I promise."

Bradley sat on the edge of the bed and released a heavy breath, one of relief mixed with trepidation.

"What is it, honey?" Claire gave his shoulder a gentle squeeze.

"I called Dad." Bradley felt Claire's hand tense ever so slightly.

"That's okay," Claire said. "You can call your dad any time."

"He's here."

"Now?" Claire pulled her hand away.

"Please don't get mad." Bradley faced Claire. "I tried finding exterminators for these spiders and got nowhere. Even the police didn't give a shit. I just knew… I knew I could count on him."

"Did you talk to Roy, about the spiders?"

Bradley wanted to say how much of a coward Roy turned out to be but decided against it. "He didn't believe me either."

Whatever anger that was simmering behind Claire's eyes softened and faded away. "I'm glad you could turn to Sam for help. You two have earned each other's trust."

"Thanks, Mom." Bradley leaned in for a hug. "I'm glad you're okay."

"Me too."

"I got to go." Bradley stepped to the door. "Oh, one more thing. Am I allergic to spiders?"

"Not that I'm aware of," Claire said. "Just bees, like me, so make sure you have an epi-pen close by."

"Yup." Bradley made a mental note to replace the epi-pen he had used on Mark. "Remember, Mom. No bouquets."

Claire gave Bradley a thumbs up before he headed toward the stairs at the end of the corridor. Before entering the stairwell, he pulled out his phone and tapped out a text.

"Alexis gone 2 far. Siempre in 30?" He hit "send" and pocketed his phone, not waiting for a response. The #14 bus would be rolling past the hospital at any moment.

BRADLEY RESENTED THE distraction that Alexis had caused. Finding the source of the spider invasion was his number one priority, but this side mission was too important to ignore.

He stepped off the bus five blocks from Taco Siempre and checked the time on his phone: 4:40 p.m. He had to hustle. Bradley secured his day pack on his shoulders and settled into a brisk jog.

With the wind in his hair and his muscles working like a well-oiled machine, Bradley propelled his body forward in a surge of positive energy. He forgot about Alexis for a moment and instead his thoughts settled on Roy and his obsession with running.

Maybe the guy isn't all that bad... or maybe it's the endorphins talking.

Bottom line: the running felt good. But as soon as he could see Taco Siempre in the distance, he tabled his thoughts about Roy for another day and returned to the problem of Alexis.

Jack and Trillian stood in the parking lot. Bradley joined them and caught his breath beside Jack's Civic.

"Spill it, bro," Jack said. "I'm dying here."

Bradley held up his hand, still breathing fast. "Just a sec."

Trillian smirked and shook her head. "Such a drama queen." Jack laughed and bumped fists with her.

"Drama queen my ass." Bradley took one more deep breath and looked at them both. "Alexis tried to kill my mom today."

Both Jack and Trillian's eyes widened, both of their mouths dropping open.

Bradley left them both in the parking lot as he strutted toward the restaurant. "You guys coming?" he said, holding the door open.

Jack and Trillian ran inside.

"What do you want?" Bradley said. "It's on me."

"Beef burrito and a coffee, black." Jack spotted Sofia behind the counter serving another customer and waved. She returned a smile and a subtle wave of her own. He strolled into the seating area and secured a table. "Thanks, bro," Jack called back.

"Trill?"

"Just a coffee, thanks. Cream and sugar." Trillian scanned Bradley's face for clues but saw none. "So, how did Alexis try and kill your mom?"

"Take a guess." Bradley stepped up to the counter, relayed the order to Sofia, and paid. "Put the order under Jack's name."

"Sure," Sofia said, casting a look in Jack's direction.

Trillian sat next to Jack as Bradley slid into the seat across from them. He placed his hands on the table.

"Look, I have no idea," Trillian said.

"Huh?" Jack looked back and forth between Trillian and Bradley. "What did I miss?"

"I ran into Alexis at the hospital today," Bradley said. "She was leaving as I arrived."

"Yeah, you were there to see your mom." Jack strummed his fingers on the table. "This is all old news, except the Alexis part."

"Confesh… I was really there to talk to Mark."

"What?" A look of mild hurt and surprise crossed Jack's face. "Why didn't you tell me that before?"

"I don't know. I didn't want to make a big deal about it."

"Hate to break up this male bonding session, but why am I here?" Trillian blew a lock of rainbow hair from her face.

"Order for Jack," Sofia called out from the front counter.

"You can thank me later," Bradley said.

Jack grinned, his hurt feelings evaporating, and leaped out of his seat. He messed up Bradley's hair on his way to the front counter.

"I don't want this to get weird, but Alexis thinks you and me are going out." Bradley tried to maintain eye contact with Trillian, which was made more difficult by the apparent ease with which Trillian returned his gaze.

"We'd have to like each other first." An inkling of a smile

began at the corners of her mouth. "So, Brad, do we like each other?"

Heat rose at the back of Bradley's neck. "Sure. We're friends, right? Friends like each other."

"And when we go out, we go out as friends, right?"

"Uh, right." Bradley looked at the counter, hoping for salvation, but Jack and Sofia appeared to be deep in conversation.

Trillian saved him instead. "Is this getting weird?"

"It's getting weird."

Hidden behind her long rainbow hair, Trillian revealed a warm smile and all at once Bradley felt at ease. He definitely liked her.

"My point is Alexis is jealous, and I think she's a psychopath." Bradley clasped his hands. "I didn't see it last year when I was dating her, but I see it now."

Jack slid the tray with three coffees, some cream and sugar, and a burrito onto the table. He returned to his seat next to Trillian and grabbed his coffee first, then the burrito, ripping into it. "What'd I miss?"

"Alexis is a jealous psychopath." Trillian took a lid off one of the coffees and poured two creamers and a sugar into it, stirring it with a spoon. She blew on it and took a sip.

"Shit, everyone knows that," Jack said through a mouthful of burrito. "What's up with your mom and Alexis?"

Bradley took the remaining coffee and added cream and sugar to his as well. "She brought her a bouquet of flowers that was loaded with spiders."

"Sporkies?" Trillian placed her cup of coffee on the table.

Bradley nodded. "I'm sure of it. We all know what they look like. If one of them had bitten her, even once, she probably would have died."

"Shit." Jack paused his furious consumption, but his cheek was still filled with food.

"They got rid of the spiders with a vacuum," Bradley said. "You would have loved it."

"Told you it was a good idea." Jack grinned. "Bet they didn't use razorblades."

Bradley sipped his coffee and shook his head.

"So, what are we going to do?" Trillian looked back and forth between Bradley and Jack. "Have you told your dad yet?"

"Fuck, no." Bradley choked on his coffee. "This stays between us. Even though my parents are divorced, my dad still cares about my mom. He would lose his shit if he found out."

"What, then? Seems to me that someone or some *thing* needs to lose their shit." Trillian dumped another creamer into her coffee. "How about we put an egg sac into Alexis's bed?"

"Girl, I like the way you think." Jack took another bite of his burrito.

"We can't physically hurt her," Bradley said, "and that might kill her."

Trillian shrugged. "From the sounds of it, it'd be no big loss."

"I think we need to get a confession. Record it on video."

Jack leaned into the table, smiling and chewing.

"You've obviously been thinking about this a lot." Trillian guided her long, rainbow locks over one ear. "What's your plan?"

"I'll tell you on the way. Do you mind driving, Jack?"

Jack gave Bradley a sideways glance and grinned. "What are friends for?"

The three took fortifying gulps of their coffees and headed for the door. Sofia caught Jack's attention, held her thumb and pinky to her face like a phone, and mouthed the words "call me." He gave her a thumbs up.

Bradley caught the exchange as he held the door for his friends. "Smooth, man."

"Damn straight."

The three piled into Jack's Civic from the passenger side and in less than a minute, they were zooming toward Alexis's house, with Bradley in the back seat laying out a plan.

JACK PARKED THE Civic a block away from Alexis's house and the three of them regrouped on the sidewalk.

"You think that's going to work?" Jack eyed Bradley with a doubtful look. "She's not going to fall for that shit."

"What else can I do? I have no proof."

"We could kick the shit out of her." Trillian didn't bat an eye. She was dead serious. "Ambush her, three against one. It'd be easy."

"Remind me never to cross you." Jack bumped fists with Trillian.

Bradley shook his head. "We can't use violence. We have to outsmart her."

"What about calling the police, or faking your mom's death?" Trillian smiled, her eyes sparkling.

"You're full of great ideas," Bradley said, "but that sounds a little complicated. Besides I tried calling the cops about the spiders before and they couldn't be bothered."

"It would sure fuck with her head, though, wouldn't it?"

All three laughed.

"Let's stick to the plan." Bradley led the way down the sidewalk toward Alexis's house.

"I still don't think she'll confess," Jack said. "I mean why would she?"

"I got to try. Attempted murder is serious."

Alexis's house was of modest size, painted white, with a verandah extending from the front door. Flanking the door were two tall bay windows that offered almost a one-hundred and eighty degree view of the front yard. Rows of hibiscus shrubs lined both sides of the property, securing it from prying eyes.

The three of them paused out of sight in front of the house next door.

Bradley took out his phone and loaded the voice recording app. He tapped the record button and placed the phone in his shirt pocket. It was just deep enough to entirely conceal the phone. "Say something."

"When you gonna get your driver's license, bro." Jack looked back at his orange Civic a block away. "Drive me around for a change. Shit."

Bradley pulled out his phone and replayed the audio. "Sounds pretty good to me. And to answer your question, a few more months. Sorry to be such a *burden*."

"I was just fucking with you," Jack said.

Bradley restarted the recorder and placed the phone back into his pocket. "Jack, you shoot video and we'll sync the audio up after."

"I'll record video too," Trillian said. "Always good to have a backup, right?"

"Right." Bradley glanced over his shoulder. "I don't see her parents' cars, so if she's home, she'll be alone. And she'll be watching from the front window."

"What if she's with her little entourage?" Trillian thought of everything.

Bradley shrugged. "I guess I'll roll with it. You ready?"

Trillian and Jack nodded.

"Recording?"

"Yes, now let's do this shit." Jack waved him off. "Go."

"Showtime." Bradley took a deep breath. He walked down the sidewalk and cut across the front lawn to the interlocking brick path that led to the verandah. He always cut across the lawn, something that Alexis's foster father had grown to despise.

He recalled the terror he'd seen in Claire's eyes earlier in the day and was surprised how easily his anger reignited.

Bradley stepped onto the verandah and skipped the doorbell, choosing to pound on the front door with his fist. He paced back and forth, stopping with his back to the door. A casual glance at the shrubs that hid Jack and Trillian showed nothing out of the ordinary. Their concealment was perfect.

The familiar sound of the deadbolt retracting caused Bradley's muscles to stiffen. How many times had he knocked on Alexis's door over the past year? Too many times to forget. Familiarity bred apprehension, but he managed to hold on to his anger. The front door creaked open.

Hector still hadn't greased the hinges.

"Finally come to your senses, lover boy?"

Bradley turned around to find Alexis leaning against the doorframe. She wore a red halter top tied only at the neck and a black leather miniskirt. Old feelings of attraction returned surprisingly quickly, but he fought them back and stepped forward.

"Stay away from my mom."

Alexis ran her hand down the doorframe. "What do you mean? Did something happen?"

Bradley took a step forward. "You know what happened."

"I brought your mom some flowers." Alexis smiled. "Nothing wrong with that, is there?"

"Where'd you get them?"

"What? The flowers?" Alexis furrowed her brow in thought. "I think it was called Daisy Days?"

"Not the flowers." Bradley forced his words through gritted teeth. "The spiders."

"I don't know anything about any sp—"

Bradley grabbed Alexis's throat and pinned her against the exterior wall of the entryway. She didn't flinch or show any signs of fear. It was like she had expected—and prepared for—this reaction.

"Bullshit."

Bradley's grip on Alexis's throat was loose enough to allow her to speak.

She smirked. "This is different. I didn't know you liked it rough, lover boy." With one of her free hands, she pressed her palm onto Bradley's crotch. He released her immediately and backed away, as if her skin had become too hot to touch.

"Where'd you get them?"

"Sorry. Can't help you." Alexis ran her hand up her abdomen and across her breasts underneath her loose halter top. "Or maybe I can."

Bradley resisted her temptations. "I have surveillance video of you with the bouquet... and the spiders."

The veil of nice on Alexis's face faded away and her eyes narrowed, revealing pure cunning. "You're a liar."

"The police won't think so."

Alexis stared at Bradley, fuming.

"Admit it," he said. "You went to the hospital today to kill my mom. Attempted murder isn't going to look good on your college applications."

Alexis balled her hands into fists, her knuckles turning white. "I think you better get the fuck off my property."

It was Bradley's turn to watch Alexis unravel. "You think you're so smart. But I know you Alexis, a lot better than you think I do."

Alexis stepped forward. "Fuck you, asshole!" She pushed Bradley backward on the verandah. Her hand recognized the size and shape of his phone in his shirt pocket. They locked gazes, and in that instant they both knew what the other was thinking.

"Insurance." Bradley grinned, tapped his pocket and stepped

off the porch. Alexis retreated into the house and slammed the door.

Bradley was almost to the curb when Alexis emerged from the house again. She had put a t-shirt on over her halter top.

"You motherfucker!" She ran down the concrete paving stones, following Bradley. "I'll fucking kill you, too! You hear me? I'll fucking kill you and—"

Bradley stopped beside the hibiscus bushes. Jack and Trillian stood up beside him, both still recording video on their phones.

"You better watch your back, Alexis." Bradley turned to Jack and Trillian. "Keep rolling," he whispered. All three walked back toward Jack's car.

"You and your friends are dead! Especially you, Rainbow Brite! You hear me?" Alexis began to run but didn't get far in bare feet.

"Hey, Alexis!" Trillian raised her middle finger and shot her arm out. Bradley and Jack followed suit. Without hesitation, Trillian turned to Bradley, pulled his face to hers and kissed him on the mouth for one… two… three seconds.

"Damn, bro!" Jack said, playing it up for Alexis.

Bradley's eyes bugged out. Trillian released him and grinned. "All for show. Don't get any ideas," she whispered.

Jack, Bradley and Trillian piled into the Civic, laughing loudly amongst each other, and peeled out, leaving Alexis fuming on the sidewalk.

"That was bad-ass!" Jack could barely contain himself as he piloted the little car down the street.

Trillian looked back from the front passenger seat. "But did you get a confession?"

"Wasn't that enough?"

"Seriously?" Trillian slumped back into her seat.

"What we *do* have is gold." Bradley reclined in the back seat and grinned.

"But we still don't know for sure where she got her spiders or if she has more," Trillian said. "That's a problem."

"It's a small problem."

Trillian turned in her seat to face Bradley again. "How is a psychopath with deadly spiders a small problem? She already tried to kill your mom."

"Trill's got a point, bro," Jack said.

"Okay, maybe it's not a small problem, but she's scared."

"Great. A scared psychopath," Trillian said. "I still don't like it."

Bradley was content to have won the battle this time around, but he couldn't dismiss Trillian's concerns.

Reparations

Mr. Silver sat at his desk at the front of the class, feet up, with his e-reader in his hand. He looked up at Bradley for only a second, enough time to register his disapproval of Bradley's tardiness.

One of the last to arrive for class this morning, Bradley heard his homeroom buzzing with conversation. He spotted Trillian and took a seat next to her.

"What's going on?"

Trillian motioned to a printed notice on his desk. "Mad Dog finally grew a pair."

Bradley picked up the notice on his desk. Across the top it read, "Pest Control at Washbrook: An Information Session."

Bradley shook his head. "Talk about burying the lead."

"I know, right?"

" 'A school event open to both parents and students'? What an asshat. No one's going to come to this."

"But there's going to be… refreshments." Trillian grinned, waved her hands and flashed her eyebrows. "Tempted?"

"Uh, no. It's probably going to be stale cookies and bad coffee made in an aluminum percolator from the seventies." Bradley propped his head up with his arm. "But it's your first info session at Washbrook. It just might rock your world."

They both laughed.

The morning bell rang. Bradley shoved the paper notice into

his day pack and followed Trillian to the classroom doors with everyone else.

"You're going… right? To the thing tonight?"

Trillian broke into a southern drawl. "Be still my beating heart. I wouldn't miss it for the world."

"Nice accent." Bradley said. "Another hidden talent of Trill exposed. You think your parents are going to come?"

"Doubtful." Trillian hid her face behind her colored hair. "I'll play it down."

"I'll bet Roy will blow it off, too."

"His loss," Trillian said. "The guy could use some education."

Bradley paused at his locker as Trillian continued down the hallway. "If I don't see you later, I'll see you tonight."

She spun around and gave Bradley a "hang loose" sign with her thumb and pinky finger, before carrying on her way.

Bradley watched Trillian walk down the hallway until she was surrounded by the mass of other students finding their way to class. The girl had style and confidence on lock, traits that he admired, and he found himself wondering if she had a boyfriend.

BRADLEY DIDN'T SEE Trillian later, or Jack, not even at lunch break. A group text to the two of them remained unanswered all day. The lack of response didn't feel right and a ball of worry began to grow in the pit of his stomach.

From the chit chat Bradley overheard in his classes over the course of the day, no one was talking about Maddox's information session either.

By the time the dismissal bell rang, Bradley couldn't stand it anymore. He grabbed his things and headed out to the student parking lot to find Jack. His orange Civic, a uniquely unnatural color that made the vehicle easy to spot, was nowhere to be seen.

Bradley's thoughts grew dark. *What if Alexis had done something to him?* She was capable of anything now.

He headed back to the school's south stairwell and spotted Trillian leaving, her knapsack slung over her shoulder.

"Hey. Did you get my texts?" Bradley's air of panic did not go unnoticed.

Trillian laughed. "I forgot to tell you. I left my phone at home today. Just in case of a run-in with Miss Psychopath."

Bradley sighed. "I can't get a hold of Jack either."

"I'm sure he's got a good reason."

Trillian scanned the crowd pouring out from the school. Bradley knew who she was looking for.

"Walk home with me?" she asked. "You know, safety in numbers?"

"Sure, because it couldn't possibly be the company."

"Well, that might be part of it too." She grinned and nudged his shoulder.

The two of them merged with the other students heading down the sidewalks on both sides of Stonehurst Avenue.

Alexis stood on the landing in the south stairwell, a spot that had become a regular surveillance point for her, and watched Bradley and Trillian through the window. Her dark eyes dropped a shade darker.

Fifteen minutes later, Bradley and Trillian arrived in front of her house on Bromont.

"Thanks, Brad." She placed her hands on his broad shoulders and planted a light kiss on his cheek. "I'll see you tonight."

"By the way, I'm not getting any ideas." Bradley grinned. "Are you?"

Trillian hopped up her front walk without saying a word, hiding her face with her rainbow hair.

"Bye." Bradley waited until Trillian was safe inside before continuing home to find the lights on in the living room. Roy was already home.

To distract himself from having to share the same space as Roy, Bradley tried texting Jack again. And again, there was no response. He tried calling and got Jack's voicemail.

Where are you, Jack?

Bradley texted O'Connor. "Pest control info sesh at my skool 2nite. Wanna crash it?"

O'Connor's response was immediate. "Fuck ya. When?"

"7:30"

"Wanna lift?"

Bradley sent a "thumbs up" emoji before pocketing his phone and heading inside the house.

As soon as he walked through the door, he was hit by the smell of burning hair, garlic and something else he couldn't be sure of.

Roy sat on the couch watching television, his bare feet propped up on the coffee table. Bradley wanted to smack them off but decided the fallout wouldn't be worth it. He kicked off his shoes and headed for his bedroom.

"Your mom forwarded me that email, about that talk at your school tonight," Roy said without looking away from the television. "Can't make it. Got other plans."

"Do they involve getting off your ass?" Bradley said under his breath. He unloaded his day pack onto his desk and contemplated doing homework. Anything to distract him from the unappetizing miasma that hung heavy in the house, and now, his bedroom.

He opened his window, letting deliciously fresh air into his room and wondered if he might see a rat on the sill. But his thoughts soon returned to the spiders—*sporkies*—that he'd encountered regularly over the past couple of weeks and he closed the window up tight again.

Roy opened the door to his bedroom.

"What the hell!" Bradley glared at him. "Don't you knock?"

"Sorry." Roy shrugged. "I made some linguine with clam sauce, if you want some. It's pretty good."

"What did you do, rub your balls in it?" Bradley muttered.

"What was that?" Roy crossed his arms. "You're always mumbling."

"I said no thanks. I'm allergic to clams. I'll make myself something else."

"Suit yourself."

After Roy closed the door, Bradley pulled his copy of *The Handmaid's Tale* by Margaret Atwood out of his day pack. It was the first book that Mr. Silver had assigned for English class. He flopped on his bed and picked up where he had left off. Despite it being a compelling read, he fell asleep, waking just after seven o'clock.

"Shit!" Bradley leaped out of bed and ran to the kitchen. Roy was still planted in front of the television. Apparently, his plans tonight did not include getting off his ass.

He reheated a frozen burrito and grabbed his shoes. The air inside the house still dripped with the essence of Roy's "linguini and clam sauce." Stepping outside and inhaling fresh air was a moment of bliss.

Bradley slipped on his shoes and wolfed down his burrito, a far cry from Taco Siempre. Jack would have smacked him for eating it.

At twenty past seven, a text chimed through on Bradley's phone.

"Need a lift?" Jack had sent the text to both him and Trillian.

"Catching a lift with my Dad," Bradley tapped out.

Trillian responded with "YP" followed by "smile" and "thumbs up" emojis.

"CU there," Jack texted back.

Minutes ticked by. After seven thirty came and went Bradley worried that O'Connor had forgotten where he lived. He hated being late for anything.

"Where R U?" Bradley texted to O'Connor.

Shortly after tapping send, a text from Claire popped up. "Got the email about the pest thing. Is Roy going?"

"No. Roy has plans." Bradley tapped.

"Ok. Let me know the deets L8R. xoMom"

Bradley smiled, distracted by Claire's attempt at teen slang in her text. He appreciated the effort. As soon as he pocketed his phone, he heard the rumble of O'Connor's baby blue Mustang convertible. She pulled to the curb and tapped her horn, just for the hell of it. Sam opened the passenger door and flipped the seat forward.

"What're you waiting for?" O'Connor called out. "Get your ass in the car. Don't want to be late."

Bradley ran to the car and hopped into the back seat. "We're already late. Did you get my text?"

Sam sat back down and closed the door. "Let it go, Brad."

O'Connor ignored Bradley's question. "Being a few minutes late ain't going to hurt no one."

"Except our credibility," Bradley said.

O'Connor swiveled in her seat, her cigar smoldering between her teeth, and sniffed the air. "Is that… you?"

Bradley blushed. "Sorry. Roy made clam sauce and it's nasty. How bad is it?"

"You smell like you've had a weekend pass at a bargain whorehouse."

Sam started to laugh.

"The ride should air you out, especially the way I drive." O'Connor puffed on her cigar. "Where the hell am I going?"

"Just go straight. You're going to want to get on Stonehurst." Bradley sniffed his shirt and billowed it back and forth. "You can't miss it."

"Buckle up!" O'Connor floored the gas and laid a fifteen foot strip of rubber down Sheldon Street.

"Just don't kill us or someone else." Bradley gripped the seat and closed his eyes to try and calm himself but ended up making his anxiety worse. It was moments like this where his raccoon tail would have helped smooth things out.

"Tone it down, Bertha," Sam said.

"Oh, boy. You know Sam means business when he calls me *Bertha*." O'Connor slowed her speed only slightly as she continued on her way.

The trip lasted a few minutes. Bradley directed O'Connor to the student parking lot. He hadn't expected the lot to be packed, but there were less than a dozen vehicles parked. O'Connor screeched to a stop in an open stall and killed the engine.

"What the f—" Bradley hopped over the side of the car, not waiting for Sam to open the side door.

Sam looked at O'Connor, then followed Bradley into the parking lot. "What's wrong?"

Bradley looked at his phone and shook his head. 7:42 p.m. "Come on. We're late."

"Late, my ass," O'Connor grumbled.

Sam and O'Connor followed Bradley to the school's main entrance. He pointed at O'Connor's cigar. "You need to put that out."

"Says the kid who reeks of a weekend fuckfest."

"Shit." Bradley pulled his shirt to his nose. "Does it still smell?"

Sam waved his hand. "You're fine." He shared a glance with O'Connor and cut her protest short. "Just do it."

O'Connor reluctantly rubbed the cigar out on the pavement and shoved it into her breast pocket. "This better be good."

Bradley led the way to the auditorium. A tall, aluminum coffee maker, exactly as he had described to Trillian, sat on a table beside the doors. Beside that, paper cups and a box of no-name brand cookies. Sam and O'Connor stocked up on both.

O'Connor jammed a cookie into her mouth as she looked

around the auditorium. "What'd I tell you?" Crumbs flew with each word. "We're not late. It hasn't even started yet."

Bradley estimated two dozen people were seated inside the auditorium. He spotted Jack and Trillian sitting in the back row and joined them.

"You were right about everything," Trillian said. "The cookies are *gross*."

"Mad Dog's nothing if not consistent." Bradley spied Fiscara sitting in the front row to the left of the stage. Mark and his parents sat in the middle of the auditorium, several rows ahead. Bradley gave him a casual wave. Mark nodded back, said something to his parents, and strolled to Bradley's row.

"Can I sit here?" Mark looked out of his element, an athlete among nerdy academics.

"Yeah, sure." Bradley turned to Trillian and Jack. "Can you guys shift down one?"

"No worries." Jack shifted down one seat, followed by Trillian.

"Keep shifting your butts." O'Connor bumped Mark over with her hip. "Two more."

The whole line of students shuffled to make room for Sam and O'Connor.

Mark turned to Bradley. "Who are these people?"

"The one on the end is Sam, my dad," Bradley said. "The woman next to you is Bertha O'Connor. She works with him, but don't call her Bertha or she'll tear you a new asshole."

Mark leaned closer to Bradley and lowered his voice. "You were right about Alexis. Bitch to the max. But Caitlin seems normal, even though it's hard to talk to her alone. She hangs out with Alexis a lot."

Bradley recalled his run-in with Alexis in the boys' washroom. "None of the *banditas* are sweet and innocent. They do anything Alexis says." He looked at Mark. "Be careful and good luck."

Principal Maddox held a piece of paper in his hand as he paced in front of a microphone on the stage. Occasionally, he looked out at the smattering of seated people waiting for the presentation to begin. He looked at his watch and his process cycled again.

O'Connor leaned toward Sam. "Who is this joker? Wait, why am I asking you?" She cackled, slapped her knee, and elbowed Sam in the ribs.

"That's our principal, Brent 'Mad Dog' Maddox," Mark said.

"Mad dog? That's rich." When O'Connor laughed her whole body shook. "We'll see about that."

Maddox ceased his pacing, stepped to the microphone and turned it on. "First, let me say thank you to all staff, parents, and students that came out tonight. I appreciate your interest." He paused and looked out onto the epic failure of his own making. "Due to low numbers, I have decided to reschedule this information session during school time."

"This is bullshit," a voice rang out.

"At least give us some details!" Mark's father raised his fist and shook it.

"Calm down, everyone, please," Maddox said.

"Calm down? My daughter might lose her hand!" a mother called out. Bradley craned his neck to see who it was but couldn't single her out from the cluster of other parents.

"What I can offer are some words from our resident expert." Maddox turned to look at Fiscara in the front row. "Miss Fiscara?"

She remained at the first row of seats and took the microphone from Maddox. "Good evening. My name is Wendy Fiscara and I teach biology. It is true that the density of spiders per square mile has increased dramatically this year over last. A few students and I have done some preliminary research on the spider outbreaks in our area. I have a theory that the lack of rain this summer pushed spiders into the school grounds and into the back yards of the surrounding homes."

"Why?" someone called out from the crowd.

"Most people like to keep their lawns green over the summer," Fiscara continued. "That requires water. More water means more insects. Spiders are exceptional hunters and go where the food is. But it's also apparent that the spiders we're seeing are more aggressive than most. You have every right to be concerned because—"

Maddox pulled the microphone cord, snatching the microphone away from Fiscara. "Thank you for sharing your knowledge, Miss Fiscara."

"But I wasn't—"

"Thank you." Maddox talked over Fiscara's protests. "Please take your seat."

"What are you going to do about this?" Mark's father called out.

"Now, there's no proof that the school is in any danger."

"How do you know? You haven't done any investigation." Mark's father stood, gripping the seat back in front of him. "Hire some damn professionals. Last thing we want is more attacks."

"Or deaths!" a voice cried out.

"No one's died." Maddox strained to maintain a calm voice.

"Not yet," someone said.

"You need to shut the school down and deal with this." Mark's father sat down, his wife placing her arm around his shoulder in an attempt to calm him.

"Rest assured that your children's safety is our utmost concern." Maddox continued his attempt to calm the small crowd. "Should a problem within the school be identified and confirmed with physical evidence, we will deal with it at that time. Until then, the school will remain open."

"Whoever said this was bullshit was right." O'Connor stood up, pushed by Sam, and marched down the aisle. Her approach interrupted Maddox's stammering, and by the time she was halfway to the stage, all eyes were on her.

"Get ready for some classic O'Connor," Sam said, grinning.

O'Connor cast a suspicious glance at Fiscara before hoisting herself to the edge of the stage. She swung her right leg up and rolled her body the rest of the way. She looked up at Maddox. "Don't just stand there. Help me up."

Maddox extended his hand. O'Connor grabbed it and pulled herself to her feet. She slid her cigar out of her pocket and placed it between her lips. Her hand produced a Zippo, the flame popping as if by magic, and she reignited the cigar's tip.

Maddox stared at her, unsure how to proceed. "Just what in the hell do you think you're doing?"

O'Connor's cheeks puffed smoke until the cigar's end glowed orange. She drew in a long toke and blew a thick smoke ring at Maddox's face.

"I think you better come up with better questions." O'Connor took the microphone off the stand, drew in a mouthful of cigar smoke, and propelled smoke rings out toward the audience.

"She taught me how to do that in New York," Bradley said to Trillian and Jack. "But the smoke's gross. You can't inhale."

"If it's gross, you ain't doing it right." Jack smiled. "And there's something sexy about a woman and a stogie."

Trillian rolled her eyes and ignored them both. "Whatevs."

"You all have questions that aren't getting answered." O'Connor channeled her inner William Shatner. "I'm here to change that. Who am I? The name's O'Connor, owner-operator of Detest-A-Pest Extermination Services from the Bronx, New York City." She pointed to the back row. "I work with Brad Shaw's dad."

Bradley and Sam offered small waves to the people who looked back.

"My job is to rid the world of the creepy crawlies that keep you up at night, and in this case, the ones that can kill you… and your kids."

Maddox stomped toward O'Connor. "That's quite enough."

"Back off, buzzcut." O'Connor held her free hand up, the smoldering cigar wedged between her index and middle finger like a red-hot brand. "Or someone out there is going to take a video and that video will go viral. You catch my drift?"

Maddox stopped, his face flushing red with anger. He looked at the audience and saw a few people had taken the hint and pulled out their phones.

"This school has a spider problem," O'Connor continued. "I've seen them, and I've seen what they can do. Some of you know exactly what I'm talking about." Nods and murmurs of affirmation echoed through the crowd. She cast a disgusted glance at Maddox. "Some don't believe it, but I'm here to tell you the threat is real."

"Why should we believe you?" a voice shot out.

"Because I know what the hell I'm talking about," O'Connor said. "And I got twenty-three years of battle scars to prove it." She dragged a chair from the side of the stage, sat down, and raised the cuff of her left pant leg.

"Here it comes." Sam grinned at Mark. "O'Connor's a master of BS."

"Not only do I terminate the vermin I face, I also survive to tell the tale." O'Connor pulled off her prosthetic leg and held it aloft to gasps in the crowd. "I lost my leg to one very bad spider bite. I have no love for those eight-legged bastards."

She folded back the suspension sleeve, slipped her leg back on and stood. "And neither should you." She kicked the chair back across the stage. "You just got to decide what you want." She held the microphone to her chest. "Action?" She pointed the microphone at Maddox. "Or inaction."

O'Connor blew a cloud of blue smoke back at Maddox and tossed the microphone back at him before turning toward the stairs on the left side of the stage. Maddox ran after her and pulled her aside.

"Who the hell do you think you are, coming into my school like this and spouting your *bullshit*. I could have you in jail so fast it would make your head spin." Maddox, who was taller than O'Connor by at least half a foot, stood glaring down at her.

"I'm the one who's going to save your school... and your career." O'Connor tapped the top of the microphone in Maddox's hand, the sound echoing through the auditorium. "Some advice? You might want to turn off the microphone before you threaten someone... *Mad Dog*."

Jack looked dreamily toward the stage. "I wish O'Connor was our principal."

"I know, right?" Trillian's eyes sparkled. "She's awesome."

O'Connor stepped off the stage stairs and passed in front of Fiscara seated in the front row. "Don't tell me you're a gutless ass-kisser, too."

Fiscara shook her head. "I've wanted pros to search the grounds from the get-go. Looks like you'll fit the bill."

"You got that right."

"Got room for one more?" Fiscara smiled. "You could use a spider expert and I'm already on good terms with the kids."

O'Connor gnawed on her cigar and blew smoke toward the ceiling. She looked Fiscara up and down, smirked, and continued toward the back of the auditorium.

"Come on," she said to Sam and Bradley. "Let's blow this Popsicle stand."

"I'll text you guys later," Bradley said to Trillian, Jack and Mark, before following O'Connor and Sam out of the auditorium.

Jack looked at Trillian and Mark. "I think our lives are going to get a little more interesting."

O'CONNOR DROVE BRADLEY home after Maddox's bungled information session, her cigar clamped between her teeth. Wisps of smoke trailed behind her head as she piloted the Mustang down Stonehurst.

"Do you always drive like this?" Bradley shifted in his seat to avoid the cigar smoke.

"Get used to it baby," O'Connor cackled. "I never believed in that 'live fast, die young, leave a good-looking corpse' shit. But just living fast, that I can get behind." She glanced at Bradley in the rearview mirror. "You driving yet?"

"Not yet. Another few months to go."

"Talk to me after you get your license. You'll see." O'Connor looked at Sam in the front passenger seat. "What's with you? *Rat* got your tongue?" She laughed. "That joke never gets old."

"Maybe for you," Sam said. "That joke is beyond stale."

Bradley placed his hand on Sam's shoulder. "You okay, Dad?"

"I'm fine." Sam patted Bradley's hand and gave it a light squeeze. "It was good to see a bit of your school and meet your friends. But your principal? What a piece of work."

Bradley nodded. "A certified asshole, it's true."

"I can't wait to serve him up some fire-roasted spiders," O'Connor said. "We've got a shipment of all sorts of anti-spider merch coming, including torches. Bought it all online, shipped to the motel."

"Cool."

O'Connor grinned in the rearview mirror. "Speaking of your friends, who's the hottie with the colorful do?"

"Oh, that's Trillian." Bradley watched the sidewalk fly by next to the car. "She's just a friend."

"Just a friend, huh? She seemed to have eyes for you."

"Yeah. Just a friend." A subtle smiled formed on Bradley's lips and he hoped the red flush moving up his neck and around his ears couldn't be seen in the evening light.

O'Connor turned onto Sheldon Street and pulled up to the curb in front of Bradley's house. "Honey, we're home. And I got to take a wicked piss. That coffee went through me like shit through a goose."

"Bathroom's the second door on your right going in." Bradley waited for Sam to get out of the Mustang before stepping out himself. O'Connor was already halfway up the front walk. "And ignore Roy. His bark is worse than his bite."

O'Connor waved acknowledgement and disappeared inside the house.

Sam took Bradley aside. "Actually, there is something on my mind. Your mom."

"What about her?"

Sam locked his eyes on Bradley's. "I need to see her."

"She's not happy you're here," Bradley said. "You know that, right."

"Even so, I think it'd be good for both of us. Briefly. But I don't want to stir up trouble between you two."

"No worries." Bradley smiled. "Me and mom yell at each other occasionally, but we're rock solid. You can't change that. She's at Sun Valley Medical Center. Want me to let her know?"

"No," Sam said. "It's probably best for everyone if I surprise her."

"She doesn't like surprises much."

Sam and Bradley heard raised voices coming from inside the house, followed by the exterior screen door slamming closed.

"Suit yourself, fucknuts." O'Connor stepped out onto the front landing, her ear cocked to one side listening to someone still inside. Sam and Bradley were too far away to discern anything meaningful.

"What did you say?" O'Connor turned and entered the house again. The audible dispute rose in volume.

"I think I better deal with this," Bradley said, leading the way up the front walk.

O'Connor pushed open the screen with her right hand and smoke swirled around her head. "You don't got no balls anyway, so it doesn't matter."

Bradley and Sam met O'Connor on the steps. "What's going on?" Bradley asked.

"There was a spider in the toilet." O'Connor hooked her thumb back through the door. "The dumb fuck doesn't believe me."

Roy appeared at the entryway of the house. "I didn't see any goddamn spider."

"Yeah, that's 'cause I flushed it, you idiot."

"Wait." Bradley gave O'Connor a sideways look. "Was it a sporky?"

"I don't fuckin' know," O'Connor said. "It was big, black, and hairy, and I wasn't putting my tush and bush anywhere near that thing."

"Maybe you should have," Roy said.

"Go choke on a bag of dicks, you douche." O'Connor pushed past Bradley and Sam, headed toward the Mustang.

Bradley took a deep breath. Since meeting Roy, opportunities to apologize to him were few and far between but it was the right thing to do. That didn't mean he had to believe the sentiments. "Sorry, Roy. O'Connor has a mouth on her, but she doesn't lie about things like that. My advice is to keep your eyes open."

"I'm taking advice from a seventeen-year-old, now? Is that it?"

Bradley shrugged. "If you're smart, yeah, maybe."

"Bah." Roy, who was still in bare feet, waved him off and disappeared back into the house.

"Spiders can be anywhere," Bradley called back to no response.

"Even in your shoes," Sam added. Bradley gave him a curious glance. "I read it online. It's a common problem in Australia."

"Good to know, not that Roy ever listens to what I say."

Sam sighed, ran his fingers through his hair, and stepped down onto the front walkway.

"What?"

Sam shook his head. "It's just that things could have been so much different. For you. But I fucked all that up."

"Don't go there, Dad. You're here now." Bradley stepped down off the landing to face Sam. "And between you and Roy, there's no comparison."

"What's the holdup?" O'Connor honked the Mustang's horn and started the engine. "I'm starving and only Mexican is going to satisfy me."

"Oh God, not Mexican again," Sam said. "You created a monster. The bathroom at our motel will never be the same." Sam turned toward the curb with O'Connor not so subtly revving the engine of the Mustang.

"There's lots of other places to eat." Bradley dug into his pocket for his phone. "I'll text you some options."

"We'll figure it out."

"Say 'hi' to Mom for me."

"Wish me luck." Sam hopped into the passenger seat of the Mustang. O'Connor wasted no time slamming the gas pedal, peeling out and leaving an acrid blue cloud of smoke in her wake. The car was gone before Bradley could respond.

He headed back inside, avoiding Roy entirely, and sequestered himself in his room. There was still the essence of Roy's clam sauce in the air, an odor he would have gladly swapped for the burned rubber from O'Connor's Mustang. Bradley glanced at *The Handmaid's Tale* on his bed, just where he had left it earlier.

"Homework first," he heard Claire say in his head.

Not tonight, Mom.

Instead Bradley reclined on his bed, closed his eyes, and imagined next steps, now that Sam and O'Connor were officially on board.

"WHAT'D I TELL you before we left?" O'Connor blocked the door to the motel room. "I do the driving."

"Fine." Sam tossed O'Connor the keys to the Mustang. "But you're waiting in the car."

O'Connor threw her head back and laughed as she pulled open the door to leave. "You don't know me very well."

"You don't know *me* very well either." Sam locked the motel door behind him.

"What do yah mean?" O'Connor laid a heavy hand on Sam's back. "You're a goddamned open book."

Sam cast a look at her. "Then you obviously don't read," he said, then lowered his voice. "You have no clue."

They piled into the Mustang and O'Connor fired up the engine.

"I'll never get tired of hearing this baby purr." She backed out of the stall and followed the driving directions being piped through the speakers wirelessly from her phone. "Phones these days. How did we ever exist without them?"

"I existed just fine."

O'Connor gunned the engine and flew down the street. "Right. They don't allow phones in prison."

"Payphones, yes. Just not cell phones. If you followed the rules, that is." Sam tried to keep his mind on his impending visit with Claire, but O'Connor's constant questions made it difficult.

"Did you follow the rules?"

"I was a model inmate." Sam's eyes fell dark and distant. "No one likes a model inmate."

"Did you get beat up a lot? Were you anyone's bitch?" O'Connor fired off questions like she was facing a deadline.

"I saw my fair share of the infirmary. And I think that's where this interrogation ends."

"Don't you leave me hanging, asshole."

Sam remained silent.

"No answer is as good as 'yes' in my book." O'Connor shot a quick glance at Sam to see if he'd break. He didn't. She returned her eyes to the road flying past her. "I think I'd be the top dog. I'd run the prison yard." She chuckled to herself. "I'd be a regular Reznikov."

"Who?"

"Red. On *Orange is the New Black*."

Sam shook his head blankly at her.

"Right, you don't get Netflix." O'Connor turned right onto San Fernando Road, with Sun Valley Medical Center looming in the distance.

"It's an Internet thing. In other words, a luxury I can't afford."

"Work for me, then. Officially. I'll throw in my Netflix password as a benefit," O'Connor said.

"Thanks, but no thanks."

"You aren't hearing me. Washington getting eaten alive left me in a bad spot." O'Connor looked for a break in traffic to make a left turn. "I need an employee I can trust and you're it."

"You really know how to sell it, O'Connor," Sam said. "The answer's still no."

"No, the answer is *yes*. You just don't know it yet."

Sam regarded O'Connor behind the wheel and grinned. "Yeah, you'd be top dog alright."

O'Connor navigated into the parking lot of the hospital and immediately found a spot close to the entrance.

"You got a horseshoe up your ass, or what?"

"A lady never gives up her secrets." O'Connor batted her eyelashes underneath a backwards baseball cap and gnawed on her cigar stub.

Sam looked at her deadpan. "Sexy."

"You know it." O'Connor pulled herself out of the Mustang and slammed the door. "Let's go find your wife."

"Ex-wife… and you're not coming." Sam jogged to catch up with her. "I'm serious."

"Did you say something?" O'Connor disappeared into the hospital's main foyer.

A few minutes at the front reception led them to the fifth floor. The two exited the elevator, O'Connor leading the way down the corridor.

"Bertha!" Sam called out.

O'Connor stopped in her tracks. Before she could turn, Sam grabbed her and pushed her into the wall. He spun her around and slammed her back into the wall again. The brim of O'Connor's baseball cap hit the wall and flipped off her head. Sam pulled her cigar stub from her mouth, dropped it to the floor and ground it with his heel.

O'Connor looked at her shredded cigar, then back at Sam. "Of course, you realize this means war."

"I'll buy you a new fucking cigar." He grabbed her shirt by the collar, his fists white with anger, and pulled her face to his. "You don't want to die on this hill."

Sam's glare proved to be too much. "Okay," O'Connor raised her hands. "You win. For now."

"You'll stay out here?"

"I'll give you five minutes."

"You'll give me as much time as I need." Sam released O'Connor and dropped his fists. "Got it?"

She grinned.

Sam gave her a sideways look, still not completely calmed down. "What?"

"Sam grows a pair," O'Connor said. "Mission accomplished."

"You're such a bitch." Sam walked toward Claire's room.

"It worked didn't it?" O'Connor laughed as Sam waved her off.

SAM STOOD AT the door to room 513. If he had a do-over, he'd have shaved and worn better clothes. But there was no point trying to sugar-coat who he was now: an ex-con on the cusp of getting the remnants of his life back.

He took a deep breath and knocked on the door.

"Come in," a voice said from within the room, a voice he hadn't heard in person for the better part of fifteen years.

He looked down the corridor at O'Connor as terror and anticipation competed for his attention. She thrust her thumb to the side and he could hear her voice in his head yelling, "get your ass in there."

Sam opened the door and walked into Claire's room. She had been reading a book on gardening but dropped it to her lap and followed him with her gaze until he stood at the foot of the bed.

"Long time." Sam tried to decipher what was going on in Claire's head, but her expression eluded him. Instead, he assumed she was angry. That was a safe bet.

"Yeah."

"I know Brad told you I was in town and—"

"You should have called first." Claire crossed her arms.

Her shields are going up, Sam thought. "I didn't think you'd want to see me."

"You're right. I don't," Claire said.

The words were expected but they still stung, even after all the years Sam and Claire had been estranged.

"The last thing I want is for this to be weird, but—"

"Too late for that."

"Please Claire," Sam said. "Just let me get this out and I swear you'll never hear from me again."

Claire shrugged indifference and waited.

"It might not seem like much, but I wanted to make sure you were okay. Brad's a great kid and all, but sometimes he's a little shy on details."

Sam drew in a deep breath and dropped his head. "I'm sorry for what I did all those years ago. Leaving you to raise Brad by yourself was the worst mistake I've ever made. But he ended up a fine young man, and that's all you."

He pulled out his wallet and extracted a photo of himself and Bradley, both screaming in fake horror as he held up a dead rat by the tail. Sam looked at it and a small smile crossed his lips.

"I want to thank you for letting me get to know Brad again," Sam said. "It's my hope that you'll continue to let him be a part of my life."

"He'll be eighteen soon," Claire said. "Old enough to decide what he wants for himself."

"Age aside, I'll respect your decision." Sam handed the photo to Claire, but her arms remained crossed. He dropped it on the bed next to her uninjured leg. "That's my favorite photo of the past summer. Maybe you could add it to a scrapbook or something." Sam stepped to the door and placed his hand on the knob.

"Wait."

Sam turned his weary eyes back to Claire.

"Sorry about the rubber rat. You know, back in New York?" Claire motioned toward her injured leg. "Maybe all this is Karma biting me in the ass."

"No," Sam said. "You didn't deserve that, not any of it." As he pulled open the door, O'Connor burst into the room.

"So, this is Claire." O'Connor shuffled to the side of the bed and presented her hand. Claire reciprocated, with trepidation at first, and shook her hand firmly.

"And you are?" Claire looked from O'Connor to Sam, confused.

"Sorry," Sam said. "This is O'Connor. She's an exterminator from New York that I've been working with on occasion."

"I'm the one that's given your ex a reason to live. And on that note, us women have business to discuss." O'Connor shoved Sam out into the corridor and closed the door, jamming her work boot against the door frame to prevent it from opening.

Sam stopped himself from pounding on the door, remembering where he was, and instead knocked. "Not fair, O'Connor. Let me in."

Muffled, unintelligible voices filtered through the door.

Sam knocked again. "Come on, O'Connor." The door wouldn't budge.

Strangely, Sam didn't feel anger, but intense relief. The talk with Claire, as short as it was, had done some good. He found a bench seat next to the room and waited for O'Connor to leave. Twenty minutes later, a nurse knocked on the door, indicating the end of visiting hours.

O'Connor stepped halfway out of the room. "Think about it, okay?" She gave a small wave to Claire and let the door close. O'Connor motioned toward the elevator. "Let's motor."

"What the hell were you two talking about?"

"You know. Woman stuff." Her phone chimed in her pocket. She pulled it out to see a group text from Bradley.

"Woman stuff?" Sam walked ahead to try and gauge O'Connor's expression. "What does that mean?"

"It means stop asking questions." She hit the down call

button of the elevator, then tapped the display of her phone. "We got spiders to catch."

The elevator doors slid open and Sam and O'Connor joined the other occupants going down.

Tally Me Banana

Sam and O'Connor flew down Stonehurst and pulled into the student parking lot of Washbrook High. The only other vehicle in the lot was Jack's orange Civic. The adjoining lot for teacher vehicles still contained a few vehicles.

O'Connor reached into her breast pocket and came up empty. "You said you'd buy me a new cigar."

"Between the hospital and here? You're crazy." Sam waved her off as he stepped out of the car. "I'll make good when we're back in New York."

"I'll hold you to that." O'Connor pulled herself out of the car and limped back to the trunk. "I never abort a cigar before its time."

She popped it open with her key. Next to the small protective case for the FLIR camera sat a propane torch and two taser canes.

"Are we going to need those now?"

"Best be prepared, and all that shit." O'Connor grabbed the FLIR case and a cane. "We're supposed to be professionals, right?"

Sam took the other cane, the torch, and closed the trunk. "You're limping," he said as they approached the front doors to the school.

"It's been one of those days." O'Connor stopped in front of

the doors, waiting for Sam to open it for her. "Too much standing and walking."

"And now we have more standing and walking to do." Sam pulled open the door.

"I'll live." O'Connor shook her cane at him. "Just don't get in my way, sonny, or I'll vaporize your balls."

They found the rest of the crew, comprised of Bradley, Trillian, Jack, Mark, and Fiscara, congregating in front of the main office. Bradley was first to approach.

"How'd it go? With Mom, I mean."

"Better than I thought it would." Sam motioned at O'Connor. "But Miss Congeniality here chatted her up for half an hour."

"More like twenty minutes." O'Connor grinned.

"Whatever."

Bradley looked a confused question at Sam.

"Yeah, that's what I thought," Sam said.

O'Connor shrugged. "What can I say? We connected on a personal level."

Fiscara corralled the group. "Now that everyone's here, I thought we'd start with my classroom. We don't have much time. Maddox is giving us until five-thirty."

"Why start there?" O'Connor fidgeted, looking for a cigar where there was none.

"We began the year studying spiders," Fiscara said. "I have a tarantula there you might want to look at, plus someone stole spider egg sacs from the classroom a couple of days ago. You might see some evidence I missed. Anything else?"

"Yeah," O'Connor said. "Who put you in charge?"

Bradley, Trillian, Jack and Mark exchanged uncomfortable glances. Sam ran his hand through his hair in exasperation. "Jesus, O'Connor."

"No, it's okay." Fiscara stepped aside. "Lead the way."

The long school hallway with branching corridors stretched

out before her. O'Connor took a step forward and realized she had no idea where to go next. "Uh, Fiscara, I think it'd be better if you led the way."

"Sure thing, Captain O'Connor. *Good* decision." Fiscara walked briskly down the hallway, the group following close behind.

Jack leaned toward Bradley, Trillian, and Mark. "Let the ego battle begin," he said. They all shared a quiet laugh.

Fiscara unlocked the classroom door and directed everyone to the back.

"Um, Miss Fiscara?" Trillian's eyes met Fiscara's with a mixture of fear and concern.

Fiscara shifted her gaze to the back of the class and in an instant knew something was wrong. "Stay back!"

Killer's terrarium was filled with a milky gauze that spilled out the top and connected to the second empty terrarium and out to the back corner of the room.

"I don't think Killer's in there anymore," Bradley said.

Fiscara scanned the room and under the desks. "I think you're right."

"Wait," O'Connor said. "Who, *or what*, is Killer?"

"Killer is a Mexican Redknee tarantula." Fiscara flanked the back desks where the terrariums sat, trying to see around and behind them. "She was the class pet."

"Where is Killer *now?*" Mark stared at the back of the classroom and followed the lines of webbing to the corner where the ceiling tiles met the walls. They were pushed aside by a couple of inches.

"Or where was Killer *taken?*" Trillian asked.

"Taken?" Sam raised his eyebrows.

"I ain't liking these questions one bit." Jack pulled out his phone and took photographs of the corner of the room.

"Up to the ceiling and into the vents," Bradley said.

"If I was to guess, some spider eggs spilled from the sacs I collected from your shed." Fiscara turned and faced the group. "They've hatched and fed."

"How many?" Sam asked.

"No way to know." Fiscara looked back at the gap in the ceiling tiles. "But now they could be anywhere."

"Wait a minute." Bradley scrunched his eyebrows. "*Sacs,* as in more than one? You said in class that only one sac was stolen."

"There were three," Fiscara said. "I withheld that piece of information. At the time, what mattered was their disappearance."

"Shit." Bradley and Trillian exchanged a knowing glance.

"Who stole them?" Sam asked.

"I think it was Alexis," Bradley said, "but I have no proof."

O'Connor opened the FLIR case, attached the thermal camera to the base of her phone, and scanned the room. Apart from the rest of the group and the window, the room displayed in shades of blues and purples.

"The room's clear," O'Connor said. "Let's start in the basement and work our way up."

"Again, you and basements," Sam said.

"Basements are closer to hell." O'Connor stepped out into the hallway, making broad sweeps with the thermal camera. "It ain't no coincidence why vermin like them."

CHARLIE JESSOP HAD been custodian of Washbrook High for thirty-three years. He was the invisible heart that kept the school running like a well oiled machine all year long. If there was anything odd or out of place in the school, inside or out, Charlie knew about it. From cherry bombs in the toilets, to shit on the ceiling, fresh vomit, and luncheon meat stuffed between the pages of books in the library, as far as school high jinks went, he had seen it all.

Charlie stood wearing navy coveralls and a matching baseball cap, mopping one of the first floor boys' bathrooms in the north end of the school. Someone had had the brilliant idea of pissing on the floor instead of the urinals. But the mess here paled in comparison to the unisex staff bathroom. He failed to understand how the toilets could clog several times a week, overflowing their contents and polluting the adjoining staff room.

After dumping the clouded mop water down a toilet and flushing, he headed out the door and into the hallway for fresh water and cleanser.

"Just the man I wanted to see."

Charlie turned to see Fiscara leading a charge of students and adults down the hallway. He recognized half the faces. "What can I do for yah, Miss Fiscara?"

"Have you seen anything out of the ordinary, down in the basement?"

Charlie squinted in confusion. "Out of the ordinary... how?"

"Like spiders," Fiscara said.

"Big spiders," Bradley said.

"Big black spiders with quills on their backs," Trillian said.

"No, Miss Fiscara, and all o' yah." Charlie scanned the entourage. "Can't say I have."

Fiscara stepped aside and motioned to the group. "We've got two professional exterminators here, plus a few exterminators in training." Sam offered a small salute and O'Connor raised her brows as she scanned Charlie from head to toe and back.

Fiscara continued, "We'd like to sweep the basement for any infestation. Can you show us the way?"

Charlies snapped his fingers. "That I can do, but I don't think you'll find anything. I run a tight ship." He rolled his wheeled bucket into a storage closet and pulled out a set of keys on a retractable cord. "Follow me."

Charlie led the crew down a flight of stairs most students used for stage performances. The corridor led to dressing rooms and the seating area for the pit orchestra. The opposite end of the corridor terminated in a locked door labeled "Boiler Room."

"I can feel the heat already," O'Connor said.

Charlie pulled his keys out from his belt and unlocked the door. "Yeah, it's warm down here. Always is."

"Hope I don't have to strip down or anything." O'Connor winked at Charlie.

"Is she hitting on the him?" Trillian whispered to Bradley, Jack and Mark.

"O'Connor's not known for being subtle," Bradley whispered back to his friends.

Charlie swung the large door open and warm air smelling of oily machinery floated past them. The room was lit sparsely with bulbs nestled within protective metal cages. The furnace and attached blower units emitted a pervasive mechanical hum through the crammed space.

"I still got jobs upstairs to finish," Charlie said, "so I can't give you a guided tour. Search around but don't touch anything. I'll know if you have."

"It's not very big," Mark said.

Charlie chuckled. "It doesn't need to be. This furnace could heat a school twice the size of this one." He jangled his keys on his belt. "The door is always locked from the outside. Make sure you close it firmly when you go."

O'Connor sidled up beside Charlie. "Are you sure you can't give me a *personal* tour?"

Charlie smiled. "No can do. Been happily married for thirty-six years." He winked and tugged the brim of his baseball cap.

O'Connor relented. "Tell your wife she's a lucky woman."

"She knows it, as do I," Charlie said. "Good luck. I hope you find what you're looking for." He stepped back through the doorway, allowing the boiler room door to swing closed with a resounding metal *clunk*.

With a wary eye Mark surveyed the boiler room and said under his breath, "I hope we *don't* find what we're looking for."

Fiscara stood with her hands on her hips. "Now that your date is over, what's the plan, Captain O'Connor?"

O'Connor raised her eyebrows and huffed. "This won't take long if we split up. If someone sees something, yell and I'll come running."

"Splitting up is what gets people killed in the movies." Jack turned on the light in his phone and began moving the light's beam around the space.

"The movies never saw the likes of me." O'Connor raised the phone and thermal camera, then pointed at Jack and Trillian. "You two, come on."

"The name's Jack."

"Great. Now you can't say 'I don't know Jack.' " O'Connor laughed. "The rest of you start on the opposite wall and we'll meet in the middle."

The group split up, the lights on their phones popping on to aid the search. Fiscara headed for the opposite wall of the room. "She always this bossy?"

"Yeah, but she means well," Sam said. "Get her on your side and she's loyal to the end."

Bradley, Mark and Fiscara scanned the walls and overhead pipes. "You getting a sense of déjà vu, Dad?"

A shiver ran up Sam's spine as he forced images of white-tailed New York City rats back into the recesses of his memory. "Don't remind me."

Sam, Bradley, Mark, and Fiscara followed the wall to the back corner, then reversed direction around the opposite side of one of the blower units and its attached ducting.

"Man, the janitor wasn't kidding when he said we wouldn't

find anything," Mark said. "Why would spiders be in here anyway?"

"I agree. Seems a little far fetched," Fiscara said. "Spiders generally don't seek out warmth."

"O'Connor's used to tracking rats and other pests." Sam squatted to look under the blower unit. "Maybe you can gently guide her to another course of action."

Fiscara saw a used rag hanging from a nearby pipe. She lifted it off, raised her finger to her lips in a "shh" gesture, and grinned.

Bradley clued in immediately, shook his head and waved his hands back and forth, pleading "no" without saying the words.

Fiscara dropped the rag on Sam's back. "Holy shit! Sam look out!"

"Step back," Bradley whispered to Mark. "Fiscara's toast."

Sam arched his back and his muscles stiffened. "Get it off," he hissed.

"It's too big," Fiscara said. "Don't move."

"Fuck that." Sam dropped to the floor and rolled away from the blower unit, knocking the rag off his back. He looked at the torn fabric on the floor and stood. "You *bitch*."

"I was just trying to lighten the mood and—"

Sam grabbed Fiscara's t-shirt just below the collar with both his fists, backed her against the blower unit, and lifted her off her feet. Nose to nose, he fought to keep his rage from exploding. "Not fucking funny."

The fury in Sam's eyes met the fear in Fiscara's and he realized that her trickery had had the best of intentions.

"I tried to warn you," Bradley said.

"Yeah, you did." Fiscara returned her gaze to Sam. "I'm sorry, Sam. Bad idea."

"Yeah." Sam released Fiscara to the floor with one last push backward, his muscular tattooed arms peeking out of his shirt. She noticed, and now respected, his strength. "Let's finish so we can get the fuck out of here."

They met O'Connor, Jack, and Trillian between the furnace and the second blower unit.

O'Connor motioned at Sam. "Find anything?"

"No. You?"

O'Connor shook her head. "Plus, it's too hot in here to see anything on the thermal."

"I've been telling her to change the threshold values." Jack shrugged, then added, smirking, "But you can't change stupid." Trillian giggled next to him, covering her mouth with her hand.

"You better watch your backs, you little shits." O'Connor pointed at both of them. "I never forget an insult. And changing the thresholds was the first thing I did."

"It's too hot in here," Fiscara said. "We better get out before we tear each other apart."

Sam sent her a look of annoyance mixed with amusement. "I'll second that."

The crew filed out of the boiler room and back up the stairs to the first floor.

"What are we going to tell Maddox?" Mark asked.

"We could lie." Trillian looked to the others for approval.

Bradley shook his head. "He'd want physical proof. Nothing's going to be good enough for him until a spider bites him in the face."

Fiscara pulled Sam aside. "Hey, I'm really sorry for scaring you like that back there."

"Apology accepted." Sam graced her with a minimal glance and rejoined the group.

Maddox was locking the office door as the crew crested the stairs to the first floor. He scowled at O'Connor and glanced at his watch, ignoring the rest of the group. "Miss Fiscara. I wasn't expecting to see you today. You have evidence for me, I presume?"

Bradley rolled his eyes at Trillian, Jack and Mark.

"Actually, no." It was clear to everyone that Fiscara had no desire to tell Maddox the truth. "We found nothing in the boiler room. But there's also the dressing rooms and auditorium and—"

"So, your infestation theory is baseless."

"As far as the boiler room, yes. But the spiders from my classroom are somewhere—"

"But not in this school."

"We don't know. With more time, we can thoroughly search—"

"I want your…" Maddox appraised the rest of the crew with a derisive eye. "…Your *exterminators* out of here."

O'Connor stepped forward and poked Maddox in the center of his chest. "Why are you such an asshole? Huh?"

Maddox took a step backward, eyes wide with surprise. "Excuse me?"

O'Connor took another step forward. "You heard me. You're the principal here. You should care about the students' and staff's well being."

Fiscara shared a look with Sam. Bradley caught the exchange and leaned close to Sam's ear. "Are you going to stop her?" he whispered.

Sam smiled and shrugged. "Why?"

"Because the school year's just started," Bradley said. "He'll make our lives a living hell."

Maddox's eyes darkened. "I care about *everyone* in this school." He stepped forward, pushing O'Connor back with one hand. "But I don't respond well to bullying tactics."

O'Connor dug in her heels. "Most bullies don't."

Fiscara placed her hand on O'Connor's shoulder. "All we're asking for is more time to search the school before drawing conclusions."

Maddox considered Fiscara's plea. "I'll run it by the school board, but I can't guarantee anything."

"It's *your* goddamned school," O'Connor said.

"And the last thing I need is mass hysteria caused by half-baked theories from a couple of washed up exterminators."

"Mother*fucker.*" O'Connor launched herself at Maddox but Fiscara managed to pull her back before O'Connor landed any blows.

"Sam!" Fiscara held O'Connor until Sam could take over. She pulled Maddox away from the rest of the crew. "This is why no one likes you."

Maddox broke away from her and headed toward the main doors of the school. "I don't do this job to be liked."

"You can be tough *and* likeable," Fiscara followed several feet behind.

Maddox stopped at the main doors and looked back at Fiscara, pointing his finger at her. "If I see those two in my school again, I'll suspend *you* without pay." He pushed open the doors and disappeared outside.

Fiscara rejoined the crew. O'Connor looked flushed but Sam and the "exterminators in training" had rallied around her and calmed her down. "Sorry about that. Maddox is a real piece of work."

"No one calls me *washed up* and lives," O'Connor said between breaths.

Bradley crossed his arms. "We need a new plan because the spiders went *somewhere.*"

"How about we figure something out after the dance tomorrow," Trillian said.

"Sounds good." Fiscara's eyes narrowed shrewdly at Sam and O'Connor. "How would you two like to be 'chaperones?' " She air-quoted the word. "With a little spider-sleuthing on the side?"

Sam and O'Connor exchanged glances and grinned at each other.

"Of course, you're going to have to dress for the role." Fiscara alternated her gaze between the two. "You got to look like parents."

"What about Maddox?" Sam asked. "If he sees us—"

"Let me worry about Maddox."

O'Connor looked at Sam, then at the rest of the crew, one by one.

Trillian sported a wide grin. "Do it!" Jack, Bradley and Mark nodded in agreement.

"Challenge accepted," O'Connor said. "Maddox can eat my shit." The group laughed and high-fived each other as they headed for the main entrance.

"Do you think I'll still have a job come Saturday?" Fiscara said.

"I don't know." O'Connor slung one arm over Fiscara's shoulder. "We may not see eye to eye most of the time, but you got my respect." She bumped fists with Fiscara before joining Sam and the trainees heading to the student parking lot.

Fiscara watched with affection, anticipation, and a touch of worry. "What have I gotten myself into?" she said to herself. In just over twenty-four hours, she'd know the answer.

DESPITE HIS ENORMOUS size and immobility, Frank Moody made sure to never be late for his daily ritual. Every weekday at ten o'clock in the morning he rolled his motorized wheelchair in front of the old RCA television console he had picked out with Henrietta during their first year of marriage.

He guessed the television weighed more than he did, the cabinet made of solid oak and stained a rich chocolate brown. When Henrietta was alive, she'd dust the cabinet every weekend, rubbing Pledge furniture cleaner into all the intricately carved nooks and crannies.

Now the cabinet was blanketed with a thick patina of dirt and dust, with Henrietta's collection of porcelain doll heads lining the top and every other surface and shelf in the vicinity.

Moody grabbed the remote, turned on the set, and keyed in channel 2, KCBS. Henrietta, always full of good ideas, had convinced him to upgrade to a digital cable box. Looking back, it seemed that Henrietta was clairvoyant. The decision allowed Moody to stay in his wheelchair.

The sound faded up first, the familiar theme to *The Price Is Right*, followed by the picture, which was still quite good despite the television's age.

Since Henrietta's fatal heart attack three years earlier, the show's theme song and the call of contestants often brought tears to Moody's eyes, and today was no exception. Game shows had kept them engaged with one another. But the show also brought up feelings of anger and resentment, more as time moved on. His life had become more difficult without her help.

The porcelain doll heads stared back at him like they were the audience and he was the host. Moody's eyes popped open wide. "Henrietta!" He looked around the wheelchair in a panic. "Henrietta!"

He reversed the wheelchair, narrowly missing the afghan hanging over a side table, and rolled out of the living room, down the hallway and into the kitchen. Doll heads followed his every move with dark, bottomless eyes.

"Henrietta?" Moody scanned the kitchen until his eyes settled on the one thing that gave him peace. He rolled the wheelchair to the counter and picked up a doll resting against a bunch of overly ripe bananas. Its frock hung by threads in places and one lazy eye rolled back into its head.

"Henrietta, you're missing the show." He placed the doll and a banana in his lap, navigated back to the living room, and parked himself in front of the television. He kissed the top of the doll's head and propped it further up on his chest. The glow of the television reflected in the doll's one functional eye. "Don't worry, we haven't missed much."

As contestants made guesses on the actual retail price of a Sea-Doo, Moody pulled the stem of the banana off like it was made of plasticine. He peeled the skin back a third of the way to reveal glistening, overly ripe fruit within. Without looking, he wrapped his lips around it and took a bite.

"Bid more!" he yelled at the television. "At least four thousand!" Drops of saliva-diluted banana sprayed from his lips. It was then that he noticed movement in the corner of his eye.

Moody shifted his gaze from the television, searching for the source of movement. In the dim light of the living room everything looked as it should. Every doll head was positioned in the correct spot in the correct orientation… except one. The porcelain head lay on its side, with its gaping neck hole facing him. His eyes darted between the television screen and the head, but there was no further movement.

"See? Forty-five hundred." Moody grunted as he returned his focus to the game show and took another bite of his banana. "You don't know a damn thing. Stupid son-of-a—"

One of the doll heads on the top of the cabinet rolled over.

"What the…" With his free hand on the joystick control, Moody advanced the wheelchair forward until his knees touched the glowing screen of the television. He leaned his massive body forward as far as he could manage.

A black spider with a body easily the size of a ping pong ball scuttled out of the neck hole of the doll head, followed by a second, slightly smaller spider. Long, sharp quills jutted out from the backs of both arachnids, expanding and contracting in rhythm. From another doll's eye socket, its black plastic eyelashes morphed into eight hairy legs as a third smaller spider worked its way out of the darkened void.

Eyes wide with horror, Moody reversed the wheelchair into a

side table, tangling the afghan into the gears and knocking Henrietta to the floor. "No, Henri…"

He leaned sideways and fished after the doll with his free hand, but knew anything on the floor was too far to reach.

The television cabinet and nearby shelving now teemed with black spiders, too many to count. They scrambled to the edge and propelled themselves into the air, tethering themselves with strands of webbing. The larger spiders landed on Moody's feet with ease while the smaller ones dropped to the floor and began scaling up the side of the wheelchair. He worked the joystick of the wheelchair, but the afghan had rendered the motor's reverse function inoperable.

The inside of his mouth felt like it had burst into flames and something *solid and foreign* rolled on his tongue.

What was it? A hair? He worked the object to his lips and tweezed it out with his fingers. A black and hairy multiple-jointed leg hung limply from his fingertips. He swirled saliva and ripe banana in his mouth and withdrew another leg. A spider leg.

He spat a mottled grey slurry with swirls of blue into his hand. Two more legs and what looked like half of a hairy black meatball worked themselves to the top of the gruesome pool.

The feeling of cold oatmeal settled on Moody's other hand and distracted him from the heat in his mouth and the horror in his palm. He realized that he was still clutching the banana. The ripe greasy fruit had been forced out of the peel like toothpaste from a tube and lay dribbled across his wrist. From within the empty banana peel a black spider crawled out and onto his hand. Its quills vibrated, flinging small pieces of banana off its thorax and abdomen, like a wet dog fresh from a romp in a lake.

Moody dropped the banana peel but the spider jumped to his chest before he could shake it off. The arachnid closed the gap between itself and Moody's face at a furious pace. From half a foot away, the spider turned about-face and sprayed webbing onto Moody's mouth.

His throat burned, spasmed, and closed up, slowly cutting off his air supply. A throng of spiders converged upon Moody's neck and head as he fell into convulsions.

Bite after bite, spiders injected their venom into Moody's bloodstream, boiling his bodily fluids from the inside out. His eyelids swelled and began to swallow his eyes. Fleshy cheeks distended around his nose until he resembled a featureless scarecrow with a yellow balloon face filled with murky liquid. A fine network of purple veins spread across his taut, jaundiced skin.

His right hand slid off his belly and struck the joystick control of the wheelchair, jamming it forward. The electrical motor strained against the strands of afghan until it broke free and drove full speed into the television cabinet. The left stirrup smashed the television screen and flipped the wheelchair onto its right side. Smoke and sparks flew out of the cracked hole in the screen, but the familiar sounds of the game show carried on.

Moody spilled sideways from the chair, his body covered with gauzy webbing and his eyes almost completely swollen shut. The flurry of oily black spiders adjusted to Moody's new position and continued to bite and wrap his body with endless strands of webbing.

The last thing Moody saw before his eyes dissolved within their sockets was Henrietta.

The doll lay in the dirty shag carpet and stared back at him with her one blank eye. The game show's "sad tuba" sound effect played from the television's smoking speakers before Moody's world fell to blackness.

IN THE THREE years Bradley had been attending Washbrook High, the first dance of the year was always well attended. Returning to school after a two month summer break was a big adjustment. A dance helped the students blow off a little steam and settle in.

Bradley, Jack, and Trillian arrived at the school just after seven-thirty in Jack's Civic. Once inside, they made their way to the gymnasium.

Trillian alternated a look between Bradley and Jack. "You think we're going to see any spiders tonight?"

"Maybe," Jack said.

"I'm keeping my eyes open." Bradley scanned the lockers on both sides of the hallway. "My spidey sense has been tingling ever since yesterday."

"Hate to break it to you, bro, but that's just your balls dropping." Jack doubled over with laughter and Bradley shoved him hard enough that Jack almost lost his balance.

"Such a comedian… *not*." Bradley pointed at the banner that had been hung above the gymnasium entrance. It read *EQUINOX ROCKS!* in large orange letters. "I see they finally chose a name."

"It's what I would have picked," Jack said. "Especially since today actually *is* the autumnal equinox."

"All facts and no play makes Jack a dull boy," Bradley said, smirking.

"Come on boys." Trillian's smile glowed. "Let's play."

Before the three of them could enter the gymnasium, they heard someone yell Bradley's name from down the hallway. They turned to look as one and their jaws dropped in surprise.

Sam and O'Connor sauntered toward them, Sam in a grey suit and coordinated tie, and O'Connor in a navy skirt and white blouse, a cane in her left hand, and a frame handbag hanging in the crook of her right arm. Her stone-faced expression exemplified her displeasure.

Jack was first to start laughing. "Ho-ly *shit!*"

Bradley and Trillian fought the urge to join Jack, but were losing the battle as giggles rose in their throats.

"Is that... *Mrs. Doubtfire?*" Jack fell to his knees in hysterical laughter.

"You better shut the fuck up." O'Connor gritted her teeth. "I'm warning you."

"Dad." Bradley held back a guffaw. "This isn't a Halloween dance."

Trillian couldn't take it any longer and turned away, holding her stomach and giggling uncontrollably.

Sam gave Bradley a sideways glance. "We're in disguise as chaperones." He looked at the three of them. "And if you keep it up, you're going to blow our cover and Fiscara's going to get fired."

"Sorry. You're right," Bradley said. "But give us a break. We've never seen O'Connor with lipstick on before. We were unprepared." He squinted at O'Connor. "Is that your real hair?"

Trillian and Jack began laughing again with renewed enthusiasm.

Sam stepped up to Bradley and lowered his voice. "It's a wig. But you know what else it is?" He hooked his finger at Trillian and Jack. The two of them noted the seriousness in his voice and stifled their laughter. "That's dedication to the job. You have no idea how hard it is for O'Connor to dress this way. And she's doing it to help *you*." Sam looked at all three teenagers. "No more jokes. Understand?"

Bradley, Jack, and Trillian nodded.

"It's just that—" Jack began.

"Jack... watch it." Sam crossed his arms.

Jack continued, "Seriously. It's just that O'Connor's one-hundred percent convincing. Us laughing should be taken as a compliment."

"Smooth," Bradley said softly.

"Okay, I'll buy that. But no more jokes." Sam looked at O'Connor. "Now that you mention it, you do rock a skirt and blouse. And that wig…" He brought his fingertips to his lips and kissed them.

"Don't make me break my foot off in your ass." O'Connor punched Sam in the shoulder. "And you know I can do it."

Sam ignored the punch and grinned. "Come on. Let's rock this joint." He followed O'Connor toward the entrance of the gymnasium.

The five of them joined dozens of students already milling about in the darkened gym. Orange paper ribbon and hundreds of fall colored lights had been strung up from the rafters. A spinning glitter ball hung over center court, reflecting rainbow diamonds across the floor and ceiling, and the bleachers had been pulled out to offer a place for students to rest between dances (or to make out if they could get away with it). A refreshment table with punch and assorted snacks had been set up on the far side of the gym.

Fiscara approached Sam and O'Connor from across the gym. She nodded at Sam, grinning. "Who's the skirt?"

Sam shook his head to indicate the taboo subject, while O'Connor brooded.

Fiscara got the message loud and clear. "Seriously though, you two look good. Very responsible. Just what you want in a chaperone."

Sam casually scanned the young crowd. "Thanks goes to the thrift store."

"By the way, don't worry about Maddox spotting you," Fiscara said. "He won't fire me. He's just a bravado balloon filled with hot air."

"You mean I didn't have to wear all this?" O'Connor looked at her clothes with disdain.

"Probably not, but it's better that you did." Fiscara wandered toward the bleachers, but turned to add, "Now mingle. Split up." She waved her hand before melding with the crowd of students.

"For fuck's sake," O'Connor said. "This isn't an episode of Scooby Doo. Splitting up just gets you in trouble."

Sam crossed his arms against his chest and sighed. "Jesus, I feel old."

O'Connor laughed and tapped her temple. "It's not the body, but the mind. Just look for spiders… and sex." She spotted two teenagers embracing each other. "Hey! You two. Break it up!" O'Connor trudged toward the two teenagers. "No kissing."

Sam rubbed his temples. "It's going to be a long night," he muttered to himself as he followed O'Connor's footsteps.

ALEXIS, DEIRDRE, AND CAITLIN had arrived at the dance early and positioned themselves on the bleachers close to the refreshments. "A good spot for surveillance," Alexis had said.

"He's here." Caitlin pointed with her bandaged hand, wrapped with red gauze that matched her red baby doll t-shirt.

Diedre popped her gum. "So's that bitch—"

"Rainbow Brite." Alexis daggered her eyes at Trillian, who was standing next to Bradley and Jack at the entrance to the gym. "She's going to get hers."

The deejay stood at a table opposite the refreshments and leaned into his mic. "Washbrook peeps! Time to rock this equinox with a little Earth, Wind and Fire!" She faded up "September" over the speakers.

"Oh God, not this again." Deirdre rolled her eyes and gnawed her gum. "They play this song every fucking year."

"It's not that bad. Isn't it from the seventies?" Caitlin's foot was tapping the bleacher seat despite Deirdre's disapproval.

"Who cares." Deirdre snapped her gum and booed the deejay. "What do you want to hear? Lex?"

Alexis hadn't heard a thing, either from her friends or the music. All her focus was on Trillian and her movements on the opposite side of the gym.

"Lex?"

"WHAT?" Alexis alternated her glare between Deirdre and Caitlin.

"Any requests?"

" 'Girl Like You' by Maroon 5." Caitlin swooned. "Adam Levine is so hot."

"*Not* Maroon 5." Alexis shook her head. "Just get everyone dancing. We need the cover."

Deirdre thought for a moment and nodded. "I got just the song."

"Which one?" Caitlin eyed her with curiosity.

"You'll see." Deirdre hopped off the bleachers and skipped to the deejay's table.

"What do you think she's going to play?"

"I don't give a shit as long as it gets everyone on the dance floor." Alexis brooded. "You know what you need to do?"

"We've only gone over it, like, a thousand times."

Alexis looked at Caitlin in her red baby doll t-shirt and denim shorts. Her outfit would work, despite the bandage wrapping her left hand and forearm. "Maybe we should go over things one more time."

"I'm good." Caitlin stood on a bleacher seat and swayed her hips to Earth, Wind and Fire.

Deirdre returned. "Okay. This dance floor's going to erupt."

"Ready?" Alexis shifted her gaze from Diedre to Caitlin. They both nodded.

"September" faded out as a familiar sequence of piano chords and finger snaps gathered volume.

Alexis grinned at Deirdre. "Loud Luxury. Brilliant."

"I love this song!" Caitlin said.

"Luckily so does everyone else." Alexis grinned. "Let's go."

The three girls stepped to the dance floor and blended in with a crush of students all hopping to the pounding bass of "Body" by Loud Luxury.

They stopped at the refreshment table. Principal Maddox stood behind and forced a smile at them, trying to monitor both the dance floor and the punch bowl. Alexis gave Deirdre and Caitlin a subtle nod and the three went into action.

Deirdre pulled two plastic cups off the stack and slid one off, passing it behind her body to Alexis. She filled her remaining cup with a ladle of punch.

Caitlin grabbed a carrot stick and walked around to the side of the table where Maddox stood. She looked up at him, slid her tongue and lips around the carrot stick and took a bite.

"Hey Mr. Maddox," Caitlin said. "You know what this song is called?"

Maddox looked left and right, this time to make sure no one was watching him. "Uh, no."

"It's called 'Body.' " Caitlin moved her eyes across Maddox's chest to his crotch and back. She licked her lips and took another bite of her carrot stick. "You like it?"

"It's, uh… catchy."

Caitlin moved her hips to the music and raised her arms, her t-shirt creeping up her midriff. "I like it."

Maddox looked at her red bandage. "What happened to your hand?"

"Spider bite."

Maddox, taken aback, swallowed hard and redirected his eyes to the dance floor. "I hope you're feeling better soon."

"Thanks."

Deirdre leaned forward to refill her cup with punch, blocking Maddox's line of sight with her seventeen-year-old cleavage.

Alexis slid her plastic cup back onto the table, upside down among the other stacks of cups. She pulled two more plastic cups from the stack and filled each with a ladle of punch. "Cait!" She held out one of the plastic cups.

Caitlin walked in front of Mr. Maddox, close enough to smell sour sweat through his rough sports jacket, and took the plastic cup of punch from Alexis. "Bye, Mr. Maddox."

Alexis, Deirdre and Caitlin took their drinks and melted back into the crowd, emerging on the opposite side of the dance floor. They ducked under the bleachers and walked back to the entrance of the gymnasium under cover.

"Cait, you were awesome back there," Alexis said.

It was rare for Alexis to offer any kind of compliment to anyone, and especially to Caitlin. She smiled broadly. "Thanks."

Deirdre finished her drink. "Do you think Mad Dog wants to fuck you now?"

"Ew. Gross!" Caitlin grimaced. "He smelled. Like *old man*."

The three girls emerged laughing at the opposite end of the bleachers where other students were still arriving to the dance.

Alexis led Deirdre and Caitlin out of the gymnasium and down the hallway. "We need to hurry. Dee, get Rainbow Bright's combination ready."

They climbed the stairs to the second floor hallway, sporadically lit with overhead fluorescents.

"This place is creepy at night." Caitlin cast her gaze at the rows of lockers and strange angled shadows.

"Shut up and keep watch," Alexis said. "They always hire a security guard for these dances." She nudged Deirdre. "What's her locker number?"

Deirdre had called the information up on her phone. "327."

Alexis found the locker just over halfway between the two doors to Mr. Silver's English class. "Ok, what's her combo?"

"38-16-22. That just happens to be my measurements too." Deirdre laughed.

"Who are you, a fucking Barbie doll?" Alexis began spinning

the number selector on the combination lock. "Now keep it down." She finished with the third number and pulled the lock. It remained closed.

Deirdre could see anger brewing behind Alexis's eyes. "That's her combination, I swear. Try it again."

Alexis returned to the lock and spun the number selector through the combination and pulled. The lock remained steadfast. "FUCK!" She kicked the locker door, denting it.

"Be quiet," Caitlin said. "Remember the security guard."

Alexis spun around, grabbed Caitlin by her t-shirt and slammed her into the adjacent locker. "You think you can do better, blabbermouth?"

Caitlin shrugged and looked at her with surprise mixed with fear. "I can try."

Alexis pushed her back and released her. Caitlin slid her bandaged hand underneath the lock like a pillow and spun the number selector several times to reset it. Then with slow determination she selected each number in turn, spinning right, left, and right. Caitlin looped her free finger through the lock, pulled, and it popped open.

Alexis stared at her. "What did you do?"

"Nothing."

Alexis removed the lock and handed it to Deirdre. "Don't lock it." She pulled the locker door open to reveal an interior that didn't appear used. There were a few stray papers inside, but no mirror or stickers on the door, pens or pencils. "Are you sure this is her locker?"

"I'm positive," Deirdre said. "I mean, we're in, right?"

"Don't be a smartass." Alexis reached into her purse and removed a small glass jar, holding it up for Deirdre and Caitlin to see. Inside was a spider egg sac, almost too large to fit out of the top. It seemed to swell like it was breathing on its own.

Caitlin looked at her bandaged hand and a shiver ran up her back. "Just keep it away from me."

"This is the last one." Alexis unscrewed the perforated lid and exchanged it with a pen from her purse. She coaxed the egg sac until it sat on the lip of the jar, then inverted it on the top shelf of Trillian's locker.

Like she was making a sandcastle, Alexis raised the jar slowly and carefully up and over the egg sac. It continued to expand and contract in its new home.

"That's really fucking creepy," Caitlin said.

Deirdre looked at her. "You got that right. Holy Toledo."

Alexis placed the jar back in her purse and pulled out her nail file. "These babies are going to look even better on Rainbow Brite's face." She directed a serious glance at Deirdre. "Get ready with the lock."

The sound of a door closing echoed back at them from the central stairwell, half the school away. A security guard emerged, his flashlight scanning the walls and lockers as he went.

"Shit. We got trouble." Caitlin vibrated in her shoes. "Twelve o'clock."

"Quiet." Alexis managed a quick glance up the hallway but remained focused. "Ready with the lock."

The security guard crossed the hallway and poked his flashlight into the boy's bathroom.

Alexis worked to secure the egg sac with the pen and nail file. Her fingers slick with nervous sweat, the pen slipped from her hand and fell to the floor. The sound echoed back up the hallway.

The security guard's flashlight found them in an instant. "You there. Freeze."

Alexis glared at Deirdre. "Get the fucking pen," she said in a hushed voice.

Deirdre looked back up the hallway as the security guard approached, then grabbed the pen off the floor, slipping it into Alexis's hand.

"You're not supposed to be up here," the security guard called out.

"Hurry up." Caitlin began chewing on her nails. "He's almost here."

There was no time left to be gentle. Alexis brought the pen down into the egg sac, skewering it, and used the nail file to rip a large hole in the side of the sac. Dozens of spiderlings, black as wet ink, spilled out and onto the shelf of Trillian's locker and began scrambling toward the locker's interior walls. As she tried to remove the pen and nail file, the sac remained stuck to it, pulling it out toward the edge of the shelf.

"Fuck it." Alexis threw the pen and nail file back onto the shelf and closed the locker door. "Lock."

Deirdre was frozen in the beam of the security guard's flashlight.

"Dee!" Alexis spoke in hushed tones through her gritted teeth. "DEE! THE LOCK!" She poked Deirdre again. Exasperated, she grabbed the lock from Deirdre's hand and secured the locker door.

The security guard approached the girls, flicking his flashlight to each of their faces in turn. "What's going on here?"

Caitlin looked at the floor and continued chewing her nails. Deirdre held her hand in front of her face to block the bright beam of the flashlight.

Alexis stepped back to the locker beside Trillian's and tugged on the combination lock. "I have an emergency tampon in my locker, but I can't remember the combination." She spun the number selector a few times and pulled, without success.

The security guard cast a suspicious eye at the three girls. "Do you want me to give it a try?"

Alexis smiled and flashed her eyes brightly. "Would you?"

"Sure." The security guard hiked his utility belt up, keys and accessories jangling. "What's the combination?"

Alexis looked at Deirdre and Caitlin with a confident twinkle in her eye. She leaned to the guard's ear, cupped her hands, and whispered the digits.

The guard raised his eyebrow at her, then approached the locker. He tried the combination twice without success.

Deirdre stared at Alexis and motioned to the top of Trillian's locker. Several black spiders had worked their way out through the gap in the locker door.

"Thanks for trying," Alexis said.

"No. Let me give it one more try." The guard went through the combination once more with the same result.

"I think Beyoncé has one you could have," Caitlin said.

Alexis looked at the security guard's name tag. "Thanks Mr. Cooper. Sorry for wasting your time."

"Not a problem, miss." The guard followed the girls back to the stairwell, shining a light on them from behind. "I hope you get… things sorted out. But stay off the second floor. Okay?"

"Okay, Mr. Cooper." Alexis waved back at him. "Thanks."

The security guard turned and headed back up the second floor hallway, sweeping the floors and walls with the beam of his flashlight.

Once back on the first floor, Alexis, Deirdre and Caitlin broke into excited giggles.

"*Beyoncé?*" Alexis laughed. "Where did that come from?"

"I thought I heard them playing 'All the Single Ladies' in the gym," Caitlin said.

"All I heard was his wheezing," Deirdre said.

"Get this." Alexis stopped and huddled with her friends. "You know when I whispered the combo in the guard's ear?" A mischievous grin spread across Alexis's face.

Deirdre's jaw dropped. "You didn't."

"I did." Alexis snickered. "I told the old loser I'd suck his dick if he could get the locker open."

Deirdre stuck out her tongue. "Oh God! Yuck."

"That's why he tried three times to unlock it." Caitlin said. "You evil bitch."

"At your service." Alexis took a bow. "And I see what you

mean about *old man* smell," she said to Caitlin. "That guard *reeked.*"

"I know, right?" Caitlin said. "It's not perspiration. It's *desperation.*"

The three girls laughed as they continued their way back to the gym.

"Now let's go watch our other plan hatch." Alexis hooked arms with Deirdre and Caitlin as they strolled back into the gym.

THE GYMNASIUM FLOOR flexed and bounced to the rhythm of four grades' worth of students. Waves of moist body heat buffeted the crowd.

"I never thought I'd ever be dancing to 'All the Single Ladies,' " Bradley said to Jack and Trillian.

"Damn straight, bro." Jack flashed a toothy grin and raised his hands up. "Beyoncé all the way."

The three of them joined up with Mark and some of his friends on the dance floor as the deejay cranked up "Feel It Still" by Portugal - The Man.

"Hey, look who just walked in." Trillian tried to motion with her head toward the gymnasium entrance, but the gesture ended up looking like a strange dance. Instead, she pointed at Alexis walking arm in arm with Deirdre and Caitlin.

"I was wondering when they were going to show up," Bradley said.

Jack rolled his shoulders and tapped his feet, confident in his dance moves. "Should we keep an eye on them?"

"I'll let my Dad know. We're here to have fun, right?" Bradley shuffled off the dance floor toward Sam and O'Connor on the sidelines.

"I got a bad feeling about this." Trillian glanced at Jack, who had begun a modified version of the Electric Slide. "What would a narcissistic psychopath do at a high school dance?"

"Make it all about her," Jack said.

"Sounds about right." Trillian stepped back to where the crowd thinned out and spotted Alexis and her two devotees perched on the far end of the bleachers closest to the gymnasium entrance. "What are they up to?"

She found a spot on the opposite bank of bleachers and sat down, high enough to keep an eye on Alexis over the crowded dance floor.

Jack appeared moments later with three cups of punch. Trillian took one and he set the remaining cup down beside him.

Trillian took a sip, then a large gulp. "Thanks. I needed that."

"Dancing's thirsty work."

"So, where'd you learn moves like that?"

Jack shrugged. "My parents love to dance so I've kind of grown up with it. Now they travel a lot so I can crank the music at home and practice any time I want."

Trillian brushed her spectrum hair around her ear and sipped her punch. "You should try out for dance squad."

"What?" Jack recoiled almost like he had been burned. "Only girls are in dance squad."

"Not so." Trillian waved her finger back and forth. "At my old school they had guys on the team too. Things are changing."

"Not here."

"Maybe you should lead by example."

A piercing scream rose from the far end of the gymnasium.

"What the hell?" Jack craned his neck, trying to isolate the source.

Trillian nodded toward the refreshment table just as Bradley and Mark approached them on the bleachers. "There's something in punch bowl."

The deejay stopped the music. "Stay calm, everyone. Don't panic."

The four friends navigated their way around the exodus of panicked students to the refreshment table.

"Someone wasn't listening to the deejay." Trillian nudged Bradley. "Look at Mad Dog."

Maddox had backed up against the wall, his eyes wide with terror. They followed his line of sight to the stack of cups next to the punch bowl, now surrounded with small moving black dots.

Trillian locked gaze with Maddox. "Now do you believe us?" She took several steps toward the table. "Asshat."

"Wait!" Bradley pulled her back.

"For what? They're getting away."

The small spiders spread out, dropping off the edge of the table to the floor. A large group made a beeline for the wall that Maddox stood against.

"Help me!" he cried out in terror.

"I think Mad Dog has arachnophobia," Bradley said.

Fiscara appeared next to Bradley. "That makes perfect sense."

"Please!" Maddox tried to make himself thinner by stepping up on his tip toes.

"Grow some balls and *stamp* on them!" Fiscara called back.

Taking her cue, Bradley, Trillian, Jack and Mark began stepping on any spider that got too close.

"Are they sporkies?" Bradley said as Trillian mashed a spider into the wooden floor.

"I don't know." Trillian shifted her stance, ready to crush her next opponent.

Sam and O'Connor joined the fray.

Sam looked up and his eyes went wide. "Holy shit."

Trillian followed Sam's sightline. "Those are sporkies all right. Look at their backs."

"Everyone, back the fuck up," O'Connor said.

"I don't think that's necess—" Fiscara followed O'Connor's pointed finger up toward the ceiling. Dangling on threads fastened to the overhead air ducting, three sporkies the size of softballs lowered themselves toward the refreshment table like a trio of eight-legged Navy SEALs. The flexing spines on their backs seemed to propel them downward faster. "Do as she says. Now."

The only one who couldn't back up was Maddox. He was pinned against the wall by a throng of fast-approaching spiderlings.

"What a pussy." O'Connor navigated around the refreshment table and approached the wall where Maddox stood paralyzed.

"Please do something." Sweat dotted Maddox's forehead and collected along the line of his buzz cut.

O'Connor looked at Maddox square in the face, noting his eyes ready to burst forth with tears. "I'll help you, not because I'm a nice person, but because you're going to pay me handsomely."

"Anything!"

O'Connor flipped a switch on her cane. A blue light glowed near the handle. She brought the end of the cane close to a marauding spider and pulled a trigger near the grip. A blue arc of electricity flashed at the end of the cane and vaporized all spiders in the immediate vicinity in a plume of acrid smoke.

Jack grinned in admiration. "Holy shit, that's *awesome.*"

"Glad to know it works, but there's too many, don't you think?"

Maddox closed his eyes and nodded.

"I need you to keep your eyes open, asshole." O'Connor handed him the taser cane. "Use it if they get too close." She reached under her skirt and unhooked a slimline propane torch nozzle. She smirked at Sam and Fiscara. "I only wear skirts for a reason."

O'Connor pulled a black rubber tube from her purse and connected it to the torch.

Mark did a double-take. "Does she have a—"

"A propane tank in her purse?" Bradley raised his brow in surprise.

"Of course she does," Trillian said, smiling.

Jack sighed. "I think I'm in love." Sam grinned and patted Jack on the back.

O'Connor removed her Zippo from her purse and lit the pilot flame on the torch. "Stay still, you candy-ass, or you're going to get burned."

Maddox nodded, his eyes darting across the floor. His uncoordinated attempts to zap approaching spiders accomplished only one thing: draining the cane's batteries.

O'Connor settled to her right knee and aimed the torch at the wave of spiderlings dangerously close to Maddox's feet. She triggered short blasts of flame at the small spiders, incinerating them almost instantly.

An inhuman screech rose above their heads from one of the three spiders descending toward the refreshment table.

Bradley instinctively covered his head and took a step back. "Holy crap. Spiders can scream?"

"Apparently these ones do," Fiscara said.

"Everyone step back." O'Connor flanked the table to get a better shot at the leading spider overhead. "Step *back*." She waved the torch's nozzle toward the crowd then cast an aggravated eye at Maddox. "And someone get Principal Fuckwit out of here."

Maddox was attempting to hit spiderlings with the depleted taser cane but kept missing the mark. Sam grabbed his arm and pulled him backward to safety.

"You break it, you buy it," he said, observing the bent taser cane in Maddox's hand.

"See you in hell, motherfucker." O'Connor released a jet of propane fire from her torch. The flames enveloped the first spider, igniting the strand of supportive webbing it hung from. Like a smoking obsidian boulder, the first spider plummeted into the punch bowl, spraying orange juice and ice cubes across the table and floor. The flames burned up the strand before fizzling out at the ventilation duct.

O'Connor re-trained the torch at the second spider and pulled the trigger. A ball of flame burst from the side of the torch and traveled down the black supply line to her purse, igniting a trapped pocket of propane gas. The side of the purse blew open in an orange fireball and propelled the small propane tank outward, where it dangled from the purse's strap, sputtering flames against her left leg.

O'Connor shook the purse off her shoulder and stepped back from the burning weapon. "Still some kinks to work out." She turned to Maddox. "Give me your coat."

He crunched his brow. "Why?"

"Just do it."

Maddox complied, slipping off his tweed sports jacket and handing it to O'Connor. She in turn threw it on top of the burning propane torch that had now scorched the gymnasium floor.

"That was a five-hundred dollar jacket!"

"And it was butt ugly," O'Connor said. "You can thank me later."

"Look!" Fiscara pointed at the two remaining spiders hanging from the ventilation ports in the ceiling. The spiders had descended almost to the floor but were now reversing direction. They sprayed a wispy layer of webbing over the floor which acted like a net.

Instead of continuing their escape path, the spiderlings reversed direction and clambered toward the temporary netting, following the two adult spiders up the main thread toward the ceiling.

"The adults are rescuing the rest of the babies," Trillian said.

Fiscara watched the spiders scramble up the threads. "I've never seen behavior like this from a spider before."

"Now's your chance." Maddox looked at Fiscara and O'Connor with wild eyes. "Do something! What are you waiting for?"

"What do you suggest, exactly?" Fiscara shot him an aggravated look.

"I don't know. Anything!" Maddox pointed up at the ceiling. "THEY'RE GETTING AWAY." His meltdown was a rarity the faculty and students had never seen before. He looked to the surrounding crowd. Some had their phones out and were now paying more attention to his outburst than the fleeing spiders. "If I see any videos of this online, you all will be permanently expelled."

Bradley leaned toward Jack, Mark, and Trillian and lowered his voice. "Do you think *this* will be enough proof?"

"Probably not." Jack scoffed. "The guy has a selective memory, too."

"I'll help him remember." Mark punctuated his words by punching his palm with his fist.

O'Connor pulled Maddox's partially charred sports coat off the propane torch and dumped the contents of the purse. She grabbed the keys to the Mustang and her phone with the thermal camera attachment and threw them to Sam.

"That doesn't mean you get to drive." She found the Zippo and unhinged the lid. "I might be down…" O'Connor ignited the Zippo. "But I'm never out." She held it to the two threads of webbing that hung from the ventilation ducts in the ceiling. They burst into flame, burning upward, catching up with the slower spiderlings and engulfing them in fire. The pungent smell of burned hair soon permeated the gymnasium. She tossed the Zippo back to Sam. "Don't lose it."

One adult spider had already made it back into the ventilation duct. The second was within two feet of the duct before the thread's flames overtook it, turning its silken lifeline into a wisp of ash.

Mark watched the screeching spider fall. "Shit. Back up! Its guts are like acid."

The crowd was able to take one step back before the spider's abdomen struck the edge of the refreshment table, releasing a gush of blue blood and rebounding onto the floor.

Mortally wounded, the spider on the floor tried to scramble away, but its legs were useless as they slid on a pool of their own blue blood. The spider safe in the ventilation duct released a screech that echoed through the gymnasium. Bradley looked to the ceiling and heard the scratchy sounds of spider legs scraping the insides of the ventilation duct, moving toward the wall that Maddox had once stood against.

Fiscara was busy staking out the two dead sporkies. If she had crime scene tape, the table and the floor would have been wrapped with it. "The refreshment table is off limits." A student stepped closer to the table to get a better shot with their phone. "Are you deaf?" Fiscara held up her hand and blocked the student's shot. "Off limits."

Maddox grabbed his jacket from the floor. "It's ruined." He threw an angry finger at O'Connor. "You're going to pay for this."

O'Connor spun around, grabbed Maddox by the collar and slammed him against the wall. "No. You're going to pay *me* to take care of this problem… and buy me a new cane. Count your lucky stars that you didn't die in that flea-bitten piece of shit."

Maddox broke free of O'Connor's grasp and headed for the exit. "Mark my words. Your days are numbered," he called back, first at O'Connor, then to the entire crew. "I'll charge all of you. Destruction of school property, reckless endangerment…" Maddox continued to mumble threats as he crossed the floor.

"We're not responsible for this," Jack said.

"No. We're not." Fiscara looked back just as Maddox disappeared from view. "Maddox is angry and embarrassed. He'll be fine by Monday."

"Who *is* responsible? Those baby sporkies didn't just magically appear from nowhere." Trillian hopped back up the bleachers and surveyed the crowd. Alexis, Deirdre, and Caitlin were nowhere to be seen.

Jack caught Trillian's gaze. "Alexis," he said to himself.

Mark appeared in front of Fiscara with a mop, paper towels, a pair of rubber gloves, and a couple of trash bags.

"Good thinking. The show must go on." Fiscara took the gloves and slipped them on. "I'll deal with the mess and you get the music going again."

Mark disappeared into the crowd. Sam looked at O'Connor and motioned at Fiscara. He picked up a garbage bag and shook it open.

Fiscara flashed him a warm smile. "Thanks."

"You going to do an autopsy on these things?"

"How'd you guess?" Fiscara surveyed the spider in the punch bowl, deciding on the best way to remove it. The slick black legs, longer and thicker than a chopstick, splayed out from the edges of the clear plastic bowl.

"If these were rats, Hope would've been all over it," O'Connor said. "Ain't that right, Sam? Or should I call you *Mr. Maxipad?*" She began to laugh, first from her belly, then her whole body following.

"Mr. Maxipad?" Fiscara grabbed one of the spider's legs and raised it out of the punch bowl. Orange juice mixed with blue blood drained back into the bowl. "And who's Hope?"

"A colleague." Sam held the garbage bag open. "She would have come with us, but she doesn't like spiders."

"He has a *thing* for her," O'Connor said, still chuckling.

"You must know by now that O'Connor's full of shit most of the time, right?"

"I'm getting that impression." Fiscara transferred the dead spider into the garbage bag.

Sam handed the mop to O'Connor. "Make yourself useful. And remember who has the car keys."

O'Connor grumbled but surprised Sam by taking the mop without protest. He followed Fiscara to the spider on the floor and knelt opposite her with the garbage bag. "What are you looking for?"

"The quills fascinate me," Fiscara said. "I want to know their function, if they hold venom, that kind of stuff. I think the rest will be typical arachnid physiology."

Sam looked at her and nodded. "Good plan."

"You think so, huh?" Fiscara grinned. "I think we'll need to get everyone on the same page. After the dance."

The deejay's amplified voice echoed across the gymnasium. "Thank your chaperones for saving this party. Now let's start a *real* fire with this golden oldie." The deejay cranked up Sean Kingston's "Fire Burning" and soon the dance floor was packed once again with sweaty dancing teenagers hopping at one-hundred twenty beats per minute. The significance of the lyrics was lost on everyone except for Fiscara, Sam, O'Connor, and the exterminators in training.

Sam furrowed his brow. "What's a *'shoddy?'* "

"It's *shaw-ty*, like your last name. It's slang for a young attractive woman," Fiscara ran her hand down beside her body in a flourish and winked.

"You mean like me." O'Connor placed a hand on her ample hips and the other pretended to coif the hair of her wig.

Fiscara laughed. "Yeah, O'Connor. You're definitely a shawty. And shawties belong on the dance floor."

"I ain't dancing to *this*." O'Connor crossed her arms.

"Chill out." Fiscara grabbed Sam's and O'Connor's arms and pulled them onto the dance floor. "Now dance, or I'll kick your asses."

And they did. One dance led to another and the evening

passed effortlessly, with the images of marauding spiders becoming a fading memory for most of the students.

The spiderlings that had survived and escaped earlier had gathered around the lone surviving adult, deep within the school's ventilation system. Having already molted once, their size and speed increased with each passing moment.

The spiders' collective consciousness took over and self-preservation became the cluster's priority. But first the spiders needed to find a way out of the school.

AFTER THE DANCE, Fiscara led the crew back to her classroom. She grabbed a metal specimen tray, a box of rubber gloves, and a tool kit from a supply locker at the back of the class and placed them on her desk. She looked up and was not surprised to find all eyes on her. "Let's see what makes these spiders tick."

"Bring it on, baby." O'Connor raised the black garbage bag containing the two dead spiders and handed it to Fiscara. She placed the bag next to the tray and unknotted the top of the bag.

"Are you sure they're dead?" Trillian eyed the bag with concern. "I mean, really sure?"

Fiscara nodded with a smile. "Quite sure. I put them in here myself." She untied the top and opened the bag, scrunching the sides down as she went.

"Flashbacks of Piper, huh Dad?" Bradley said.

A shiver ran down Sam's back. "Don't remind me."

"Who's Piper?" Jack asked without taking his eyes off the garbage bag.

"It was a cat that was eaten alive by rats," Bradley said. "Remind me to tell you about it later."

"Nah, bro. That's okay."

Mark recoiled, covered his nose, and took a step back. "Ugh. What's that smell?"

Fiscara had opened the bag down to its base and was in the process of transferring the two spiders to the specimen tray. She paid particular attention to the quills, positioning the sharp ends facing away from everyone looking on. "That's essence of spider." She sniffed, crinkling her nose. "It's a lot stronger than tarantula."

"Spiders are a delicacy in some countries." Jack grinned. "A little soy sauce and down the hatch."

Trillian gagged. "Gross."

"I bet they taste like chicken," Bradley said.

"No. More like crab."

"So, everything with eight legs tastes like crab now?" Trillian gave Jack a sideways look.

"Or so I've read," Jack said. "Everything on the Internet is true, you know."

"This thing isn't even on the Internet yet," Mark said.

"Further than that, this species hasn't been classified yet. The guts look like other large spiders I've seen, but the quills are the unique feature." Fiscara picked at the exposed innards of one of the spiders with a metal probe. The drop to the floor in the gymnasium two hours ago had caused massive disruption to the spider's internal organs, mixing it all together like a custard gone bad. She turned to look at the crew gathered around the table, starting with O'Connor. "To my knowledge, there are no spiders on the planet that have long quills like this."

"In other words, we're sitting on a cash cow of fame and fortune." O'Connor flashed her eyebrows. "And we have to kill them? Shouldn't we keep them alive?"

"I get the money-making attitude," Mark said, "but since I'm the only one here who's been attacked, I vote to kill the fuckers." Everyone except O'Connor appeared taken aback by his language. "Come on. I could've died."

Fiscara nodded a smile at Mark. "He's right. Preventing injury and death is our primary concern. If we're lucky, there might be some fame in it for all of us."

She moved to the charred but intact spider and lifted it up slightly from the front. "You see the eight eyes, right here? And the chelicerae?" Fiscara glanced up at Sam and O'Connor. "Chelicerae are similar to the claws on a crab." They both nodded.

"But on a spider, the chelicerae…" Fiscara looked to Bradley, Trillian, Jack, and Mark.

"Don't look at me," Jack said. "I'm not taking biology."

"The chelicerae are attached to the fangs." Mark leaned toward Bradley and Trillian and grinned. "You need to study more."

"I'll get *right* on that," Bradley said, smirking.

O'Connor lowered herself onto her right knee. "Show me the fangs."

Fiscara placed the metal probe underneath the spider's head, just behind the chelicerae and moved it forward. Two black needle-sharp fangs the size of her fingernail and curved like the blade of a scythe appeared in the classroom light. "Venom is pumped through the fangs, immobilizing the spider's prey."

She moved to the quills on the back of the spider. "But these quills, they're an oddity." Fiscara exchanged the probe for a pair of forceps. "Spiders are usually covered with fine hairs that break off, making ingestion difficult. But these quills look lethal. The million dollar question is if they just fall out, like a porcupine."

She positioned the jaws of the forceps around the base of one of the quills and gave it a gentle tug. The quill didn't budge.

Trillian crouched next to Fiscara. "Maybe they're permanently attached, like armor."

"Good hypothesis." Fiscara squeezed the forceps, locking the clamp, and gave the quill a twist. "They also might've fused to the exoskeleton when it was blasted with fire."

O'Connor sighed. "That was a moment of beauty, wasn't it?"

"Except for the explosion," Sam said.

O'Connor shrugged. "Gotta fail to succeed, right?"

"Speaking of failing…" Fiscara unclamped the forceps, moved them to an adjacent quill, and began twisting again.

Without warning, the spider's legs curled up on themselves and contracted underneath its body, forming an oily-black cage. The quills spread out like a Japanese fan and shot out of their anchor holes in the spider's thorax.

There was no time to react. The forceps that had been in Fiscara's hand a second before remained attached to the quill, now embedded in the blackboard. Dozens of quills surrounded it in the walls and ceiling.

Everyone jumped back a step.

"Holy shit," Jack said. "Forget sporky. You should call them the Death Blossom spider."

Trillian crossed her arms. "Sporky is easier to say."

"But it doesn't sound scary enough."

"Sam." Fiscara's eyes widened. "Don't move."

"What?"

"Don't move." Fiscara grabbed another pair of forceps and maneuvered to Sam's right arm, at the shoulder. A shorter quill sat three-quarters of the way through Sam's suit jacket. "Do you feel any pain?"

Sam shook his head.

Fiscara clamped onto the quill with the forceps and wiggled it. "How about now?"

"Nothing. Why?"

Fiscara motioned at the blackboard. Drops of liquid had begun to flow down the walls and drip from the ceiling where the quills had penetrated. "It's probably venom. We need to clear the area."

Fiscara led Sam to a nearby desk and sat him down. A small cloudy droplet had formed at the tip of the quill in Sam's jacket.

Working fast, Fiscara pulled the quill out in the direction of the point and threw it into the waste basket. "Take off your jacket. If the quill broke the skin, you're going to have problems."

Sam slipped out of his suit jacket, revealing a corresponding set of entry and exit holes in his white dress shirt.

"Sorry, but shirt too," Fiscara said. "There's no blood visible, but we have to be sure."

Sam sighed.

"What?" Fiscara looked at O'Connor, to Bradley, then back to Sam. "Did I say something wrong?"

Sam looked at Bradley. "You okay with this? I won't do it unless—"

"I'm fine, Dad. Really." There was concern in Bradley's eyes, but also love for his father. "I'd rather know you're okay."

Sam nodded. He began to untie his tie when Fiscara stopped him.

"You can't move your arm," she said. "Let me do it."

Sam heaved a sigh. "Go ahead."

Fiscara untied Sam's tie and unbuttoned and removed his shirt slowly but surely, revealing a collage of prison tattoos covering his chest, arms and back. Jack and Mark exchanged surprised looks. Sam heard Trillian gasp and a faint wistful smile crossed his lips.

O'Connor pulled on rubber gloves, grabbed a pair of pliers and began to remove the quills from the walls.

"Get the ones from the ceiling first," Fiscara said. "Stand on my desk if you have to."

"Got it, Chief." O'Connor laid the garbage bag on top of the spider corpses and moved the specimen tray to a nearby desk. Once standing on the top of the desk, she worked at the quills from the outside in, tossing each one in the waste basket. Sam and O'Connor regarded each other with respect.

Fiscara focused on Sam's right arm as she looked for any sign of skin abrasion, but his lean upper body, muscular arms, and profane artwork proved to be a distraction. The words "Motherfucker for Life" and "Murderer" across his chest drew her eye.

"Should we be worried?" she asked.

"No." Sam closed his eyes and bowed his head. "I've paid my dues."

Fiscara gave Sam's arm one last look. "Looks like you lucked out. That quill missed you by less than an inch." She handed him his shirt.

"You're going to have to be careful cleaning this classroom," O'Connor said. "There's drops of venom everywhere." She dropped another quill into the waste basket. "And how about some help?"

Sam threw his shirt back on and joined the others donning rubber gloves and grabbing either forceps or pliers. The quills were collected and disposed of with the dead spiders.

"I'll come in on the weekend and scrub down the walls," Fiscara said.

"Burn the desk, too." O'Connor eased herself off the desk to the floor. "Fire works wonders."

Fiscara smirked. "So I've seen."

"What's the plan now?" Jack said.

Sam slipped back into his suit jacket. "Sleep sounds good to me."

"Sleep when you're dead." Jack looked at the rest of the crew. "Afterparty at my place?"

O'Connor narrowed her eyes. "Will there be burritos involved?"

Jack returned a toothy grin. "Does a sporky have deadly quills?"

"Now you're talking." O'Connor hooked her arm around Jack's neck and led the group out of the classroom.

Jack, Trillian, and Mark had squeezed into Jack's Civic. They waved as Jack peeled out of the student parking lot. Bradley waved back. The only other car left in the student parking lot was O'Connor's blue Mustang.

"Last to leave. Just the way I like it." O'Connor held out her hand and beckoned toward Sam. "Keys, please."

Sam pulled the Mustang's keys out of his pocket and tossed them to her.

"I'll take the Zippo, too." O'Connor popped the trunk and loaded the bent taser rod and the faulty propane torch into it. She planted herself in the driver's seat and slid a cigar box out from underneath. O'Connor pulled out a pristine Cohiba and ran it under her nose, sniffing along its length. She bit one end, spitting bits of tobacco onto the asphalt, and placed the cigar between her teeth.

Sam handed her the Zippo from the passenger seat.

"It's been too long, baby." O'Connor ignited the Zippo and held the flame to the tip of the cigar, rotating it with her other hand to ignite the cigar evenly. Plumes of thick, grey smoke jettisoned from the side of her mouth like a steam-powered locomotive. She tossed the Zippo into a tray under the console and started the engine.

Bradley sniffed his shirt. It smelled of a mixture of cigar smoke and burnt arachnid. "Can we drop by my house so I can change?"

"Want to splash on the aftershave for… what's her name. Tilly?" O'Connor winked at Bradley in the rearview mirror as she pulled out of the parking lot and turned down Stonehurst.

"Her name is Trillian," Bradley said. "And no. I just don't like smelling like shit."

"Hammered shit, more like."

Sam took a quick whiff of his jacket. "I think we all could use a change of clothes."

"Damn straight," O'Connor said. "First stop, Casa del Brad."

A few minutes later, O'Connor rolled up in front of Bradley's house on Sheldon Street. The blue light of late-night television flickered in the window. Roy was still up.

Bradley hopped out of the car.

"Make it snappy, Casanova," O'Connor said. "I'm getting a rash down under."

"Too much information," Bradley called back as he ran down the walk and up the front steps. He unlocked the door and disappeared inside.

O'Connor turned to Sam. "He's sweet on that Trillian girl, you know."

Sam nodded. "I got eyes. But he'll never admit it."

"He's a good kid. They all are."

"Just don't ride him too hard on the girl stuff," Sam said. "He's a bit of a late bloomer."

O'Connor puffed her cigar, blowing rolling smoke rings into the breeze. "Sure, Sam. No worries."

"Speaking of crushes, I think you got your jones on for Jack."

O'Connor raised her eyebrows. "I ain't no cradle robber, but I swear, if I was seventeen again, there'd be some full-on jungle fever happening."

Sam grinned. "Old cattle eat young grass."

"You calling me a cow?" O'Connor punched Sam's shoulder. "Fuck you."

"Just saying."

They both settled into mutual laughter but yelling from within the house caught their attention.

O'Connor turned to look at the house. "What the hell is going on now?"

Sam gritted his teeth. "Roy would be my guess." He stepped out of the Mustang and headed toward the front door.

"Oh, yeah. That dipshit." O'Connor followed Sam across the street. "I should introduce his balls to my prosthesis."

Sam stopped and faced O'Connor. "Let me handle this, okay? Please?"

"Sure, just as long as his ass gets a whupping."

The front door opened and Bradley's shouts burst out of the house. "Fuck you! I'm almost seventeen." He stepped onto the landing and Roy grabbed his arm, pulling him off balance and back into the house. "Let go of me!" He pulled his arm back and stepped out onto the front landing. Sam and O'Connor arrived at the base of the front steps.

Roy stumbled to the entryway, cradling a can of beer in one hand. "It's almost eleven. Your mom's going to be—"

"You don't know shit about my mom, you dick swab." Bradley recoiled from Roy's breath. "Ugh. One thing my mom can't stand is a drunk."

Roy stabilized himself and grabbed Bradley's wrist. "Get your ass back in this house, *now!*"

Sam's muscles tensed under his suit. He formed white-knuckled fists, preparing to storm the steps, but O'Connor stopped him with a light hand on his shoulder. Her head shake and subtle grin prompted Sam to rethink his actions.

"Fuck YOU!" Bradley pried Roy's hand off his wrist and pushed him backward into the door. Beer sloshed from Roy's can and slicked the floor of the entryway. "You're not my dad, either."

"Yeah." Roy grabbed the door handle to steady himself and pointed at Sam down on the front walkway. "Your washed up, ex-con, murdering loser of a father is down there, coming to your fucking rescue." He spat a stale beer-infused gob of saliva into Bradley's face. "You're a goddamn pussy."

Bradley had had enough and wasted no time landing a fist into Roy's face. One punch was all it took.

Blood exploded from Roy's nostrils. His feet stumbled back in surprised steps and slipped on the spilled beer. He landed hard on his ass, the half-full can of beer flying back down the hallway leaving a trail of beer along the way.

Bradley stood in a combination of silence and shock, his fist shaking as the energy of the moment washed off him. He wiped the spittle off his face although the essence of cheap beer remained.

"Is he dead?" O'Connor asked.

Roy groaned and rolled onto his side, clutching his face with his hands. "I think you broke my nose, you little shit."

Bradley closed the front door and joined Sam and O'Connor as all three walked back to the Mustang. "I didn't want him dead. I just don't want him living in our house."

Sam gave Bradley's shoulder an affectionate pat. "You handled yourself well back there. The guy had it coming."

Bradley smiled. "I guess. I didn't want to hit him, but I kind of lost it."

Sam glanced at O'Connor as they all sat down in the convertible. "I probably would've killed him. Glad you got to him first."

O'Connor started the ignition and revved the engine. "We'll get some ice for your hand at the motel." She peeled out down the street. "Jack wouldn't mind if we crashed at his place, would he? I mean the motel is nice and all, but..." She rubbed her thumb and fingers together miming money. "You know, contribute to the cost? I got supplies, expenses, and Washington's estate only goes so far."

"Jack's cool and his parents are away."

"Music to my ears."

O'CONNOR PULLED UP in front of Jack's house. Music droned from within. "Nice digs." She hopped out of the Mustang like she was waking from an eight-hour sleep.

"Jesus, you're twenty-five years older than me and I get tired just watching you," Sam said.

"It's the way of the Cohiba, baby." O'Connor blew toward the night sky. "Less stress means a longer life. That's a fact."

"You're not going to be able to smoke in Jack's place either." Bradley held a bag of ice on his hand.

"Mother*fucker.* No one smokes in this town."

"Lots of people smoke," Bradley said. "Just not in buildings."

"I'm stressed out now." O'Connor tapped Bradley's shoulder. "You're endangering my life. If I die, that's on you, Brad." Instead of arguing, O'Connor butted out her cigar on the driveway.

Sam stood at the front door, poised to knock, but Bradley rang the doorbell instead. "No one ever hears the knock."

The doorbell echoed five notes within the house. O'Connor cocked her head, recognizing them immediately. "Was that from…"

"Close Encounters?"

"Yeah."

Bradley nodded. "Not only is Jack a nerd, he's a movie fanatic too."

"There are worse things to be," Sam said.

The front door flew open, revealing a smiling Fiscara standing at the interior landing of the split-level home. She had changed clothes as well. "We thought you guys had bailed on us."

Trillian spotted Bradley from the upper floor. She skipped

down the stairs, holding a can of Orange Crush in one hand. She reached out to grab Bradley's hand and stopped. "What happened?"

"I kind of punched my mom's boyfriend."

"Kind of?"

Bradley shrugged and grinned. "He was being an asshat."

"Would've liked to see that. Come on. Everyone's upstairs." Bradley followed Trillian up the stairs and out of sight. Sounds of "Highway Tune" by Greta Van Fleet and laughter floated back into the stairwell.

"Surprised to see you here," Sam said to Fiscara.

"I'm here in an unofficial capacity. We're still the chaperones."

"We are, huh?" Sam smiled.

"Step aside, lovebirds." O'Connor kicked off her boots. "There food at this shindig?"

"Lots."

"Good. I'm starving." O'Connor trudged up the stairs, with Fiscara and Sam following closely behind.

The open concept living room still exuded a 1970s interior design style, despite the updated furniture. The walk-around fireplace had a black slate tile seating area on three sides, with a grey granite chimney rising to the roof. Hardwood floors contrasted tastefully with the black leather sectional sofa and tan area rugs.

One side of the living room joined with the kitchen and dining room. An art deco style chandelier hung from the ceiling, which, after their recent run-in at the dance, looked like a bunch of silver spiders impaled on spikes. On the adjacent wall sat a computer desk surrounded with shelves of books about music and art history, travel, computer science, and a diverse collection of fiction. Jack had pushed aside the computer's keyboard and placed his laptop in front of the monitor.

Bradley scanned the room. "Where's Mark?"

"We drove him home." Jack walked to the entertainment

center and turned down the volume on the stereo. "His parents are still a little freaked about his spider attack."

"I hope he doesn't say anything about tonight," Bradley said. "He'll never go to Washbrook again."

"He won't." Trillian sipped her soda, grabbed a few potato chips and began to munch on them.

O'Connor claimed the bowl of tortilla chips for herself. "Just what the doctor ordered." She strolled through the living room, observing the framed photos and artwork, and reading the titles of the shelved books. "What do your folks do to afford this place?"

"They write travel books for cyclists," Jack said.

"Hmm." O'Connor nodded in approval. "Business must be pretty good."

"They aren't complaining," Jack said. "As a result I'm basically an orphan, but that's beside the point."

Bradley's phone chirped in his pocket. He slid it out of his pocket and saw a text from Mark with a photo attachment. "Look what I found in our garage," the text read.

Bradley enlarged the photo, revealing a tube of webbing with a black spider halfway inside. The spider had quills expanding outward from its thorax.

"Holy shit. Look at this," Bradley said. He handed the phone to Trillian and Fiscara.

Trillian's eyes widened and Bradley noticed a shiver move through her back. The fine hairs on her arms stood up like the bristles on a hairbrush.

"Where does—" A second text chirped, interrupting Fiscara.

"Crushed the fucker," Mark texted.

Fiscara handed the phone to Jack's outreached hand. He looked at it, then showed it to O'Connor.

"Crushed the fucker? Hah!" O'Connor said between handfuls of tortilla chips. "Kill it and ask questions later. My kinda guy."

She handed the phone to Sam. He gave the image a casual glance before handing it back to Bradley.

Fiscara tried again. "Where does Mark live?"

"About halfway between here and the golf course," Jack said.

Fiscara motioned toward Jack's laptop. "You need to add his house to your map."

"Good idea." Jack scribbled a note on a piece of paper and set it next to his laptop. "Is anyone thirsty? There's soda in the fridge, plus some beer that my dad left."

"Beer me," O'Connor said.

"If you're drinking, I get to drive Baby Blue." Sam crossed his arms.

"Forget the beer." O'Connor munched on chips. "No one gets to drive Baby Blue except me."

"Miss Fiscara? Mr. Shaw? Beer?"

"Thanks, but no," Fiscara said. "We're still chaperones."

"And I don't drink," Sam added. "But I wouldn't turn down a Coke."

Fiscara studied Sam's face. Some of the tattoos he revealed earlier could be seen peeking out from his t-shirt collar. "Make it two."

"Make it three." Tortilla crumbs flew from O'Connor's mouth as she spoke.

Jack fetched the Cokes and tossed them one at a time to Sam and Fiscara. He hand-delivered the last Coke to O'Connor.

O'Connor draped herself on the sofa, taking up one side of the sectional. "So, you're an inventor, huh?"

Jack sat on the slate bench surrounding the fireplace. "I've made some things, yeah."

"What have you made?"

Jack looked around the living room. "The music you're hearing is playing from my phone. I rigged a Bluetooth headset to a cassette adapter. I use it in my car mostly."

O'Connor raised her eyebrows. "What else?"

"Made this retractable metal arm for holding stencils on a spray paint can." Jack mimed the arm's action with his own. "I just squeeze, tag, and run. I could make one for Detest-A-Pest."

"I've seen it," Bradley said. "It's pretty cool."

"I'm down for one. What else?" O'Connor narrowed her eyes. "Any killing devices?"

Jack thought for a moment, then his eyes lit up. "The razor vacuum attachment!" He looked at Bradley. "Bro, remember that drawing I showed you?"

Bradley nodded. "Yeah. You got a build?"

Jack ran down the stairs to the lower level of the house. "It's in the garage," he called back as he descended. "Back in a sec."

"It's pretty cool," Bradley said. "You ever heard of a Flowbee?"

O'Connor cackled. "Who do you think you're talking to? You remember that thing, Sam?"

"Yeah. The infomercials were so cheesy. The thing scared me."

"You guys ever had the pleasure of getting your hair cut with a razor comb?" Fiscara ran her fingers through her hair for effect.

Trillian scrunched her brow. "What? A comb with a—"

"A razor blade embedded in it," Fiscara said. "Yeah. Literally."

Trillian grimaced.

"Maybe at a barber shop?" Sam shrugged. "But I've had a buzzcut for most of my life." He exchanged a knowing glance with Bradley.

"Whatever. Blah blah blah." O'Connor waved her hands, flinging chip crumbs around. "What's the story?"

"When I was twelve, my mom decided to cut my hair herself, to save some money," Fiscara began.

O'Connor started to chuckle, her stomach bouncing. "No happy story ever began with 'my mom cut my hair.'"

"I know, right? Anyway, she saw this thing called 'The Home Barber.' Let me tell you, it should've been called 'The Home

Butcher.' It was triangular and had a different comb on each side, and razors embedded in two of them."

First Bradley joined the laughter with stifled giggles, then Trillian and Sam not too long after.

"I'm sitting in a chair in the kitchen," Fiscara said, "a sheet tied around my neck. My mom starts running this thing through my hair, which was longer than it is now." She let her hair fall through her fingers. "At first it seemed okay, but then the thing snagged. Instead of stopping, she pulled harder and the tangled hair in the comb and blades just got worse."

Everyone was laughing now, including Fiscara, and she fought to maintain her composure.

"She wasn't cutting my hair but pulling it out in clumps. I was in tears, but my mom was determined to make it work. She only stopped when she drew blood."

Trillian placed her hand over her mouth. "Oh shit."

"Yeah." Fiscara pulled back her hair and revealed a small bald spot at the back "Hair doesn't grow on that part of my head anymore, but the rest covers it up."

Sam raised his brow. "She threw that thing away, right?"

"Actually, no." She sipped her Coke, grinning. "Get this, she tried it on my younger brother, saying it was *my* hair that was the problem."

"And?" O'Connor was hooked.

"He's been bald ever since."

Everyone erupted with laughter. A text chime sounded from Bradley's phone.

"But seriously, the same thing happened to him," Fiscara said between giggles. "Me and my brother took that 'Home Barber' into the back yard and smashed it with a hammer. My mom never asked where it had gone, but I think she knew."

Bradley's phone chimed again.

"Did Mark find something else in his garage?" Sam asked.

Bradley looked at his phone and his face drained of color. "Oh *fuck*."

O'Connor raised an eyebrow. "What?"

"It's Jack."

BRADLEY LED THE way down the stairs, followed closely by the others. The lower hallway connected with the recreation room to the left, a laundry and bathroom combo, two spare bedrooms and the garage at the end to the right. The interior door to the garage was open and the light was on. Jack was nowhere in sight.

The smell of metal and motor oil intensified with each step. As Bradley approached the door frame, his field of view within the garage increased. He spotted Jack to the right, crouched down on the concrete floor with his "spider vacuum," his eyes wide in a mixture of fear and excitement.

Jack raised his index finger to his lips, shushing Bradley, then pointed at the corner of the garage opposite where he sat.

Bradley first turned to the rest of the crew and relayed Jack's instructions, then turned to look where Jack had pointed moments before. He inched his head past the door frame and peeked into the corner of the garage. A funnel web at least three feet tall had been built in the corner, woven in and around a set of metal shelves containing tools and seasonal household supplies.

Bradley brought out his phone and loaded the photo app, framing the web on the screen. Trillian sidled up next to Bradley and saw Jack signaling frantically. She tapped him on the shoulder and motioned at Jack.

Jack mouthed the words, exaggerating each syllable. "No light."

Bradley and Trillian had no idea what he was saying. They shrugged and mouthed back "What?"

Jack tapped a message on his phone with one hand and held it up instead of sending it. "No light. No flash. No sound."

Bradley and Trillian gave him a thumbs up. He tapped the word "sporky?" into his phone and held it for Jack to read.

Jack nodded.

Bradley turned the flash off and snapped a picture in the dim light of the garage. He turned to Jack, held up his index finger, and mouthed, "Be right back."

Bradley backed into the hallway and presented the photo to the rest of the crew.

"Funnel web," Fiscara whispered.

Bradley nodded and whispered back, "Sporky."

"What's the plan?" Sam's whisper came out gravelly and harsh.

"Vacuum," Bradley said, low and quiet.

O'Connor rubbed her hands together. "That's the main attraction, baby." She spoke louder than anyone.

Bradley shushed her. "Keep it down," he whispered. "You want to get him killed?" He turned and approached the door frame again.

Jack held up his phone with a message on it. "You, lite. Me, vac. 3-2-1 ON. OK?"

Bradley nodded in agreement. He prepared his phone for flashlight mode.

Jack set his phone down and locked gaze with Bradley. "Ready?" he mouthed.

Bradley gave a thumbs up.

Jack extended three fingers, then two, then one. He turned the vacuum on just as Bradley flooded the corner with light.

Jack moved fast, shoving the razor-edged nozzle of the vacuum into the center of the web, cutting it away from the shelving and sucking it through the nozzle. Shredded web flew out the bottom side of the nozzle and onto Jack's feet.

"It works!" Jack spotted the black spider in the back of the nest, the size of a football with its quills flexing. He pressed forward with the nozzle's end.

"Great, kid," O'Connor said.

The flexible tubing reached its maximum length and pulled free of the vacuum. The suction at the nozzle's end dropped to zero and the spider leaped to the end of the nozzle. Jack knocked the spider onto the shelving.

Jack panicked. "It's getting away!"

"Shit!" Sam hopped over the tubing and into the garage, lifted the vacuum with one muscular arm, and reconnected the tube. "Now, Jack!"

Jack followed the spider through the shelves. Blocked by a box of rat poison, it attempted to scurry around the obstacle only to be caught by the suction of the vacuum.

But the spider had hooked its legs around the edge of the nozzle, stopping it from being pulled through the spinning blades within.

Jack repositioned the nozzle's end and pressed it into the drywall, cutting off the spider's legs and finishing the job. A glob of bluish-green paste ejected from the bottom side of the nozzle and sprayed against Jack's pants.

"Shut it off." Jack said between breaths, his face slicked with sweat. "You see that? Fucking thing *works*."

Sam toggled the power button and the vacuum's motor wound down.

"You better take off your pants." Trillian said.

There was a moment of awkward silence. Sam and Fiscara shared a glance.

"I thought you liked Brad," Jack said grinning, already unzipping his fly. Bradley glared at him, embarrassment evident on his neck and cheeks.

Trillian gave Jack a sideways look and crossed her arms. "Idiot." Trillian pointed at the bluish-green splatter. "Remember what happened to Mark, asshat."

"Right." Jack kicked off his pants and rolled them into a ball. "Look out. Toxic waste coming though."

"Add your house to the map now too," Fiscara said as Jack moved past.

"Noted," Jack called back.

Ten minutes later, everyone had regrouped in the living room. Jack placed his ruined pants in the fireplace and set them ablaze. He sat on the slate bench to monitor the flames.

Sam and Fiscara reclined on the longer side of the sectional sofa, with O'Connor stretched out reclaiming her earlier spot. Bradley and Trillian sat at the dining room table nearby, snacking on potato chips and talking to each other quietly.

"That was a nice gadget you made back there," O'Connor said.

Jack shrugged and ran his hands across his clean khakis. "It was my first prototype. It needs a lot of refinement."

O'Connor interlaced her fingers behind her head. "I used to work with an inventor just like you, but in the end, the rats ate him."

Bradley fell silent.

"Ate him?" Fiscara looked surprised. "I've never heard of rats eating people before, at least not in the last hundred years."

"Stick with me, honey," O'Connor said. "You'll see things that'll turn your shit white. Ain't that right, Sam?"

Sam closed his eyes. "Washington. He was a good man."

"Damn straight." O'Connor's eyes went dark and distant for a moment. "I still prefer killing shit with fire."

"Yeah, you've got a point." Jack tapped his temple with his finger. "And I have some ideas to harness the power of fire."

O'Connor rubbed her hands together. "Do tell."

Jack yawned. "Got to finish the prototype first."

"Tease." O'Connor felt the cigar in her breast pocket. "Shit, I need a smoke."

Trillian had been watching the reactions of Sam and O'Connor, then refocused on Bradley. "Hey, are you okay?"

Bradley nodded.

"Washington," she said softly.

Bradley nodded again. Trillian placed her hand lightly on his shoulder. Both felt the comforting warmth of the other.

"So, Jack," O'Connor said. "I see you got some spare bedrooms. Mind if Sam and I crash here for a couple days?"

"They kind of checked out of their motel already," Bradley said.

"Kinda?" Jack raised his brow. "You don't mind sleeping downstairs after what just happened?"

"The fucker's dead, right?"

Jack looked at the fireplace grate. A pile of ash sat where his ruined pants had been, wisps of smoke rising in weak tendrils. "Yeah."

"No problem then," O'Connor said. "Right?"

"Sure." Jack stood. "Just don't trash the place." He turned to Bradley and Trillian. "Want a lift home?"

"It's okay, Jack." Fiscara sat forward. "It's late. I'll drive them home."

"Thanks."

"Well…" Fiscara stood, her eyes flitting from person to person and settling on Sam ever so briefly. "I have to say, this has been the most exciting chaperoning experience in all my years at Washbrook."

"But we still haven't found the source," Bradley said.

Jack smiled sleepily. "Don't worry, bro. We will."

Fiscara looked at Bradley and Trillian. "Shall we?" The two of them nodded.

Jack escorted Fiscara, Bradley, and Trillian to the door and saw them off. He returned to the top of the stairs. "Look, I got to work tomorrow and I need some sleep. The rooms downstairs are made up, but you can sleep anywhere. Good night."

"Good night, Jack," Sam said. "And thanks."

"Yeah, thanks," O'Connor added.

Jack had already shut his bedroom door and was out of earshot.

"So…" O'Connor looked at Sam and batted her lashes. "Want to have sex?"

"What?" Sam stared back at her with surprise mixed with a little terror.

O'Connor burst into hysterical laughter. "Just busting your balls. You're not my type. Should've seen your face, though." She rolled off the sofa still laughing, walked behind where Sam sat, and patted his shoulder roughly. "Good night."

Sam sat alone in the living room. He spied his tattoos peeking out from the cuffs of his flannel shirt and reminded himself that he'd be a free man in three months. Then he'd have to make a real decision about what to do about his life.

But for now, he was content to try and think like a spider. He looked at the screensaver on Jack's laptop, beckoning him from the desk on the opposite side of the living room.

"It couldn't hurt to take a look," he said to himself. "Maybe I'll learn something." Sam sat himself down and began to browse, not knowing where it would take him.

Bad Things Come in Threes

Five-thirty Saturday morning came fast. Jack groaned and rolled over, silencing his alarm. He could give himself an extra fifteen minutes of sleep if he gave up his morning shower, but after battling spiders at the dance *and* at home, his body odor convinced him otherwise.

The shower woke him up. He dressed and grabbed some breakfast. Sam lay asleep on the couch, right where Jack had left him five hours ago, a low rumbling snore emanating from his nose. Jack thought of recording some video just for fun but reconsidered after noting the time. In his head, Jack pictured Mr. Toscano with a stopwatch in his office at the back of Food Fresh, noting each employee's time of arrival.

"Not today, Toscano." Jack backed the Civic out of the garage and peeled out. Speed limits were rarely an issue at this time of the morning.

He rolled into his favorite parking spot at the market and noted the time on his phone: five minutes to spare. From bed to shower to the market in under thirty minutes—a performance approaching epic status.

But Jack's luck had run out. Mr. Moody was on his list of deliveries again. Bananas and a jug of milk with no additions or substitutions, his standing Saturday order. He threw on an apron and began stocking shelves, saving his deliveries for later in his shift.

By the time Jack rolled into Mr. Moody's potholed driveway, it was approaching ten in the morning.

Move faster, Jack thought. *Got to get in and out before his shows begin.* He had made that mistake once before during an episode of *The Price Is Right* and the bastard had refused to answer his door until the show was over. Even though it was Saturday, Jack had vowed never to make that mistake again.

Today he carried the bananas and milk in a paper bag instead of a box, double-bagged for strength. That was another lesson he had learned early on. Jack could have been delivering a bag of cotton balls, but if it wasn't double-bagged, Moody would complain.

"You got nothing to complain about today, Mr. Moody," Jack grumbled as he knocked on the door.

After what seemed like a minute, Jack checked the time on his phone and knocked on the door again. In the back of his mind, he could see Mr. Toscano making notes in his little black book.

"Food Fresh Delivery, Mr. Moody," Jack said as he knocked a third time. There was no response. He tried to look through the window in the door, craning his neck to gauge any movement inside, but the windowpane was frosted over with a mixture of dust, dirt, and grease.

"Fuck this shit." Jack grabbed the doorknob and twisted it. The door wouldn't budge. "Dammit." He was left with the choice of leaving the delivery on the doorstep, and risk the wrath of both Moody and Toscano, or finding a way in. He could break a window or find a way to jimmy the lock.

In all the times Jack had delivered food to Mr. Moody, he had never noticed the lack of a deadbolt. That made the choice easy. He valued his job too much, but he had to act quickly.

He set the groceries down and trotted to his car. Jack dug around in the back seat and collected a shoe box lid and an empty soda can. Back at the side door, he fished into his pocket and retrieved a Swiss Army knife. He cut a strip of cardboard and jammed it in between the door and door frame, working it against the latch and strike plate. The cardboard buckled under the pressure.

Jack cut the top and bottom off the soda can, then down one side to form a flat aluminum sheet. He folded it in half for strength and tried to pop the latch out of the strike plate again as he had before. The aluminum wouldn't budge.

"Fuck!" Jack's mind raced, trying to come up with an alternative. He glanced at his phone, reminded of the time ticking away. He collapsed the blade of the Swiss Army knife into its handle, then stared at it. The solution had been in his hand all along.

Jack opened the knife half-way, forming a square angle between the blade and the handle. He inserted the tip of the blade into the keyway in the door handle and rotated it, placing tension on the lock cylinder. He slid out the set of tweezers from the knife's handle and inserted it into the keyway, jiggling it as the tweezers moved further into the door handle.

Jack heard a *pop* on the other side of the door. He twisted the doorknob and to his surprise and excitement the door slid open. "Just like the fucking movies," he said to himself, grinning.

A waft of something sweet but overpoweringly wrong floated past his nose. Jack held back the urge to vomit. "Hello? Mr. Moody? It's Jack from Food Fresh."

The house wasn't silent. He could hear the television from the living room, but it sounded more like sports than game shows.

He dropped the knife back into his pocket, picked up the bag of groceries, and stepped inside. The smell grew stronger the farther in he walked.

Jack unloaded the bananas and set them on the counter. "What the hell?" The bowl that Moody used for bananas still had a couple left in it, but the skins had many gaping holes, like someone had jammed and lit small firecrackers within the fruit.

Normally he let Moody put away the milk, but something in his gut told him that he should do it today. He pulled open the refrigerator expecting to see a den of filth and rot. Instead, a quarter-full jug of milk, a can of freeze-dried instant coffee, and a pot of congealing oatmeal sat on the center shelf. It was the cleanest part of the house.

He folded the empty paper bag twice and jammed it and the receipt into his back pocket.

Jack held his hand over his nose. "Mr. Moody? You okay?" He stepped out of the kitchen and moved further down the hallway, toward the living room where the television was. College basketball was what he was hearing, Jack was sure of it.

The smell was terrible. It stung his nose and the air felt wet against his skin. Every step was a battle to control his revulsion.

Jack reached the entrance to the living room and peered around the edge of the wall. The last time he had ventured this far into Moody's house was to unsnag his creepy-ass toenails from his afghan. What he saw in front of him today made him freeze in terror.

Moody's body—which was more a *rounded shape* than a body—lay slumped to one side in his motorized wheelchair. His body was grossly bloated and stretched the fabric of his clothes so much that some of the seams had begun to rip and unravel. Globs of cloudy mucus dripped from his swollen hands and Moody's head lolled back unnaturally far on his shoulders, such that he'd be able to see Jack, if he still had eyes.

But Moody's face was gone, the peaks and valleys of his nose, cheeks, and chin leveled and encased in grey webbing. A funnel of webbing descended from the corner of the ceiling and the wall, and connected to a dark hole in Moody's head, where Jack guessed his mouth had been. The horror on display short-circuited any rational thought.

A black spider, complete with its requisite quills, crawled

onto Moody's head and disappeared into the dark open end at the funnel web's terminus.

Moody's mouth.

"Ho... ly... *shit.*" The words escaped from Jack's throat in a hoarse whisper as he stumbled backward, knocking a table into the wall.

The sound echoed through the small space. Everything became dark, but not due to lack of light. Morning sun still filtered through the translucent curtains. The darkness moved toward Jack like living paint, over Moody's body and onto the floor. And as it moved, Jack heard clicks and scratches.

Move! Run! Jack's brain screamed at him, but he was frozen, unable to move. The dense clutter of black spiders continued their steady approach.

Jack could hear noises from the kitchen now too. Soon all avenues of escape would be closed. An ad for 1997's *Starship Troopers* blasted from the television speakers, distracting Jack just enough to hear the film's tagline. He put his own spin on it.

"The only good spider is a dead motherfucking spider." Jack turned and ran down the hallway toward the mudroom and the side door. The distance felt much longer now that his life was on the line.

He passed the kitchen and the countertops were covered with spiders. Jack leaped down the ramp into the mudroom and slammed his body against the side door before he remembered that the door opened inward.

Jack pulled the door open, stepped through and slammed it closed. He slid down the door to sit on the landing. His stomach finally overtook him. He leaned over the edge of the balcony and vomited into an overgrown flowerbed. He spat, wiped his mouth, and reclined against the door again.

"Kill it with fire," he whispered to himself as he caught his breath. "Kill it with fire." He looked at the detached garage and remembered his newest invention. A key component of his idea lay within.

He pictured Moody's ring of keys hanging from his wheelchair and briefly contemplated going back in. "Fuck *that* shit." Going back into the house would be suicide. Jack's hand fell to the pants pocket containing his Swiss Army knife. "If I can pick this lock…"

With renewed vigor, Jack stepped to the side entrance of the garage. The door was secured with a padlock, but installed backward so that anyone with a screwdriver could get in. His Swiss Army knife was equipped for the task.

He extracted the knife from his pocket and pulled out the flathead screwdriver. He began loosening the screws from the padlock bracket when he realized that the padlock was unlocked and hanging by its lock loop. Whoever had access to the garage had grown tired of asking for Moody's keys.

Jack tightened the screw, unhooked the lock loop and opened the door. If he had had more time, he would have browsed the small space, which was filled to the rafters with vintage machinery. However, the item he had come for, a gas-powered power washer, sat right next to the door.

He's not going to need this now, Jack thought. *Plus, I'll be using it for the greater good.* He left the lock loose as he had found it and carried the washer to his car. It fit perfectly into the passenger footwell, but he covered it with a blanket just in case.

He pulled out his phone and had already tapped out 9-1 before he stopped himself. Being young and black, he was keenly aware of how he was perceived, especially by law enforcement. He had just entered a house with a dead body inside, and now had stolen property in his car. He pocketed his phone, slid into his car through the driver-side window and backed out of the driveway.

With the prevalence of cell phones, public phone booths had

become harder to find as time moved forward. But Jack knew there was a bank of them at Stonehurst Hills strip mall.

He parked the Civic a block away and walked to the mall. The parking lot was half full of Saturday shoppers. Most of the pay phones were out of order or missing the handset. The second to last phone in the cluster gave him a dial tone. He dialed 9-1-1.

"I want to report a death." Jack relayed the details to the 9-1-1 operator and hung up. As he walked back to his car, he could hear the sirens approaching. Once in his car, he sat and waited for the emergency vehicles to pass before starting his engine.

He docked his phone and cranked the tunes, noting the time. "Shit, Toscano is going to fire my ass," Jack said to himself. He hoped that he would catch a break, seeing that he had just made a delivery to a dead man.

He headed back home to drop off the power washer, purposely driving under the speed limit and avoiding Mr. Moody's neighborhood entirely. He rolled the Civic into his garage and removed the washer from the back seat. He looked to the corner of the garage where he had encountered a sporky less than twelve hours earlier. Wisps of webbing and oval marks on the walls from the nozzle were all that remained.

Kill it with fire. Jack nodded and grinned. *This invention's going to be epic.*

THE SUN BEAMED down from a clear blue afternoon sky when Claire was discharged. It was officially Fall but it sure didn't feel like it.

Roy drove the Nissan Leaf home from Sun Valley Medical Center, with Claire in the passenger seat and Bradley sitting in the back. Roy had tried to sneak out alone, but Bradley was one step ahead of him and waiting by the car when it came time to leave.

"How are you feeling, Babe." Roy punctuated his words with quick glances at Bradley through the rearview mirror. "Leg still okay?"

Bradley narrowed his eyes and gritted his teeth. It was hard to be in the same small space as Roy after their fight, but Claire was more important. He'd keep the peace for her.

"Roy, stop fussing," Claire said. "My leg's fine. I'm just glad we're so close to the hospital."

"Why? Are you hurting?" Roy shot a concerned look at Claire.

"I'm *fine*. I'm more concerned about your nose." Claire returned a look of her own. "The shower door?"

Roy shot a look at Bradley through the rearview mirror. "What can I say? I slipped."

Bradley grinned, reached out, and squeezed Claire's shoulder lightly. "I'm glad you're okay, Mom."

She pulled his hand to her lips and planted a light kiss on his fingers. "Thanks honey. Glad to be *going* home."

Once on Sheldon Street, Roy flipped on his turn signal and prepared to turn down the alley to the detached garage.

"I think parking out front would be better," Bradley said.

There were those angry eyes in the rearview mirror again. "I got it covered, thanks."

"Brad's right." Claire caressed the back of Roy's neck. "That way I can go straight into the house and flop onto the sofa."

Bradley offered a satisfied grin and made sure that Roy saw it in the rearview mirror.

"Okay." Roy turned off the signal and pulled up in front of the house. "Stay put. I'm coming around to get you." Roy jumped out of the car, ran to the passenger side, and opened the door.

"You're fussing." Claire gave a half-hearted attempt to wave him off, but it was clear that she was enjoying being fawned over.

Roy helped Claire out of the car. She wore the same coveralls that she had worn when she was bitten, but with the fabric cut away on the left side. Her exposed left leg was wrapped in a purple compression bandage below the knee that matched her painted toenails. She steadied herself on the side of the car.

Claire's purple crutches were propped up against the back seat. Roy leaned in to grab them and glared at Bradley. "Not a fucking word, hear me?"

"Or what?"

Roy's cheeks flushed crimson. "Bring in your mother's overnight bags." He pointed an angry index finger at Bradley and backed out of the car. He handed the crutches to Claire and guided her across the street, down the walk, and to the front door.

Bradley followed with Claire's overnight bag and small suitcase. "You can go park the car, Roy. I've got it from here."

Roy glared at Bradley.

Claire touched Roy's arm. "I'll see you inside, okay?" She smiled at him and kissed his cheek. That seemed to diffuse some of his anger.

Bradley passed Roy going down the steps and bumped shoulders with him. He unlocked the front door and stepped into the house, holding it open for Claire.

"My spidey-sense is detecting a strange vibe." She looked at Bradley as she navigated the entryway on her crutches. "What's gotten into you both?"

Bradley shrugged. "I don't know." He dropped the suitcase and overnight bag near the door and helped Claire onto the sofa. He placed a pillow under her left leg, raising it up.

"Thanks, honey. How was the dance?"

Bradley smirked, recalling the evening. "Interesting. I went to Jack's place afterward to hang."

"Late night?"

Bradley grinned. "Not too late."

"Any luck finding the spider that bit me?"

"Yeah, actually. There were a bunch of spiders at the dance too, the same kind. Big ones," Bradley said. "Jack and Trillian and me, and Dad and O'Connor and my bio teacher too, we exterminated them and examined their bodies after. We all went to Jack's to chill and talk about it and he was attacked in his garage."

"Oh no!" Claire's eyes went wide with concern. "Is Jack okay?"

The back door opened and slammed closed.

"He's fine. He killed that spider with this cool vacuum attachment he made."

"I've got no love for those things," Claire said, "but I don't like all this talk of killing like it's no big deal."

Bradley sat on the sofa next to her. "But those *spiders* are killing things." His blue eyes shone clear and strong. "If you weren't a nurse, you could have died."

Claire took a moment to study her son's face, the angle of his jawline, his eyes, his concern.

"What?"

She placed her hands on his cheeks. "I've missed you." She leaned forward and hugged Bradley tightly. He reciprocated.

Roy entered the living room from the kitchen. "Babe, can I get you anything?" His eyes went dark upon seeing Bradley in Claire's arms.

She planted a light peck on Bradley's cheek and thought for a moment. "A nice cup of tea would be wonderful."

"Coming right up." Roy disappeared back into the kitchen. "What kind of tea?" he called back.

"Chamomile, please."

Sounds of cupboard doors opening and closing echoed back to the living room.

Claire lowered her voice to a whisper. "Go show him where the tea is, honey."

Bradley gave her a sideways look. "Come on, Mom."

"Please?"

Bradley sighed and made his way to the kitchen. He opened a cupboard above the coffee maker and kettle, and pulled out a box of chamomile tea from the back.

Roy grabbed Bradley's shirt and pinned him against the counter. "If you say anything about Friday night, I will fuck you up," he hissed. "I will become your *worst* nightmare."

Bradley pushed the box of tea into Roy's chest. "Sometimes a simple *thank you* is all you need to say." As he walked out of the kitchen, he called to Claire in the living room. "I'll be in my room. I've got some reading to do."

For the first time in his life, Bradley wished for his parents to reconcile. He closed his bedroom door, removed his phone from his pocket, and was about to place it on his charger when he noticed he had missed a text from Jack.

"Sporkies killed Moody." the text read.

ROY ROSE EARLY the next morning. From the bedroom window, he could see reds and oranges had just begun breaking across the horizon, and the rest of the sky faded into a cloudless sapphire blue.

He kissed Claire's cheek, causing her to stir. "Going for a run," he whispered. She murmured something unintelligible in response and fell back asleep.

Roy dressed in his usual red jogging suit and positioned the white headband around his forehead. As he padded in bare feet down the hallway to the kitchen, he stopped at Bradley's door. He raised his fist to knock, then decided against it.

He filled a water bottle and found his red jogging shoes in the mudroom off the kitchen. He sat on the bench and picked up the right shoe. A black spider fell out onto the floor.

Roy let out a little shriek and flinched back. He instinctively looked around to see if anyone had seen his reaction and quickly regained his composure. He chased the spider across the floor and pounded it into a black smear on the linoleum with the heel of his shoe.

"Take that you little fucker." He tapped the heel of each shoe to make sure there were no more hidden eight-legged surprises, then slipped them on and tied the laces in neat bows.

Roy stepped out the back of the house and inhaled a cleansing breath. The analog thermometer's needle hovered around 65° F. Too hot for a marathon, but perfect for a morning jog.

He stowed his water bottle into a pouch at the small of his back and checked his watch. The sun would rise in less than an hour. After some warm-up stretches, he ran around to the front of the house and pulled out his phone. He opened his running app and tucked the phone back into a zippered pocket. The suburb of Stonehurst had just begun to wake up to another Monday morning as he headed southwest on Sheldon Street.

Roy's usual six mile loop circumnavigated Hansen Dam Golf Club, returning on the bike path over the dam. It took him just over an hour to complete, using Claire's house as home base. He had run the loop in the opposite direction a few times, but it didn't offer as beautiful a view. This morning he estimated that he'd be crossing the dam just as the sun broke the horizon.

A definite photo op, Roy thought.

He turned north up Wentworth Street, jogging in the bike lane—which doubled as a horse lane—but neither cyclists nor equestrian riders were out this early.

Roy crossed Wentworth at the southeast foot path access to Hansen Dam Golf Club. He followed the winding path around the southern edge of the front nine until the path joined with Montague Street and later, Glenoaks Boulevard. He followed the road northwest along the border of the back nine, dwarfed on his right by an eighteen foot tall golf backstop.

Roy glanced at his watch. He was making good time and might even manage a personal best. He followed Osbourne Street northeast and ducked right onto the Hansen Dam bike path. The valley was considerably brighter now. The sun had just started to peek over the horizon, flooding the San Fernando Valley with golden warmth. He pulled out his water bottle and took a swig.

The light will be just right on the opposite side, Roy thought as he replaced the water bottle back in its pouch. *That'll be my photo op.*

The top leading edge of Hansen Dam had been turned into a path two miles long. Signs described it as a "bike path," but everyone used it, walkers, joggers, and cyclists alike. As the path approached and crossed the dam's spillway channels in the middle of the structure, nearby vegetation thinned out to nothing, replaced by barren flats on one side and coarse, rocky scree on the outflow side.

At a brisk jogging pace, it usually took Roy about twenty minutes to run from the west side of the dam to the east. As he approached the spill gates, the path narrowed between chain-link fencing, the face of dam to his right and the dam's solitary maintenance building to the left.

The sun broke the horizon and shot bright rays of sunshine into Roy's eyes. He held his hand up to block the intense light, but the aftereffects of the sunspots bounced in his vision like a photographer's flash, distracting him from the dark pebbles lining both sides of the path.

Yet some of pebbles were too big to be pebbles. And they moved when he moved. His foot fell on one and instead of rocking like a pebble, it squished with an audible *crunch*.

Roy slowed his pace as he realized what he was seeing. Spiders were surrounding him, black, ugly ones, and turning back wasn't an option. The only escape was forward.

A two-hundred foot long concrete corridor between chain-link walls stretched out before him. Spiders of all sizes, some as big as footballs, spilled up, over the edge, and under the fencing in coordinated movements.

I could outrun them if I just kicked it up a notch.

But Roy's body protested, his judgment overoptimistic. Increasing his pace would be a challenge after forty minutes of jogging. The influx of spiders making a run at him forced his hand. He had no other option.

Roy's muscles screamed at him with every stride, and for a brief moment he thought he'd make it. Exhaustion and incoordination tangled his feet together three-quarters of the way in. He tripped, hitting the concrete path hard on his right side. Any chance of making it past the impending cluster of spiders was lost.

Roy pushed himself off the ground, ignoring his bruises and scrapes, and hobbled to the locked chain-link fence that surrounded the maintenance building. He grabbed the fence with both hands and rattled it, as if that would magically unlock it. But the fence remained locked, just as the spiders continued their attack. His only escape was up, even though the top of the fence was lined with coils of barbed wire.

Roy didn't need any convincing. The white noise of hundreds of black legs propelling themselves across the concrete was more than enough reason to begin climbing. He hooked his fingers as high as he could reach, jammed one foot into a link of the fence, and raised himself up. His thighs protested the exertion, but he followed with a second step, then a third.

The bare concrete where he had stood seconds ago was swallowed up by a mass of spiders, the quills on their backs quivering as if sensing his fear. They flowed across the concrete like a slick of black oil.

Roy took another step up the fence and reached over the barbed wire with his right arm. *If I can just get to the roof of the maintenance building, I can—*

A searing pain shot through his left ankle and he lost his footing. His right arm was dragged back through the barbed wire, ripping though the sleeve of his track suit and into the flesh and tendons of his arm. Roy could feel his warm blood flowing down his right arm and soaking into his jacket and pants.

With his uninjured limbs, he pulled himself back up far enough to see three spiders on the back of his left leg. Roy tried to shake them off, but his left leg hung limp from his hips, unresponsive to command.

The spiders had no trouble climbing the chain-link fence. Larger spiders left strands of webbing bisecting the openings in the fence, making it easier for the smaller spiders to climb. They were working together, coordinating their efforts toward a common goal.

Roy watched in horror as the spiders attacked his right leg now. He was able to shake off the first few, but each spider's nimble legs allowed for fast, evasive movement. He couldn't keep up. The intense pain of individual bites melted into an overall fiery sensation, as if he was being burned alive.

His body began to swell, first at his feet, followed by his calves and thighs as the venom coursed through his veins. Thoughts became disjointed as delirium and paralysis set in.

Spiders reached the height of the fence and advanced toward Roy along the top rail and through the coils of barbed wire. He flailed with this left arm, the only limb obeying his brain, and almost connected with the closest spider. The arachnid spun around and sacrificed itself by launching its volley of quills at Roy's face. The sharp ends embedded themselves across his face, piercing through his cheeks, nose, and eyelids. The spider's spent body tumbled off the fence replaced by dozens more.

The Monday morning sunrise basked Roy in a warm glow as his life bled away. The spiders made quick work of encasing his inflated body in a silken sac with strands as strong as spun steel.

JACK'S TEXT THE previous night had lit a fire under Bradley and he planned to give Jack hell for leaving him hanging. He had arrived at the school by eight o'clock, but twenty minutes later Jack still hadn't graced the student parking lot. The first attendance bell would ring any minute.

"What's up?" a voice said from behind.

Where the hell are you, Jack? Bradley paced as he watched the student parking lot filled up.

"Earth to Brad," the voice said. "Come in, Brad."

Bradley turned to find Trillian, the bright smile on her face faltering once she saw trouble in his eyes. He didn't hide it well.

"What's wrong?"

"Jack's late," Bradley said.

"You're worried about Jack's attendance record?"

"No. Sorry." Bradley switched gears. "You know he works at Food Fresh, right?"

"Yeah, everyone knows that."

"He also does deliveries and there's this one guy, a really big guy, we're talking *huge,* who never leaves his house because he's stuck in a wheelchair. All he eats is oatmeal and bananas." Bradley's words flowed out like a torrent.

Trillian placed a hand lightly on the center of Bradley's chest. "Slow down. Breathe." She pulled her hand back after sensing the warmth and strength of his body. It was too much of a distraction.

Bradley gave her a sideways look. "You need backstory."

"Okay," Trillian said. "Jack delivers to a fat invalid who likes old-school breakfast. So?"

"The guy's dead." Bradley scanned the parking lot and street. "Killed by spiders."

"Sporkies?"

The echo of Jack's high performance Civic announced his arrival. He turned into the lot and found a parking stall in no time.

"I swear he's got a lucky horseshoe up his ass." Bradley set off toward Jack's car. "Come on." He was about to beckon toward her, but Trillian was already matching his strides. She took the lead and arrived first.

Jack had just stepped out of the passenger side door when he was accosted by Trillian and Bradley.

"Spill it," Trillian said.

Bradley rapped his knuckles on Jack's shoulder. "You haven't been returning my texts or calls, dude. What gives?"

The school bell rang and the three friends headed toward the school.

"I had to lay low for a while." Jack looked over his shoulders and back toward the street. "You know, cops."

"What did you do?" Trillian asked.

"I didn't do nothing, but I'm black *and* I was the last person to see the guy. He was way past dead when I got there." Jack shivered, then pulled Bradley and Trillian aside just before entering the school. "I kinda stole something from his garage, too."

"See, *that's* the kind of thing that gets you arrested," Bradley said.

"Keep your fucking voice down." Jack looked for potential eavesdroppers. "Shit."

Trillian smirked and crossed her arms. "What was so important that you had to steal it from a dead fat invalid?"

"A power washer."

Trillian burst into laughter.

"You're joking," Bradley said. "You planning on cleaning—"

"Think outside the box for a second, idiots." Jack looked at them both, dead serious. "A power washer would make a great flame thrower."

Trillian raised a brow. "Okay, you're redeemed." She pulled open the door to the south stairwell. "Let's go or we'll be late."

FROM THE FAR edge of the parking lot, Alexis watched Trillian, Bradley and Jack enter the school. She was flanked by Deirdre and Caitlin. "It won't be long now."

"I hope they just scare her," Caitlin said as she caressed her bandaged hand. Her gauze wrap was yellow today to match her t-shirt. "Getting bitten really sucks."

"Going soft, Cait?" Alexis smirked. "I hope they all get bitten. I hope they all *die*."

"Jesus, Lex."

"What?" Alexis turned to Caitlin and pushed her chest with both hands. Caitlin stumbled backward. "WHAT?"

"Nothing." Caitlin stared at the pavement.

"You sure about that?"

Caitlin nodded.

Deirdre looked up from her phone. "Sure about what?"

Alexis knocked the phone out of her hands and into the grass. "Put that fucking thing away."

"Hey!" Deirdre chased after her phone. "Don't be a bitch."

"Then join reality," Alexis said. "Because sparks are going to fly."

ONCE ON THE second floor, Trillian made a beeline to her locker and began rotating the combination wheel. Her first attempt failed.

Bradley stopped in front of his locker. "So how are you going to test it? Huge fireballs kind of stand out around here."

Jack shrugged. "I'll figure that out later."

Trillian popped open her combination lock on the second try and pulled open her locker. The cubby at the top was encased in webbing and tore apart as the door swung open. Dozens of black spiders—most the size of ping pong balls, some larger—poured out, clambering fast across the wall to the ceiling, their quills pulsing.

AS IT TURNED out, word of Mr. Moody's death was already common knowledge among the students and faculty. The story led the local news section of the San Fernando Valley Sun, in both the paper and online versions.

When Maddox stopped by the Washbrook staff room for a coffee, it was the single topic of conversation.

Fiscara appeared beside Maddox, sipping from a mug. "I guess you've read the news?"

"Don't start, Fiscara." Maddox tore open two packets of sugar and dumped them carelessly into his travel mug. "I'm in no mood."

"Spiders at the dance. A mysterious death nearby. Coincidence?" Fiscara focused on something distant outside the staff room window. "Just saying."

Maddox poured coffee into his mug and screwed on the lid. "Keep your baseless theories to yourself." He headed for the door.

"Nice suit." Fiscara grinned as she sipped.

Back at his office, Maddox had the newspaper spread out on his desk in front of him. "Mysterious Death Rocks Suburb of Stonehurst," the headline read.

"Jesus fucking Christ," Maddox grumbled.

Although the story didn't mention spiders explicitly, it did say that insects may have been partly to blame for the deteriorated condition the body was found in.

The school board would be on his case now, since Washbrook was the closest high school in the vicinity of the death. The fact that he had asked about extermination services previously wouldn't help his case.

"Jesus fucking *Christ*." Maddox slammed his fists onto his desk, knocking over his coffee and soaking the paper. As he cleaned up, he could hear screams emanating from within the school, screams that were increasing in volume.

He swung open his office door, striking the adjacent wall and rattling the glass surrounding his office. Mrs. Bischoffe jumped in her seat and almost dropped the phone in her hand.

"What the hell is it now?" Maddox stood with his hands on his hips, his face flushed with anger.

Mrs. Bischoffe placed a hand over the receiver of the phone. "Several teachers are reporting a spider attack on the second floor."

"Fuck this school." Maddox stepped back into his office and slammed the door. "*Fuck* it!"

"What should I tell him?"

Maddox yelled through the glass. "DON'T GET BITTEN!"

Mrs. Bischoffe relayed her own edited version of Maddox's message as she watched him pace back and forth in his office. In response, Maddox pulled the blinds on the windows.

TRILLIAN DROPPED HER knapsack, screamed, and recoiled to the opposite side of the hall. Students protested being shoved out of the way until they realized what was going on.

"Oh *fuck!*" Jack pulled Bradley back to where Trillian stood. Students scattered up and down the hallway. "Stay back!" He held up his hands and waved off unaware students coming up the stairs.

Trillian looked across the hall and saw Mr. Silver leading a charge of his homeroom students to the door. "No! Mr. Silver! Close the door!"

Mr. Silver saw Trillian waving at him and furrowed his brows. "Trillian? Brad? What's—"

Bradley, Trillian, and Jack all began yelling in unison, but their words overlapped, making the message unintelligible.

"Close the door!"

"Stay back!"

"Don't come out here!"

Mr. Silver approached the door, holding back his class. He knew something wasn't right. He slowed at the door frame and looked out. From his vantage point, he couldn't see the spiders above the door. With slow steady movement, he reached out for the doorknob.

"Shit shit shit shit!" A tear fell to Trillian's cheek as she watched Mr. Silver reach farther into the hallway.

He grabbed the knob and gave it a strong pull. The door arced closed, but two spiders dropped down on threads of silk anchored on the top of the door frame just before the door latched closed.

"Kill it! Kill it!" Trillian and Bradley yelled. From within the

Mr. Silver's classroom, they could hear muffled screams and the rumble of running feet.

Trillian closed her eyes. "Please be okay. Please."

The spiders on the walls thinned out, with most disappearing into gaps in the ceiling tiles and vents. Bradley scanned the hallway left and right, down the stairwell. The school was almost clear of students.

"What are you, in love with him or what?" Jack said.

Anger flared across Trillian's face. "Dude, it's okay to like teachers, you know. And Mr. Silver's a good teacher. So go pound sand."

"Pound sand?" Jack raised his eyebrow.

"Look it up," Trillian said. "While you're there, look up 'asshole' and make sure your picture's next to it."

The school's P.A. system buzzed on. Maddox's staticky voice echoed through the halls. "Attention staff and students of Washbrook High. This is an emergency drill. Please make your way outside to the playing field and await further instructions."

"Talk about an asshole. Mad Dog doesn't even recognize *this* as proof. You'd think after the dance he'd be on board." Bradley focused on Trillian's open locker across the hallway. "This shit doesn't just happen." He shook his head then looked at Trillian. "Your locker was clear on Friday, right?"

"Yeah."

Bradley surveyed the area. "Hey Jack, can you go back and get O'Connor and my dad? We got some hunting to do and we're going to need some reinforcements."

"I'm on it." Jack turned to leave, then turned back. "Trill? I'm sorry, okay?"

Trillian looked at him and nodded.

"Back in a flash." Jack bounded down the stairs and out of sight.

"Have you seen Mark?"

Bradley shook his head. "No texts from him since Friday, either."

Trillian pulled out her phone and began tapping out a message. "I'm going to text him to make sure he's okay."

Mr. Silver's door cracked open and he peeked out. "Is it safe to come out?"

Trillian heaved a sigh of relief. "Yeah, but no sudden moves. There's still a few spiders around."

"We killed the two that got in here." Mr. Silver ushered his homeroom students out of his class, then approached Bradley and Trillian. "What the hell happened?"

Bradley pointed at Trillian's open locker. "Spider infestation." He shared a knowing glance with Trillian. "We've been telling Mad Dog… uh, sorry. I meant Maddox. We've been telling Maddox since school started."

Mr. Silver laughed. "Calling him Mad Dog is fine by me."

"My dad's an exterminator. He's on his way."

"Going over Mad Dog's head." Mr. Silver crossed his arms over his ample belly. "Good call. Takes guts. If you need a teacher in your corner, let me know." Mr. Silver's eyes flitted over the wall above Trillian's locker and his classroom door. "On that note, I'm heading outside. I never liked spiders much. You two going to be okay?"

"We're here. The spiders are there." Bradley pointed at Trillian's web-encrusted locker. "We'll be okay."

"Adios." Mr. Silver shuffled down the stairs.

Trillian's phone chimed a text alert. "Mark says he's out on the field."

"He can join us if he wants."

Trillian tapped out a quick response as she and Bradley stood in the empty hallway. They watched stray spiders traverse between the ceiling and the open locker, making quick work of extending the web in all directions.

"Ugh. This has—"

"Alexis's name all over it?" Trillian asked.

Bradley nodded slowly. "Yup."

"You know what?" Trillian slid her hand around the back of Bradley's neck, pulled him toward her, and planted a full kiss on his lips. Afterwards, she said, "Alexis has hatched her last plan."

WHEN JACK RETURNED with Sam and O'Connor, the field behind the school was filled with students. Alexis, Deirdre and Caitlin stood at the fringe of the group.

Mark stood close by. He caught Caitlin's eye and gave her a warm smile and a small wave. She looked around as if his greeting was meant for someone else. Both Alexis and Deirdre were focused on the school and Jack's arrival. Caitlin offered a timid wave back when she realized Mark was interested in her.

Jack parked and all three tumbled out of the passenger door.

"That's the first and last fucking time I'm sitting in the back of your sardine can of a car." O'Connor stretched her back and her joints popped like a string of firecrackers.

Sam surveyed the field. "They evacuated the school?"

"People were leaving on their own when I left to get you guys." Jack opened the back hatch and began pulling equipment out. "Sure you brought enough?"

The back of the Civic was packed with equipment: tasers, propane torches, pellet guns, a Super Soaker, and Jack's spider vacuum.

"Best be prepared." O'Connor chewed on the end of her cigar and tapped Sam's shoulder. "Ain't that right, Sam?"

Sam ignored the question. "How many spiders are we talking about here?"

"Hundreds, at least." Jack picked up the Super Soaker. "What's the idea behind this?"

"Fill it with insecticide and you've got one hell of a lethal weapon." O'Connor pushed the barrel of the Super Soaker to the side. "Just don't point it at me. That stuff causes cancer."

Jack narrowed his eyes. "You realize we're going into a school with hundreds of students? Insecticide is a bad idea. You'll never get this past Maddox… or the propane torches."

O'Connor raised the propane torch onto her back. "He didn't have a problem with fire at the dance."

Sam grabbed two taser canes. "That's because he was going to die."

"Bingo." Jack lifted his spider vacuum from the back of the Civic.

O'Connor dropped the Super Soaker back into the trunk and blew a cloud of cigar smoke from the corner of her mouth. "The guy's a massive pussy. Still, I'm gonna wear one. Just in case."

"Don't forget your thermal camera," Jack said. "That's the most important thing. We need to find the source."

O'Connor tapped her front breast pocket. "Let's rock."

The three of them crossed the parking lot looking a lot like Ghostbusters and entered the south stairwell. They heard a booming voice echo from the second floor.

"Hear that?" O'Connor placed her hand to her ear. "That's the sound of a gutless turd in its natural habitat."

They rounded the landing between the first and second floor just in time to see Maddox press Bradley against the lockers with his right forearm. Bradley pushed back.

"Get your fucking hands off him." Sam's confident voice caught Maddox by surprise. He backed off as Sam led Jack and O'Connor up the final flight of stairs to the second floor. "I don't know why you're even here." He motioned at spiders on the wall. "With your arachnophobia and all."

Maddox glared at the five of them, then singled out Bradley and Trillian. "You're expelled. Both of you. Don't bother returning to school tomorrow." He shifted his gaze to Jack. "You, too."

"What about us? Huh?" O'Connor motioned at Sam and herself. "You going to throw us out too? We're providing a valuable service."

"Forget that." Sam's eyes narrowed at Maddox. "Four witnesses who'd love to see you fired just watched you just assault a student."

Maddox forged down the stairs past Jack, Sam, and O'Connor, swinging a bullhorn in his left hand. "I got plans brewing for all of you. Just wait." He disappeared from view. "And put out that fucking cigar."

"What a wind bag," Sam said.

Jack set the spider vacuum next to Bradley and looked a question at him. "So… when did you start wearing lipstick?"

Bradley wiped his face as Trillian grinned sheepishly next to him and shielded her face with her hair. A red flush spread over Bradley's neck and ears.

Jack lowered his voice. "It's okay, bro." He looked at Trillian's locker and spoke in a normal voice. "Any changes?"

"They built out the web," Bradley said. "And they're fast. But they're also disappearing somewhere, like they've been signaled."

O'Connor scanned the area with her thermal camera. Bright yellow spots peppered the walls. "We're never going to get them all."

"Most went up toward the vents in the ceiling," Trillian said. "And a few headed toward the boy's bathroom next to Mr. Silver's class."

"Let's start there." Sam led the crew toward the bathroom, moving slowly along the lockers. He approached the bathroom door. "We good? See anything?"

O'Connor monitored her phone. "Nope."

Sam pulled open the door and held it so O'Connor could

sweep that area with her camera. Several spiders scuttled into a vent in the ceiling and one sat on a drain cover in the tile floor.

"Vents get my vote." O'Connor stepped into the bathroom and opened the door to each stall, one by one. "Nothing." She paused beside the small spider on the drain cover and crushed it with a slow twist of her boot. "Drains lead to sewers and I don't do sewers."

Sam turned to Bradley, Jack and Trillian. "Can we get to the roof?"

MADDOX EMERGED FROM the school to find the crowd of students thinning out. Mr. Silver sat on the grass chatting with a group of kids from his homeroom, recounting their recent spider encounter. Other teachers were doing the same.

Maddox raised the bullhorn to his lips and pulled the trigger. His voice squawked across the field. "Everything is under control. The school is completely safe. Please return to your classes in an orderly fashion."

Mr. Silver stood and approached Maddox. He raised his voice so the rest of the students could hear. "You sure about that? I saw a hell of a lot of spiders outside my classroom and we had to kill a few that attacked us. My students are still rattled."

Maddox lowered the bullhorn. "The school is safe."

"No. It's not." Fiscara stood up beside Mr. Silver and addressed the crowd. "We need to let the exterminators do their job." She stepped forward. "The spiders in the school are extremely dangerous."

She bolted toward Maddox and grabbed the bullhorn from his hand. "Go home! You're safer there." Maddox reached out to intercept her but Fiscara evaded him. The scene played out like an adult game of keep away. "Silver! Heads up!" She tossed the bullhorn over Maddox's head and Mr. Silver caught it easily.

"Listen to Mrs. Fiscara," Mr. Silver's voice crackled out of the speaker. "She's the voice of reason here. She knows her stuff." Some laughter floated through the crowd of students and many were turning to walk home.

"You getting this shit?" Alexis asked Deirdre.

"Yup." Deirdre held her phone steady, capturing Maddox's meltdown.

Caitlin's concerned eyes were on the school, scanning the windows of the south stairwell for activity. She turned around looking for Mark but couldn't spot him.

Alexis nudged Caitlin. "You watching this? Totes brill."

Maddox chased Mr. Silver, but it was more of a speed walk than a run. His suit wasn't made for running. "Give me the megaphone." Maddox's face flushed with anger. "Give it to me *now!*"

Mr. Silver ignored Maddox, glanced at Fiscara, and grinned. "Go home, everybody. Our principal has some work to do." He clicked off the bullhorn and tossed it at Maddox, who caught it and promptly turned it back on.

"Those of you who go home today will be suspended indefinitely."

"He can't do that," Mr. Silver waved his arms and yelled at the crowd. "Don't believe it."

"And you two…" Maddox alternated his glance between Fiscara and Mr. Silver, aiming the bullhorn at them like it was a handgun. "You're both fired."

"What?" Mr. Silver shook his head. "You can't be serious."

"Oh, I am serious," Maddox said. "Mark my words."

"You're endangering lives. You know that, right?" Fiscara glared at Maddox before turning toward the school. "You're a real… piece of work."

Mr. Silver pulled his car keys from his pocket and made a

beeline toward the staff parking lot. Over the next several minutes, Maddox watched the crowd disperse. Very few re-entered the school, and those that did were mostly teachers.

Maddox marched back to the front entrance to the school. "If they think I'm bluffing, they're in for a big surprise," he said to himself, but loud enough for anyone nearby to hear. He pulled open the main doors just as Mrs. Bischoffe was heading out.

"Where are you going?"

"I'm deathly afraid of spiders, Mr. Maddox." Mrs. Bischoffe looked around the parking lot. "Everyone else is going. I'd just feel safer at home until this is dealt with."

Maddox cross his arms against his chest. "You've bought into this nonsense now, too? I'm disappointed in you, Wendy. I was counting on your support, but I guess you're just like all the rest of them."

"Sorry, Mr. Maddox." Mrs. Bischoffe continued toward the staff parking lot.

Maddox observed the parking lots steadily empty of vehicles. "You'll all be sorry." He paced down the hallway toward the office, letting the front door close behind him.

The few teachers who had re-entered the school had already collected their things and were making a hasty exit.

"Sure. Just go on home," Maddox muttered under his breath. "I'll fire all of you and solve this problem myself." He crossed through the main office and into his inner office, closed the door, and lowered the blinds. He stripped off his sport coat and tossed it on a chair.

Maddox paced in front of his desk in an attempt to cool himself down. "Fuck this shit." He pulled a binder out of his bookcase labelled "Washbrook High School Code of Conduct." Tucked into the back pocket of the binder was a small silver flask. Only Maddox and maybe Mrs. Bischoffe knew that it was filled with Southern Comfort. He unscrewed the cap and took a pull.

Relaxation washed over him. *They call it Southern Comfort for a reason.* He took another drink before planting himself in one of the two swivel chairs in front of his standing desk.

Maddox spun the chair around and propped his feet on the other swivel chair, leaning his seat back. He slipped his phone from his front suit pocket and began playing music from his seventies playlist. His wireless portable speakers semi-hidden in the bookcase began pumping out "Staying Alive" by the Bee Gees.

Maddox felt the Southern Comfort spread through his body. He took one more ample drink before closing his eyes, nodding his head to the beat of the music.

As the Brothers Gibb hit the chorus, Maddox sang along. He pictured himself up on stage in front of millions of adoring fans, belting out "Staying a-live!" in an extended vocal hit.

Dozens of young black spiders the size of quarters scuttled out of the air vent above him and launched themselves toward his face on nearly invisible strands of silk. The first two spiders missed the mark, landing on the seatback of the swivel chair. The third spider brushed his chin as Maddox hit the chorus but he was so in the moment he didn't feel it. The spider landed on his tie and scrambled up toward his neck.

"Staying ALI-IVE…!" Maddox held the vocals, controlling his breath, when the fourth spider hit the bullseye at back of his throat. His eyes popped open as he righted himself in his chair. He pushed the spider from his mouth to his lips and tweezed it, now soddened with saliva, off his tongue. Maddox stared in horror as a black spider wriggled to get free from between his thumb and index finger.

In the second it took for Maddox to follow the strand of webbing to the ceiling, the remaining cluster of spiders, many now larger than a quarter, had lowered themselves toward his face, spraying webbing on his mouth and eyelids, blinding him into darkness.

The spider still at his fingertips fell to his palm and sank its small fangs into the fleshy pocket of his palm. The pain of this bite was followed by dozens more, concentrating around his head and neck.

Maddox felt like he was on fire, burned alive. The feeling of his flesh spontaneously combusting overtook the pleasure of Southern Comfort. His heart convulsed in his chest as "Staying Alive" progressed into its final chorus and faded into the next song on his list: "Tragedy."

Maddox's phone continued to play seventies favorites as his frantic legs scrabbled at the floor, slowed, twitched, and fell still. His fight for his last breath—and his career as Principal—was over.

CHARLIE WAS MAKING his rounds in the boiler room as he sipped coffee from a thermos his wife had prepared for him that morning. The rich black brew kickstarted his day the way coffee was meant to, not like the undrinkable swill they served in the staff room.

The machinery hummed and rattled in all the right ways. Charlie could read the boiler room's inner workings like a book and everything checked out. A heavy knock sounded at the door. Upon pulling it open, he found Bradley standing in the doorway.

"Mr. Jessop? Uh, do you have a moment?"

Charlie set his thermos down. He looked at Bradley and narrowed his eyes in thought. "Brett?" he asked, pointing with his free hand.

"Close. It's Brad."

"Right. Brad. What can I do for yah?" Charlie craned his neck past Bradley and into the lower hallway. "And where is everyone?"

"That's kind of why we need your help again. The spiders are back."

"Not flippin' possible."

"We have proof this time. I'll show you." Bradley explained the need to access the rooftop as he led Charlie to Trillian's locker on the second floor.

As Charlie approached the rest of the crew, O'Connor eyed him up and down. "Now there's my tall drink of water and I'm thirsty as hell."

Sam nudged O'Connor in the ribs.

Charlie stood, one hand on his hip and the other rubbing his stubbled shin. Spider webbing in the shape of a funnel stretched from Trillian's locker to the ceiling vent. But the web was empty. "Well, I'll be darned. Ain't like anything I've ever seen before."

"They've moved into the vents," Trillian said.

"But there's not many sources of food in the ducting," Fiscara added. "They're probably following the air current through the vents, and the higher they are, the easier they can take flight."

"Wait," Sam said. "Spiders can fly?"

"Technically, it's more like floating," Fiscara said.

A lightbulb went off behind Jack's eyes. "You're talking about ballooning, aren't you?"

Fiscara pointed at Jack. "You got it. Spiders can detect electrostatic changes in their surroundings. The farther they are from the ground, the more charge there is in the air around them, and subsequently, the farther they can travel."

"What she said." O'Connor blew a smoke ring at Fiscara. "That's why we need to get on the roof."

"But why are they flying away?" Trillian followed the train of thought. "Maybe that will lead us to—"

"A bigger nest." Jack grinned as the gears in his head began to grind.

Charlie raised his brow. "You're the experts. I'll unlock the roof hatch, but I ain't going up there. Not in my job description."

Charlie led the crew past the water fountain to a small alcove with an unmarked access door. He unlocked and opened it, revealing a narrow vertical chute with a red iron ladder bolted to the wall. He climbed up the rungs, lighting the way with a penlight clamped in his teeth. Sounds of jangling keys echoed down from above.

"Don't—" The scraping sound of the metal hinge stopped Fiscara's words before they started. Daylight flooded the access chute.

"Did someone say something?" Charlie called down.

"I was going to say 'don't open it too quickly', but it looks like I was worrying for nothing."

Charlie backed down the chute. "Fill yer boots. But like before, last one out locks up." He held up an open padlock. "Who's gonna be the gatekeeper?"

"If you're the key master, that's a no brainer." O'Connor winked at Charlie and took the lock. "No point everyone going up," she said to the rest of the group.

Everyone shrugged indifference except Fiscara. "Someone who actually knows something about spiders would be helpful."

O'Connor rolled her eyes. "You mean *you?*"

Fiscara crossed her arms. "Who's the biologist?"

"You don't need to be a biologist to be an exterminator."

"It wouldn't hurt."

"For fuck's sake. How different can spiders be from rats or cockroaches?"

If Fiscara were wearing glasses, she'd be looking at O'Connor over the rims. "Bitch, please." She pushed past her and hooked her hand on a rung of the ladder. "You definitely need my help."

"By all means, *Fiscarella.* Be my guest." O'Connor followed Fiscara up the ladder. "She always like this?" she said to Bradley.

Bradley chose to keep quiet.

"Wendy could *never* be as egotistical as you. You got that mastered," Sam said, a grin wide on his lips.

"Shut the fuck up." O'Connor blew cigar smoke at Sam before disappearing up the chute.

"Huh. I've never seen a pissing contest between two women before," Jack said.

Trillian's eyes bugged out. "Excuse me?" Bradley began to laugh.

"You know what I mean."

Trillian whacked Jack's shoulder with the back of her hand. "You're an idiot."

"Every minute of every day is a pissing contest with O'Connor," Sam said. "And it's best if you let her win. She's a lot like a Wookie in that way."

"I can hear you, jackasses," O'Connor's voice echoed down the chute. She reached the lip of the hatch and Fiscara extended her hand down to help. Instead, O'Connor struggled to pull herself up on her own.

"You done?"

O'Connor brushed herself off and caught her breath. She pulled out her phone with the thermal camera attachment.

Fiscara shook her head. "That's not going to work out here. Too hot today."

"What do you know?" O'Connor opened the thermal camera app and adjusted the temperature threshold, but the detail on the screen appeared in bright yellows and oranges. She sneered at Fiscara before pocketing the phone. "Lucky guess."

The roof had smaller air intake vents scattered across its surface, with the main exhaust vents located on the south end of the school.

"Look." Fiscara pointed to one side of the main exhaust. Gauzy webbing flowed from one side of it. "And above it. Do you see that?"

O'Connor squinted and stepped closer to the exhaust vent.

Small black spiders lined up along the top edge of the vent, casting threads of silk from their spinnerets. Then, one by one, they took flight, drifting away from the school, across the field and over nearby homes.

"They're ballooning," Fiscara said.

O'Connor nodded and blew smoke into the blue sky. "No shit. Where are they going?"

Fiscara shrugged. "Not sure. The suburbs of Stonehurst are in that direction, and maybe the golf course and the dam beyond that."

"You got a dam here?"

"Flood control. It doesn't get much action." Fiscara stepped closer to the exhaust vent. The small spiders took turns launching themselves, like there was an organized plan. "They're sporkies. I can see their quills."

"I'll take your word for it." Something dark caught the corner of O'Connor's eye. "I'd also take a step back if I were you."

"Why? You—"

"We got company, that's why." A large spider with a thorax the size of a football scrambled around the exhaust vent, its back legs coiled in a defensive pose.

Fiscara caught sight of the spider and reversed her advance. With every step backwards, the spider moved forward as if she was tethered to the spider by an invisible line. "Mama spiders appear to be just as territorial about their young as other wildlife."

"*Appear* to be? I thought you were the expert."

"I've never gotten this close to an active cluster before. So sue me."

"I just might." O'Connor looked behind her. The open hatch was about twenty feet away. She dug out her Zippo and lit the pilot light on the end of her propane torch. "Hey fearless leader. I don't think there's much we can do up here, so—"

"I hear you." Fiscara took a larger step backward and the

spider advanced again, closing the distance between them. She could see the spider's fangs pumping behind its chelicerae and the quills on its back spreading and retracting.

"I want you to run to the hatch as fast as you can."

"I can't turn my back on it."

"Then run backwards."

Fiscara shot a fearful glance back at O'Connor. The chip on her shoulder was gone: O'Connor had switched to protection mode. She raised the torch's nozzle, a small orange flame flickering beside it. "I've literally got your back."

Fiscara began to run backwards, but increasing her speed was easier said than done. The spider followed, gaining on her with ease. The heel of her shoe caught on a strip of upturned flashing and she fell on her backside. "O'Connor!" She continued to scramble in a sitting position, her hands and feet seeking purchase on the tar and gravel roof.

"You're fired!" O'Connor leveled the torch at the mama spider, almost upon Fiscara's feet, and triggered a blast of flame. Fiscara felt the heat wash by her as she scrambled to the hatch, lowering herself in.

"O'Connor! Come on!"

The spider halted its attack. Its quills were singed and smoking, and the small hairs covering the front half of its body had been burned away. It seemed like the spider had been momentarily blinded as well.

O'Connor seized the moment and stepped into the hatch. She looked back as the spider resumed its attack. She reached out and pulled the hatch door closed but the front edge caught on the nozzle of the torch, propping it open.

The spider was on the hatch door in seconds, working at the opening. O'Connor blasted the torch, but the flames missed their mark.

She raised the hatch door just enough to pull the torch nozzle into the chute, but this allowed the spider more room to jam one of its legs into the chute after her.

Heaving with all her weight, O'Connor pulled the hatch door down and amputated the spider leg with a *crunch*. The disembodied appendage fell to the floor below where it writhed next to the base of the ladder. O'Connor thought she heard screams. "Pussies," she muttered.

She dug in her pocket for the padlock and fastened it around the latch. A dozen ladder rungs later, she emerged from the chute on the second floor. She turned off the gas to the torch and extinguished the pilot flame.

"Well, that was pointless," she said.

Fiscara was still catching her breath. "Not necessarily. We know where they're headed."

O'Connor picked up the lifeless spider leg, easily twelve inches long. The exoskeleton was hard and smooth, with all its micro-hairs burnt off. "How about we shove this up Maddox's ass?"

Everyone laughed.

"How about we give him a report instead," Fiscara said.

"If he gives us any shit, I reserve the right to bury this where the sun don't shine." O'Connor pulled a mouthful of cigar smoke into her mouth, releasing it in a cloud that floated back up the chute, then used the pointed tip of spider leg to pick something out of her teeth.

"Gross," Trillian said.

The crew headed down the hallway toward the stairs. Fiscara hung back and pulled O'Connor aside. "Thanks."

O'Connor grinned. "No problemo. I'm the exterminator, after all."

Fiscara slapped O'Connor's back with affection. "Let's tear Maddox a new one."

THE CREW PASSED Trillian's locker, still connected to the vent in the ceiling by a conduit of gossamer.

"We should probably deal with that," Sam said.

"Yeah, I mean I feel a little exposed. I don't want anyone to steal my stuff." Trillian scanned the expanse of webbing emerging from her locker and shivered. Bradley noticed and placed his hand gently on her shoulder and gave it a brief squeeze.

O'Connor held up the nozzle of her torch. "Just say the word."

"I think setting the inside of the school on fire would be bad for business," Fiscara said.

"Sam's got tasers, and I got this razor vacuum." Jack held up the business end of his contraption. "Let's just pull the web down and deal with any spiders as we go."

"I don't think we'll find many more spiders," Fiscara said. "They were all ballooning north from the roof, like they were regrouping."

O'Connor stowed the torch nozzle on her belt. "Taser me."

Sam handed her a taser rod and both began to dig out the web from inside the top cubby of the locker and pull it off the ceiling vent. They collected the silk web in a translucent pile in the middle of the hallway.

A small spider emerged from underneath the webbing and Jack was first to respond. He turned on the vacuum's motor and shredded the spider into a blackened splatter on the floor.

"Now that was fucking cool, don't you think?" Jack looked at the rest of the group. "Got to admit, it works pretty well."

Trillian grimaced. "I guess."

"Now can it do the same thing with rats?" O'Connor smiled and flashed her eyebrows.

"Uh, probably not," Jack said. "Rats are too big."

"Well, let me know when you build a version that shreds rats." O'Connor gnawed on her smoldering cigar. "I'll be first in line to buy a couple."

"Okay…" Jack's voice trailed off as he became lost in thought.

"Let's move." Bradley led the way down the south stairwell.

The first floor hallway was deserted, an odd sight to see on a Monday morning. The group's footfalls echoed from the polished concrete floors as they headed for the office, located in the center of the school.

Something caught Trillian's attention. "Hey, guys. Do you hear something?"

Bradley and Jack shrugged.

"Like what?" Fiscara asked.

"Stop. Stop for a second." Trillian cocked her ear to one side. "You hear that?"

"I don't hear jack shit," O'Connor said.

"But did you hear me fart?" Jack laughed and high-fived Bradley.

"Everyone. SHUT UP." Trillian glared with exasperation at the rest of the group.

A different sound rose up just above the white noise of the ventilation system.

Fiscara nodded. "Yeah, I hear it too."

"What is it?" Bradley asked.

"Only one way to find out." O'Connor resumed walking down the hallway.

"It's music," Sam said. "Coming from the office."

Fiscara and O'Connor exchanged glances, and both stepped up their pace toward the office, Fiscara leading the way. Once in the main office, the music was muffled but clear.

"What the...?" Bradley looked at Trillian and Jack. They shrugged in response.

Sam scrunched his brows. "Is that—"

" 'Don't Fear the Reaper', yeah," Fiscara said.

"Blue Oyster Cult." O'Connor blew smoke and smiled. "It's been years."

Fiscara stepped to Maddox's office door. She raised her hand to knock, hesitated, then followed through, rapping the glass pane in the door with her knuckles. "Mr. Maddox?"

The music continued to play without a response from within.

Fiscara knocked again, a little harder, rattling the blinds on the opposite side of the window. "Maddox?" She placed her ear against the glass. "Brent?" Fiscara placed her hand on the doorknob and looked back at the group.

Sam shrugged. "What have you got to lose? We're all either fired or expelled."

"Good point." Fiscara twisted the knob and pushed the door open.

O'Connor was first to push past her. "Sweet red pepper Jesus." The rest of the group crowded around her to get a look.

Maddox's body reclined in a swivel chair facing the doorway, his legs propped up on a second chair facing him. His face looked as if it had melted and slid to one side. His arms resembled the filling of a sausage casing, with his shirt sleeves stretched tight to the breaking point. What little of his skin they could see appeared fractured by raised black veins and a pool of viscous bodily fluid leaked out next to the chair and under his desk.

"Mother*fuck*," Jack said.

"Ugh." Trillian held her nose. "What's that smell?"

O'Connor stepped around pools of human waste. "Melted Mad Dog appears to have shit himself in his final seconds."

Blue Oyster Cult transitioned from instrumental to chorus.

"I guess that makes forty-thousand men and women and one Mad Dog," O'Connor said.

Trillian stepped back into the main office and vomited into Mrs. Bischoffe's waste basket.

Bradley sat on the edge of the desk next to her. "I know how you feel. There was this guy, back in New York—"

"It's okay, Brad." Trillian wiped her mouth. "You don't need to say anything."

O'Connor stepped farther into the office, navigating around the desk and slickened floor. She looked under his legs, already bending unnaturally backward at the knees under the weight of his swollen flesh between the two chairs. She tossed the spider leg onto his chest, took out her phone, and snapped a photo. "Reality bites."

The group stepped slowly inside the office, spreading out, their eyes locked on Maddox's body in morbid fascination. Fiscara searched the opposite side of the desk. Trillian leaned against the doorframe, cradling her stomach.

"You ever see anything like this before?" O'Connor asked Fiscara.

"Like what exactly?"

"Like spiders killing for sport," O'Connor said.

"Or revenge," Bradley added.

"Bingo." O'Connor looked around the small office. "There's none of those little black bastards anywhere. They didn't stick around. And the webbing on his face is minimal. Not like the locker upstairs."

Fiscara stood up and blew a lock of hair away from her face. "Nothing about these spiders is normal."

"I've got a feeling there's not going to be school tomorrow," Jack said.

"Or the day after," Trillian added.

"Probably not." Fiscara looked at Sam, Bradley and Jack. "We need a new plan and I need a coffee. Let's get the hell out of here."

Bradley used Mrs. Bischoffe's phone to call 9-1-1. Less than ten minutes later, police and emergency crews arrived at the school to search the premises. It didn't take long for them to find Maddox.

At the same time, Jack was unlocking his front door for the rest of the group and putting coffee on to brew.

180 Degrees

Trillian cooled her coffee with a splash of cream and sugar. "I'd love to be a fly on the wall in Maddox's office right about now."

"Really? With all the spiders around that's pretty risky business." Bradley winked at her as he blew on his coffee to cool it.

"You know what I mean."

"First Moody, then Maddox," Jack said. "Maybe now would be a good time to get the city to hire you on officially."

"Too much red tape," Sam said. "And O'Connor hates red tape."

"You got that right. Bureaucratic sons of bitches, all of 'em. Vermin like this needs a fast response." O'Connor sat reclined on one side of Jack's sectional. She had claimed the spot for her own from the first moment she entered Jack's house. "Shovel Maddox into a garbage bag and be done with it."

"Do you think Charlie would sell us out?" Fiscara stirred sugar into her coffee.

"Charlie? My darling boytoy?" O'Connor widened her eyes and fluttered her lashes. "He'd never do such a thing."

Fiscara laughed. "In your dreams."

"Why?" Sam said. "We did nothing wrong. We followed his instructions to the letter."

"You've Got a Friend in Me" by Randy Newman sounded

from Bradley's pocket. He walked to the corner of the living room and pulled out his phone.

"Who's that?" Trillian asked Jack.

"His mom," Jack said. "She loves the Toy Story movies."

Trillian shrugged. "Never seen them."

"What?" Jack nearly fell over with surprise. "You got to see them before the next one comes out."

"They're really good," Sam said. "I saw the first one when I was about your age. Lines around the block."

"Brad?" Fiscara set her coffee down on the dining room table. "What is it?"

Bradley approached the rest of the group, his face as white as a ghost with an expression to match. "That was my mom."

O'Connor propped herself up on the sofa with her elbows. "And?"

Bradley's eyes roamed the room, finally settling on Sam. "Roy's dead."

EVEN THOUGH BRADLEY had only known about Roy for a few weeks and despite their dislike for each other, he was affected by the news of his death. Claire had seen the good in Roy, something Bradley never experienced. Still, the first place Bradley's mind went to upon hearing the news was his mom. Ironically, he felt some anger toward Roy about that, mixed in with the sadness and shock of it all. He was a bundle of conflicting emotions.

Trillian guided Bradley to the sofa to sit and everyone else corralled around him. At that moment he realized how good it was to have friends.

"My mom said they found him on top of Hansen Dam. There's a path that runs the length of it."

"Yeah," Jack nodded. "One side comes out pretty close to Taco Siempre. I used to ride my bike across that path."

Bradley swallowed hard. "Another runner phoned it in. He was all caught up in the barbed wire at the top of the fence, near the spillways."

Sam handed Bradley his coffee and he took a sip. "Take your time, son."

Bradley looked to Sam and nodded. "The police used his phone to call Mom."

"Any spider webs on the scene?" O'Connor asked Bradley.

"Hey, cool your heels for a goddamned moment, huh?" Sam glared at O'Connor.

"Excuse me." O'Connor held up her hands in surrender. "Just looking for clues because it sounds a lot like Maddox."

"That can wait."

"It's okay," Bradley said. "Mom didn't say anything about spider webs."

O'Connor looked at Jack. "We're going to have to check it out."

Jack was fiddling with his phone. "Already on it."

Bradley felt a wave of sorrow fill his chest and tears spilled from his eyes. He placed his hands over his face and again was thankful to be surrounded by friends.

Fiscara knelt in front of Bradley and gave him a brief but strong hug. "I'm sorry for your loss."

"Thanks, but I didn't even know the guy," Bradley said. "I don't even know why I'm crying. If anything, I feel sorry for my mom's loss."

Fiscara nodded.

"She needs to identify the body. Officially," Bradley said. "She can't drive herself, yet."

"I'll drive her." Sam reached toward O'Connor. "Give me the keys to the Mustang."

"Uh, Dad, I don't think that's a good idea," Bradley said.

"Damn straight." O'Connor jangled the keys in her hand. "No one drives Baby Blue except me."

"Okay. We'll hang back and re-evaluate," Fiscara said.

As O'Connor headed out the front door, Fiscara turned to the rest of the group. "Anyone have a problem with me leading the charge?"

No objections all around. Sam watched Fiscara step into teacher mode.

"Okay," Fiscara said. "We need to pinpoint where Roy died."

Jack pulled up Washbrook High School, Hansen Dam and the surrounding area on his laptop and the group went to work.

THE DOORBELL RANG. Claire grabbed her purse, hobbled to the front door on her crutches and pulled open the front door.

O'Connor took a bow on the front steps. "Your ride awaits, my lady." She took a drag from her cigar, blew a cloud of smoke over her shoulder, and placed the cigar back between her teeth.

"You aren't who I was expecting to—"

"Look, Claire. Do you want a ride or not?"

Claire locked the front door and stepped gingerly down the steps to the Mustang. She stowed her crutches on the back seat.

Once they were buckled in, O'Connor floored the gas and left another strip of rubber behind on the road.

"Sam put you up to this, didn't he?"

"The only person I take orders from is me."

O'Connor motioned toward Claire's left leg, the purple compression bandage peeking out from under the cuff of her jeans. "You're lucky you didn't lose it. Being an amputee ain't no walk in the park."

"Sorry. I didn't know."

"If it had been my right leg, Sam would probably be driving you right now."

"Then I'm glad it's your left." Claire shook her head. "Sorry, that sounded wrong. I didn't mean I'm glad you're an amputee."

"You know, I've only known Sam for a short while, but he seems like a stand-up guy," O'Connor said, smoke trailing from the corner of her mouth. "He's been through a lot."

"You don't know the half of it." Claire looked at O'Connor's left leg. "You know, I can't tell if it's real or not."

"That's part of the magic, baby. I use it to my advantage."

"How did you lose it, if you don't mind me asking."

O'Connor pulled into the Sun Valley Medical Center parking lot. "Long story short. Shark attack in Hawaii, twenty-five years ago." She pulled Baby Blue into a stall. "But we got bigger fish to fry." She butted out her cigar and slipped the stub into her breast pocket.

O'Connor and Claire soon found themselves in an elevator descending to the basement levels of the hospital.

"You know why morgues are in the basement?"

Claire shrugged and adjusted her grip on her crutches. "No idea."

"So the dead can be closer to hell."

Claire fell silent and looked down at the floor.

"Sorry. Bad joke. Didn't mean nothing by it," O'Connor said.

"Bullshit." Claire pinned O'Connor in place with her fiery stare. "You only saw one side of Roy. He could be hard to be around sometimes, but he only showed me love and compassion."

"If Sam had been here, he would have elbowed me in the ribs for that one."

"You deserved it." The elevator doors opened and Claire stepped out first. "You two seem pretty tight."

"When you've helped each other escape death multiple times, you grow on each other."

"Like a fungus."

O'Connor laughed. "Yeah, that's accurate."

Claire followed the main hallway and around a corner to the reception desk.

"You really know your way around," O'Connor said.

"You know I work here, right? When I'm not all fucked up?"

"Uh, must've missed that part."

Claire let the reception nurse know they were here to identify Roy. The nurse led them into a room warmly lit with pot lights. Soft music played in the background.

"You can turn the music off here if you prefer." The nurse indicated a volume knob next to the door. "If you require a medical examiner or a crisis counsellor, just let us know through the intercom. And take all the time you need." The nurse closed the door, leaving Claire and O'Connor alone.

The room was painted a light yellow and was sparsely decorated with plants. Two picturesque images of Venice Beach and the Santa Monica Pier hung on the wall.

There was a comfortable couch against one wall facing a coffee table, with a box of tissue and a touch tablet. "Roy Detmer" and "Press start to begin" below it displayed on the screen. Even with the amenities, the room still bore an antiseptic hospital smell.

Claire sat down and looked at the tablet. O'Connor could see she was struggling to maintain her composure.

O'Connor shifted uneasily on her feet. "Maybe it would be better if I waited outside."

"No. Stay. You don't need to sit down. I just need someone else here." Claire took a deep breath.

O'Connor sat next to Claire. "I won't look at the pictures."

"Don't you think you should?" Claire turned to her. "If spiders got him like they got me, I'd think you'd want as much information as possible."

O'Connor nodded. "Lead on."

Claire tapped "Start."

The first screen displayed a disclaimer stating that only parts of the body with identifiable markings would be shown. For further information, they would have to contact the active medical examiner.

"I don't know what to think of that," Claire said.

"It's probably better that you don't."

Claire tapped the "next" button on the tablet. A photo of an enlarged ear appeared. The skin was pale and stretched thin, with a small mole on the ear lobe.

"He had a mole like that," Claire said, "but his ears weren't that big."

"Would you recognize your own foot if you saw a photo of it?"

"Probably." Clair looked down at her foot in the purple compression bandage, her toes peeking out at her. "The nail polish would be the giveaway."

"My point is, from what I've seen so far, swelling is part of the reaction that causes death."

Claire advanced the image on the tablet. Roy's right wrist showed a deep groove where his fitness watch would normally be.

The next image sucker-punched Claire in the gut. Part of her wanted this all to be imaginary. Seeing the photos in a comfortable room on a tablet helped reinforce that myth, but when a photo of Roy's right calf appeared, Claire began to sob uncontrollably.

Across Roy's right calf was a port wine stain birthmark in the shape of a lightning bolt, stretched due to swelling, but recognizable just the same.

O'Connor handed Claire the box of tissues.

"Thank you." Claire wiped her eyes and blew her nose, then traced the birthmark with her finger. "Lightning legs. He was born to be a runner."

"And he was doing what he loved."

Claire looked at O'Connor, her eyes red-rimmed. "He didn't deserve this."

"No. He didn't."

Claire took a fresh tissue and blew her nose one last time. "I don't need to see anything more. Please take me home."

"You got it."

They both stood and made their way back to the elevators.

"Did seeing those photos help you any?" Claire asked.

"Yeah." O'Connor dug out her cigar stub and clamped it between her teeth. "I think we've been digging in the wrong place."

O'CONNOR PULLED INTO Jack's driveway to find the rest of the crew gathered around the Civic in front of the open garage. Bradley was at the side of the Mustang before O'Connor could step out. He was vibrating with anxiety but trying to restrain himself out of respect.

"How's my mom doing?"

"As good as she can be," O'Connor said.

"Was it really Roy?" A touch of short-lived sorrow crossed Bradley's face.

"Damn straight it was. Pretty much a repeat of Maddox," O'Connor said. "You should give your mom a call. And soon."

"I will. But we made a huge discovery while you were gone."

"Let me guess." O'Connor spat the remnants of her current cigar onto the driveway and went through the ritual of preparing a fresh one. She nursed the end of the cigar into a cherry-orange coal and drew in a mouthful of smoke. O'Connor targeted Bradley's head with a meaty smoke ring. "There's no spider colony at the school."

"Yeah. How'd you know?"

"I had my suspicions when me and Fiscara were on the roof," O'Connor said between puffs. "The spiders were jumping ship, leaving the school, like they were on a mission."

"Exactly." Bradley pulled open the Mustang's driver side door. "But there's something else. Come on."

Bradley led O'Connor back to the rest of the group. On the hood of the Civic, Jack was fiddling with a quadcopter.

"Just the person I needed to see," Jack said. "I'm going to need your thermal camera."

"You up to speed?" Fiscara asked O'Connor.

"Getting there."

"Coles Notes version: The spiders…" Fiscara glanced at Trillian. "The *sporkies* are regrouping. And we think they're communicating collectively in some way, which is extremely rare because spiders are usually solitary creatures."

O'Connor blew smoke over her head and motioned at Jack. "You planning on following them with a drone? You'll never see them. They're too small."

"Jack's plotting a course from his map of sightings," Trillian said.

"To the dam? Where Roy was found?"

"Bingo," Jack said. "And there's only a small section on top of the dam where there's barbed wire. That narrows things down a hell of a lot."

O'Connor turned to Sam. "You're awfully quiet. Anything to add?"

Sam shrugged. "Not really. This is all pretty amazing to me, what you can do. I'll be first to admit I'm living in the Dark Ages when it comes to technology."

"Well watch and learn, Bucko," O'Connor said. "I'll be relying on you when we get back to New York."

"I don't work for you."

O'Connor cackled with laughter. "That's what you think."

"O'Connor, I need your thermal camera." Jack beckoned with his hand. "I want to get this done before the sun gets too high."

O'Connor pulled it out of her pocket, the thermal camera attachment still fastened to the bottom, and handed it to Jack. "If you break it, you buy it, capiche?"

"As long as the battery holds and it's not shot out of the sky, we'll be golden."

"How many times have you flown this contraption?"

Jack grinned. "Today marks its first official flight."

"What?" O'Connor's eyes bugged out as the rest of the crew began to laugh. "Okay, we ain't doing this. Find a different plan. And give me my phone back."

"Relax." Jack spoke in calm tones. "I've flown other drones before. It's practically foolproof. You'll see." He attached O'Connor's camera to the gimbal under the quadcopter. "I've transferred the route to the onboard computer. All I need to do is begin a video call and press start. We'll be able to watch the signal live."

Jack held his phone out to the group. "Who'd like to do the honors?"

Fiscara redirected Jack's hand toward O'Connor. "As much as I'd love to do it, I think it should be you, O'Connor. It's your camera after all."

O'Connor looked to the group then singled out Jack. "Sure this is going to work?"

"What's the worst that could happen? I buy you new gear." Jack said. "Do it."

O'Connor tapped the red "Start Flightpath" button on the screen. The four rotors on the quadcopter spun up and within a second it was airborne and enroute to the top of Hansen Dam.

"Well I'll be dipped in shit." O'Connor watched the quadcopter disappear from sight. "Look at that little mother go."

Sam shook his head in wonder. "Completely amazing. Honestly."

Jack smiled, monitoring the video feed from his phone. "I programmed the drone to make a couple of passes in front and behind the dam, around the area where they found Roy."

It was almost noon and the sun bore down on the valley, warming everything up. The video feed on Jack's phone showed patches of yellows and oranges on the roofs of the surrounding houses, with small patches of red and purple in the shadows. It was like looking at live video that had a vibrant posterization effect applied to it but offered enough detail to discern structures and roads.

"How long does the battery last?" Fiscara asked Jack.

"Maybe twenty minutes? I've never officially timed it."

"And how fast is it traveling right now?"

Jack thought for a moment. "About forty miles per hour. It's pretty speedy."

It took the quadcopter just over two minutes to arrive at the dam.

Trillian pointed at the screen on Jack's phone. "Is that it? The dam?"

"Yup. I programmed the drone to shoot the south face of the dam first," Jack said. "See that structure at the top? The maintenance building or whatever? That's probably where they found Roy. It's the only section that has barbed wire fencing."

"And those darker areas are the spillways," Bradley said. "I remember them from when I was looking for missing pets a while ago."

"Yeah, the spillways are always in shadow." Jack passed his phone to Fiscara and Sam so they could get a better look. O'Connor budged in between. "They're a great place to hang out during a hot day."

"I got to get me one of these drones," O'Connor said. "A Detest-A-Pest value-added service, baby."

Fiscara grinned. "You're one high-tech grandma."

"Who says I'm a grandma, you Southern-fried trollop?"

"If you're not a grandma, you should have been." Fiscara laughed, ignoring O'Connor's taunt. "I would have loved to have a grandma like you."

"Well, all right then." O'Connor said, caught off-guard.

Trillian poked her head in to get a better view. "That must be the back side now… but what is that bright spot?"

"Where?" Bradley squinted at the phone as if that might help identify the detail.

"Right… there." Trillian pointed at an orange spot in one of the upper spillway openings. "You see it, right?"

"I do now. Jack? Any ideas?" Bradley handed him the phone.

Jack shrugged. "I don't know. The camera detects temperature. So I guess it could be anything. A person, an animal…"

O'Connor blew a smoke ring, then jetted the rest of the smoke through the center. "A big-ass spider?"

"Spiders, as in more than one," Fiscara said. "Technically a cluster. That's where they're regrouping."

"More like a cluster*fuck*." O'Connor looked at Bradley. "That's what got Roy."

"So that's where we need to go." Sam looked at the others. "I've never seen this dam up close, but I know they're massive structures. We're going to need more people."

"I've got Washbrook's student email distribution list," Jack said. "I could just contact everyone and ask for volunteers."

"How the hell did you manage that?" Bradley asked.

"A hacker never reveals their tricks."

"I think that might be a little overkill," Fiscara said. "Can you imagine if half the school showed up? Or even a quarter? We don't want to have to worry about crowd control too."

The buzz-whine of the quadcopter's rotors rose overhead,

then descended to land on the hood of Jack's Civic, precisely where it had taken off less than ten minutes ago.

"Damn," Sam said. "Can we get drones to take those spiders out?"

"That would be *sweet.*" Jack tapped at his phone. A second later the quadcopter's rotors spun down. "In a parallel reality, maybe."

"So how many people do we really need?" Sam looked to the group.

"This 'A-Team' moment brought to you by coffee, as in I need some, right fucking now." O'Connor bounded up the front steps of Jack's house, a trail of blue smoke following her head. "What are y'all waiting for? Let's plan this shit out and kick some spider ass."

Jack picked up the quadcopter and followed O'Connor inside. "I think I'm in love."

Trillian leaned close to Bradley. "What the hell is an 'A-Team moment?' "

"I don't know," he said, "but I think we're going to find out."

Bold Plans

O'Connor, Sam, Fiscara, Bradley, Trillian, and Jack sat around the kitchen table, all with beverages in hand. O'Connor had helped herself to a banana, temporarily stowing her smoldering cigar between the thumb and fingers of her other hand.

O'Connor turned to Jack. "How damn big is this dam?"

The sight of partially chewed banana in O'Connor's mouth dredged up a flashback of Mr. Moody. Jack raised his eyebrows in surprise while he tried to conceal his shiver of revulsion. "Have you ever toured a dam? They're massive."

"Prepare to get schooled." Bradley settled into his chair.

A smile curled at the corner of Jack's lips and he gave Bradley dap. "The Hansen Dam is two miles long, with a path on top. But unlike other dams that are used for storing water, you know like Hoover Dam, Hansen redirects water to avoid flooding." He called up a satellite view of the area on his laptop.

"Ever thought of becoming a teacher?" Fiscara asked.

Jack shook his head. "Nah, I don't have the patience. But back to what I was saying… most of the time there's very little water flowing through the dam. Good news for us. The part of the structure we need to worry about are the spillways, and all together they're about one hundred feet across. Even better news for us. But—"

"I knew there would be a but," Trillian said.

"There's always a but." O'Connor turned to Jack. "Please continue, Professor."

"But there's ten spillways, eight lower and two upper, for emergencies."

"What kind of emergencies?" Sam asked.

"I don't know," Jack said. "Flash floods, maybe? I don't know as much history as I'd like to."

O'Connor quickly tallied heads. "So, we got six people. We each take a channel. A few of us can take more than one."

"Don't forget Mark," Bradley said. "He'll be helping out too."

"Okay, seven people." O'Connor looked around the table. "Easy peasy, right?"

"You don't want to go through these channels alone," Jack said.

O'Connor began flapping her arms and clucking like a chicken. "Is Jack scared of the dark?"

"Generally? No. But in there? Fuck yeah and I'm not ashamed to say it." Jack locked eyes with O'Connor. "If you were smart, you'd be listening instead of swinging your dick."

"Enough." Sam alternated his glare between Jack and O'Connor, finally settling on O'Connor. "Why is everything a competition with you?"

"Because I'm a bad-ass bitch."

"You want to be a *dead* bad-ass bitch?" Sam didn't wait for O'Connor's response. "Jack knows more than you about this. What he says might end up saving your life."

O'Connor relented but everyone sensed her reluctance. "Whatever you say, *Dad*."

Sam rolled his eyes and shook his head.

Jack looked around the table for his cue to continue. "Going in pairs would be better. You know, safety in numbers."

Fiscara sipped her coffee. "No story ever ended well when a character said 'Let's split up. We'll cover more ground.' "

"Okay, we go in pairs. You convinced me," O'Connor said. "But we're going to need weapons… and *that* is something I know a little bit about."

"Go." Jack gave the floor to O'Connor and produced a pen and a pad of paper.

"We've got taser rods, propane torches, flashlights, pellet guns, and Supersoakers filled with insecticide."

"You got enough torches for everyone?" Jack asked as he scribbled.

"No but…" O'Connor saw Jack was shaking his head across the table. "What?"

"No one goes in there without a torch of some kind. Kill it with fire, remember?"

O'Connor leaned back and crossed her arms. "You got the extra equipment?"

"Not fueled by propane, but I have alternatives."

"Like what?"

"You'll see." Jack glanced at Bradley and grinned. "It's my own special design. But no insecticide."

"Here we go again." O'Connor pushed her chair back in frustration and puffed on her cigar.

"Hear me out," Jack said. "Insecticide is a good idea, except for one thing. It's toxic. I don't want anyone getting cancer in six months."

"No one will get cancer."

"Can you guarantee that?"

O'Connor shrugged. "No."

"I'm seventeen and you're seventy," Jack said. "No disrespect, but I got a lot more years left in me than you."

Fiscara raised her hand. "I also vote no insecticide."

"Me too," Trillian said.

"All right. No insecticide." O'Connor gnawed on her cigar. "But for the record, I'm not seventy."

"How old are you?" Jack asked.

"Take me to bed and I'll tell you." O'Connor blew a smoke ring across the table and made a kissy-face at Jack.

There was a moment of silence before everyone at the table burst into laughter, breaking the tension.

"I thought you were serious for a second," Jack said.

"Who said I wasn't?" O'Connor flashed her eyebrows at him.

Jack cast a quick glance at Bradley and Trillian. "Oh-kay…"

Sam nudged O'Connor. "Anyway, moving on."

"What about spray paint?" Trillian asked. "You know, to blind them."

"Good idea except they don't die."

"Knives?" Trillian continued. "Bug zapper rackets?"

"Girl's on a roll," O'Connor said, "but I'd take a taser rod over a zapper racket any day."

Jack wrote the ideas down as fast as he could.

"Knives could work. A spider uses internal pressure to move its legs," Fiscara said. "But you'd have to get really close to do any real damage. Closer than with a flame thrower. Not sure if I'd want to do that."

"It'd be good as a backup, a last resort." Bradley smiled at Trillian, then turned to O'Connor and said, "How many pellet guns do you have?"

"Just two, and one of 'em is mine."

"You're going to need four arms to operate all your weapons."

"They don't call me Queen Bitch for nothing." O'Connor leaned back in her chair, rocking it on two legs. She clasped her fingers behind her head and grinned.

Sam chuckled. "Who calls you that?"

O'Connor waved him off, causing her to lose balance on her chair. The table edge was too far to reach and she tipped in an accelerating backward arc. The back of the chair hit the floor, transferring the impact through O'Connor's torso, but her cigar remained firmly clamped between her teeth.

The rest of the group peered down at her, showing expressions of surprise mixed with laughter.

"Well, don't just sit there. Let's get this show on the road." O'Connor blew a puff of smoke out of the corner of her mouth. "And someone help me the fuck up."

MONDAY HAD BECOME a free day for all the students of Washbrook High and Alexis used her time wisely. She ditched Deirdre and Caitlin and headed home.

Having ultimately failed at getting spiders to do her dirty work, she needed to change her tactics.

A squirt gun filled with insecticide was Alexis's new idea, one that came as quickly as her journey back to her house. Ironically it was a small-scale version of O'Connor's Supersoaker idea, even though the two had never met. Great minds think alike, but only a true psychopath would think to use the weapon on humans instead of insects.

It took less than thirty minutes of searching on the Internet to determine the insecticide her father had talked about: Emtix. She read that the insecticide was extremely toxic to mammals and a more powerful poison than arsenic. A teaspoon could kill a full-grown rhino. Criminals used the insecticide to kill guard dogs during robberies. The more Alexis read, the wider her smile got.

Alexis threw on a long sleeved shirt, grabbed a knapsack, a plastic garbage bag, and rubber gloves. She arrived at the Hansen Dam Golf Club just after eleven-thirty in the morning and made a beeline to the main equipment shed. Chances were good she'd run into her dad there.

Before Alexis entered the shed, she removed the rubber gloves from her backpack and put them on. She stepped to the door of the equipment shed, already ajar, and knocked, causing the door to swing open a bit more. Her nose was flooded with the smells of oil, gasoline, metal, and sweet grass.

Tools, equipment, and supplies lined the shed on rows of shelving units, some free-standing and some anchored to the walls. There was more to look through than Alexis had anticipated, and she began scanning for anything labelled Emtix, including its logo.

She could hear someone working in the back out of sight. "Dad?" With that one word, she set her plan into action.

A voice from behind. "Can I help you?"

Alexis spun around to find a young man, she guessed a few years older than her. Her rubber gloves resisted the tight denim of her back pockets as she jammed them inside. "Just looking for my dad." She turned on her charm and blinked at him.

"Who's your dad?"

"Oh. Hector Delarosa." Alexis hesitated. "He doesn't know I'm here."

"He's in the back. My name's David, by the way." He extended his hand in an offer of greeting.

Alexis balked, feeling the sweat build up within the rubber gloves on her hands.

David pulled his hand back. "Sorry. I haven't washed up recently. What's your name?"

"Alexis."

"You want me to get your dad for you?"

"Yes, but before you do, I'm doing a project on the environment for school."

David rested his elbow on a shelf and leaned in. "What school?"

"Washbrook." Running into someone hadn't been part of the plan and Alexis felt her nerves heating up. But she was ready for the challenge. She strolled in a slow circle, taking in her surroundings.

"Cool. I went there a few years back."

Alexis could feel David's eyes on her. "My project is about insecticides used in the environment. Could I ask what the golf course uses?"

"We recently made a switch to a safer mix of insecticide." David walked to one of the shelving units and pointed out some containers. "Atinaz is one of the newer ones but we use a combination of a few that aren't a risk to humans or animals."

"What were you using before?"

"It was highly effective, but too toxic. We never used it on the grass. Too much human contact. Only on the shrubs along the rough." David paused to think, then rummaged though a few rows of containers behind the Atinaz.

"Was it called Emtix?" Alexis asked.

"Yeah! That's it. You know your stuff."

"According to my research, lots of places used to use it."

David pulled out a plastic jug with "EMTIX" written across it in bold letters. He held it up with one finger hooked around the handle. "Yeah. This stuff is nasty. Going to have to wash my hands now."

"Where do you dispose of insecticides like that?"

David shrugged and set the container down. "I think they call someone to take it away." He looked at his watch. "Look, I got to get back to it. I'll go get your dad." He took a few steps before turning around. "Maybe we can hang out sometime."

"Yeah, maybe." Alexis tilted her head to offer a flirty smile from behind her hair. She rocked her shoulders back and forth and flipped her hair back. It was an enticing move that had proven very effective on boys in the past. Judging how David's eyes roamed Alexis from head to toe and back, it appeared to have worked again. He grinned and disappeared into the back.

Alexis sprang into action. She slipped off her backpack and unzipped it, realizing one thing she hadn't considered: the Emtix container was too big to fit into her backpack. She needed a smaller container.

Voices floated from the back. Alexis zipped up her backpack, looped one strap over her shoulder, and jammed her gloved hands back into her back pockets.

Hector bounded in from the back of the shed. David stood next to him, grinning stupidly. "Alexis! What a surprise. Wait." Hector checked his watch. "Why aren't you in school?"

"We had a spider infestation," Alexis said. "So, I thought I'd drop by to see if you'd like to take me for lunch."

"If you don't, I will." David still sported his lovestruck grin. He felt Hector's stare and cleared his throat. "Sir."

"You must have work to do somewhere besides here," Hector said.

"Right." David hustled out of the shed. "Nice meeting you, Alexis," he said just before he disappeared out the door.

"How about taking your dear ol' dad out for lunch for a change. We can exchange spider stories."

"Sure," Alexis said. "Can I have my allowance then?"

"An advance?"

Alexis shrugged as a sly grin slid across her face.

Hector looked at his watch. "We'll negotiate. Give me five minutes to change and we'll head out."

"Great, I'll meet you in front of the Club House."

Hector trotted out of the shed, happy as a pig in shit. Alexis's smile vanished and she got to work looking for a container.

In an equipment shed as large as this, it should have been easy to find a suitable container. But it was like an insanely difficult game of Eye Spy where the future depended on her finding just the right item. The containers were either too small, too large or didn't have lids. And she was running out of time.

On the back work bench, Alexis spotted a travel mug. It could have been Hector's, but she didn't keep track of dumb details like that from her foster parent's lives.

She grabbed the mug and ran back to the container of Emtix. Alexis dropped her pack off her shoulder and knelt close to the ground. She unscrewed the lid of the mug and found it was half full of hazelnut latte.

Yup, it's Hector's mug alright.

She recoiled from the sickly sweet smell and dumped the contents in the corner.

Alexis lifted the container of Emtix and found it surprisingly light. She unscrewed the cap and tipped the container over the mug, her fear confirmed. Empty. "Shit!"

She peered behind the stacks of eco-friendly insecticide that David had shown her and saw one other container that looked to be the same size and shape.

Alexis grabbed it, reassured by its weight. It was a full container of Emtix. She heaved a sigh of relief and twisted open the cap. An industrial odor that reminded her of mothballs mixed with gasoline floated up to her nose. She remembered the health risks of the chemical and held her breath.

She positioned the spout over the travel mug's opening and tilted the container. Alexis was expecting a liquid, but a white sandy powder flowed into the mug instead. She filled it three quarters full and recapped the container.

Her lungs were hot and screaming for air. She twisted on the travel mug's top, closed its sippy opening, and threw it into the garbage bag in her backpack. Alexis gasped for one more breath and held it as she knotted the garbage bag and rezipped her backpack

She carefully placed the Emtix containers back where she'd found them, stood and ran out of the equipment shed. Halfway to the parking lot in front of the Club House, she realized she still had the rubber gloves on. She peeled them off and stuffed them into a trash can beside the tee-off area for Hole 1.

Plan complete, breathing fresh air again and her pulse

returning to normal, Alexis spotted her dad in front of Fairways, the course's restaurant. "We're not eating here."

"Where have you been?" Hector eyed her curiously. "I've been ready to go for five minutes."

"It hasn't been five minutes. I was here waiting. When you didn't show, I went back to the equipment shed to see if you went back there for some reason."

"You must not have waited very long."

Alexis shrugged. "Long enough. So where are we going?"

"What about Taco Siempre? Can't go wrong there."

"Are you buying?"

Hector hooked his elbow around Alexis's neck, pulled her close, and kissed her on the head. "Let's go."

As the two of them walked to Hector's car, Alexis thought about pursuing acting as a career. She had just pulled off a great performance. But her best performance was yet to come.

THE SUN HOVERED in the middle of a blue, cloudless sky, marking a slow descent toward the horizon. Monday was coming to a close and there was still a lot to do.

Bradley, Trillian and Jack strolled out of Stonehurst Hardware, their arms and hands stacked with supplies. Between them, they carried half a dozen headlamps, two flats of WD-40 lubricant in aerosol cans, a bag of disposable lighters, elastic bands, and two bags of heavy duty hot glue refill sticks.

"Kill it with fire," Trillian said. "I'm starting to *warm* up to the idea."

"It's *smokin' hot.*" Bradley grinned.

"Damn you guys." Jack shook his head as he dug for the Civic's keys. "Find some better jokes." He unlocked the back hatch and set down the bag of supplies.

Trillian placed a flat of lubricant behind the back seat. "I just want to see what you've come up with."

"I've got a pretty good idea." Bradley stacked his flat of lubricant beside Trillian's. "But shit, that's a lot of WD-40."

"O'Connor paid for it." Jack held up her credit card. "It's like she's grooming me to be an employee."

"Or her sex slave." Trillian poked Jack in the ribs. "Better watch it, buster."

"She was joking about that."

Trillian hopped into the front passenger seat.

Jack closed the back hatch and glanced at Bradley. "She was joking, right, bro?"

"I don't know for sure. Her only other employee was black. Besides, didn't you say once that you were in love with her?"

"I wasn't *in love* with her." There was an element of panic in Jack's voice. "I just liked her ideas."

"Keep telling yourself that, Casanova," Trillian called back.

Jack hoisted himself through the driver's side window. "You're not helping."

Trillian scrunched her nose and stuck her tongue out in response.

Bradley knocked on the passenger door. "I need to get into the back seat." He propped himself up on the open window, eyeing Trillian with dreamy eyes. "Unless you'd like me to sit on your lap."

Trillian opened the door, forcing Bradley backward, and pushed the seat forward. "It's not your lucky day." Bradley crouched into the back seat. Trillian slapped his butt as he went by.

"Talk about being *in love*." Jack rolled his eyes. "Get a room."

Trillian hopped back into the car and gave Bradley a quick flash of her brown eyes. Jack threw the Civic into gear and blazed a path back to his house.

Sam and O'Connor had collected all the equipment they had

and lined it up along the side of the driveway. Now that they had the equipment out in the open, it didn't seem like enough to make a dent in the clusters of spiders they had seen earlier.

O'Connor twisted her lips around her cigar in frustration. "I'm still ticked about the Supersoakers. They would have worked great."

"The insecticide may not have," Sam said. "Fire is best."

Jack popped out of the driver's side window. "Did I hear someone talking about 'fire?' "

O'Connor approached Jack and gave him a friendly shove on the shoulder and beckoned with her hand. "What have you got for me?"

Jack dropped O'Connor's credit card and receipt in her hand. "It's something you're going to like." He opened the back hatch and the three teens unloaded their supplies.

O'Connor looked at the receipt. "For a hundred-fifty bucks, it better be."

"You worry too much, O'Connor." Jack set one flat of WD-40 on the grass and disappeared into the garage.

"Where's Viscera?" Trillian asked.

"Apparently she's got an extensive hunting knife collection," Sam said. "She'll be back in a bit."

O'Connor looked at Bradley and Trillian. "You guys know what that son-of-a-bitch is cooking up?"

"Not exactly, but…" Bradley pulled a can of WD-40 out of the plastic wrap and held it up next to a disposable lighter. "Oh look. Contents under pressure. Keep away from heat, sparks, and all other sources of ignition." He gave O'Connor a sideways look. "I wonder what's going to happen?"

"Smartass."

"Like father, like son," Bradley said.

Sam leaned against the house grinning and watching the drama play out. Freedom felt good. "Speak for yourself."

"But what about the plastic part?" Trillian pointed to the long red tube attached to the lubricant's spray nozzle. "It's going to melt."

"Yup. But we're not going to use those." Jack emerged from the garage jangling a bag of silver metal tubes. In his other hand was a hot glue gun and an extension cord. "These pen ink tubes are exactly the same size. I knew I was saving them for a reason."

Trillian raised a brow. "You save… pen ink tubes?"

"He saves all sorts of shit," Bradley said. "Lucky for us."

"Okay. Show me your work of art, da Vinci." O'Connor took a seat on the steps.

"It's pretty simple, really," Jack said. "Hey Sam, could you plug in the power, over there by the wall?"

Sam plugged the extension cord into an outlet just inside the garage. He exchanged a look with Bradley. "You feeling a little *déjà vu?*"

Bradley nodded. "Totally."

"Oh, yeah!" O'Connor began to cackle. "I almost forgot about that. We almost died that day. Fun times. And I shot you in the leg. Remember that?"

"Still got the mark to prove it," Sam said.

Trillian sat next to Jack. "What are you guys talking about?"

"Hunting vermin a few months ago in New York," O'Connor said. "Brad will tell you about it later, right Brad?"

Bradley nodded. "One of the best summers of my life."

While the group was talking, Jack had been busy hot-gluing a disposable lighter perpendicularly near the top of the aerosol can. Trillian watched him closely. He jammed a metal pen tube into the nozzle of the WD-40 can. "Hey Trill, can you hand me the rubber bands?"

She tossed him the bag. Jack ripped it open and took one out. He slid it around the aerosol can in line with the disposable lighter.

"The gang's all here." Fiscara appeared behind O'Connor and

squatted. Her belt was adorned with at least a dozen different hunting knives in their protective leather sheathes.

O'Connor eyed Fiscara's beltline. "Nice blades."

"Thanks. What's Jack up to?"

"A new invention," O'Connor said. "Better be worth the Benjamins of mine he spent on it."

"You're just in time, Miss Fiscara." Jack stood up and looked around the front yard. "I call it Port-A-Torch. You hook the elastic onto the disposable lighter's gas release and spark it."

Jack rolled the flint and ignited a small orange flame from the lighter. "Now it's just a matter of point and incinerate. We good, Brad?"

Bradley checked the road for cars. "All clear."

Jack pointed the aerosol can away from the group and depressed its nozzle. A five-foot blast of flame shot from the metal pen tube, singeing a nearby shrub. He turned to the group, grinning. "Fucking sweet, huh?"

O'Connor shrugged. "Hate to break it to you but my torches can shoot twice as far."

"Yeah? How much did yours cost?" Jack held up the can, his annoyance simmering. "This baby cost about six bucks."

O'Connor spotted Sam's glare and clenched her teeth. "Yeah, yeah. I get it."

"I can make twenty-three more of these. Just say the word." Jack looked around the group. "Everyone needs to be able to protect themselves. Right?"

"Do it," Sam said. "Build them. Whatever we think we'll need, we'll probably need more. And Jack, I for one thought it was pretty cool."

"Thanks." Jack relaxed.

"So much for my knives," Fiscara said.

"No, Miss Fiscara." Jack sat next to the flat of WD-40. "The known problem with this is once the lighter's burning, you have about ten minutes before the plastic gets soft... unless you're turning it on and off. We're going to need extra weapons. So your knives will come in handy."

"Thanks for the vote of confidence, Jack," Fiscara said.

O'Connor picked up Jack's Port-A-Torch. "No offense, but I'll be using my propane torch before this thing."

"The same one that exploded at the dance?" Jack smirked at O'Connor.

"Yep."

"Just make sure you have a couple as a backups," Jack said. "You never know."

"Will do."

"You going to show O'Connor the mother of all flame throwers?" Bradley asked Jack.

Jack offered a wide smile and nodded. "Damn straight, bro. I was saving that one." He disappeared into the garage again.

Trillian gave Bradley a sideways look. "This isn't going to be another dick swinging contest, is it?"

Bradley looked at O'Connor. "Well? Are you going to be swinging your dick?" Bradley began to laugh.

O'Connor swung a hand at Bradley, narrowly missing his head. "Watch your mouth, you little shit."

From inside the garage, Jack's voice boomed, "Presenting… either the best or the worst idea I've ever come up with." He stepped out from the shadows with a pair of aviator sunglasses on and struck a pose. Strapped to his back was Moody's power washer. Jack had fastened a modified barbeque lighter to the end of the nozzle and extended the trigger with a metal lever.

O'Connor took her cigar from her mouth and scrunched her brow. "You planning on cleaning my car?"

"Ha ha," Jack said. "It's gas powered. And instead of water, I'll be shooting gas. Well, a mixture of unleaded and diesel."

"Your plan is to strap a gallon of gas to your back?"

"That's one way to put it."

"It's been nice knowing you." O'Connor turned to Bradley. "No dick swinging here. I'd get burned."

Jack slid the power washer off his back and carefully set it down. "So, what do you think? 9 a.m., Hansen Dam. We take those fuckers out."

"Abso-*fucking*-lutely." Trillian pumped her fist. Everyone looked at her, surprised. "What? I'm no angel!"

"Abso-fucking-lutely," Bradley echoed.

"I'm in." Sam looked at Fiscara. "Wendy?"

"You better believe it," Fiscara said. "Those bastards ate my tarantula."

Sam tilted his head toward O'Connor. "Bertha?"

O'Connor's eyes narrowed and her lips curled in a smirk around her cigar. "I live for this shit."

Bradley pulled out his phone. "I'll text Mark the deets."

"Who's going to help me make more Port-A-Torches?" Jack asked.

Trillian held up two WD-40 cans she had already glued disposable lighters to. "Couldn't help it. I've got a thing for arts and crafts and incendiary devices."

"Hand me the pen tubes," Bradley said. "We'll be done in no time."

With the three teenagers assembling the Port-A-Torches, Fiscara turned to Sam and O'Connor. "What next?"

"Food run," O'Connor said. "I'm thinking burrito feast."

"Abso-fucking-lutely." Jack's ears never failed to perk up when burritos were mentioned.

"Let's go." O'Connor stepped into the Mustang and revved the engine. Sam hopped in the back, leaving the front for Fiscara.

When the Mustang was just an echo in the distance, Trillian paused her gluing. "You think this is going to work?"

Jack and Bradley looked at each other. "It has to," they said in unison.

They resumed construction of the Port-A-Torches, all three wondering if they'd be alive to tell the tale in twenty-four hours.

ASSUMING THERE WOULD be no school, Deirdre had stayed up later than usual watching movies and surfing social media on her phone. She awoke at four minutes to four in the morning, her ear buds still in place and her phone resting on her chest.

Deirdre propped herself up on her elbows and scooted back onto her pillow. She rubbed her fists in her eyes and looked at the phone's screen. A text from Alexis awaited in the center of the display.

"Cait's 2morrow @ 8am," Alexis's text read.

Eight in the morning? Seriously?

Deirdre plucked a wad of gum off her bedside table and stuck it in her mouth. She was always surprised at how the flavor would bounce back after a night without chewing.

Her mom said it was a disgusting habit.

"Fuck you, Mom." Deirdre snapped her gum, now softened and renewed between her teeth. She contemplated blowing off Alexis's text but knew the risk would be greater than the reward.

But the phone almost made the decision for her. Her battery sat at three percent.

"Shit!" She swiped to reply and sent back, "OK" with a "thumbs up" emoji.

Deirdre plucked out her earbuds and placed their jumbled wires and the phone on the induction charging pad on the bedside table. She swung her legs off the side of the bed, sat up, and stretched.

The house was silent except for the usual clicks and creaks all houses make at night. Deirdre peeled off her shorts, shirt, and bra and dropped them in a heap beside the bed. She grabbed her favorite night shirt, extra large with the words "DON'T WAKE ME UP EVER" written on the front, and pulled it over her head. The cool white cotton felt soothing on her skin.

She padded to the bathroom in bare feet and closed the door as quietly as she could. One bathroom wall was bathed in blue light coming through the frosted window.

The moon must be full tonight.

She turned on the small nightlight next to the sink, pulled her panties to her knees and sat to pee.

Facing the partially open shower curtain, Deirdre saw something dark move across the tile in the shadows of the shower enclosure. Her mind drifted back to the school storage alcove the night Caitlin was bitten by a spider. She stopped chewing her gum.

What if there's a spider in the shower? Or worse, in the toilet?

Deirdre rose from the toilet seat in slow motion, her panties still stretched between her knees. She looked into the toilet bowl, relieved to find no dark spider hiding in there, ready to pounce. She tore a wad of toilet paper, wiped herself, then froze.

Please don't be there please don't be there... Deirdre pulled up the hem of her shirt slowly to get a clear view of the cotton gusset between her knees.

No spider. All clear. She heaved a sigh of relief and pulled up her panties. With renewed bravery, she looked behind the shower curtain.

Again, no spider.

You're such a drama queen, Deirdre.

She quickly washed her hands and splashed fresh water on her face. Rivulets rolled over her lips. They tasted cool and sweet and suddenly she was thirsty. She snapped her gum as she grabbed a navy blue plastic cup from beside the sink, one that she had used since she was five, and filled it with water.

Deirdre brought the cup of water to her lips and began to

drink. Cold and refreshing, she drank, tipping the cup up to get every last—

Drop.

The plastic cup hit the floor and clattered across the checkered linoleum. Something that had been in the cup was now in her mouth, on her tongue, *through* her tongue.

The red hot pain was overpowered by the horror of not knowing the cause. Deirdre opened her mouth and stuck her tongue out.

Horror seized her and her gum fell to the floor. Reflected in the mirror, on the tip of her tongue, was a black spider the size of her thumb, its two fangs buried in the muscle.

Tears poured down her cheeks and despite her attempts to control her terror, a scream rose in the back of her throat. But it was stifled by her own tongue, which had swollen well past its normal size and had begun to block airflow to her throat. She heaved panicked breaths through her nose.

The spider retracted its fangs and scrambled out onto her cheek next to her left eye. Too close to focus on it, Deirdre watched the spider advance up her cheek in the mirror. Her face frozen in fear, she raised a trembling hand to her cheek, but the spider detected the motion as a threat. It sank its fangs into her lower left eyelid, close to the tear duct, and a fresh bolt of pain shot through Deirdre's head.

Her knees buckled and she fell forward, catching herself on the lip of the sink. In the mirror she saw black veins stretch out from her left eye socket. The swelling spread to her nose and cut off her remaining source of oxygen.

Deirdre's right eye darted erratically across the sink's splash back for something sharp. She could give herself a tracheotomy, just like in the movies.

Her lungs burned and spasmed for air. She fumbled for a pair of tweezers in a plastic caddy behind the tap, knocking the entire contents into the sink.

Her left eye clouded over and useless, Deirdre used the fading eyesight in her right eye to guide her shaking hand to the tweezers, before collapsing to the floor.

In a fist that grew weaker by the second, she positioned the tweezers to her throat and pushed with all the strength she had left.

The sharp end of the tweezers pierced her throat but not far enough to make a difference. Deirdre felt no pain. She had nothing left. No strength and no air to breathe.

Black veins spread out like a web across her face and neck and her world faded to black.

Shake, Freeze, Burn

AFTER A FEAST of every kind of burrito Taco Siempre served compliments of O'Connor, the crew disbanded, agreeing to meet back at Jack's place at eight-thirty the next morning.

Bradley walked Trillian home.

"That kind of felt like our last supper," he said.

"You're so dramatic." Trillian took on a solemn tone and held up her hands like she was proselytizing. "Truly I tell you, one of you *will* betray me."

Bradley gave her a sideways glance. "What?"

"Sorry. I went to Sunday School for a while. Some of the verses stuck," Trillian said. "Like you said before, our plan has to work." She looked at him through strands of rainbow hair. "Besides, we haven't gone on our first official date yet."

Bradley gulped, his throat instantly dry. "Date?"

"Don't say you haven't been thinking of it. I know I have."

"Yeah, I've been thinking of it. But what about the whole 'don't get any ideas' thing?"

Trillian shrugged and rested her head on Bradley's shoulder for a moment. "All of that means it wasn't our *last supper*. It can't be."

The two of them arrived at Trillian's house.

"Am I ever going to come in?" Bradley asked.

"Yep. On our first official date." Trillian grinned, grabbed his shirt with both her fists, and pulled him down to her level. Her kiss was warm and smelled faintly of chilies and corn tortilla. A definite step up from jasmine. "I'll see you tomorrow," she said as she walked toward her house.

"I'll be here at eight. We can walk."

"I'll be waiting," Trillian called back. And like so many times before, she slipped into her house without so much as a wave.

But Bradley had another kiss to hold him over. He walked on air all the way back to Sheldon Street. The front door was unlocked and silence greeted him when he entered.

"Mom?"

No response. He passed the living room. The couch had been recently slept on and a plate littered with crumbs sat on a nearby coffee table. The television offered no clues.

He passed the entrance to the kitchen and proceeded down the hallway. "Mom?"

"In here, hon." Claire's voice rose softly from her bedroom.

Bradley pushed the door open and peered in. He could see Claire curled up on her right side, a pillow raising her left leg up. He sat on the corner of the bed and all at once, he knew. For him, it had been easy to forget, with his head buried in battle preparations and young love.

"I'm sorry about Roy," he said.

Claire rolled onto her back, wiping a stray tear away with her wrist. She repositioned the pillow under her left leg. "Thanks." She reached out and squeezed Bradley's hand. "I know you two didn't see eye to eye—"

"We're going to get them, Mom, those spiders," Bradley said. "We've got a crew and we've got weapons."

"Promise me you'll be careful." Her eyes pleaded with his, just as they had done from her hospital room days earlier. This time her terror was replaced with concern.

"I promise." Bradley offered a confident smile, one Claire found irresistible. "Can I make you some chicken noodle soup?"

"That would be wonderful." Chicken noodle soup, the salty kind in the packets, was one of Claire's comfort foods.

Bradley went to work. In no time they were sharing soup in front of the television, and later, popcorn for an encore presentation of "Jaws."

The morning came fast for Bradley. He hadn't slept this well since returning home from New York City. His friends were here, his dad and O'Connor were here, and they had a plan that would work. Everything had fallen into place, although Roy's death cast a spectre of doubt over everything.

Bradley shoveled a bowl of cereal into his mouth and made a pot of coffee for his mom. He met Trillian just after eight o'clock and they joined the rest of the crew at Jack's twenty minutes later.

Mark waved down Bradley and Trillian at the end of Jack's driveway, a partially eaten donut in his hand. "I was beginning to think that you weren't going to show."

"I'd look pretty stupid not showing up to my own hunting party."

"Well…" Mark motioned at Trillian and flashed his eyebrows. Tact and subtlety were not in his wheelhouse.

Trillian caught the gesture and glared at Bradley.

"I don't know what *that* was about, but I haven't said anything." Bradley could see the fire in Trillian's eyes. "That's the truth."

"Jerks." Trillian pushed past Bradley and Mark and stormed forward to join the others.

"Dude, what'd you do that for?"

Mark shrugged. "Sorry. It's no secret that you and her have *a thing*. Plus, she's a looker, so—"

"Your timing's shit," Bradley said. "Next time, talk to me first."

"Sure, sure. Oh, and guess who has a date with Caitlin on Friday?"

Bradley raised an eyebrow. He was beginning to regret including Mark in their crew. "I don't know if I should say 'good luck' or 'be careful.' "

" 'Congrats' is enough." Mark pumped his fist. "It's going to be *sweet!*"

"Come on." Bradley grabbed a donut, poured himself a cup of coffee, and stood next to Trillian. He could feel the heat coming off her.

Trillian took an angry bite of a donut.

Bradley leaned toward her. "Sorry for Mark back there. He didn't mean anything by it."

"You think I'm stupid?" Trillian faced him, her eyes gleaming. She lowered her voice. "He thinks we're *smashing.*"

"He does have a one track mind," Bradley said. "But I prefer to think he sees the same thing I do. You're smart and beautiful, Trill. The whole deal."

Trillian's eyes softened but she maintained her veneer of annoyance.

"He's got a date with Caitlin on Friday," Bradley whispered. "God help his soul." He saw a slight smile form in the corners of her mouth and knew his attempt at repair had begun to work.

"Seems confident enough to me."

"You lovebirds going to join us?" O'Connor locked eyes with Bradley. "In case you haven't noticed, some serious shit is about to go down."

Bradley gave Trillian's hand a brief squeeze and straightened up. "We're listening."

"Uh huh." O'Connor dunked a donut in a paper cup of coffee and chomped a bite. "Jack's got the schematics all worked out and he'll brief us at the dam. Let's load up and rollout. Sam, Fiscara, you're with me."

Sam smiled at Fiscara. "Lucky us."

The seven members of the crew loaded up the back of the Mustang and the Civic with everything they had. Now with the two dozen newly assembled Port-A-Torches and Jack's power washer flame thrower, storage space was tight.

Mark held a Port-A-Torch in his hand. "These things really work?"

"Hell, yeah." Bradley took the torch and placed it next to the others in the Civic. "We tested them yesterday. Shoots a five foot flame."

There were enough donuts left for at least one more per person. Bradley grabbed the box. "Hey, everyone. I'd like to quickly say something."

"Don't tell me. You're getting married." O'Connor cackled as she pulled out a partially burned cigar and placed it between her teeth.

Bradley ignored the joke. "The next steps are dangerous, and our lives will be on the line. Everyone here has shown dedication and a willingness to help. But if you want to back out, now's your chance, no questions."

Everyone exchanged looks, as if expecting someone from the group to bail out, but no one did.

"I'd raise a glass to you all, but all I have are these donuts." Bradley selected a cruller. "Take one and pass the box along."

The box floated from hand to hand, ending with Mark. "There's two left so..." He grabbed both and tossed the box aside.

Bradley raised up his donut as if it were a glass of wine. "Here's to Mis Fiscara—"

"That's Viscera," Fiscara smirked.

"Thanks for your knowledge and expertise. And the coffee and donuts." Bradley turned to Sam. "To my dad and O'Connor, who travelled from New York to help us, we couldn't have gotten this far without you. And to my friends Jack, Trillian, and Mark. Thanks for standing by me. You must think I'm nuts."

"Yeah, you've always been nuts," Jack said. Soft laughter rose from the rest of the group.

"May the Force be with us," Sam said before taking a bite of his donut.

Everyone glanced at Sam at the same time.

"What? Did I say something wrong?" Donut crumbs flew from Sam's mouth.

"Nope," Jack said. "Works for me." He took a giant bite of his donut.

"Okay, jam those cake holes into your cake holes and let's hit the road." O'Connor consumed her donut in two bites and washed it down with her remaining coffee. She pulled out her keys and headed to the Mustang. "Sam, Fiscara. Ándale!"

Jack gulped his donut and swung his body through the driver side window of the Civic. Bradley and Trillian squeezed into the back and Mark in the front.

"Let's do this." Mark looked as if he might burst from excitement.

Bradley leaned toward Trillian and lowered his voice. "About earlier—"

"We're good." She grabbed his hand and smiled at him through strands of multi-colored hair.

Jack started the engine and stretched his neck out the window. "O'Connor, follow me."

"Why? Are you the leader now?"

"Because you don't know where the fuck you're going," Jack said.

O'Connor blinked. "Right. What are you waiting for, then?"

Jack gunned the engine and peeled out onto the street, O'Connor following close behind. They turned onto Sheldon Street and followed it to a right turn onto Glenoaks Boulevard. Their destination was the Hansen Dam Recreation Area parking lot. Jack had calculated this to be the most direct route.

Trillian clutched the seat. "Guys? Did you feel something?"

Mark twisted in his seat. "Like what?"

"I don't know." Trillian squeezed Bradley's hand. "I felt something."

"Was it in Brad's pants?" Mark laughed. "You two need a room?"

Bradley punched the back of Mark's seat. "Knock it off."

"Holy shit. Look!" Trillian pointed at a fallen telephone pole across the road in front of Singer Fence Company. It had toppled to one side, stopping askew thirty degrees off vertical. The power lines, now taut, snapped in a shower of sparks.

All four teenagers gazed at the spectacle as they zoomed by, as if passing the wreckage of a car accident. Jack looked in his rearview mirror and saw O'Connor tailing him close behind.

"I think we're having an earthquake." Jack's frenzied eyes scanned the road ahead for obstructions or cracks, but never slowed his speed. Instead he jammed his foot on the gas.

The connected telephone pole further down the road pulled free of its base and a chain reaction began to unfold, power poles falling over like a row of toy soldiers.

Telephone poles on the right side began to topple, one after another every which way until one fell out into the road.

"Look out!" Bradley shifted in his seat and instinctively covered Trillian's head.

Jack swerved wildly, narrowly missing the impact of a thousand pounds of wood. He checked the rearview mirror and saw O'Connor steer the Mustang around the tip of the splintered pole.

"We need to outrun them," Mark said.

"Yeah." Jack floored the gas, tearing down Glenoak Boulevard and pushing the Civic to its limit. For the time being, luck was on their side, with most of the heavy telephone poles located on the opposite side of the boulevard.

"Watch for cops," Bradley said.

"Forget that. I'm more worried about getting to the parking lot in one piece." Jack navigated around debris on the road and blew through a red light at Montague Street. "We're close. The golf course is on our right."

Jack checked the rearview mirror and the baby blue Mustang was nowhere to be seen.

Bradley saw the concern and panic in Jack's eyes and looked through the hatchback window. "Where's O'Connor? My dad?"

Jack gripped the steering wheel. "I don't know."

"We got to go back for them."

"We can't."

"WE GOT TO." Bradley grabbed the back of Jack's seat and rattled it.

Jack slammed on the brakes and skidded to a stop. He turned to Bradley, wild-eyed. "I can't drive over telephone poles and live electrical wires."

The two teenagers stared at each other, both unwilling to back down.

"Look. O'Connor's a good driver," Jack said. "They'll make it." He juiced the gas pedal and resumed his route toward the parking lot. "The best thing we can do is get to the parking lot."

The Civic continued down Glenoak. There was less debris on the road in front of the golf course, making driving easier. Jack turned right onto Osborne Street and into the Hansen Dam Recreation Area parking lot.

The lot was almost deserted. Jack pulled into a spot next to the main entrance to the walking trails and his blood ran cold.

"Brad, we got a problem."

"No shit," Bradley said, still looking out the back window of the Civic. The Mustang was nowhere in sight.

"No, we got another problem." Jack rapped his knuckles on Bradley's knee.

"Hey, Caitlin made it. Cool!" Mark jumped out of the Civic and walked over to where she stood.

"What... the... *fuck*." Trillian shifted her eyes from the front to Bradley. "The asshat invited Caitlin and—"

"Caitlin brought Alexis," Jack said. "What are we going to do?"

Bradley's mind raced between concern for Sam, O'Connor, and Fiscara, and having to deal with Alexis. "There's only one thing we can do."

The three friends stepped out of the Civic and approached Mark, Caitlin and Alexis.

O'CONNOR FOLLOWED THE Civic as closely as she could, but her nerves were worn thin. The first of the telephone poles on the right side of Glenoak Boulevard began to rip from their foundations, crumbling the concrete sidewalk like it was meringue.

"Stay on him," Fiscara said.

"What do you think I'm doing?"

The first few poles fell away from the road but the third had heavy transformers attached to the top. The weight pulled the pole to the left, bringing everything crashing down across the right lane.

The Civic ahead cornered sharply into the oncoming lane, narrowly missing the telephone pole and its transformers.

O'Connor followed but wasn't as lucky, ripping a gash into the Mustang's right side.

Sam shook baby blue paint flakes out of his hair. "There goes our damage deposit."

"Don't start." O'Connor spoke through clenched teeth, clamped to her cigar. She glared at Sam briefly in the rearview mirror.

"Look out!" Fiscara pointed at the telephone pole ahead. Its connected power lines pulled taut in the same direction as the pole they had narrowly missed. She raised her arms to shield her face.

O'Connor slammed on the brakes too late. The telephone pole glanced the front left corner of the Mustang. The left headlight exploded in a shower of glass and metal. The transformers behind them burst into blue electrical flames, popping and fizzing, filling the air with rancid ozone.

The Civic was nowhere to be seen, having somehow outmaneuvered the telephone pole that had blocked the Mustang in its tracks.

O'Connor sat gripping the steering wheel. Her body trembled and her lungs fought for air in panicked breaths. The ground undulated beneath the tires and all three felt the low rumbling deep within their core.

Fiscara shot Sam a brief worried look. "O'Connor, we got to go."

"I can't."

"What do you mean *you can't?*"

"I can't." O'Connor maintained her grip on the steering wheel, knuckles white with fear. "I don't do earthquakes."

"You don't do—"

Sweat poured from her brow and threatened to douse her cigar. "I'm a diagnosed seismophobe. A card carrying member."

Fiscara looked at Sam. "You have any issues with me driving? Because we *got* to move."

"Nope. Go for it."

Fiscara unbuckled O'Connor's seat belt, pried her fingers from the steering wheel, and the two of them moved O'Connor into the back seat.

"Remember back in New York when I told you to lay off the pound cake?" Sam grinned as he labored under O'Connor's weight. "You didn't listen to me, did you?"

"Fuck you and your pound cake."

"There's the O'Connor I know." Sam buckled her into the back seat and got in. "Just relax." He looked at Fiscara. "Go!"

Fiscara threw the Mustang into reverse, then turned right onto the crumbled sidewalk. The undercarriage scraped against the raised chunks of broken concrete. She juiced the gas pedal and zoomed down the sidewalk.

"You're definitely not getting your damage deposit back," Fiscara said.

Sam admired the skill with which Fiscara handled the Mustang. "Where'd you learn to drive like this?"

"My father was a NASCAR driver."

"No shit." Sam grinned at her in the rearview mirror.

"I'm not just a pretty face."

A clearer path opened up when Fiscara arrived at the intersection of Montague Street. The chain link fencing lining the southern edge of Hansen Dam Golf Course had remained upright throughout the quake. Fiscara carved a path straddling the right side of Glenoak Boulevard and the sidewalk, swerving to avoid lamp standards that miraculously remained standing.

"ETA two minutes out," Fiscara said.

O'Connor leaned forward. "Not a fucking word to anyone about this or you'll be eating my torch."

"You're welcome." Fiscara turned right onto Osbourne Street, the parking lot and Jack's orange Civic visible in the distance. A police car, sirens engaged, flew down the street in the opposite direction.

"You ready to rock?" O'Connor asked Sam.

"Yeah." He gave O'Connor a once-over. "The real question is, *are you?*"

"Bring it on."

Fiscara turned into the parking lot and backed into the stall next to the Civic. She peered into the rearview mirror and furrowed her brow. "Alexis? What the…"

JACK PULLED HIMSELF out of the driver side window of the Civic in one fluid motion, an attempt to impress as well as intimidate. More muscle on his thin frame would have helped.

Bradley and Trillian stepped through the passenger door. He cast a wary glance at Jack and Trillian before straightening and approaching Mark, Caitlin and Alexis.

Alexis was dressed in black tight-fitting shorts, a black leather vest over a white t-shirt, black work boots, and black driving gloves. Her hair was tied back in a tight ponytail. "Loverboy and Rainbow Brite. Why am I not surprised?"

Caitlin thumped Alexis with her bandaged hand and lowered her voice. "You said you'd be nice." The purple gauze wrapped around her hand matched her t-shirt, but now her thumb was separated and her fingers were wrapped two at a time, allowing for more manual dexterity. She looked like she had one three-fingered alien hand.

Alexis scowled at Caitlin but before she could respond, Bradley had marched forward, stopping nose to nose with her. His approach had come so quickly that she had to take a step back to maintain her balance.

"Why are you here?" The muscles in Bradley's jaws stood out in angry angles.

"She came with me," Caitlin said.

Mark approached the three of them. "And I invited Cait. I figured the more people we had the better."

"You figured wrong." Bradley stood his ground. "Where's Deirdre? You never fight your own battles."

Alexis narrowed her eyes. "She'll be here." She leaned forward and whispered into Bradley's ear. "You're dead." She grinned and winked, close enough for only Bradley to see, then summoned tears to her eyes as if she had just flipped a switch. "My dad was bitten and he might die." Alexis shifted nervously on her feet. "I know we're not exactly friends… but I want to kill those things too."

"Bullshit," Bradley said. "You're a liar." He turned to the rest of the group. "Can't you see she's lying?"

"Call him then." Alexis held out her phone, wiping tears from her face.

"Good idea." Instead of using Alexis's phone, Bradley pulled his phone from his pocket instead. "I still have his number." As he dialed he saw a momentary look of panic cross Alexis's face.

"Well?" Trillian asked.

Bradley hung up and redialed. "The call's not going through."

"Probably because of the quake, although I still have a signal." Jack looked at an app on his phone. "A magnitude 4.1. You saw the damage getting here."

Caitlin stepped closer to Mark. "Can't we all work together?"

Bradley squared off with Caitlin. "Did you know that she tried to kill my mom? With spiders?"

"Fuck you." Tears streamed down Alexis's face.

"And the spiders at the school, that was Alexis too."

Caitlin and Alexis shared a look. "You have no proof," Caitlin said.

Bradley stepped back. "Isn't that convenient?"

The Mustang squealed into the parking lot, its engine rumbling. The remnants of the left headlight hung from its socket by wires and the hood and part of the bumper were crumped. Fiscara pulled up behind the Civic and backed into an adjacent parking stall in one smooth move.

Bradley's beef with Alexis momentarily forgotten, he made a line toward Sam. "Fiscara drove?"

Sam shook his head and lowered his voice. "Don't ask." They shared a brief hug.

"What happened?"

"A telephone pole zigged," Sam said, "and unlike you guys, we failed to zag. But we're here now."

Alexis leaned toward Caitlin's ear and whispered, "Where the *fuck* is Dee?"

Caitlin shrugged. "I have no idea. Maybe the quake delayed her." She cast a nervous eye across Alexis's face. "We're going to have to do this without her."

"Fucking bitch. I'm going to beat her sorry ass when I'm done here," Alexis mumbled to herself.

Fiscara stepped out of the Mustang and unlocked the trunk. Jack followed suit and popped the back hatch of the Civic.

O'Connor swung her leg over the side of the car. "What are you all standing around for? Haven't you felt the earth move before?" She spotted Caitlin and Alexis. "Who the hell are you?"

Mark stepped forward. "This is Caitlin. She's been bitten too. And that's her friend Alexis. She used to date Brad."

"Jesus Christ, Mark." Brad grumbled. "Not important."

"The team needs to know each other," Mark said. "History is important or we'll be doomed to repeat our mistakes."

O'Connor sent a disapproving look at Mark, moved on to face Alexis, and blew cigar smoke into her face. O'Connor raised a brow and looked at Bradley. "This ain't going to get weird, is it?"

"Fuck, no." Bradley placed his arm around Trillian's shoulder. "I'll protect what's important to me."

"You got to be useful if you're going to roll with us," O'Connor said to Caitlin and Alexis. "Let's see your weapons."

In her good hand Caitlin held up a can of purple spray paint, the color matching everything else. "To blind them."

Bradley leaned to Trillian's ear. "Was your idea first."

Trillian offered only a small smile in response.

O'Connor took in the mass of purple. "You're quite the

fashion plate. You know you're going to have to get really close with that, right?"

"Yeah," Caitlin nodded. "No bigs."

"No bigs." O'Connor chuckled. "We'll see about that." She watched another police car sped down Osbourne Street, sirens wailing and lights ablaze, before switching her gaze to Alexis. "How about you, Doll-face? What do you got?"

Alexis rummaged in the back pocket of her tight shorts and pulled out a knife handle. Bradley recognized it immediately. She clicked a button on the handle and a stiletto blade popped out.

"Another close-range weapon," O'Connor said. "You got the balls to match?"

Alexis ran a finger along the edge of the blade. "I'll be fine, *grandma*." She retracted the blade and slid the hilt back into her pocket.

O'Connor puffed her cigar. "Honey, you better not go chickenshit on us." She pointed at herself with her thumb. " 'Cause *this* grandma's a fucking *bitch*."

"Let's suit up and move out." Jack grabbed a Port-A-Torch. "There's too many cops around."

O'Connor grabbed four walkie-talkies and clipped them to her belt. She lifted a propane torch from the back of the Mustang and hung it off her shoulder. "Jack, we got enough of your little torches for Miss Purple and Doll-face?"

"Plenty." Jack and Bradley shared a look of frustration, then waved Alexis and Caitlin to the back of the Civic. Mark tagged along like a lost puppy.

"Don't forget the headlamps," Bradley said.

"Got it." Jack handed them each a Port-A-Torch and one headlamp. "You know how to use one of these?"

Alexis scowled at him. "We're not stupid."

"Light the lighter. Press the nozzle. Burn spiders." Caitlin batted her eyelashes at Jack. "Am I right?"

"Yeah, but use the rubber band to keep the fuel release open,"

Jack said. "And you got ten minutes before the end of the lighter melts."

"What happens then?" Caitlin asked.

"You're fucked." Jack looked at Alexis, Caitlin and Mark and handed them each another torch. "Take one more, for back up."

Sam handed a taser rod to Fiscara.

"You sure *you* won't need that?" she asked.

"I'll have a big torch and a couple of little torches. I'll be fine." Sam winked at her. "If I need one, I'll take O'Connor's."

"Only from my cold, dead hands," O'Connor said as she clipped her taser rod to her belt.

Jack divided the remaining Port-A-Torches and headlamps between the rest of the crew before slipping into the harness of the power washer. A strong odor of gasoline floated from the back of the Civic. One of the fuel reservoirs on the power washer had a leak, but there was no time to isolate it. He grabbed a coil of rope and slung it over his head and shoulder.

Trillian and Bradley took three Port-A-Torches each, one in hand and two jammed into their pockets, plus ample rubber bands for the fuel release valve.

"Let's move out," O'Connor said.

Dozens of walking paths criss-crossed the Hansen Dam Recreation Area. Bradley, Trillian, and Jack led the crew through a copse of trees until their chosen path joined at the leading edge of the dam. To their right, a rocky scree two-hundred fifty feet deep rose seventy-five feet to the bike path above.

"That's the path Roy died on," Jack said.

"We'll avenge him." Trillian looked at Bradley. "For your mom."

Bradley nodded in silence.

Mark, Caitlin and Alexis were last in line, following behind O'Connor, Sam and Fiscara.

"I don't know if Jack told you, but these spiders have things on their backs that—"

"Would you shut up?" Alexis rolled her eyes.

Mark recoiled as if touched by something hot and attempted to hide his hurt feelings. "Just trying to help."

"You'd help by shutting the fuck up," Alexis said.

Mark fell silent and quickened his pace.

Caitlin glowered at Alexis. "Who pissed in your cornflakes this morning?" She ran to catch up with Mark, leaving Alexis at the rear of the pack.

Alexis had stowed one Port-A-Torch in her front pocket and held the other. With her free gloved hand, she smoothed out her denim shorts. The switchblade in her back pocket embossed the denim in the distinctive shape of the knife's hilt. She dipped her fingers in the pocket, reminding herself of the hilt's smooth pearl inlay. What everyone had failed to notice was the other pocket where an equally distinctive shape sat concealed: Alexis's secret weapon.

She grinned to herself and followed the others as the dam's scree ended, replaced by the enormous fenced-in maw of the dam's opening.

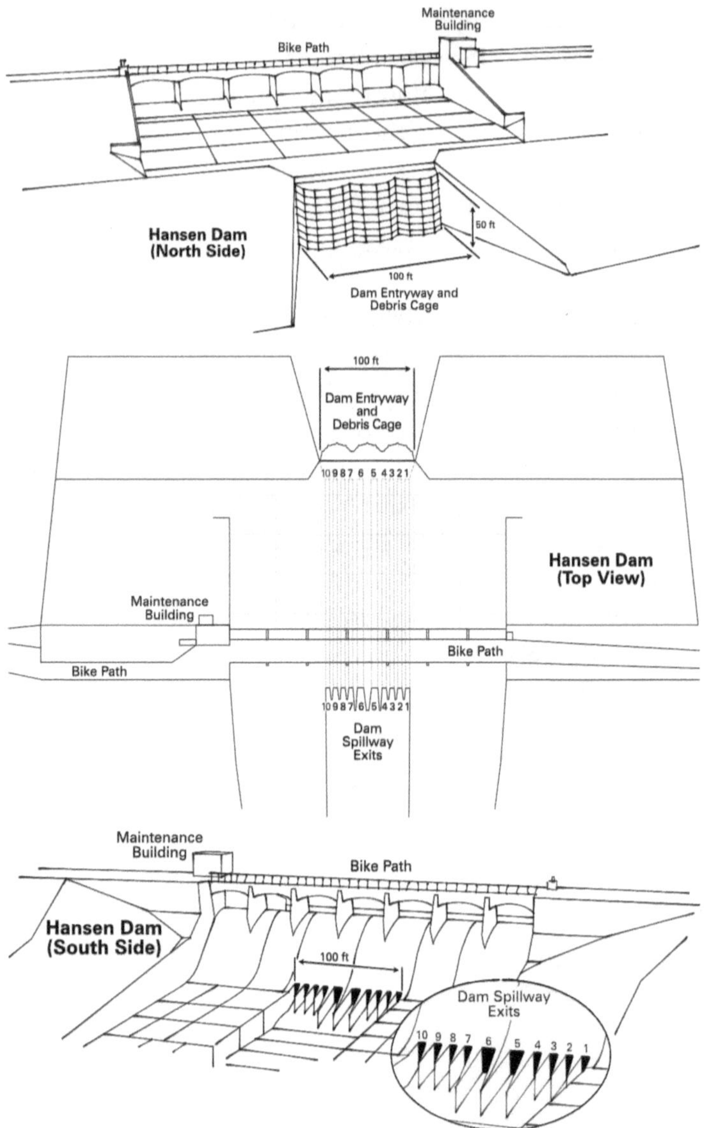

(For 3D views, go to LeeGabel.com/hansendam.)

JACK LOOKED UP at the wrought iron debris cage spanning a hundred feet across the entry of Hansen Dam and fifty feet above his head. He glanced back at the rest of the crew. "Impressive, isn't it?"

"Indeed," Fiscara said. "I've been all through the recreation area, but never in the dam itself."

"We're going *in* there?" Mark swallowed hard and glanced at Caitlin.

"Yup." Jack beamed. "Through all the spillways. It's the only way to find all the spiders."

"Uh, cool." Mark failed to conceal his lack of confidence but Caitlin didn't seem to notice.

Trillian reached for Bradley's hand. "Why not just the spillway we saw from the drone?"

"Got to be thorough," Jack said. "Kill 'em all."

O'Connor grabbed Jack's shoulder and gave it a firm, friendly shake. "I like the way you think. Any chance of rats in there?"

Jack shrugged. "Probably."

O'Connor gnawed her cigar. "Hear that Sam? We might see some rats too."

"Great," Sam said. "This trip is getting better and better."

Jack led the crew through the wrought iron debris fence, having to duck and twist sideways between the bars, and into the protected area of the dam's opening. Damp and putrid air flowed from the eight ground-level spillway channels. The smoothly rounded concrete walls were covered with graffiti as if a tagging competition had taken place between all the gangs in the San Fernando area. The violent painted designs didn't help settle the sense of unease and insignificance that the crew felt within the dam's entryway.

The ground-level spillway channels were separated into two groups, four on the left and four on the right, with two emergency spillways separating them, twenty-five feet above. The crew spread out to examine their surroundings.

Jack slipped the rope and power washer off his back and trotted over to Mark, Caitlin, and Alexis, ignoring Alexis's scowl. "Cait, can I use your spray paint for a second?"

"Sure." Caitlin handed her spray can to Jack and he jogged to the farthest channel. "But don't use it up."

"I won't." Jack popped the lid off and sprayed the number "10" next to the dark opening. One by one he labeled the channels, counting back to "1" and added arrows pointing up at channels "5" and "6" for the two emergency channels above. Jack recapped the spray can and handed it back to Caitlin. "Thanks," he said.

"No bigs." Caitlin shrugged and smiled.

"Shit, that can't be good." O'Connor pointed out a crack in the wall an inch wide, traveling from the floor to just under the emergency spillways above.

"Earthquake damage?" Bradley said.

"Probably, but I wouldn't be too concerned." Jack ran his hand across the wall, stopping at the crack. "The U.S. Army builds these dams to be practically indestructible."

"Practically?" Mark fidgeted with his hands, flicking the flint of his Port-A-Torch. "So maybe an earthquake *could* destroy it."

"If it was strong enough, sure," Jack said. "But this dam survived the massive earthquake of 1971. That was a 6.5 and it destroyed the valley. What we just experienced was a 4.1. Am I worried? No."

"If the expert ain't worried, neither am I." O'Connor walked a few feet into one of the spillways. "Detest-A-Pest! For the win!" Her voice echoed from the spillway channel and through the entrance.

Trillian pointed up at the rightmost emergency spillway.

There were wisps of webbing hanging down from the ledge. "Jack? Is that it?"

"Yup."

"How are we going to get up there?"

Jack grabbed the rope, tied it around his waist, and began scaling the wrought iron debris fence. "I'll climb up with the power washer and have a direct line of fire." Once at the top, he looked across to spillway channel "6." A few feet in, gauzy strands plugged the entrance to the channel. "Holy shit."

Bradley watched Jack secure his footing. "What do you see?"

"A buttload of webbing," Jack said. "This nest is massive. We're going to have to split up and attack from both sides." He fastened the rope to the top of the debris fence and rappelled back down.

Mark looked up at spillway "6", then around the expansive entranceway to the dam. "Anyone get the feeling that we're unprepared for this?"

"No," Sam, O'Connor and Jack said in unison.

"Yeah but you all have heavy duty flame throwers." Mark looked at the Port-A-Torch in his hand. "Not candy-ass candles like these."

"Candy-ass?" Jack gave Mark a sideways look. "Seriously, bro?"

"Give it a try," Bradley said. "Get the lighter burning, use an elastic to keep the fuel release open, and press the nozzle."

Mark lit his lighter and affixed the elastic with ease. He pressed the nozzle and a five foot flame shot out. "Holy shit."

Bradley flinched. "Whoa, dude! It'd be better if you pointed it away from the rest of us."

"Yeah, sorry." Mark turned and blasted another ball of flame in the opposite direction.

"Convinced?" Jack asked.

Mark looked back with a sheepish grin. "Sorry. Looks are deceiving. This isn't candy-ass."

"Remember to put out the lighter when you're not using it," Jack said.

Alexis tapped her foot on the concrete floor. "Are we going to stand around talking all fucking day? Or are we going to kill some fucking spiders?"

All eyes shifted to Alexis.

"How would you suggest we proceed, Miss Delarosa?" Fiscara asked.

"Easy." Alexis shifted her weight and placed a hand on her hip. "There's eight channels. We each take one. Then we attack the ones up top."

"You seem to have it all figured out," Bradley said.

Alexis tapped her temple. "Yeah, that's because I'm fucking smart. Unlike all of you."

"We don't have enough headlamps for eight people," Sam said.

"Or walkie-talkies." O'Connor walked over to Alexis and blew a cloud of smoke in her face. "I'm liking you less and less."

"We pair up and take two channels each." Jack pointed at the first and second channel from the left. "Go down through one, come back through the next. It's safer and it'll take the same amount of time."

"See? Genius speaks." O'Connor poked Alexis in the chest. "Who's *fucking smart* now?"

"Don't touch me again." Alexis's free hand went to her back pocket and she wasn't subtle about it.

Caitlin flashed her eyes and caught Alexis's attention. She shook her head and mouthed the word "stop."

"Okay, enough. Break it up." Fiscara looked at O'Connor. "You're supposed to be an adult. Act like it."

"Jesus, *Mom*." O'Connor gnawed her cigar as she flipped her middle finger at Fiscara. "Let's do this. I need to burn something in a bad way."

Fiscara singled out Alexis. "We're all here for the same reason. Don't screw it up."

"Don't worry. I won't." A small, devious smile crossed her lips as her hand smoothed over the back pocket of her denim shorts.

"OKAY, LET'S FORM pairs." The crew had begun to self-select before Jack had finished talking.

"Isn't this when bad things start happening?" Mark pulled Caitlin close. "We cover more ground but get picked off one by one." Caitlin reveled in the attention, even if Mark's motives were based on self-preservation. For once she didn't have to take the back seat.

Bradley and Trillian paired up. He gave her the headlamp and between them they had six Port-A-Torches. "You ready to do this?"

Trillian looked up at him. "I think so."

Bradley could see trepidation in her eyes. He dug into his pocket and pulled out an elastic band. He held it up for her. "For your hair."

"Thanks." Trillian smiled and collected her hair into a multicolored ponytail.

Alexis alternated her glare between Caitlin and Bradley. "I wish I had an AR-15. I could be *so* much more productive."

"Nice idea in theory, but I think that'd be a little overkill." Jack pulled on a headlamp.

"That's kind of the point," Alexis said to herself.

O'Connor looked at the remaining crew. She pointed at Fiscara and waved her finger. "You're on my shit list. And you…" She glared at Alexis. "There's no way I'm pairing with bitchy

Doll-face. That leaves Jack. Will you be mine?" O'Connor batted her eyelashes awkwardly and began to cackle.

Jack backpedaled. "I think the Detest-A-Pest team should work together. You stick with Sam. I'll join Fiscara and Alexis." He handed a headlamp to Mark and Sam. "Ready?"

"I'm *so* ready," Alexis said.

Caitlin looked as if she was vibrating. "I know, right? Me too. It's like I'm excited and scared at the same time."

Alexis shrugged and rolled her eyes.

"O'Connor, I'm going to take over a bit," Jack said. "You okay with that?"

O'Connor took a bow. "I defer to your inherent brilliance… for now."

"Okay. Sam and O'Connor, you take channel one and two. Brad and Trill, channel three and four. Mark and Cait, seven and eight. And Fiscara, Alexis and I will take the last two channels." Jack felt around on his belt. "Shit! Walkies."

O'Connor unclipped three of the walkie-talkies from her belt and handed them to Jack. He turned them on, gave one each to Bradley and Mark, and kept the last for himself.

Jack joined Fiscara and Alexis at the far end of the dam's entrance. "Don't feel like you have to hurry. We don't know what we'll find in there."

"It's a creepy, dark tunnel," Bradley said. "Why would we hurry?" Trillian squeezed his hand.

"Real funny." Jack flipped on the switch to his headlamp. "Lights on?"

"Check," Sam said.

Mark turned on his headlamp, the beam cutting every which way except into his assigned channel. The light didn't ease his peace of mind.

Trillian clicked the switch for her light. "How do I look?"

"Brilliant," Bradley said, then leaned close to her ear. "Brilliant and beautiful."

Trillian grinned at him. "Smooth, Brad."

"Let's head in," Jack said. "Check in with your walkie when you get through to the other side or if you see anything weird. And torch any spider you see, especially if it's a sporky."

"Sporky?" Alexis cast a dubious glance at Jack.

"Fiscara will fill you in." Jack called out to the rest of the crew. "Good luck. Be careful and see you in a few."

THE FOUR GROUPS stepped into the channels at the same time, but Mark balked just past the opening.

Caitlin was already further into the channel and she tugged his arm. "What's wrong?"

"I'm a little claustrophobic."

"Isn't everybody? I mean a bit?" Caitlin scanned the concrete. Graffiti disappeared into the darkness. "At least we got light. Can you imagine having only our lighters?"

Mark shivered. "No."

Caitlin held out her bandaged hand. "Come on. We don't want to be the last ones out of here."

Mark's hand was clammy with cold sweat, but he took Caitlin's hand anyway. Her bandages disguised how scared he really was.

As they walked the graffiti became sparser. The dirt and silt on the floor were damp and mucky and stuck to the soles of their shoes.

Caitlin stopped. "Can I wear the light?" Her voice echoed in the channel. "You're kind of making me dizzy, moving around all the time."

"Oh." Mark looked back where they had begun, and the bright entrance already seemed so far away. "Sorry. Here." He took off the headlamp and gave it to Caitlin.

She slipped the light on her head. "Shh. Can you hear the rest of them?"

Mark and Caitlin stood silently for a moment. There was no sound except a low and hollow howl from the ripe breeze funneled through the channel.

Until a rustling sounded ahead them, about twenty feet away.

"Oh, shit," Mark said. "I knew I shouldn't have volunteered for this."

"Take it easy. We got this." Caitlin held up her Port-A-Torch. "Light me up."

Mark managed to ignite the lighter and fasten an elastic around it, all with trembling hands. He passed the torch to Caitlin.

"Follow me," she said.

Mark followed Caitlin forward through the channel toward the source of the rustling, crouching behind her back and looking over her shoulder.

The headlamp illuminated the source of the noise: a piece of newspaper rustling against the base of the wall.

"Is it the wind?"

"Let's find out." As Caitlin approached the newspaper, a small furry tail flicked out from underneath. "Take the paper off."

"No," Mark said. "What if it's a sporky?"

"Sporky?"

"Spider. Whatever. I know what those things can do and I—"

"Just use your foot," Caitlin said. "I'll back you up with the torch." She crouched, supporting the torch with her bandaged hand and finger on the nozzle. "Just hurry up."

Mark inched his foot toward the newspaper, placed his foot on the corner and pulled it a bit. An emaciated cat popped its head up from behind the paper. The small cat was skin and bones and much of its fur had fallen off. Its eyes glowed a feral yellow back at them.

Mark let out a yell, stumbled backward and landed on his backside. The cat yowled, hissed and scrambled into the darkness. Startled by both the cat's and Mark's reaction, Caitlin pressed the nozzle on the torch and a ball of orange flame erupted forth, missing the cat entirely but illuminating a further fifty feet down the channel. In that second or two, Mark and Caitlin glimpsed skeletal remains.

The kitten disappeared into the dark recesses of the channel.

"Shit, you scared me," Caitlin said.

"Me? What about that fucking cat?" Mark stood and brushed himself off.

"It was starving and alone, poor thing."

Mark's walkie-talkie squawked and Jack's voice crackled through the speaker. "Heard a yell. Everyone okay?"

Mark grabbed the walkie-talkie and pressed the talk button. "Uh, we're fine. Where are you?"

"Approaching the exit of nine."

To Mark, the exit of the seventh channel seemed like a pinprick of light in the distance.

"Almost there too. Over and out." Mark clipped the walkie-talkie to his belt.

"You're such a liar." Caitlin grinned at him in the low ambient light from her headlamp. She unhooked the elastic from her torch and extinguished the pilot light.

"Let's just get the hell out of here."

The two of them hurried their pace toward the end of channel seven, kicking skeletons aside without looking. During that time, Sam and Bradley both checked in over the walkie-talkie and began their return trips.

"We're officially last," Mark said.

"It's not a race."

The channel dipped sharply toward the end before exiting into sunshine.

Mark closed his eyes and faced the warmth of the morning sky. "I never thought I'd be so happy to see the sun as I am now."

"I know, right?" Caitlin bumped Mark's shoulder with her bandaged hand. "But we got to go back now."

Mark grimaced. "I think those tunnels are now my number one worst places to be."

"Imagine my naked body at the end." Caitlin winked at him and kissed him on the cheek. "Lead the way."

Mark's brain derailed in a mixture of fear, imagination and anticipation. "Alright. We can do this." He advanced into the exit of spillway channel eight. "Wait."

He removed a Port-A-Torch, lit the lighter's pilot flame, and secured it with an elastic.

"Do you think we can get through this before the lighter explodes in a ball of flames, consuming us both?"

Caitlin gave him a sideways look. "Are you always so dramatic?"

Mark shrugged and stepped into the shadows of channel eight. He let loose a blast from his torch every few steps, but they didn't get far before the ground began to shake.

Jack led the way through channel nine, followed by Alexis and Fiscara. The light from his headlamp cast warped shadows that danced in awkward angles. An intense odor of rotting fish mixed with dirt, urine, and wet concrete filled their noses.

"I hope you like fish. We're going to end up tasting this smell for weeks," Jack said.

Alexis watched the graffiti become sparser as they moved deeper into the channel. "Sleep with the fishes," she said to herself, but the curved walls of the channel amplified even the slightest whisper.

"Did you say something?" Fiscara asked.

"Godfather. 1972." Jack managed a quick glance back at Alexis. "Great movie."

Alexis shrugged and looked away.

"I'm surprised you came out, Miss Delarosa," Fiscara said. "You were never into extra-curricular activities."

"Quit the *Miss Delarosa* crap. And this ain't school-related." Alexis stopped and faced Fiscara's silhouette. The entrance to channel nine looked like a small window in the distance. "Those spiders bit my dad. No one hurts me or my family without facing payback."

"I hear you," Fiscara nodded. "Want this taser thing? Frankly I'm a little scared to use it."

"No." Alexis raised her hand, the hilt of her knife in her hand. With a click, the blade engaged, reflecting their darkened faces on the stainless steel surface. "I like to get up close and personal." She clicked the hilt again and the blade disappeared.

"Suit yourself."

Jack flashed his eyebrows and shook his head subtly at Fiscara as if saying "don't poke the bear."

"We're almost through," he said. "There's a steeper decline in the channel up ahead."

"This was your idea, wasn't it Jack?" Alexis asked.

"Yeah. To look for stragglers."

"Kind of a huge, stupid waste of time, huh?"

Jack shrugged, Alexis's indirect insult sliding right off. "Had to be done."

A muffled scream echoed through the channel. All three of them stopped to listen but there was nothing more except the echo of the morning wind.

Jack plucked his walkie-talkie from his belt. "Heard a yell. Everyone okay?" Waiting for a response seemed to take minutes instead of seconds.

"Uh, we're fine." Mark's staticky and faded voice responded. "You okay?"

"Ugh, Mark," Alexis scoffed. "That guy is a pussy. For once I feel sorry for Caitlin."

Jack shushed Alexis. "Approaching the exit of nine," he said into the walkie-talkie.

"Almost there too," Mark's voice crackled. "Over and out."

Jack reclipped the walkie-talkie to his belt.

Alexis's eyes, ice cold and black as night, found his in the dark. "Don't shush me."

"I do what I need to do to get the job done."

"You might end up regretting that."

"Whatever." Jack turned and continued toward to the exit of channel nine.

Fiscara shook her head. "Did everyone wake up on the wrong side of the bed this morning?" She followed Alexis and Jack out of channel nine and into ten.

"I bet we find nothing in this channel too," Alexis said.

"That would be great." Jack's walkie-talkie squawked updates from Bradley and Sam. "I'm all for finding nothing."

Halfway through channel ten, the three of them felt the entire dam shift and shake beneath their feet.

"Aftershock!" Jack said. "Run!"

WITH A PORT-A-TORCH in one hand and two in their pockets, Bradley and Trillian navigated channel three side by side instead of single file. Their hands brushed knuckles a few times on the way in until Trillian seized the moment and grabbed Bradley's hand, their fingers meshing together. Being connected—feeling the warmth of each other's skin—made the darkness seem not quite as dark.

"Jack's idea is great and all," Trillian said, "but I hope we don't have to use these torch things."

Bradley had enabled the light on his phone to boost the strength of Trillian's headlamp. He kicked some bones out of their path. "So far so good."

They continued in silence. Once inside, the channel seemed longer than Jack's estimate. Trillian stopped and faced Bradley. He squinted at the blue-white beam of light shining from her headlamp.

"Sorry." Trillian aimed the light up at the ceiling.

Bradley locked his gaze with hers. "What is it?"

She balked on her words until she found the courage to speak. "Do you still have feelings for Alexis?"

"What?" Bradley's eyes widened. "God no. Why are you asking me this?"

"Why did you let her join us then? After all she's done. I mean she tried to kill your mom, and me too."

Bradley sighed. "That was a tough choice. She said her dad had been bitten and her dad's alright. Her mom too. She may be a psycho most of the time, but I would hope for the same treatment if things were flipped."

Trillian dipped her head down to Bradley's chest. "Okay." Her voice sounded small.

"Wouldn't you want that too?"

Trillian burst into tears.

Bradley, a little taken aback, placed his arms around her and held her as gently as he could. His mind raced for something to say, but he drew blanks. As it turned out, the silence held more power than any words he could have said.

Trillian turned her head against Bradley's chest. "My parents are dead. They both died of heart attacks. The doctor said my mom was first. While my dad was trying to revive her, his heart stopped too."

"Oh my God." Bradley felt his face go cold and drain of color. "I'm so sorry, Trill."

She wrapped her arms around his body and held tight. "I've lived in four foster homes in the last three years."

"And that's why you've never invited me in at your place."

"Partly. I moved there in July and it doesn't feel like I belong yet."

"Well you belong here," Bradley said.

"In a grungy concrete tunnel that reeks of rotting fish?"

Bradley laughed. "No. In my arms."

Trillian stepped back. "You're quite the marshmallow, you know that?"

"Duck!" Bradley raised his Port-A-Torch over Trillian's head, ignited the lighter's pilot flame, and blasted fire against the ceiling of the channel. A spider fell to the floor, tendrils of smoke rising from its charred body. He stamped on it to be sure.

"Sporky?"

"I think so." Bradley wiped her tears with his thumb and planted a quick kiss on her forehead. "I think we better get moving."

As they approached the end of channel three, a scream echoed dimly from somewhere within the dam.

"What the hell?" Trillian looked back into the darkness they had just come out of. "Did you hear—"

Mark and Jack's conversation squawked back and forth on Bradley's walkie-talkie and Trillian heaved a sigh of relief.

Bradley side-stepped a pile of fish carcasses. "I hope bringing Mark wasn't a mistake. Scoring is his number one priority."

"Just like an athlete," Trillian said.

"He needs to discover how versatile his hand can be."

They both laughed as they emerged into the Tuesday morning sunshine. Bradley checked in on the walkie-talkie before entering channel four.

Twenty feet into their return trip, Bradley stopped. There was still enough natural light to see without a flashlight.

"What?" Trillian gave Bradley a sideways look. "Why are we stopping?"

"You ever get a feeling like something is going to happen?"

"Like what?"

Bradley produced a warm grin. "Kiss me, Trill."

Trillian returned his grin with one of her own. "Don't get any ideas." She leaned into him, placed her hands on his chest, and rose up onto her tiptoes. "Are you doing that?"

"Doing what?"

"Trembling."

Their lips came within an inch of touching when the dam's walls began to shake. Years of dirt and dust rained down on them.

Bradley took Trillian's hand. "Run!"

A chunk of concrete broke from above and blocked the exit, leaving them with no option but to proceed into the darkness.

The channel amplified the rumbling as if a fleet of eighteen-wheelers were bearing down on them. Light from Trillian's headlamp and Bradley's phone danced on the walls with each frenzied step.

Seconds felt like minutes. When they burst out of the entrance to channel four, the only member of the crew visible was O'Connor. She sat on the floor right next to the entrance to channel two, her back against a pastiche of territorial graffiti.

Bradley grabbed O'Connor's shoulder and shook it. "Where's Dad... Sam?"

O'Connor looked at him with lost, confused eyes.

"Where's *Sam*?"

O'Connor hooked a thumb at channel two. "Went back in."

Bradley's and Trillian's eyes met. Without words, Trillian knew what he planned to do.

Bradley ran into channel two.

"No, Brad! It's too dangerous."

He stopped and ran back to her. Bradley held Trillian's face in his hands and kissed her deeply. "I'll be back, I promise."

Before Trillian could respond, Bradley was gone. His phone's flashlight disappeared into another black hole of hell. She hated this place.

Trillian dropped to her knees in front of O'Connor, making no attempt to hide her tears. "Are you okay?"

"Except for the quake, never better."

Trillian gazed into channel two, tensing her muscles and trying to raise the courage to follow.

O'Connor placed her hand on Trillian's arm as if reading her mind. "Don't. Brad and Sam keep their promises."

"Are you sure?"

"A hundred percent."

But the dark shadows, dank air, and particulate flowing out from the channel did nothing to dampen her fears.

Then the concrete floor cracked open.

"Channel one clear," Sam said. "Starting two."

O'Connor gave Sam a quick once-over as she checked her thermal camera. "No rats. Disappointed?"

"Are you kidding? No." Sam grinned at her. "If I was a rat, I'd be eating at that taco place not to far from here."

"I hear you," O'Connor said. "But I have to say, you did a lot better in there than I thought you would."

"I've spent a month in solitary confinement. Most things are easier now by comparison." Sam looked up at the exit to spillway channel two, a large toothless throat, cold, dark, damp, and ready to consume them. "You think you could put out your cigar while we're in this channel?"

A grin spread across O'Connor's face. "Nah. You lead. I'll be the exhaust."

"Yeah, that fits," Sam said. "You're always full of hot air." He adjusted his headlamp and checked the pilot flame on the propane torch slung over this shoulder.

"Just move it." O'Connor nudged Sam forward with her boot.

The two of them trudged up the gravelly slope of channel two and entered its cold darkness. The graffiti on the exit side of the dam was less frequent but more violent. Sam guessed that the gangs that had tagged the channels this far in had had more to prove.

"Why earthquakes?"

"Why not?" O'Connor released a plume of smoke which ended up floating forward past Sam instead of backward. "I don't like shit I can't control. That includes natural disasters. But earthquakes tend to follow me around."

"You're shitting me," Sam said.

"Swear on my life. First quake I can remember was Yellowstone, 1959. I was six and camping with my parents. It was late, probably close to midnight, but my mom and dad were still up, probably fooling around. The whole tent was vibrating and the ground felt like it was turning soft, like mud."

Sam stopped to listen.

"When my Dad unzipped the door to the tent, I thought he was standing, but he was lying on his stomach, reaching down and yelling 'grab my hand!' I did and he pulled me out."

"Holy shit."

"The tent didn't sink, but the ground level fell about three feet." O'Connor drew in a large mouthful of cigar smoke, releasing it slowly as if to calm her nerves. "Listening to the radio later, in some places the ground fell twenty feet or more. I remember it like it was yesterday."

"Sounds terrifying," Sam said.

"And there was this other time when I was sixteen and…" O'Connor stopped, eyes wide, darting back and forth.

"What's wrong?" Sam aimed his headlamp forward and back. "O'Connor?"

O'Connor opened her mouth to speak, her cigar falling to the moist concrete floor. It landed lit end down, fizzling in the muck. "You feel it?"

"Feel what?"

O'Connor held her hand up. That's when Sam heard the low rumbling noise. Dirt chipped off the curved walls onto their heads.

"This is it. We're going to die." The propane torch rattled in O'Connor's trembling hands. "Fuck, not like this. No no no no…"

They were almost halfway through channel two. Either direction would get them to safety but regrouping with the rest of the crew made the most sense.

Sam grabbed O'Connor's shoulders and shook her firmly against the concrete wall. "O'Connor, get a grip. We got to run."

O'Connor was delirious with panic and wasn't hearing anything Sam was saying.

"BERTHA! MOVE YOUR ASS."

O'Connor's eyes cleared just for a moment, but long enough to register Sam's attempt to get her attention.

"Fuck this." Sam slid his shoulder under O'Connor's arm and hoisted her up, half-dragging half-walking her toward the entrance to channel two. As the open space lightened, O'Connor joined Sam's gallop with steps of her own.

"Glad you could join me," Sam said between breaths.

The two of them burst out of the second channel, into the graffiti-covered cathedral they had left less than ten minutes earlier. Sam sat O'Connor against the wall and knelt in front.

"Are you okay?"

O'Connor's breath remained harried, but she managed a nod.

She checked her pants pockets, then her breast pocket. "Ca… cam…"

Sam shook his head.

"Camera." O'Connor closed her eyes and laid her open hands on the cool concrete wall. The earthquake had stopped but her hands still had a visible shake to them.

"I'll go get it."

Sam disappeared into channel two without hesitation. His headlamp cast dancing shadows as he ran, and the walls seemed like they were closing in on him.

"Just halfway," he reassured himself. And less than a minute in, he spotted the glowing screen of the phone. Beside it stood O'Connor's cigar. He grabbed both but caught his foot on a crack in the floor.

Sam hit the concrete hard and knocked the wind out of himself. The phone and cigar tumbled forward out of reach. The pilot light of his propane torch burned a hole in its supply line and caused a jet of uncontrolled orange flame to burst forth.

He pushed the torch's support strap from his shoulder and tried to roll away from the flames, but the curved walls and ceiling kept him within the flame's reach.

Sam kicked the torch with his boot and scrambled forward, his nails raking across the silt. At some point during his struggle, he had knocked off his headlamp. In blackness tinged with orange firelight, a familiar hand grabbed him and pulled him forward and onto his feet.

"Dad?" Bradley guided Sam back through the channel. "You okay? Dad?"

"Yeah." Sam matched his son's stride. "Just got a little cooked is all… wait! The—"

"Phone?" Bradley tapped his pocket. "Got it."

Once out of the channel, Bradley sat Sam down next to a still recovering O'Connor. Trillian ran to Bradley and wrapped her arms around him in a tight embrace.

"Told you I'd be back," Bradley said.

"Don't do that ever again." Trillian kissed Bradley's neck, slicked with grime and sweat.

Bradley handed the phone to O'Connor. She gave him a "thumbs up" and slid it into her breast pocket.

Sam turned to O'Connor. "Bad news. Couldn't save your cigar."

O'Connor waved him off. "I'll let you live… this time." She managed a chuckle.

The two of them sat against the wall, silently celebrating cheating death one more time.

Jack, Fiscara, and Alexis emerged from channel ten at the far end of the dam's entrance, followed by Mark and Caitlin from channel eight.

Jack ran toward the center of the space. "I think it's over. Everyone okay?"

"I think I shit my pants," Mark said.

Caitlin recoiled. "Gross."

"Joking."

"You sure?" Caitlin crinkled her nose in disgust. "You *do* smell weird, and not in a good way."

Mark began backpedalling in a hushed voice only Caitlin could hear.

Bradley stood at the edge of a widening crack in the dam's floor. "I thought you said these dams were indestructible?"

"They're supposed to be," Jack said.

The crack divided the main entrance almost exactly in half. Concrete crumbled under Bradley's feet and he took a step backward. "What's the plan now?"

Everyone looked to Jack for answers.

Do or Die

JACK SCANNED THE crack in the floor, which was quickly becoming a dark, apparently bottomless chasm. He jumped the expanding void while he could still get to his power washer flame thrower and pulled it onto his back. He grinned at Bradley, a sparkle in his eye. "Same plan. We break out the big guns, except we got to mind the gap now."

"I think I know why earthquakes follow you around," Sam said.

"Yeah?" O'Connor glanced over at him. Her face was covered in sweat. "Why?"

"It's the pound cake." Sam stood and offered his hand. "A fuck-ton of pound cake."

"Was funny once, smart-ass." She took his hand and Sam hoisted her to her feet.

Sam gave her a once-over. "You okay to go on? You don't look so good."

"Legs are a little rickety, but I'm good."

"Sure? You're white as a ghost, your skin's clammy, and—"

"And you look like a bucket of shit." O'Connor brushed herself off. "I'm fine. End of story."

Jack pulled out his phone and tapped at the display. "Holy shit. That was a 5.5. Twenty-five times bigger and a hundred twenty-five times stronger than the last one."

"Jack? A word of advice," O'Connor said. "If you want to live to see tomorrow, keep the earthquake stats to yourself."

Fiscara stepped to the edge of the chasm, crouched, and ran her hand across its jagged edge. Concrete broke away like it was dried mud. "I thought aftershocks were supposed to be weaker?"

"Not necessarily," Jack said. "This will probably be logged as the main quake, and the one before as a foreshock."

"Stop it with the goddamn quake talk." O'Connor clenched her trembling fists. "Fuck."

Sam shot a look at Jack and shook his head. He placed his arm around O'Connor's shoulder and took her aside to calm her down.

"So there *is* a hole in your armor," Alexis said. "Good to know."

O'Connor pushed Sam's arm off her shoulder and locked gazes with Alexis across the chasm. Everyone, especially Sam and Bradley, expected a clever comeback but O'Connor remained silent.

"Yeah," Bradley said to O'Connor in a hushed voice. "She's not worth it."

Fiscara stepped close to Alexis. "What is with you?"

Alexis shrugged. "I call it like it is."

Jack stepped up onto the wrought iron debris fence and maneuvered his way across the chasm. He stepped off the other side and said, "O'Connor, you good to go?"

"If you're asking, you don't know me very well."

"Well, I don't, really," Jack said.

Mark scanned the crack up the wall to the remaining spillway channels five and six, twenty-five feet above their heads. "Let's just get to it. Blast it with the flame thrower 'cause I'm getting hungry."

"Yes. A voice of reason." O'Connor looked at Sam. "Where's your torch?"

"Burning out of control in channel two."

"How the fuck—"

"Saving your sorry ass… and that damn phone of yours."

O'Connor got the hint loud and clear. "Okay, then."

"Bradley and Trillian, you flush out channel five," Jack said.

"Got it." Bradley took out an additional Port-A-Torch, now one in each hand. Trillian did the same.

"Sam, O'Connor, take channel six and use your remaining torch to force the sporkies out here. We'll burn them to a crisp with this mother." He tapped the power washer. "Sound good?"

"Fuckin' aces!" Mark pumped his fist, more for Caitlin's benefit than anyone else's. "Let's do it."

Sam, O'Connor, Bradley, and Trillian moved into channel four, headlamps lighting their way through to the other side.

Jack grabbed the rope he had tied to the debris fence earlier and began to scale the iron lattice. The remaining crew watched his ascent.

He secured himself with the rope twenty-five feet above the concrete floor. From his vantage point, he could see into channel six and partly into five. A pervasive odor of wet decaying concrete rose from the newly formed chasm in the floor. It still appeared bottomless, even from Jack's elevated view.

Fiscara looked up at Jack. "What can you see?"

"I can see the nest in channel six, just barely," Jack said. "It's darker up here." He craned his neck to adjust his line of sight. "Can't really see anything in channel five. I'm at a bad angle."

Jack unhooked his walkie-talkie. "I'm in position, where are you guys?"

A second later Bradley's electronically filtered voice echoed through the entrance chamber. "Approaching the end of channel four. About to split up between five and six. Over."

"Ten-four, over." Jack looked around the dam's entrance. "It's good we have four…"

"What is it?" There was concern in Fiscara's voice.

"Where's Alexis?"

Fiscara, Mark, and Caitlin turned themselves around, looking for Alexis. She was nowhere to be seen.

"Good riddance," Fiscara said to herself.

"Mark, did you or Cait see where she went?

Mark shook his head. "With the earthquake and everything else happening all at once, I lost track."

"Cait?"

Caitlin looked around once more before looking up at Jack. "Sorry. I didn't see anything."

"You didn't hear any secret plans, like a double cross or something?"

Caitlin placed a hand on her hip. "Are you accusing me of something?"

"Uh, no. Of course not," Jack said. "It's just that you're friends. You and Alexis wouldn't be caught dead hanging with us."

"All I know is she was here because her dad was bitten." Caitlin raised her bandaged hand. "Just like I'm here because I was bitten."

"Okay." Jack raised his walkie-talkie to his mouth. "Alexis has gone AWOL." His message echoed from Mark's walkie-talkie, almost causing a feedback loop.

A second later, "What the hell?" Bradley's urgency came across clearly through the speaker of the walkie-talkie.

"No one here saw anything either," Jack said. "Just keep your eyes peeled, bro."

"Will do. I know what she's capable of. Over and out."

Jack clipped his walkie-talkie back on his belt.

"What does that mean, Jack?" Fiscara looked up at him. "What is Alexis capable of?"

Jack stalled, looking for the right words.

Fiscara turned to Caitlin. "Should we be worried?"

Caitlin avoided Fiscara's eyes. "I don't know."

"You don't know? Bullshit. You're practically joined at the hip." Fiscara pulled the walkie-talkie off Mark's belt.

"Hey!" Mark took a step forward.

Fiscara held up her hand, glared at him, and raised the walkie-talkie to her lips. "What has Alexis done?"

Dead static buzzed through the speaker.

"Brad! Spill it or I'll make sure you repeat your senior year."

"She's a psychopath, Miss Fiscara." Bradley's voice on the walkie-talkie sounded small. "I know for a fact that she tried to kill my mom. And I think she was responsible for the school infestations, but that proof is circumstantial."

"And you thought it would be a good idea to invite her into our team *and* give her weapons?" Fiscara's face was red with anger.

"It was a bad call," Bradley's voice said. "I take full responsibility."

"And if she injures or kills one of us?"

Bradley had no answer.

"Wendy, this is Sam," the walkie-talkie buzzed. "The only thing we can do at this point is finish the job we came here to do. We're moving into five and six. Sam out."

Fiscara paced back and forth next to the chasm.

"I agree with Sam," Jack said. "Let's finish this."

"You're damn lucky you're not in my class, Jack."

"I know." Jack grinned. "By the way, you remind me of Ellen Ripley."

A hint of a smile in return crossed Fiscara's lips. "Flattery will get you everywhere."

"Can you cross the chasm," Jack said, "using the debris fence? We need that escape route covered."

Instead of answering, Fiscara ran to the fence and side-stepped across the void to the other side. "Better?"

Jack nodded and raised the walkie-talkie. "We're all ready here."

Sam's voice broadcast through the speaker. "Approaching nest. We'll give you a countdown."

Mark's stomach growled, loud enough to echo through the entranceway.

Caitlin raised her brow. "You're hungry? Now?"

"I'm always hungry."

"Stay alert," Jack said. "You're not the only thing that's hungry in here."

Fiscara, Mark, and Caitlin each held a Port-A-Torch in their hands. Jack's finger twitched on the modified trigger on his power washer flame thrower.

They waited for Sam's countdown.

But something didn't feel right, and not just Alexis's disappearance.

IN THE MAYHEM of the earthquake, Alexis made sure she was the last out of the channel. She took off her shoes and left them back in channel ten. Underneath her black work boots, she had worn thick black socks. No one would suspect a thing.

"Bradley and Trillian, you flush out channel five." Jack's voice echoed within the entrance.

That was Alexis's cue to put her plan in action. As Jack continued to drone on about "the plan," she backed up toward channel ten, rolling each step on the balls of her feet to minimize the noise. As it turned out, her sock-footed steps made no noise at all. Alexis grabbed her work boots and disappeared back down channel ten.

She broke the lighter off one of her Port-A-Torches and cranked up the flame level. The firelight was nowhere near as efficient or bright as a headlamp would have been, but after her eyes adjusted to the dark, the lighter's flame was more than adequate to guide her way.

Halfway through channel ten, Alexis stopped and peeled off her socks, now caked with gravel and dirt. She pulled on her work boots and carried on her way. Alexis emerged into the sunshine of the dam's exit less than a minute later.

She was prepared to make a beeline for spillway channel five but realized she didn't know from which channel Bradley and Trillian would emerge on their way there.

Channel one is my best chance, Alexis thought. It was farthest away from channel five and those scaredy-ass fucks wouldn't want to walk more than they had to. *But can I make it there in time?*

Alexis figured she had to run about a hundred feet to get to the opposite side of the dam. It shouldn't take more than ten seconds. Or she could hold her ground and wait.

"Fuck that." Alexis bolted down the incline of the dam's exit toward emergency spillway channel six and slid on the gravelly surface at the left side. She peeked out, saw that she was in the clear, and carried on to the right side of channel five.

She took a careful glance around the concrete divider separating channel five and four. She could hear echoes of conversation. It was now or retreat and Alexis didn't believe in retreat.

She sprinted out from behind the divider, channel one in her sights. The gravel strewn over the dam's exit worked against her. She caught a boot lace in a crack in the dam and fell hard against the concrete. Sharp pebbles embedded themselves through her jeans and into the flesh of her left thigh. Pain lit up in the back of her eyes like fireworks and she clenched her teeth.

The sounds of footsteps and conversation grew louder.

You're blowing it, you bitch.

An image of Bradley and Trillian holding hands floated into

her head. The anger she felt smothered her pain and she forced herself to scramble the rest of the way to channel one.

Now hidden from view in a position no one would have suspected, Alexis caught her breath as she watched Sam, O'Connor, Bradley and Trillian emerge from channel four. Bradley and Trillian *really were* holding hands and her anger ramped up to white rage.

The four of them stopped between channel five and six. Bradley spoke into his walkie-talkie, but he was too far away for her to hear anything.

Alexis didn't care. Her plan was moving along without a hitch and it allowed more time to regain her strength. But her rage remained. She crouched and stuffed her laces into the sides of her boots.

One final slow look around the wall of channel one saw Sam, O'Connor, Bradley and Trillian bump fists before splitting up. Sam and O'Connor took channel six, and Bradley and Trillian headed up into channel five.

Alexis envisioned Bradley and Trillian moving up the steeper incline of channel five and after a minute she ran to the concrete divider and peered up. She could hear scratchy footsteps and the occasional echoey word emanate from the dark channel.

Alexis carefully ascended the incline into the darkness of channel five. At the top, the channel leveled off. She slipped off her boots and placed her feet on the grimy cold concrete. Her lighter was of no use this time, but it didn't matter because Trillian's headlamp gave away their position.

Alexis continued her silent pursuit, her grin as cold as the concrete walls that surrounded her.

SAM, O'CONNOR, BRADLEY, AND TRILLIAN moved swiftly through darkened spillway channel four.

"Going through these channels doesn't get any easier," Bradley said.

"Especially when there's cracks in the walls that are big enough for my arm to fit through." O'Connor pointed out the damage as the group passed. "How many tons of concrete do you think is above our heads right now?"

"You're not helping." Trillian shivered. "Being in here is bad enough without you inducing claustrophobia."

"I hope those cracks don't create more escape routes." Bradley looked back at the entrance, now a small window of light. "The earthquake was never part of the plan."

"Focus on the exit," Sam said. "We'll be out of this before you know it."

"How long before another aftershock?" O'Connor cast a concerned glance back at Bradley. "I don't want to be anywhere near this tomb for the next one."

"Minutes, hours, days?" Bradley shrugged. "No one knows, not even scientists."

"Well you're no fucking help."

"I know that's sunshine up ahead." Sam quickened his pace.

Sam and Bradley's walkie-talkies crackled to life in unison. "Alexis has gone AWOL," Jack's tin-can voice said.

The group stopped short of channel four's exit.

Bradley exchanged a knowing glance with Trillian. He raised his walkie-talkie to his mouth. "What the hell?"

Trillian's face drained of color as Bradley and Jack discussed details. She couldn't have understood his words if she had tried.

The group resumed their exit of channel four and made their way down the sloped concrete to where channels five and six exited.

"Should we be worried?" Sam asked Bradley. "Alexis seemed okay back there. If anything, a little bitchy, maybe."

"If she's going to come after anyone, it's going to be me."

"Then let's regroup," Sam said. "I'll go with Trillian and you can go with O'Connor. She's got the big guns."

"No." Bradley looked at Trillian. "I'm sticking with Trill. We can take care of ourselves." She managed a smile from behind her rainbow hair.

"Brad!" Fiscara's voice zapped through the Walkie-Talkie's speaker. "Spill it or I'll make sure you repeat your senior year."

"Jesus Christ," O'Connor said. "Wendy doesn't fuck around."

"Nope."

Bradley came clean as quickly as he could. Fiscara was livid and rightly so. He had kept the adults in the dark and withheld information that affected the plan; a bad move.

Sam paced between the exits of channels five and six, trying to sort out his thoughts. All roads led to the same conclusion. He grabbed his walkie-talkie. "Wendy, this is Sam. The only thing we can do at this point is finish the job we came here to do." He looked at O'Connor, Bradley, and Trillian. "We're moving into five and six. Sam out."

O'Connor turned to head up channel six, but Sam hesitated.

"If you need help, call me." He tapped his walkie-talkie. "And if there's nothing up there in five, join us in six. We'd love the company."

"You got it." Bradley and Trillian scrambled up the silty slope and into channel five.

Sam watched them leave until they merged with the darkness.

O'Connor poked him in the ribs. "Our turn."

The inclined surface of channel six harbored considerable sand and grit, making their ascent a game of two steps forward, one step back. O'Connor's prosthetic leg restricted her mobility but with Sam's help, they both reached the apex where the channel leveled out.

"Here we are again, you and me, alone in the dark." O'Connor elbowed Sam. "Must be love, huh?"

"Let's go, Bertha." Sam lit his Port-A-Torch. "You can hold my hand if you want."

"I'd rather you hold my—"

"Oh Jesus. Just follow me." Sam moved into the shadows, O'Connor a step behind with the pilot flame of her propane torch flickering.

They moved past wisps of silken webbing that hung slackly from the curved walls just within the channel.

"I guess that's a good sign," O'Connor said.

Sam's foot bumped against a pile of animal bones and only some of them were fish. "I think you spoke too soon."

"I don't give a shit unless it's human." O'Connor peered around Sam's shoulder. His headlamp didn't penetrate far into the channel's darkness. She slipped her phone out of her pocket and pushed in front. She called up the thermal imaging app and a blue and purple version of the channel appeared on the display.

"Watch for trip wires," Sam said. "They're not going to show up on that thing."

"Always got to piss on my parade, huh Sam?"

"If it's going to save your ass, yeah."

The two of them continued forward through the channel. The strong smell of decaying life and animal waste was inescapable, and Sam wished he had some Vick's VapoRub, just like Hope had used back in New York.

There was no light at the end of the tunnel to guide them this time. Both knew the channel was blocked by a nest of spiders. The question was how big it would be.

"There. See it?" O'Connor pointed out a small reddish orange dot in the center of a sea of blue on her phone's display. "That's the power of thermal."

"Yeah, I see it." Sam lowered his voice and squinted down the channel, but his headlamp wasn't strong enough to reveal exactly what they were looking at. "Maybe you could talk louder? Really let them know we're coming."

O'Connor looked back at him and grinned. "Sarcasm looks good on you, Sam." She roamed his body from head to toe and back, and winked at him. "*Real* good."

"You better get yourself laid after this is done," Sam said.

"I promise."

The image on O'Connor's phone increased in size with every step and soon it wasn't just a pinpoint of orange they were looking at, but an expanse of reds and oranges with isolated yellow hotspots. And the hotspots moved.

Sam's headlamp revealed the nest twenty feet ahead. Gossamer tripwires spread out in multiple directions. There were at least two woven entry tunnels facing them and several others joining where the walls met the floor.

Sam crouched next to O'Connor's ear and whispered, "You got enough juice in that thing?"

"I could ask you the same thing," O'Connor whispered back, a smile in her voice. "But if you mean the flame thrower, don't worry. I got gas." She ripped a fart that echoed throughout the channel.

Sam shook his head as he ignited the lighter on his Port-A-Torch and affixed an elastic to keep it lit. "You ready?"

O'Connor gripped the nozzle's handle with one hand and checked the line to the small tank with the other. "That's not propane you're smelling, that me. Just in case you're wondering."

"Thanks for that." Sam unclipped the walkie-talkie from his belt. "Jack?"

"Sam, what's up?" The walkie-talkie's volume was turned up and Jack's electronically distorted voice boomed in the small space. Sam fumbled with the volume knob until Jack's voice was barely audible, but their attempt at stealth was over.

The yellow hotspots on O'Connor's phone converged near the base of the nest. Sam could see patches of dark scuttling out from the nest.

"Shit's about to get real." Sam clicked off the walkie-talkie and returned it to his belt.

Sam and O'Connor exchanged a knowing look that said, "this is it." They stood side by side and engaged their flame throwers, lighting the channel with orange heat.

"YOU HEAR THAT?" Jack called down from his position on the debris fence. "It's go time."

Fiscara lit her Port-A-Torch and secured the fuel valve with an elastic.

Mark equipped Caitlin and handed her a torch. She gripped it with her good hand and held her bandaged hand at the ready over the nozzle.

Mark pulled out two Port-A-Torches. "Double the fire, double the fun." He gave Caitlin a warm smile as he pulled out a couple of elastics and prepared his torches for action.

From Jack's position he saw the shadows within channel six light up in a soft orange glow. He expected the entire nest to burst into flames, but reality ended up being much different. Tendrils of smoke and hot air flowed out at the top of the channel opening. Then the shadows began to move.

"I see them!" Jack said in a mixture of excitement and terror. "Remember, five feet is all you got to work with."

Spiders of all sizes crested the channel's entrance and scuttled away from the heat, smoke, and light. Their black inky bodies stood out from the concrete and seemed to flow down the wall toward the floor where Mark and Caitlin stood. All at once, the peril became real.

"And watch out for the quills," Fiscara said. "They're just as deadly."

"Quills? Oh, shit oh shit oh shit. I can't do this." Caitlin's first reaction to seeing the spiders up close was retreat. She stepped backward. "They're fucking huge."

"But they burn real good." Mark, riding a high of bravado, ran toward the wall and released a double-barreled blast of flame. "Die, you motherfuckers."

Smaller spiders curled up and popped in Mark's flames. The larger ones reversed direction and headed toward Fiscara, casting webbing across the crack in the wall for the others to scramble over. The remaining critically injured spiders released their quills in a fleeting attempt at survival.

Mark and Caitlin were unprepared for the speed at which the spiders traveled. He took several steps back in trepidation, but Caitlin looked at the bandage on her arm and stood her ground. Seeing the Port-A-Torches in action summoned her courage. "You're not fucking biting me again!" She charged at the dark tide of arachnids and engaged her Port-A-Torch, blasting a path through them.

"There's too many," Jack called from above. "Force them into the crack."

"No shit." Fiscara took an apprehensive step toward the wall and let loose a jet of flame, redirecting the spider exodus into the chasm. Graffiti paint bubbled under the heat as spiders changed their downward direction. The first few spiders were easy targets but as their numbers increased, combined with the fluctuating flames from the Port-A-Torch, doubt and a sense of dread rose on Fiscara's face.

Mark, impressed by Caitlin's assault, mustered what little courage he had and ran around her right side to redirect escaping spiders back toward the crack in the floor. "Go to hell, you bastards!"

"Shit!" In her haste, Caitlin had allowed the path to close behind her, surrounding herself with spiders. "I'm trapped!" She spun around in place, jetting flames at the floor. The heat kept the spiders away, but it was a losing battle—there were too many and they were closing in.

Quills from spiders in their in their death throes penetrated Caitlin's denim pant cuffs and shoes. She swatted at them with her bandaged hand.

"No! They've got venom in them." In a lateral sweep, Mark laid a fire trail that blew through the spiders like a leaf blower. The floor, now coated in WD-40, began to burn on its own in patches. He forced the spiders from around Caitlin's feet and pulled her back to relative safety.

But the spiders also spread up the wall toward the ceiling, toward channel five and beyond the reach of the Port-A-Torches. Fiscara looked up the wall back at the entrance to channel six as more spiders breached the edge. Her Port-A-Torch sputtered out, its fuel spent. She dropped is and grabbed a replacement from her pocket.

"Jack! We're losing down here." Fiscara sent a panicked look up at him. "When you going to light that bastard?"

Jack surveyed the floor and walls below. Despite the heat and smoke flowing out of channel six, spiders had begun to use the ceiling of the dam's entryway as an additional escape route. His time window for containment was closing a hell of a lot faster than he had anticipated.

Jack had one option left and he carried the weight of that decision on his shoulders.

BRADLEY'S WALKIE-TALKIE crackled to life with Jack's frantic voice on the other end. "Brad? You near five's entry?"

About fifty feet away, Both Bradley and Trillian quickened their pace toward the entrance. Both their Port-A-Torches were already lit and ready to go. He pulled his walkie-talkie to his mouth. "Almost there."

"Use your torches on the spiders heading to the ceiling," Jack said. "For fuck's sake, hurry."

"On it." Bradley skidded to a stop just before the entrance to channel five. The grit on the ground caused his feet to slide an extra few feet, with one foot shooting right past the edge.

Trillian grabbed him by the collar and pulled him back to safety in the nick of time. His walkie-talkie hit the ground and bounced back into the channel.

"I owe you one." Bradley wiped beads of sweat from his brow.

"You owe me a few." Trillian winked at him.

"I'll go first." Bradley leaned out of channel five. His eyes widened at the hundreds of spiders emerging from channel six.

Below them, Fiscara, Mark, and Caitlin corralled the spiders from ground level, but it was difficult to tell if they were winning the fight.

Bradley turned his head to the left and was faced with dozens of spiders scuttling across the wall toward his head. "Holy shit!" He engaged the nozzle of his torch and sent flaming lubricant toward the advancing cluster. It adhered to the wall and formed a temporary burning barrier.

Cheering rose from below but before Trillian could add to Bradley's flaming barricade, she heard footsteps approaching from the darkness. She turned and her headlamp revealed Alexis holding a lit Port-A-Torch in one hand.

"Long time no see, Rainbow Brite."

Trillian's voice nearly left her behind. "Brad," she said.

Bradley fired another blast of flame. "Just a sec, there's too many."

"Brad!"

He leaned back into channel five. "What's wrong—"

"Loverboy." Alexis smirked. Her eyes looked as black as her hair and the shadow that surrounded her.

Bradley went for his walkie-talkie and realized it was on the ground by Alexis's feet.

"Looking for this?" She picked up the walkie-talkie, keeping her eyes glued to Bradley and Trillian, and tossed the device over her shoulder into the darkness. Sound of plastic cracking and a hiss of static echoed back. "I don't think you'll be needing it again."

Bradley whispered something into Trillian's ear, then took several steps toward Alexis. "What are you doing?"

Alexis stood her ground. "Don't come any closer or I'll fucking fry you. Now toss me your torches."

"How about we fry you?" Bradley said.

Alexis scoffed. "You can try, but I'll get one of you… The torches. Now!"

Bradley and Trillian shared a knowing look, crouched and set their torches on the ground.

"All of them."

Bradley and Trillian complied. A total of six Port-A-Torches sat on the ground in front of them, two with pilot flames still lit.

"Kick them over here," Alexis said.

Again, Bradley and Trillian did as they were told and pushed the torches with a sweep of their feet. The gritty surface prevented sliding and the cans toppled and rolled toward Alexis.

"Brad? You okay?" Jack's voice echoed from behind Alexis. Static broke his voice into unintelligible pieces as the walkie-talkie shorted out. "Brad—" One last *pop* and the radio went silent. The acrid smell of ozone floated out of the channel.

Bradley stepped in front of Trillian. "I won't let you touch her."

"Always the hero. You underestimate me, Brad," Alexis said. "Did you learn nothing while we were fucking?"

The question flustered Bradley. He cast an embarrassed

glance at Trillian, as if to say *I'm sorry.* "I'm tired of your bullshit." He launched himself at Alexis but the grit on the floor slowed him down. Her free hand was already in her back pocket, anticipating his move. She pulled out a syringe with a protective plastic cap covering the needle.

Bradley's eyes widened when he saw Alexis's new weapon, but it was too late to stop now. He body-checked her to the floor and sent the syringe flying.

Trillian ran to help Bradley but Alexis sent a ball of flame toward her. She ducked to the side as the burning lubricant fell to the ground, drawing a fiery line in the floor grit.

Bradley grabbed Alexis by the throat but she smashed her Port-A-Torch cannister against the side of his head, dazing him. She followed the hit by raising her knee to his crotch.

Bradley lost his breath, groaned, and rolled off Alexis, clutching his groin. Trillian pulled Bradley to a sitting position.

Alexis was on all fours in a flash, crawling and searching through the silt and sand in the dark, until her fingers uncovered the syringe, still intact. She turned, a wicked grin on her face and her eyes blazing in the dim ambiance of the channel. Alexis stood and pulled the protective cap off the needle, flicking it aside.

Bradley instinctively worked his legs to get away but the fiery pain in his groin short-circuited his brain. Trillian hooked an arm around him and helped him stand. Both had their eyes glued to Alexis's syringe with its exposed needle glinting in the channel's low light.

Alexis took a step forward. Bradley and Trillian stepped backward in response. They had nowhere to go.

SSAM AND O'CONNOR were so focused on the base of the nest that they failed to see a silken conduit fastened to the ceiling of the channel and stretching out from the top of the nest.

When spiders began launching themselves out of the conduit's opening, Sam was first to strike. His blast of flame was just long enough to reach the ceiling. The conduit ignited and burned back toward the main nest, incinerating spiders within it. Quills shot out of the burning conduit in a multitude of directions, some burning, some penetrating the concrete wall. One quill pierced O'Connor's left boot.

"Wrong foot, motherfuckers!" O'Connor joined the barrage of ceiling fire with a burst of her own until she spotted more spiders on the walls and ground and readjusted her aim. Her propane torch was set on a wide coverage pattern that was great for breadth but lacked distance.

The burning conduit sputtered itself out after reaching the main nest.

"We need to get closer," Sam said. "And focus your flames or we're going to die here."

O'Connor presented her arm. "Ladies first."

"Fuck you."

"There's the Sam I know."

They both charged forward another fifteen feet. The spiders that they encountered either retreated along tripwires back to the main nest or burst into flames.

"This seem too easy to you?" O'Connor blanketed the front of the nest with fire.

"It's almost like we were..." Sam turned around to find a massive spider blocking their retreat. Its chelicerae and fangs pulsed, moist with venom. "Lured for ambush." He blasted flame at the shiny black monster, but his Port-A-Torch had run out of fuel. Sam plastered himself against the opposite wall. "O'Connor? A little help?"

O'Connor backed up next to Sam and sent a fireball across the channel. "I love the smell of burnt spider in the morning."

The large spider, easily two feet across, swiftly shifted to one side, avoiding the flame.

"Let's fall back and regroup." Sam moved against the wall toward the exit of channel six. His headlamp cast wildly distorted shadows as he looked for more spiders.

"Yeah, I think you're right." O'Connor followed Sam, but her boots tangled up on thick tripwires along the floor. She pointed the nozzle at her feet and managed to burn only one side of the entanglement. Her left leg remained tied up and the more she struggled, the more the strands stuck to her boot. She could only use short blasts of fire or her clothes would ignite, and shorter blasts no longer had any effect.

"Get ready. We're going for a ride." Sam grabbed the back of O'Connor's collar and yanked her backward. Her prosthetic leg separated from her left stump.

"No, goddamn it! That leg was practically brand new." She pulled her stump up and smoothed out the protective sock covering it.

"You can buy a new one." Sam ran as fast as he could, pulling O'Connor behind him. His feet fought for purchase on the gritty ground, but the friction made moving O'Connor's bulk easier.

The spider launched itself onto the prosthetic leg and sank its fangs through the foam rubber calf, striking the titanium support post of the leg. The spider recoiled and scuttled after Sam and O'Connor, now with a healthy head start.

O'Connor lit the channel with short bursts of fire. At first there had been nothing but blackness as they retreated from the charred nest. But soon O'Connor could see the spider gaining on them, casting an echoey *clickity-click* like raindrops on dry sidewalk.

"You're filling my ass with sand," O'Connor said, "but you

need to go faster." She blasted flames behind her but the spider outmaneuvered the fire with ease.

"Maybe this will help." Sam crested the top of the channel where it shifted into a steep slope down toward the exit. The two of them gained speed, O'Connor still on her back and ejecting fireballs behind her as if she was rocket propelled.

They emerged into the morning sunshine once again. The spider stopped at the line between sunshine and shadow, initially hesitant, before launching itself down the spillway channel's exit toward Sam and O'Connor.

ALEXIS TOOK ANOTHER step forward. Her gloved hand held the syringe between flexed fingers and her thumb, ready to inject.

Bradley considered rushing her again. Alexis was devious and had no issue inflicting grievous harm on people if it suited her. That was common knowledge. But the unknown fluid inside the syringe stopped him. He'd never forgive himself if he ended up causing Trillian harm.

He took a quick glance behind him. From Bradley's current position, he could see the debris fence but not much else, including the mayhem that was taking place on the concrete floor twenty-five feet below.

Trillian stepped beside Bradley. His eyes flitted over her, head to toe and back, and they shared a brief look. There was a smile on her face, ever so subtle. Then it was gone.

Trillian motioned at the syringe. "What's with the needle?"

"Oh, look. Rainbow Brite has a question." Alexis moved one more step forward. A bead of whatever was in the syringe leaked from the tip, glinting like a jewel.

"Are you smart enough to answer?"

"A twenty foot drop *might* kill you." Alexis held up the

syringe. "But this will. Guaranteed. There's enough of my dad's favorite insecticide in this to kill you both ten times over." She took a step forward. "And you're not leaving here until you both get a taste."

"Bullshit," Bradley said. "That's just water."

"Come closer and I'll prove it."

"It's twenty-five, by the way," Trillian said.

Alexis gave Trillian a sideways look. "What?"

"It's a twenty-five foot drop, not—"

"Shut the fuck up."

This time Trillian took a step forward. Bradley put his hand on her shoulder to pull her back, but she brushed it off. "This is insane. Why are you doing this?"

"He's mine." Alexis's nostrils flared with each breath. "If I can't have him, no one can."

"We're just friends," Trillian said. "Frankly, I'm surprised you ever dated his scrawny ass. I mean look at him."

Alexis looked at Bradley and Bradley at Trillian, both confused.

"Too tall, too lean." Trillian winked at Bradley then turned back to Alexis. "It was the feet, wasn't it? Is it true what they say about guys with big feet?"

"What? Shut up."

"You're forgetting the fact that *she* dumped *me*," Bradley said.

"True." Trillian took a step forward. "So you *want* the person you *don't* want? You're either very confused or fucking stupid."

Even in the low light of the channel, Alexis's face was reddening by the second. The bead of fluid at the needle's tip dripped down the syringe and onto her glove.

Trillian took one more step. She now stood less than five feet away from the needle, well within striking range if Alexis lunged fast enough.

"You're too close," Bradley said quietly.

"You're right." Trillian grabbed a Port-A-Torch from her back pocket, the pilot flame amazingly still alight, and held the torch at arm's length. "Suck on this, bitch."

She engaged the nozzle with her thumb and flooded the channel with firelight.

JACK GRIPPED THE starter cord of the power washer flame thrower, the handle slick with unleaded and diesel mixture. Everything moved in slow motion as he watched Mark, Caitlin, and Fiscara battle smaller spiders at ground level, but the onslaught was far from over. Bradley and Trillian had inexplicably ceased their defense of channel five and were no longer responding over their walkie-talkie, adding a new, unanticipated worry to his mind.

There was no time left. Kill or be killed. Jack yanked the starter cord and the power washer's engine chugged into life. He triggered the lighter he had bolted to the nozzle of his power washer. "It's time for the big guns! Watch out below."

Fiscara, Mark and Caitlin looked up and stepped back to a safer distance. Barriers of flaming WD-40 flickered on the concrete floor, temporarily keeping the spiders at bay.

Secured to the debris fence, Jack aimed the flame thrower's nozzle at the entranceway ceiling where hundreds of spiders were scuttling to their escape. Across the space in channel six, a spider with a foot long leg span burst through the woven wall of the nest.

"It's broken through!" Jack divided his attention between the smaller spiders on the ceiling and this new larger threat. "Fall back and watch out!"

Jack engaged the nozzle's trigger and several large undirected fireballs burst forth as the supply line cleared itself of air. He soaked the ceiling and the advancing spiders with gasoline mixture until the fuel caught fire with a sudden *whomp!*

The heat was intense and unexpected, but thankfully short-lived. Jack turned his attention on channel six. The large spider crested the edge of the channel's opening and scuttled down the wall as his flame thrower jetted an arced stream of liquid fire across the entryway.

Mark, Caitlin, and Fiscara scattered, avoiding droplets of burning fuel that didn't make it to the opposite wall. Jack's blast of fire missed the large spider but coated the cracked concrete wall, floor, and remaining fleeing spiders in flame. He adjusted his aim and drenched the nest in channel six in fire.

The large spider dropped to the ground of the dam's entrance. Mark and Caitlin blasted it with their Port-A-Torches but their fuel was running out, weakening their attack. Mark's torch sputtered and extinguished itself.

Fiscara aimed her waning torch at the spider as it leaped the chasm. With no time to light her backup torch, she unclipped the taser rod at her belt and jammed it into the arachnid's abdomen. Arcs of blue electricity buzzed from the end and exploded, destroying the taser rod and sending the eight-legged marauder careening into the shadows below.

"Premature electrocution," Fiscara said to herself with a grin. A *pop-hiss* sounded from the darkness and a volley of quills flew out, embedding themselves in any exposed concrete within range.

A quill punctured the side of Fiscara's spent Port-A-Torch and the remaining pressurized lubricant ejected a cloud of flame, partly igniting her shirt.

"Viscera!" Jack yelled.

Fiscara dropped to the concrete and rolled herself in the grime, choking out the fire. She gave Jack a thumb's up and grabbed her second Port-A-Torch. "I'm okay."

Despite the fire in channel six, smaller spiders still manage to escape, but instead of fleeing, they reversed direction and charged down the wall toward Mark and Caitlin.

"Climb the cage!" Mark pointed to the debris fence.

"What about you?" Caitlin stepped backward, away from the approaching spiders.

"No time." Mark looked around and saw only one option. "I'll jump."

Before Caitlin could argue, Mark bolted toward the chasm. His foot hit the edge and the concrete crumbled under his weight, taking the power of his jump with it. He landed on the opposite side of the chasm, but short of his goal. Mark scrambled for something to hold but his muscular frame slipped back and disappeared into the darkness.

"Mark!" Caitlin ran toward the edge of the chasm.

"Cait! Get to the fence," Jack called down. "Don't worry. I can still see him from up here." The fuel leak he had smelled earlier had soaked through his shirt to his skin, but he figured he had one more shot left.

Caitlin jammed her Port-A-Torch into a front pocket and ran to the debris fence. Spiders scrambled across the floor, closing the gap between her and the chasm. One step at a time, she traversed the bottomless black crack, but her bandaged hand slowed her progress.

Jack aimed at the floor and arced a jet of fire on the spiders pursuing Caitlin. He slipped the flame thrower off his back and hooked one shoulder strap around an exposed bolt from the wrought iron fence.

"Help!" Mark's voice echoed out of the darkness.

Jack untied the rope from around his waist and the debris fence and threw it to Fiscara. She retied it to the base of the cage.

"Your headlamp!" Fiscara yelled up at Jack.

Caitlin hooked the elbow of her bandaged hand around a wrought iron bar and pulled off her headlamp. "Take mine!" She tossed it to Fiscara.

Fiscara pulled the headlamp on and peered over the cracked and crumbling edge of the chasm. "Mark?"

"Over here," Mark said.

Fiscara still couldn't see Mark but she had a good sense of where he was. She dropped the rope into the chasm. On the opposite side, spiders that had eluded Jack's final volley of fire breached the edge and spilled into the inky black below.

The rope pulled taut as Mark began to pull himself out of the chasm.

"Hurry, Mark!" Caitlin stepped off the debris fence and ran to where the rope disappeared down into the depths of the dam's structure. She hit a patch of loose dirt and slipped, landing square on her butt. As if the impact had given Mark a boost, his arm appeared over the edge of the crumbling concrete grasping the rope with a white-knuckled fist.

He pulled himself onto the floor of the entryway on his stomach. Fiscara bent down to give Mark her hand when both she and Caitlin realized with horror that his back was covered with spiders.

Caitlin pulled out her Port-A-Torch. "Cover your face." Mark had barely registered the words when Caitlin let loose the last of her fuel. Fiscara joined in and together repelled the spiders back into the chasm.

They pulled Mark out to safety and rolled him onto his back, extinguishing the smoldering sections of his shirt. Caitlin pulled Mark into her arms and hugged him tight.

"Take cover! This is going to be big." Jack grabbed the nozzle and aimed a bolt of burning fuel into the entire length of the chasm, emptying the reservoir. He lifted the flame thrower off the fence and threw it toward the chasm, where it hit the edge and exploded in a shower of burning gasoline.

"Holy shit," Fiscara said. "You weren't kidding."

Fire reflected in Mark's eyes. "Nothing's getting out of that inferno alive."

But Jack spotted movement within the growing flames of the chasm. "Fiscara! Look out!"

Fiscara followed Jack's line of sight to see two black smoking spider legs hook into the softened concrete close to her feet. The large spider's palps and all its quills had been incinerated but the rest of its body appeared intact. Four more legs breached the edge, followed by the last two. The eight legged freak collected itself on the ledge as if it was deciding how to attack. Fiscara stared at the spider, her face reflected in the thing's eight miraculously unburned eyes.

"Kill it!" Caitlin scrambled backward with her legs, pulling Mark with her.

"Already on it." Fiscara pulled her largest knife from its sheath on her belt. "This is for Killer!" She flipped the knife in her hand, grasping the blade, and launched it at the spider. At the same instant, the spider jumped into action and scrambled toward her. The blade of the knife hit its mark and sliced through the spider's abdomen up to its hilt. But the blow was not enough to stop it.

Feet became inches in seconds and Fiscara had enough time to grab one more knife. With the spider nearly upon her, she thrust the knife's blade into the head of the advancing arachnid and twisted the hilt. As thick blueish-green fluid flowed out of the wound, Fiscara pulled the knife out and stabbed the spider's thorax from underneath, twisting again.

The spider's legs retracted to form a cage under its body and rolled to one side. Fiscara stood, pulled her knives free and kicked the spider back into the burning chasm.

"Ho-ly shit!" Jack grinned from ear to ear. "You got some skills, Fiscara."

Mark swallowed hard. "Remind me to never hand in an assignment late."

"What you saw here today…" Fiscara returned her knives to

their sheaths as she alternated her gaze between Jack, Mark and Caitlin. "You keep that between us. Understand?"

All three nodded.

Jack scaled down the debris fence and joined Fiscara, Mark, and Caitlin on the floor of the entryway. The walls, floor, and ceiling were charred black and peppered with burnt spider husks. He looked back at the chasm, flames burning a couple feet above the ground like a moat. "You can thank Mr. Moody for that."

O'CONNOR SLID DOWN the steep sloped exit to spillway channel six and was first to hit the bottom.

The queen spider followed in hot pursuit. Even halfway down the channel's exit, Sam could see the spider's glistening fangs and pulsing quills.

"Blast it!" Sam pulled out his last remaining Port-A-Torch.

O'Connor pushed herself up to a sitting position, then used her stump to balance herself on her right knee. She twisted the nozzle to focus the spray, aimed her flame thrower at the spider, and released a narrow burst of flame.

The spider tried to avoid the fire but the silty ground along the spillway affected its traction as well. Its hairs and most of its quills burned down to stubs before it latched onto the dividing wall between channel six and five.

Sam anticipated the spider's direction and ran to the adjacent spillway exit.

The spider crested the dividing wall and scaled down into channel five, safe from O'Connor's fire but headlong into the flames from Sam's Port-A-Torch.

Its thorax and abdomen trailing tendrils of smoke behind it, the spider scrabbled up the inclined spillway and into the shadowy exit of channel five.

"Goddammit." Sam wiped his brow. "You're afraid of earthquakes but not those things?"

"I can't see an earthquake," O'Connor said.

Sam pulled the walkie-talkie from his belt. "Brad, a big-ass sporky headed your way." He waited for a response but received none. "Brad?"

"Sam? Jack here," the walkie-talkie buzzed back.

"Hold up, Jack." Sam looked up the incline of spillway five, then at O'Connor. "I got to go back for him."

"And I got to go back for something too." O'Connor tapped on her stump. "No one takes my leg and gets away with it."

"You'll be okay?"

O'Connor gave Sam a sideways smile. "Who the fuck do you think you're talking to?"

"Right."

O'Connor clambered up spillway six on her hands and knees, singing a badly out-of-tune version of "Ring of Fire" by Johnny Cash.

Sam smiled and raised his walkie-talkie to his mouth as he set off up spillway five. "Sam here. Heading into channel five, following one big-ass sporky."

THE PILOT FLAME on O'Connor's torch lit the way back to the nest. Her hands and knees were scraped to ribbons from the bones, gravel, and sand she'd had to crawl over.

Her prosthetic leg was right where she'd left it, now with two gaping holes in the foam cover where the spider had thrust its fangs. The venom had melted away some of the foam covering exposing the titanium pylon "bone" inside.

O'Connor grabbed the leg and pulled but it was still tangled up in the nest's tripwires. A burning sensation erupted on her right hand and she realized too late that her hand had brushed against some venom the spider had injected into the foam.

"Fuck." She rubbed her hand in silt to stop the spread of irritation. "Not today."

Without access to a knife, O'Connor centered each tripwire on the nozzle of the flame thrower and burned through it with a few seconds of fire. Each blast lit up the channel with amber light, exposing a cluster of young spiders, inky black and covering the walls and ceiling a few feet away.

O'Connor pulled her prosthetic leg free and extracted the liner. She rolled up the cuff of her pant leg, brushed her frayed stump sock free of debris, and guided the liner back on. The prosthetic's socket slid snugly over top and O'Connor pulled up the suspension sleeve. The leg needed some adjustment, but it would have to do for now. The immediate discomfort was an acceptable temporary trade-off for having the ability to walk again. Imitating a human limb took a huge amount of work.

She stood up and stamped her feet, sending dirt and silt to the ground in a cloud.

"So, who likes toast?" O'Connor sprayed a jet of fire up the left wall, across the ceiling, and down the right. The small black spiders that had been clinging to the walls fell to the ground like ashen stones.

She stepped forward, crushing charred spiders under her boots, until the partially burned nest blocked the rest of her passage. Evidence of morning sunlight (or fire) sliced through the less dense sections of the nest.

O'Connor poked at the base of the gossamer warren with the nozzle of the flame thrower. Hundreds of semi-translucent eggs lined the woven walls, some showing movement within. It looked like a scene from *Alien*.

She took a step back and clenched her teeth. An imaginary cigar would have to do. "Ellen Ripley, eat your heart out."

Starting in the center of the nest near the floor, O'Connor

released a clockwise jet of flame, moving forward a step at a time, boring a charred path through the intricate web.

An acrid odor similar to burned hair filled the channel. Spider eggs boiled, popped, and burst into flames and the nest began to self-combust. Eggs that didn't burn were crushed by O'Connor's heavy work boots.

Her jet of fire burned through the last of the nest and the eggs it contained. She stooped to walk through the charred hole and stepped to the edge of the channel.

O'Connor pointed her torch back into the dark opening. "Now *that's* a tarantula burger. Well done, just like I like it." Twenty-five feet below, Jack, Fiscara, Mark, and Caitlin huddled next to the debris fence. The heat and black smoke from the flames belching out of the crack in the concrete below made her hair curl. "You good down there?"

Jack answered with a wide, exhausted smile and held up his thumb.

"We got them all." Fiscara spotted a crippled straggler scratching its way over the lip of the chasm. She blasted it with her Port-A-Torch. "Well, now we do."

"Brad?" Jack asked between breaths. "Have you seen Brad?"

"Probably in channel five. I'll check on my way back." O'Connor stepped back into channel six, sweeping ash out of the way with her feet. She began to whistle "Ring of Fire" again, her tone-deaf rendition echoing back through the channel and into the dam's entranceway.

Trillian had had the good sense to reclaim a lit Port-A-Torch while Alexis had been scrambling for her syringe in the dirt. She'd jammed it into the back pocket of her jeans before helping

Bradley to his feet. And Alexis was so hell-bent on killing them both that she never noticed one torch was missing.

The blast of burning lubricant from Trillian's torch seared Alexis's leather vest and soaked into her shorts.

Alexis slapped the fire out with her free hand before it did any real damage. She looked to the ground and counted five Port-A-Torch canisters instead of six. "You little *bitch*." Alexis rushed her.

Trillian stepped back and responded with another blast of flame, this time at Alexis's head.

Alexis turned away, shielding her face. Her ponytail flipped back, caught fire, and flash-burned right up to the hair elastic tying it back before the flames snuffed themselves out.

"Hair today, gone tomorrow—" Trillian's grin melted away as she realized Bradley had turned ash white. She followed his eyes to the ceiling, where a massive spider clutched the concrete. They both began taking small steps backward.

"What the fuck?" With nothing to hold it back, Alexis's hair sprang forth like it was charged with static electricity. She ran her free hand over her head, feeling the grit of ash where her ponytail used to be. "My hair! Fuck! What did you do?"

Alexis turned toward Trillian and Bradley, who were stiff as boards inching their way backward. Their eyes flicked between Alexis and the spider clinging to the ceiling.

"Alex, you got bigger problems," Bradley said softly.

"Who said you could speak?" Alexis's pupils had taken over the whites of her eyes, leaving nothing but black hatred behind. The hand that clutched the syringe shook with anger.

"Above you." Trillian motioned at the ceiling.

"What was that, Rainbow Brite?"

"A spider as big as your fucking head," Trillian said. "Right above you."

"You expect me to believe that a spider—" Alexis heard a wet drop land on her vest. She touched the milky white liquid with her free hand, rubbing it between her gloved finger and thumb.

Alexis and Trillian locked gazes. They both knew what was going to happen next.

Trillian held the Port-A-Torch in her hand, her thumb on the nozzle. "Sorry, not sorry."

Alexis looked up just as the spider, now hovering on a line of silk two feet above, dropped onto her face. Moving faster than she could react, the spider plunged its fangs into her neck.

A network of red and purple veins erupted under the tendons of Alexis's neck. Rapid swelling took over, rendering her left arm useless. Her throat began to close up as she fell to her knees, struggling for breath.

Alexis grasped the syringe in her gloved fist and brought it down hard, but the spider's thorax was harder. The needle glanced off the spider's exoskeleton and plunged into her chest, injecting most of its insecticide payload.

Startled, the spider released Alexis and backed up against the wall.

Bradley looked at Trillian. "Kill it, or we're next."

Trillian aimed her torch at the spider and blasted it with fire. "This isn't going to be enough."

Bradley grabbed his Port-A-Torch from the ground, but the pilot flame was out. The elastic holding the lighter's fuel valve open had burned off. He snapped the lighter off the canister where it was glued and held it under the pen tube nozzle.

Together, Trillian and Bradley covered the spider with flame, yet it was still able to escape down the channel. Its quills had been burned to charcoal nubs.

Sam appeared from the darkness and used his torch on the spider. It reversed direction and darted up the wall back toward Bradley and Trillian.

They continued their onslaught of liquid flame. The spider lost its grip on the wall and fell to the floor.

O'Connor appeared next to Sam. "The cavalry's here,

bitches." She leveled the nozzle of her propane torch at the spider and pulled the trigger. There was no getting away now.

The spider moved its legs furiously but was unable to propel itself any longer.

"I think it's a goner," Trillian said.

O'Connor holstered her torch and pulled out her taser rod. She jammed it into the thorax of the spider, still smoldering and sputtering with flame, and discharged the weapon. "I honor Washington on every job now."

Bradley turned his head toward Alexis. "We've got one last detail to take care of."

BRADLEY WALKED TO where Alexis lay on the ground. Extreme edema radiated from the bite on her neck and it was worsening by the second. Her chest, left arm, and most of her face was swollen beyond recognition. With her short charred hair, Alexis looked like she had been boiled alive. A faint wheeze of breath escaped from her lips.

Bradley knelt next to her and placed his ear next to her grotesquely swollen lips. A whisper of slurred words escaped through her thickening saliva.

Alexis's body tensed up. Even though more than half of her body was swollen, Bradley could still feel her muscles convulse underneath her doughy flesh. He pulled out the syringe and tossed it aside.

Bradley looked where Alexis's face used to be, a face he used to love and lust over, then gazed up at Trillian, Sam, and O'Connor. "I have to try."

"Just don't get any of that venom on you," O'Connor said. "It already destroyed the covering on my leg."

Bradley squeezed open Alexis's fattened lips, guided by her

perfect teeth buried beneath, teeth that had felt so smooth against his tongue half a year ago. He placed his mouth overtop and blew in a breath. Her cheeks puffed out but her chest refused to rise. Bradley tried again but his attempts at breathing life into Alexis ultimately failed. Either her throat had closed up, her lungs were full of fluid, or both. He hung his head and felt hot tears building behind his eyes.

A warm hand fell on his shoulder. Bradley looked up to find that it was Trillian's. Her face was sorrowful but warm with understanding. "Brad, she's gone."

That's all it took. Bradley's flood gates opened. Tears that he didn't understand flowed down his cheeks, dripping and soaking into the silt on the ground. Time seemed to stand still. There were no questions or answers. Just silence.

Until a familiar voice echoed up from below. "Brad?"

It was Jack.

Bradley stood and wiped his eyes. He walked close to the opening to channel five and looked down into the entryway of the dam. Jack and Fiscara stood looking up at him. Caitlin was absorbed in taking care of Mark up against the debris fence. "We'll be down in a sec."

Concern reflected in Jack's eyes. "You okay?"

Bradley answered with a weak "thumbs up" and stepped back into channel five.

"We got to get her out of here." Sam crouched in preparation for lifting Alexis up.

Bradley placed his hand on Sam's shoulder. "No, Dad. I'm carrying her out."

Sam nodded, stepped back and glanced at Trillian. She offered him a somber look in return.

O'Connor shut off the gas to her flame thrower. "It's a long way back to the parking lot. Ask for help if you need it."

"Especially down the incline," Sam said.

Bradley lowered himself to one knee and rolled Alexis onto

her back. He slipped one arm under her legs and one under her arms and back. Her body was entirely swollen and warm to the touch, reminding him of a plastic bag full of gravy. He pushed the thought aside as he lifted her body up.

Alexis's dead weight rolled in Bradley's arms. Her torso twisted and slumped against his chest like she was giving him one last hug, except her arms hung lifelessly down his back.

One step at a time, Bradley made his way back to the dam's entryway, with Sam leading the way and O'Connor and Trillian following. There they rejoined the rest of the crew and walked back to the parking lot a mile away.

Except for a short breather in the dam's entryway, Bradley didn't ask for help once. He carefully laid Alexis's body on the dry grass next to the lot.

He sat up against a tree and dialed 9-1-1 on his phone. Much to his surprise, his call connected with an emergency operator who remained unfazed upon hearing about a "death by spider bite." Bradley relayed their location and specific details and hung up.

"It might be a while, since there's no—" Bradley looked at Alexis's lifeless body. But it wasn't Alexis at all, not anymore. Just a strange swollen vaguely human form that would haunt his memories. "Since there's no one who needs immediate medical attention."

"I'm in no hurry." O'Connor pulled her box of cigars out from under the driver's seat of the Mustang and slid out a fresh cigar. She bit the end off and lit it with the warm flame of her Zippo. "A cigar, a snooze, and I'm good."

Fiscara pulled a trash bag from the back seat of Jack's car. "You need this?"

Jack shook his head.

She draped the trash bag over Alexis's head and torso and turned toward O'Connor. "Doesn't it bother you that someone died? Especially a teenager?"

"What can we do? Besides, no one forced her to make bad choices." O'Connor puffed dense smoke out the side of her mouth, closed her eyes and appeared to melt a little bit. Cigars hit O'Connor's relax button.

"How about show a little respect? She didn't have to die like *that*." Fiscara gestured at Alexis's body.

"We all knew the risks going in."

Fiscara shook her head in disgust. "You're such a heartless bitch."

"And damn proud of it." O'Connor said. "Being a bitch has kept me alive."

"Enough." Sam's voice cut through the tension. "We've all been through a lot. Everyone just relax."

Mark and Caitlin sat themselves down in the shade of a nearby tree and fawned over each other.

Jack caught a whiff of O'Connor's cigar and had had enough of smoke and flame. He popped the back hatch on the Civic, pulled out a partially used flat of bottled water, and set it on the car's hood. "For emergencies. Anyone want one?"

Everyone except Bradley nodded in unison. Jack began to dole out the water. "It's a bit warm."

Trillian grabbed two bottles and handed one to Bradley. "Okay to sit?"

He nodded.

Trillian plopped herself down beside him. She cracked open her water and took a sip. She looked at Bradley, studying his face, then rested her head on his shoulder.

Bradley's phone chirped in his pocket. He pulled it out to find a text from his mom.

"Are you okay?" the text read.

"👍 talk 18r," he tapped out before sliding his phone back into his pocket.

Trillian traced Bradley's hand with her index finger. "You think school's cancelled tomorrow?"

"I think school's going to be cancelled for the rest of the week at least." Bradley took Trillian's hand and wove his fingers through hers.

The crew waited in silence for emergency personnel to arrive.

A Picture's Worth

O'CONNOR TOOK SIDE streets back to Bradley's house, which had escaped the damage from the earthquake. "I was thinking about driving Baby Blue back to New York. You know, make it a real road trip," she said. "Want to come?"

Sam looked at her, surprised. "Sorry. Parole. But that ends in three months."

O'Connor nodded, gears working in her head and a smoldering cigar clamped between her teeth like an anchor. "Keep your calendar open."

She turned onto Sheldon Street and rolled the Mustang to a stop just across from the house.

Bradley and Trillian sat close together in the back seat behind Sam to avoid as much of the cigar's acrid miasma as they could.

Claire perched on the lower step of the front landing, her purple compression bandage wrapped tightly around her left calf and foot, and her purple crutches propped up beside her. As O'Connor killed the Mustang's engine, she pulled herself up with her crutches. O'Connor waved and Claire waved back.

"See that, Sam?" O'Connor nudged Sam's shoulder. "We're besties now."

"Great." Sam stepped out of the car and flipped the seat forward to let Bradley and Trillian out.

"You can thank me later," O'Connor said.

The four of them crossed the street to the front walk, Bradley and Trillian, hand in hand, leading the way.

Claire wrapped her arms around Bradley, her crutches falling to the ground. "I'm so glad you're home safe."

"Me too, Mom." Bradley hugged Claire back and kissed her on the cheek.

Claire gave Trillian a head to toe once-over then turned back to Bradley. "Well?"

"Well what?"

Trillian gave Bradley a sideways look that said, "Introduce me!"

"Oh!" Embarrassment spread up the back of Bradley's neck in a hot flush.

O'Connor leaned closer to Sam. "Smooth."

Sam chuckled. "He gets it from me."

"No shit, *Mr. Maxipad.*"

Bradley cleared his throat and placed his hand on the small of Trillian's back. "This is Trillian Stark. We've been hanging out a lot and—"

"Suckin' face," O'Connor said.

Bradley glared at O'Connor. "Shut up," he said through clenched teeth.

"You *haven't* been suckin' face?"

"Behave yourself, *Bertha.*" Sam crouched to pick up Claire's crutches and handed them to her. "Trill's a fine young woman. Brave and strong."

"Thanks, Sam, er, Mr. Shaw."

"After everything we've been through, Sam's good."

Claire took the crutches from Sam but avoided his eyes. "I'm looking forward to getting to know you, Trillian."

"I hate to kill a party, but we got a plane to catch," O'Connor said.

"Old Mother Hubbard is getting restless." Sam smiled at Bradley and held his arms out. Bradley accepted the invitation and the two shared a short embrace. "Good to see you again so soon." He motioned at Trillian. "Behave, huh?"

Bradley smirked. "Thanks for coming out. And for all the help."

Sam switched his gaze to Trillian. "Can I give you a hug?"

Trillian nodded and gave Sam a hug and a light kiss on the cheek. "Safe flight."

Sam nodded, then motioned at Bradley. "Text me if he *doesn't* behave."

Sam offered Claire a friendly nod and a wave before stepping back toward the sidewalk.

O'Connor blew a cloud of blue smoke toward Bradley. "I don't do hugs."

"Bullshit." Bradley wrapped his arms around O'Connor's bulky frame and gave her a tight hug. "You're just a teddy bear deep down."

O'Connor patted Bradley's back and pulled away. "I've never been so insulted." She smiled and winked at him.

"A teddy bear that eats rats and spiders for breakfast." Trillian stuck out her hand.

"Now *that* I can get behind." O'Connor and Trillian exchanged a firm handshake. "I like your style, Trill."

Trillian beamed. "Thanks."

"You hear that?" Bradley said.

"What?" Sam cocked his head to one side, listening. "I don't—"

Sounds of squealing tires on pavement arose from down the street. Jack's orange Civic slid around the corner onto Sheldon Street and screeched to a stop behind the Mustang.

"Good, I didn't miss you guys." Jack pulled himself out of the driver's side window and grabbed a white plastic bag from the passenger seat.

Sam met Jack at the front of the walk and shook his hand.

"Nice to meet you, Jack. Keep inventing with that brain of yours."

"You can count on it."

O'Connor jutted her hand forth. "If you ever need a job, or a little *Mrs. Robinson* action, you know where to find me."

"Uh, I'll keep that in mind," Jack said as he shook O'Connor's hand. "The job that is."

"Bah. Sex is wasted on the young." O'Connor blew a cloud of smoke into the sky and trudged across the street to the Mustang. "Let's hit the road, Muchacho."

Sam offered one last wave and trotted toward the passenger side of the Mustang.

"Sam." Claire hobbled to the sidewalk on her crutches.

Sam looked back to see Claire set the grips of her crutches on the street and move toward the car. "Hold up, O'Connor." He ran back and met Claire halfway across the street.

They both looked at each other, unsure what to do next.

"Here." Claire reached into her back pocket and pulled out Sam's favorite photo. "You should have this."

Sam took the photo. It always brought a smile to his face. He flipped it over to reveal Claire's mailing address and telephone number, with the message "Let's talk" written below.

"Thank you." Sam slipped the photo back into his wallet. "If you need anything…"

Claire nodded.

Sam hopped into the Mustang and O'Connor started the engine. "Catch you on the flip side." She pulled away from the curb.

"What's in the bag?" Bradley gestured at the plastic bag in Jack's hand.

"Shit!" Jack ran down the street after the Mustang. "O'Connor! Wait!"

A block ahead, the brake lights glowed red and the Mustang screeched to a stop. O'Connor shifted into reverse and began to back up slowly. Jack caught up with O'Connor and Sam, breathless.

"Change your mind?" O'Connor grinned and flashed her eyebrows.

"Just something for the road," Jack said between gasps for air. He handed the plastic bag to O'Connor.

She opened it up and inhaled the aroma inside. "Taco Siempre?"

Jack nodded. "Burrito Extreme. Fully loaded."

O'Connor smiled. "Mrs. Robinson *approves*." She kicked the Mustang into gear and accelerated down Sheldon Street, leaving a strip of rubber behind. She raised one hand, thumbs up, and waved it side to side. "See you in New York!"

In less than a minute the Mustang was out of sight.

April 4, 2018 - May 29, 2019
Victoria, BC

Continue the adventure with
Molerat 2.0: Terror Burrows (Detest-A-Pest #3)
coming in 2020.

Note from the author: *If you like this book, may I ask three things? First, please leave a review. I must manage my time and since I write in multiple genres, I will pay more attention to the books/genres with the most reviews. What I focus on next depends on you, the reader. Help me to make the most of my time. Second, please join my reader group at LeeGabel.com/signup. There, I can keep you informed of future books and giveaways. And third, please recommend this book to your friends. You can also ask your local library to order it for you if they don't have it yet. My sincere thanks.*

TITLES BY LEE GABEL

Detest-A-Pest Series
Molerat 2.0 (Coming 2020)
Arachnid 2.0
Vermin 2.0

Standalone
Snipped
David's Summer
Tied

Afterward

Like it? Rate it. Share it.

If you enjoyed *Arachnid 2.0*, please rate it and spread the word. With your rating, you take part in this book's success. If you're interested in joining my Reader Group for updates and advance notice of upcoming releases, please sign up by going to LeeGabel.com.

Note from the author

Thank you for reading my fifth novel. The first novel in the "Detest-A-Pest" series had always intended to be a standalone story. But readers expressed so much interest in a sequel, I was compelled to continue. This time the seed of the idea was simply a request from a reader. "Write a sequel about spiders."

I must admit that spiders have creeped me out in the past. They've made me jump as they scurried across the floor as I watched late night television.

I based the "sporky" on the Australian funnel web spider, one of the most lethal spiders in the world. Making them enormous wasn't enough. Adding porcupine-like quills made a fearsome spider even more dangerous.

I enjoy writing about real places. As with my previous novels so far, I have used real street names where appropriate, but have changed addresses and made up most locations and businesses.

This is my longest book to date. I hadn't initially planned on writing such a long story, but I found that the world and characters I had created demanded it.

Many thanks go to my wife and editor Sheila. She has a command of the English language that makes my kneecaps sweat. I couldn't do this without her, nor would I want to. I'll always owe a debt of gratitude to David Hoselton for his feedback on earlier books and for helping me find my writing voice. Watch David's work on *The Good Doctor*, which airs on ABC. And to my family and friends who supported my decision to quit my job to write full time, you were right. I am your number one fan now.

About the author

Since 1992, Lee has worked within the visual and dramatic arts landscape as a graphic designer, illustrator, visual effects artist, animator, screenwriter and author. He's contributed to an Emmy award and once walked 63.5 kilometers in 13 hours. Traditionally trained as a screenwriter, Lee has moved to writing books in order to share his stories.

Lee has spent most of his life living on an island in the Pacific Northwest and he writes in multiple genres that interest him. Why? In his own words: "Writing is magic. I'll never understand how it works the way it does, but I do know if I put energy into writing, it rewards me in strange and wonderful ways. Even if I know where I'm going in a story, often I'll end up being pulled in directions by my characters that I least expect. What ends up on the page never ceases to surprise me, and that's super cool. Writing continues to be one of the most difficult and most rewarding aspects of my life."

Find Lee on the Internet:

Want to join Lee's Reader Group or find out more about Lee and the books he writes? Please go to:

LeeGabel.com

LeeGabel.com/facebook
LeeGabel.com/twitter
LeeGabel.com/instagram
Or follow Lee at BookBub - LeeGabel.com/bookbub